MW00586783

For testimonials from law enforcement,
visit Carolyn Arnold's website.

ALSO BY CAROLYN ARNOLD

Detective Madison Knight

Ties That Bind
Justified
Sacrifice
Found Innocent
Just Cause
Deadly Impulse

In the Line of Duty
Power Struggle
Shades of Justic
What We Bury
Girl on the Run
Life Sentence

Brandon Fisher FBI

Eleven
Silent Graves
The Defenseless
Blue Baby
Violated

Remnants
On the Count of Three
Past Deeds
One More Kill

Detective Amanda Steele

The Little Grave
Stolen Daughters
The Silent Witness

Black Orchid Girls
Her Frozen Cry

Matthew Connor Adventure

City of Gold
The Secret of the Lost Pharaoh

The Legend of Gasparilla and His Treasure

Standalone

Assassination of a Dignitary
Midlife Psychic

A gripping heart-stopping crime thriller

SACRIFICE

Finding the truth sometimes comes at a high cost...

CAROLYN ARNOLD

A Detective Madison Knight Mystery

HIBBERT & STILES
PUBLISHING INC.

Hibbert & Stiles Publishing Inc.
hspubinc.com

Names: Arnold, Carolyn, 1976
Sacrifice / Carolyn Arnold.
Description: 2021 Hibbert & Stiles Publishing Inc. edition. |
Series: Detective Madison Knight Series ; book 3

Identifiers: ISBN (e-book): 978-1-988064-13-0 | ISBN (4.25 x 7 paperback): 978-1-988064-14-7 | ISBN (5 x 8 paperback): 978-1-988064-31-4 | ISBN (6.14 x 9.21 hardcover): 978-1-988353-08-1

Additional formats:
ISBN (large print editon): 978-1-988353-08-1
ISBN (audiobook): 978-1-989706-57-2

SACRIFICE

To Sherry, a sister whom I had lost for a time.
I'm blessed to have her back in my life.
She's a motivating force to just "be"
and to let my light shine.

PROLOGUE

He equated his past deeds to shades of gray with no distinction between black and white, right and wrong, good and bad. He knew others would see things differently, but it didn't matter. Few people possessed the ability to intimidate and influence him. The man he was meeting had the power to do both.

He walked into the dimly lit Fairmont Club, and as he followed the maître d' to a back table, he inhaled the smells of grilled steak mingled with imported cigars. Appreciatively, he watched her hips sway as if she was putting extra effort into it.

"Patrick, how nice of you to join me." The man in the pressed Armani, whom very few conversed with on a first-name basis, sat at the table. A glass of Louis XIII Black Pearl, priced at fifteen hundred an ounce, was in front of him.

Patrick noticed the man's bodyguard sitting at a nearby table. He was Armani's prized stallion, who, instead of being stabled, was toted about and showcased. The man went by Jonathan Wright, but Patrick doubted that was his real name. He was super intelligent and a former marine. Wright nodded his approval and went back to his steak and red wine.

A lovely Asian woman, who could have easily been a model, stood at the edge of the table. "Your regular, sir?"

"French with a twist." Patrick smiled at the waitress, remembering the feel of her skin and the smell of her musky dew. Although a married man for thirty years, he didn't think his wife had noticed him missing that night.

A few minutes later, the waitress came back with his Perrier water and lime in a rocks glass. The weight with which she set it on the table told him her memories were back, but she had to act like a civilized woman. After all, she was working. She had to know, with a body like hers, she was begging men to take advantage of her. He still believed he could have her again if he were at all inclined.

Armani held up his glass in a toasting gesture before swirling it lightly and inhaling deeply. He followed with a small draw on the cognac. "When are you going to join me and have a real drink?"

"I'm on the job." Not Patrick's only reason for not drinking, but it would suffice for now.

"Time for that new chair, my friend."

"Is that why you called me here?" Patrick smiled. Maybe the time had come to be repaid for past favors?

Armani let out a laugh. "Hardly. I need your help with something."

Patrick's heart palpitated with adrenaline, as it did every time this man made that statement. It was too late in his life to change to a path of innocence. Should his past deeds ever require an accounting, his only option would be a bullet to the brain. "You name it."

Armani played things smart, though. He always reminded him of the stakes involved first. "You help me with this, and I'll ensure you make mayor."

CHAPTER ONE

The pungent odor hit Madison instantly upon opening the morgue doors. She pinched the tip of her nose, but it did little to save her from the smell of decomp embedding itself in her lungs and sinus cavities.

"Whoa, he's a ripe one." Terry, her partner, stepped through the doorway behind her. He grabbed for a cloth mask from the dispenser mounted on the wall and handed her one.

Cole Richards, the ME, stood by the body, looking like a tall, dark guardian. "It's the exposure to the air accelerating the putrefaction process. That's why the autopsy must be done tonight," Richards said.

Madison noted Richards talked while keeping his eyes on the dead, an unusual thing for him. Maybe something about this death touched him on a personal level? She looked from Richards to the body.

The male victim, estimated in his early twenties, lay on the metal slab, a white sheet draped over his distended abdomen to his shoulders. His skin was almost black and appeared separated from the bone, as if one could peel it off like the rind of an orange. His face, like the rest of him, was distorted and bloated beyond recognition. His eyes were open and vacant, clouded by death. His arms lay above the sheet to his sides. Some of his fingers were missing nails. The skin of one fingertip had been removed. Madison deduced Richards had taken it for identification purposes and forwarded it to the lab.

There was no wallet found on the body, nor any identifying marks to flag him in the missing person database. He'd been wearing jeans and a gray hoodie, and the only things on him were a metal card holder that was empty except for a folded-up napkin with a woman's name and number, a wad of cash, and a cell phone. He wore a gold chain with a pendant that had the letters CC engraved on it.

The body had washed up on the shore of the Bradshaw River, which ran through the city of Stiles and fed from a lake an hour away. The property belonged to a middle-aged couple, without children, by the last name of Walker. The wife had found the body when she went to get wood for their woodstove. She said he hadn't been there the day before. They had interviewed the couple at length and obtained their backgrounds, which came up with nothing noteworthy.

"How long do you estimate he was in the water?" Madison asked.

"As a simple deduction based on what is before me, I would say at least two to three weeks." Richards pulled his eyes from the body to look at Madison.

Was pain buried there?

Richards returned his gaze to the body as if he'd read her thought. "I'm basing this on when he surfaced. In cooler water, bacteria causing decomp multiplies more sluggishly. If this was a warmer season, and it was three weeks later, we'd have a skeleton. Stomach contents will provide the approximate time of his last meal and what he ate. I'll also be consulting with a friend of mine, Wayne McDermott. He's a forensic climatologist. He can provide us with recent temperatures so we can get a closer estimate for time of death."

"So, what are your thoughts? Dead when he went in, or did he drown?"

"This is still to be determined. He is young and appears to have been in excellent shape."

Madison's eyes diverted back to the body. The currents of the Bradshaw River had swept away any trace of a fit male adult. His bloated features made him appear more like a character from a sci-fi movie than a once living human being.

"Assuming he was alive when he hit the water, it is unlikely that he had a heart attack on entry. Quick results would show frothy liquid in the lungs, but because he was submerged for a considerable time, any trace of this would be gone. Tissue samples from his lungs, however, will be taken and sent to the lab for further analysis. We'll also extract bone marrow in search of diatoms." He must have clued into their confusion and added, "These are microscopic organisms that are specific to a region. If it made it to his bone marrow, he was alive when he went into the water. We could also find evidence of this in his kidneys, should this be the case. This will prove whether he drowned in the Bradshaw or was dumped in the river after death." His eyes went to the body. "We're not going to get these answers just by looking at him."

"Anything else you can tell us?" Terry asked.

"His neck is broken, but that might simply be from the trauma the body experienced as it went down the Bradshaw. I'll also require a full tox panel be run on him. We might be able to find out if he had any drugs or alcohol in his system, though it's more like a shot in the dark. If he did consume, any trace might be long gone."

Madison latched eyes with the ME. "Well, let's assume he did drown. How would we know it was homicide?"

A faint smile touched Richards's lips, exposing a slit of white teeth. "It is dubbed the perfect murder. But until we can establish his identity, concrete his background, and get the tox results back, I will not be finalizing COD on paper."

Cause of death.

"He could have jumped in. Suicide?" Terry rubbed at the back of his neck.

"Possibly, but unlikely. The reason for this is the natural tendency to surface. Drowning suicides usually involve the use of a heavy object to counteract the instinct to save oneself."

"Maybe he didn't think things through and acted on impulse. Most suicides are executed in the moment. He could have gotten caught in the current and pulled under the ice. His restraint could have broken free from the body."

"I prefer not to speculate." Richards's eyes scolded Terry. "But at this point, I would treat this case as suspicious leaning toward homicide. Look at this." He lifted the left hand of the victim.

There was a circular impression on the backside of the hand.

"Cigarette burn, or possibly something larger." She studied it and then glanced at Richards. "It's almost large enough to be a car lighter or a cigar."

Richards's eyes narrowed, pinching the dark skin around his eyes.

"So our vic was definitely in some sort of struggle before ending up in the river. But intention is going to be hard to prove."

Madison glanced at her skeptical partner. "Hard, but not impossible." She went back to Richards. "So, you don't have an ID and only a speculative conclusion as to the cause of death. Why did you call us down here?"

Richards pulled back the sheet and pointed to the victim's shoulders. "This."

There were darkened lines, a subtle contrast, the two widths a mirror image of each other, on each shoulder close to the neck.

"Bruising," Terry said.

"Yes, contusions."

"From what? What would cause something like that?" Madison asked.

"That I'll leave for you to figure out." Richards placed the sheet back over the body. "But if our guy did drown due to forcible action, these marks could have come from our murder weapon."

CHAPTER TWO

Stepping out of the morgue, Madison braced a hand on her hip above her holster. "So, we're left without an identity and only have a surmised cause of death."

"Richards seems pretty certain it was a drowning, even though he didn't want to speculate," Terry said, mocking the ME.

Madison had noted that, too. Richards was typically a person who ran based on facts, not assumptions. She had found it strange how he kept coming back to drowning as the COD without being certain.

"And here we are, another Sunday night spent on the job."

"Terry, what else would you be doing?"

"Hmm."

Her phone rang, but she ignored it. "If he was drowned intentionally, we have to prove someone did this to him. It's not going to be an easy case."

"Even more fun." He plastered on a fake smile and passed a glance to her phone. "And figures we get the case, instead of Sovereign."

Toby Sovereign was another detective in Major Crimes, and on a personal note, Madison ex-fiancé.

"The only reason we got it is because he's got the flu." Or so she had heard. It wasn't like she was in communication with him anymore. When their engagement ended so had their relationship, and all that had been years ago now.

"Think they're calling it a super bug."

Madison shrugged it off. Her phone kept ringing, bringing with it the reminder she had to take care of something. "Gotta go."

She headed for the elevator, pushed the up arrow, and answered her phone without consulting the caller ID. "Knight."

"Don't worry about coming for me." It was Blake, a man she had been seeing for a few months.

She looked at her watch. *11:00 PM.*

Hours had passed since they last talked. They had been at her sister's for dinner and a get-together with her parents, who were up from Florida. Originally, Madison had staged a fake call to leave early, but then the real one came in. Blake, playing the good boyfriend, stayed behind.

"I can come get you now."

"Don't worry about it. I'm home now and you're on the hunt. I get it. Just don't get on me when a case loads me down."

She detected amusement in his voice. That was the one benefit of dating another professional. Blake was a defense attorney and understood what it was to forfeit all else to focus on what needed to be done. "Who drove you?"

"Chelsea. She even wrapped you up a take-home platter. You'll have to come over here to get it."

Chelsea was her younger sister, the perfect one, at least in the eyes of their mother. A family woman, a mother of three, married to the perfect man, living in the perfect neighborhood. One thing that wasn't perfect about her, though, was her cooking. Now Blake would know this.

"Yum." Madison laughed, but it cooled rather quickly as thoughts of Blake being left with her family slapped her.

"Are you upset with me for some reason?" He must have sensed the mood shift across the line.

She'd been surprised when he'd decided to stay but she was more mad with herself for allowing it.

"Madison?" he prompted.

"I'm fine. How did it go anyway?"

"Not too bad."

Next liar take the stand…

"And Mom?" Madison didn't know why she asked because she really didn't want the answer. She was sure she already knew it.

Blake's end went silent.

"She's not happy. You can say it." She felt as though a stranger had invaded her world. He didn't need to see this side of her life, the side her mother tried to dominate. *What was I thinking by inviting him to meet my family in the first place?*

"Well…" He cleared his throat. "Things came to an impasse. I defended you. Your father seemed to like that, with me being a defense attorney and all."

"I don't need you defending me."

"I was just—"

"Don't bother telling me. Mom told you how my job eats people alive, probably tried to talk you out of a relationship with me." Her voice rose with each word. She turned around to face Terry, who diverted his eyes.

"She's just concerned."

"But she doesn't need to be."

"Maddy, may I see you tomorrow?"

The elevator chimed its arrival. It seemed to have taken forever to reach the basement today. Terry came on beside her.

"Can I get back to you?" she said to Blake.

"I'm sensing a brush-off, and after you took me home to meet the parents?"

"Night, Blake." She hung up without waiting for him to respond.

What did all this say about her as a person? Was she getting defensive because her mother had a point? Maybe it was selfish of her. Not when it came to her career, but that she had pulled someone else into her life. In some ways, things would be less complicated if she stayed completely unattached. What was she thinking allowing her heart a small chance at a real relationship? As long as there were killers to catch, she really didn't have time for one.

"You took him to meet your parents?" Terry pointed to the phone she held clenched in her hand.

She shoved it into a pocket. She should have taken the stairs. After all, she only had to go up one floor. She'd have gotten some exercise and some privacy.

"So…how did it go?" Terry said when she didn't speak, and he was grinning. "Your relationship must be progressing. Before you know it, there will be a wedding."

"Terry, shut up before I punch both of your shoulders hard enough you'll lose all feeling." She stared at him, daring him to say one more thing before she turned toward the lit floor number. She would never let the relationship get to the point of marriage. And to think she could have avoided this conversation—if only she'd taken the stairs.

"Did they like him?"

The elevator chimed to notify them they had reached the ground floor.

"Night, Terry."

CHAPTER THREE

Madison had been to Blake's condo before. With its fifty floors, valet service, a lobby atrium, and front-door security, it was a showy display. Blake nestled himself into the forty-ninth floor, and she was certain the only reason for that was the penthouse had been purchased by an old man who had refused to sell his spot on the fiftieth. She often wondered where Blake's money came from and assumed his affluent lifestyle required more than even a successful defense attorney's salary could accommodate.

A uniformed doorman opened the front door. "Detective Knight."

She nodded in response, still not sure why she ended up here.

Inside, the elevator operator stood to the side of the open elevator doors. He was all of five-five but carried a confident air, one no doubt required when dealing with the type of people living in such a building. Except for his height, Madison could picture this man guarding Buckingham Palace with those high hats and straight faces. It seemed nothing would faze him.

"The forty-ninth floor, Miss?"

She nodded, and he closed the doors.

The journey up was a long one, during which she continued to question herself as to why she had come. She was still upset with Blake, and he was likely in bed already. It was nearing midnight.

In the end, loneliness had compelled her over there. Everyone else had someone to go home to. Terry had his wife; Cynthia, who worked in the forensics lab and was her best friend had her current man—she dated a lot; and Cole Richards had his wife.

Madison had a dog—Hershey, a chocolate lab—who would do his best to housebreak her into a responsible, domestic person. She would have to make this visit quick so she could get home to him. Her stomach rumbled, and she found herself desperate enough for her sister's leftovers. Maybe this was a bad idea. She could just forget it, grab a burger on the way home, and settle in there. The elevator chimed their arrival.

The elevator operator stood to the side. "Good evening, Miss."

Blake greeted her from the other side of the doors. "Quite a nice surprise." He extended a hand for hers and pulled her in to him.

The front desk must have called up to notify him he had a visitor. He owned half the floor, the elevator being in the middle of it with doors that opened to either side, dependent on which the elevator operator requested. If the other side was a mirror image to Blake's, a small foyer inlaid with marble tile greeted visitors. Ahead of this, double oak doors set a regal tone and separated private space from the lobby.

"I didn't expect to see you tonight." He swept back a stray hair from her forehead and kissed her.

The touch of his lips made her come alive, despite exhaustion. With all the death she saw on a continual basis, it was a welcome comfort.

She cocked her head into the nape of his neck and walked with him into the condo. He smelled of expensive cologne. It mingled with his personal scent and drugged her thinking.

Did it mean something more substantial than simply that? She knew there were studies out there that concluded women picked their mates based on scent. *Ridiculous.* She was getting more analytical by the hour.

He cupped his hand behind her neck, pulled her in tighter, and took her mouth. His kiss, his taste, made her hungry, but no longer for the food she had craved earlier. Rather, for him.

The passion was reciprocal, and it felt so good to be wanted. But as they kissed, her defenses recalled the betrayal she felt earlier in the day. She pulled back from him.

"Why did you do that to me?"

"Do what?"

"Pick my mother over me."

"Do you even hear what you're saying?" A smile teased his lips.

She waved her hand. "It was a bad idea to come here."

"Actually, it was a smart one because now I can tell you to your face that you're crazy."

"Excuse me?"

"Come on, Maddy, a choice between you and your mother? I'm not into older women. Simple pick."

Madison crossed her arms. "I didn't mean it like that. I meant—"

He put a hand on her shoulder. "You think because I stayed with your family that I somehow betrayed you and your need to leave."

She nodded.

"Do you want your family to like me?" he asked.

"Yes." The response was instant and said aloud so she couldn't reel it back.

"Well, I couldn't exactly just leave. You were called away. I wasn't." He ran his fingers through her short hair. "Even if the first call was a fake. You're such a bad actress." He smiled.

"Oh, shut—"

He put his mouth on hers. She didn't fight it, but let herself melt into him. She excused her weakness as a natural appetite that needed satisfying. He led her to his bedroom.

...

Madison looked over at the clock on his dresser. *1:15* AM.

It was time for her to leave, to get some sleep in her own bed, and spend time with her new four-legged responsibility.

She leaned across the bed and kissed Blake's lips. "I've gotta go."

He rolled over and pinned her. "Not even time for a shower?"

It sounded wonderful. His shower had seven jets, which covered every part of the body in a massaging pulsation that rid the body of stress, but there wasn't time.

"Not tonight." She reached for the light on the nightstand, and Blake moved back to his side of the bed. "I've gotta go. I'm a momma now."

"A momma? I wish I had recorded that."

She narrowed her eyes, yet played along. "You've just got to know where you stand. You can't have all my free time." She was smiling. "Besides, he's not that bad."

Truth was, even though Hershey demanded much of her time, she was willing to extend what she could. Maybe it had something to do with Terry's brainwashing with phrases such as, *One day he'll be a great friend* and *His love is unconditional.*

She could be putting too much faith in her partner's words, but when her relationship with Blake went down, which they always had a way of doing, at least her chocolate lab would be there to lick her wounds. Right now, though, all the thinking was only further exhausting. She had to get home before she fell asleep in Blake's bed.

He must have sensed her hesitation to leave and poked her side. "Get going then."

She kissed him on the lips, wishing she had time to stay, time to savor him again. She pulled herself out of the bed.

"You know, if you lived here, you wouldn't have to leave."

Dear God, please don't tell me he's going where I think he is…

"You said you loved me," Blake said. "I love you. Why throw your money away on rent?"

Her first thought was that she didn't need anyone to take care of her. Her second was what would her share of a place like this would amount to.

"My portion here would be more than what I spend now. I couldn't afford it." She pulled a sweater over her head and pulled up her jeans, while doing her best to keep her eyes off him.

"We could work something out."

She detected the smile in his voice. "Uh-huh. So you'd cover the monthly expenses, and I'd put out in exchange?"

"Sounds good to me. Of course, I'd also expect some light domestic duties to be taken care of. The cleaning, the cook—"

The pillow she threw hit him directly in the face.

Her ringing phone on the nightstand felt like part of a dream. Only, in a dream you could turn it off. This noise was insistent, and through slit eyes, she could see the blue glow shrouding her bedroom. By the time she'd settled into bed after going out with Hershey, it had been past two, and she remembered seeing three thirty on the clock. Thoughts of Blake's proposal kept her mind going and sleep at bay.

The ringing continued.

Figures. I was just about to dip into an REM cycle…

"Hello?" she answered. It hurt to speak. Just a few more hours… What time was it, anyway? She lifted her head enough to read her alarm. *6:03 AM.*

"Maddy?"

"Yes." She didn't have patience at the best of times, let alone when she was waking from a deep sleep, one that morphed her ringing phone into a distant church bell. *Why a church bell?* The implication gave her a headache.

"It's Cyn."

Madison sat up. "We have an ID?"

"Sort of."

"I don't get it."

"I've been here all night, and before you say anything about it, you know I hate loose ends."

Madison smiled into the receiver. That was just another aspect of Cynthia's personality that drew her in.

"The fingerprint came back with a match."

"Who is it?"

"The file number is eight-three-four-five-seven-nine-two-three."

"A file number?" Nothing was making sense right now.

"Here's the thing. The file is locked. I don't have a name to give you. The vic was wearing a gold chain with a pendant. Initials CC."

"Okay. I knew about the pendant, but why would his file be locked?"

"Obviously, our dead guy has a record we're not supposed to know about."

"Crap." She knew the fastest way to get that file unsealed, but she didn't like it. "Looks like I'm going to have to speak to McAlexandar."

Patrick McAlexandar was the chief of police, and they never saw eye to eye, but if she was going to get her answer, he would be the best place to start.

CHAPTER FOUR

"You're sure? File number eight-three-four-five-seven-nine-two-three?" Chief McAlexandar sat in his city-appointed chair bought by the votes of the people, as if he were royalty.

Madison stared at him blankly, viewing his question as rhetorical.

McAlexandar leaned across the mahogany desk, bent at the elbow, the one finger wagging at Sergeant Winston across from him. "I don't like the way your girl is looking at me."

The four of them, including Terry, were pressed into McAlexandar's fancy office. Only high-end furniture adorned the room. Expensive carpet, recently installed, modernized the space and complemented the mahogany cabinetry.

While Winston sat across from McAlexandar, Madison and Terry remained standing.

His office was on the fifth floor, on an outside corner, allowing windows to frame two of the four walls. The sun was bright and glistened off snowflakes as they fell.

Winston passed a glance to Madison, but instead of silencing her, it prompted her to speak.

"We need to know who he is. He is dead. His family has a right to—"

"Yes, I realize that." McAlexandar's temper was evident in the tone of voice, the reddened cheeks, and the intensity in his eyes.

If Madison were to guess, McAlexandar knew the person behind that specific file number—and quite well. "Who is it?"

His eyes went from Madison to her boss.

"Knight." Winston silenced her with a glare.

The room went quiet but thundered with the questions that weren't being voiced or satisfied.

Who is this man in the morgue, and what is his connection to the chief?

"I want to be the one to tell him." McAlexandar drew his hands down his face. The action brought attention to both his age and the deep-set creases on his forehead. He leaned back in his chair and swiveled side to side.

"Chief, this would give us a place to start, an ID. We could establish timeline, the situation surrounding his death—" Her words stalled with his eye contact. She stepped back again, looked at Terry, let out a puff of air, and rolled her eyes.

"The file belongs to Chris Randall."

"*The* Chris Randall, as in business tycoon Marcus Randall's son?" Terry's words were animated, but McAlexandar's unimpressed look quashed his excitement.

Marcus Randall owned the largest investment firm not only in Stiles but the entire state. The man was worth billions of dollars, and that was after the economy hit of 2008, when the markets plunged.

"We'll need his file unlocked." Madison's mind was calculating how McAlexandar knew just by hearing a file number whom it belonged to. She wanted to ask what Randall meant to him. A discrepancy that stood out to her was the pendant with the letters CC. If it was in fact Chris Randall, shouldn't it be CR?

"This situation is to be handled delicately. It must be kept from the media." McAlexandar's beady eyes steadied on Winston, a finger pointed at him. "I will notify Mr. Randall myself. How did he die?"

"Exact cause of death has not yet been confirmed," the sergeant answered.

"I would think that would be a terrific place to start."

"It seems to be a drowning, but Richards hasn't made his conclusion yet," Madison began. "He still needs to summarize his autopsy findings. He's also waiting on tox results."

McAlexandar wagged his finger again as he spoke to Winston. "Get things moving on this. Rush the results." He swiveled to look out the windows, lowered his voice, and mumbled to himself.

Madison thought she'd heard something to the effect of, *What am I going to tell him now?*

McAlexandar turned back around. "Now, as far as accessing his file, it was closed by court order and will remain such until a court order releases it. But seeing as he's dead, that should be the least of our problems." He paused. "I can't believe it."

The thought went through her mind again. Exactly how personal was the relationship between Marcus Randall and Chief McAlexandar? And if they were as close as it seemed, how could she allow him to visit the father alone? What if he was involved somehow? The relaying of that news was crucial to reading and gauging the relationships of the deceased. The Randalls, no matter who they were or how much they had, shouldn't be exempt from scrutiny.

"I can get started on releasing the file." Winston offered, and McAlexandar nodded authorization.

"Chief, if I may," Madison said. "It's important that we be there when you give notification."

Seconds passed.

She continued. "We need to gauge his relationship with the deceased—"

"The boy's own father. Really?" McAlexandar stated sourly. "Why? Do you think he killed his own son?"

It didn't seem like a good time to point out that was a possibility. Instead, she remained silent but kept steady eye contact.

"And you're questioning my ability to feel out their relationship." He had a way of phrasing questions like statements.

"I'm not questioning that."

"Then what do you question, Knight?"

It was rare for her to feel pressured, but the situation presented was delicate. She needed to speak her feelings aloud. "You're close to the Randalls?"

McAlexandar clenched his jaw in a manner she had only seen a few times. It normally came just before a suspension. She knew that from being an eyewitness to a couple of altercations. He had been her sergeant prior to police chief.

"You can come with me." He directed his next comments to Winston. "But if she says one word—I'm telling you, *one* word outta line, she's finished. You hear me?"

Madison felt slightly nauseated because she knew her ability to stay quiet was minuscule to the point of being almost nonexistent.

With them out of the room, McAlexandar opened a desk drawer he had avoided for some time. Up until now, he had always possessed the strength to refrain.

He looked at the bottle of scotch that was on its side and put a hand on it. Some might consider it foolish for a recovering alcoholic to keep a reserve so readily accessible. He viewed it as instilling character. After all, what good was a test if it wasn't before you? All he could think now was that maybe he didn't know Marcus Randall as well as he thought.

That night at the lounge, Randall had been sketchy about the details of what he needed help with. He just said the time was coming soon, and that he'd be notified. Was that time now? Had he murdered his own son?

And with Madison at his side, he would have to deal with her prying curiosity as well. He had to take her out of the equation before his world came crashing in on him.

CHAPTER FIVE

One would expect a multibillionaire to own a large estate. From the gatehouse, which resembled a small house itself, you couldn't see the main house. Madison sat in the front seat of McAlexandar's Lincoln MKS.

A man wearing a gray uniform, complete with a hat, opened the window. "Go ahead, sir. Mr. Randall is expecting you."

Madison didn't miss the quick pass McAlexandar received from the front gate. Even if McAlexandar had called ahead, it didn't explain the apparent familiarity between the chief and security guard. The latter never passed a second glance in the chief's direction but paid more attention to her. She was the outsider.

The paved drive seemed to wind forever. They passed a tennis court and a walking trail that headed out into a wooded patch on the estate. As they neared the house, she noticed an atrium at the one end that was large enough to accommodate an Olympic-sized swimming pool.

McAlexandar pulled to the top of the curved drive and parked in front of a wide brick staircase. He faced Madison. "Remember, you're here as an observer only." He repeated his earlier direction, *not one word*, and drilled it in with that wagging finger of his.

Waiting at the door, Madison turned and looked over the property. The house was elevated, affording it a good view of the river. Beside it was a boathouse larger than her apartment.

As she turned around, the door to the house opened, revealing a man in his midthirties. He had short, neatly groomed dark hair. His face was pleasant, and he had a small chin dimple. But whoever this was, Madison knew it wasn't Marcus Randall.

McAlexandar went rigid. "We're here to see—"

"Yes, I know." The man stepped back, allowing them room to move past him. He kept his eyes on her and smiled when her eyes met his.

Marcus Randall walked into the great room with a muscular man trailing him. "To what do I owe this visit?"

Randall looked just like all the photos she had ever seen of him. A distinguished man of the world, aged to maturity with a head of silver hair, complete with bushy eyebrows and lying eyes. With one sweeping glance from him, Madison knew he deemed her inferior. He viewed her even more of an outsider than had the guard at the gatehouse.

Randall walked around her and addressed his words to McAlexandar. "I trust it's an important matter."

"Do you have somewhere we could talk privately?"

Her head snapped in the direction of her superior. He knew fair well she'd come to get a feel for the relationship between father and son.

"You should know I do."

The muscular man who Madison deemed was Randall's bodyguard clung to his master's back as if a shadow.

Randall stopped walking and cast another glance that told her she was insignificant. He then turned to the large man. "You stay out here with these fine people, Jonathan."

"As you wish."

Randall and McAlexandar entered a room to the left.

The bodyguard stood braced in front of the doorway. He clasped his hands in front of himself, his one hand twisting a pinkie ring on the other. His unsettled energy would suggest he was used to being included in his boss's meetings.

"Where are my manners?" The man who answered the door walked over and extended a hand to her. "I'm Tony Medcalf, and this is Jonathan Wright." He casually waved a hand in the guard's direction.

Madison acknowledged Jonathan but returned her attention to Medcalf. She smiled at him. From the way he spoke to her and the way his eyes danced over her, she knew he found her attractive. She would take advantage of that. If she didn't have access to Randall himself, she'd get information from the two men in front of her. "I'm Detective—"

"Don't say it." Medcalf held up a hand and flashed a charming smile. "Your reputation precedes you, Madison Knight."

"Impressive, but how do you…"

"I make it a point to know who works to protect this city. Where's your partner, Detective Grant?"

He hadn't really answered her question to her satisfaction, but she'd let it slide for now. Pressing the matter would have her breaking McAlexandar's stipulation for coming: *Not one word.*

She paced the perimeter of the great room. Hallways sprouted from it in several directions. The windows were floor to ceiling, allowing natural light to flood in, and the furniture was laid out like a hotel lobby with groupings of chairs, marble-top tables, and large potted plants.

She paused in front of Randall's bodyguard. "How long have you been with Mr. Randall?"

"Should you wish to discuss that, you can speak with Marcus." Wright looked right through her and squared his shoulders.

"Never mind him. He's not that talkative." Medcalf moved over to them. "I've been with Mr. Randall for—" his face screwed up in thought "—two years now. Jonathan here came before that. I believe he may just be another son." Medcalf attempted a laugh but struggled with the performance.

Madison picked up on the strain between the two men and the differences in their relationships with their employer. Wright had more intimacy with Randall, calling him by his first name. Medcalf referred to his employer formally. The other thing engraving itself in her mind were Randall's words to McAlexandar about a private place to talk: *you should know I do.*

Randall went over to the bar cart and poured himself a scotch. "I'd ask you, but I know better." He raised his glass and took a swig. "Cheers."

McAlexandar experienced discomfort, despite being familiar with Randall's office. He had been called there and pulled from dinners and benefits held in the home many times, but they had been happier occasions. Normally the purpose involved minor things to be taken care of or a bonus wad of cash for a job well executed.

Today was not such an instance. Today, McAlexandar had initiated the meeting, and it placed him in a vulnerable position. The words from their meeting a month ago had haunted him since he found out about Randall's son. Just the vagueness of Randall's request filled him with unease.

I need your help with something. *Something*—as if that one word said it all when it really disclosed nothing.

He rarely experienced nausea, but this was certainly one of those times. If he were to bury the murder of Randall's son, he risked jeopardizing everything. He had asked himself how far he was willing to go. His mind refused to formulate the answer.

Randall stared at him from over his drink. McAlexandar opted for the direct method. "Chris is dead."

"What in blazing hell do you mean?" He took another sip of his drink, swished the amber liquid in his glass. He walked behind his desk and sat down.

McAlexandar dropped into a leather chair across from him. "We found his body—"

"Impossible. He's away on business. I sent him myself on the jet, January eleventh, to the Caymans for a few weeks."

"The Caymans? Did you ever confirm he got on that flight? That is the alibi you want to establish?" With that last question, he knew he had crossed a line.

Randall's face hardened. "Patrick, let me remind you that I am the one to ask the questions. An alibi, why in hell would I need one?"

McAlexandar's throat constricted, and it was a hard swallow.

Randall made no move to call his pilot and confirm the flight. He asked, "What happened?" as if he were inquiring about a business deal gone bust, not the death of his son.

McAlexandar sank further into the leather of his chair, seeking it as an asylum. "Cause of death is still being determined, as is the *manner* of death. Whether it was suicide, accidental, or homicide."

"Well, determine it. That's my son we're talking about." He drained the glass. "I want his body released for burial immediately."

McAlexandar would rather avoid what he had to say next, but he needed to explore all the avenues. He felt his cheeks heat. "Would he have had any reason to kill himself?"

Randall's lips tightened and pursed. A flick of fire bolted through his eyes. "My son would not have killed himself, are we clear?"

McAlexandar pinched his right earlobe until it throbbed. Anything to quiet his wild thoughts. "And as far as you know, he got on that flight a few weeks ago?"

Randall's eyes were cold and seared through him. "I don't—*didn't*—babysit my son, Patrick. Now, his body. I'd like to see it, confirm it's him."

"I don't think you'll want to do that."

"He was my son." The statement hung in the air as a divider between both men for a solid thirty seconds. "After I see him, I want his body released for burial."

"I'm not sure if I can right—"

Randall walked over to him, bent over, and spoke in his ear. "If you can't arrange it, I will find someone who can. And you know what that means about our little agreement?"

"So, what do you do for Mr. Randall?" Madison asked Medcalf. It was apparent she would get nowhere with Wright. He hadn't moved a foot from his original station, only shifted his weight from left to right.

"What I *don't* do would be a better question." Medcalf laughed.

Madison passed a glance at Wright, whose mouth twitched as though he was going to say something, but he didn't. She called him out. "You disagree?"

Silence.

Why does this man refuse to communicate?

"Never mind him; he can be like that. His job, as you can you tell, is to play mute and carry out all of Mr. Randall's requests. He's pretty much his PA."

"And here I thought you were his personal butt-kisser?" Wright slapped back.

The tension between the two men had been given voice. Without company, or the supervision of their employer, she feared for Medcalf's safety, and all it took was the look in Wright's eyes.

Medcalf turned to Madison. "We'll leave him to his hand-holding. I must start preparing lunch. Would you like to come with me?"

Madison followed Medcalf into the kitchen, which would be any chef's dream. The room itself was monstrous with its high ceiling and skylights. Windows framed the outside walls just as the great room, and granite counters lined the wall in an L-shape. In the middle of the cabinetry and counters was an island with a double sink, and overhead, stainless steel cookware hung from a pan rack, dangling as if they were gigantic wind chimes. Her gaze settled on a tap that came out over the stovetop.

"It's for filling a pot on the stove. It makes it a lot easier than hauling it from the main sink." Medcalf must have followed the direction of her gaze and read the inquiry on her expression.

She nodded, dismissing it like she had foreknowledge, but the extent of her culinary skills ended with mac and cheese. "You obviously cook for him," she said in hopes of getting a dialogue started.

Medcalf moved toward meat wrapped in butcher's paper that sat on a wooden chopping block. Next to it were a few grocery bags. The corner of a cigar box poked out of one of them.

Circular impression on the backside of the hand... Almost large enough to be a car lighter or a cigar.

Madison leaned in to read the brand name, but Medcalf pulled the bag back and, in the process, tucked the box out of sight.

"Cooking is one of my responsibilities." He smiled, pride in his expression, and he started to unwrap the meat. "Every morning I go to Hanigan's Market and get fresh ingredients. I just got back before you got here. Almost missed meeting you."

Madison had been to Hanigan's Market once or twice in the past. Numerous vendors set up under one roof—except for in the summer when the market spilled out into the back parking lot. The market offered everything from butchered meat, imported and local fruits and vegetables, and freshly baked goods, to artwork and candles.

Medcalf took a large knife out of a drawer and sliced the chicken breasts in half lengthwise. "Along with cooking, I answer his door, the telephone..." He paused. "Maybe *I* am Mr. R's PA." He dismissed the title with a wave of the knife.

Madison noted how Medcalf switched to a more personal address for Marcus Randall than he had been using. The relationship between Medcalf and Randall was an uncomfortable one. She let that pass and focused on the one between him and Wright. "I sense you and Jonathan don't get along."

"I'm not the one with the issue."

The topic was obviously now closed. She watched his hands work on the meal. "What is it today?" It pained her to make small talk with this guy.

"Brie-stuffed chicken breast with a green salad misted with balsamic."

Madison needed to direct the conversation and dredge up some information that could prove enlightening. But how could she do that without getting herself into a heap of trouble?

"Chris not home?" She posed the question casually, even though it bordered on distasteful.

"Nope, I haven't seen him in weeks, not that that's unusual." Medcalf's hands stopped moving. "Women are always curious about that boy. I don't know what charm he has over them." He went back to meal preparation. "And he has a way of finding trouble. I thought he must have done something when I saw the two of you."

Two of you. While McAlexandar's presence was common, the fact he had company, her, meant something different. She thought of the locked record. "Does that happen often? Chris getting into trouble?"

Medcalf's gaze remained on the food. Another avenue of conversation hit a dead end. Maybe it was more a roundabout. She'd pick it up from another angle.

"Chris takes off a lot? You mentioned it's not unusual not to see him for weeks?" It was hard to carry on speaking of Chris in the present tense with flashes of him on the metal slab hitting her.

"Mr. R keeps him busy. He travels for the company, seeking out new clients for investments. The economy's still recovering here, but the global markets are strong."

"Guess I never realized the impact of Randall Investments."

"They are worth billions due to their global market share—"

"Are we interrupting something?" Randall stepped into the room with McAlexandar at his side and Wright behind.

Medcalf hesitated briefly. "I was just showing Detective Knight here your beautiful kitchen."

"And apparently, my lunch."

"Actually, we just finished with the tour," she said, finding it hard to decide whether to look at Randall or McAlexandar, so she didn't look at either one. She certainly didn't need to glance at the chief to sense his displeasure: she felt it.

Randall turned to McAlexandar. "Now, it would be quite rude of me not to ask you to join me."

"We should go. Again, my sympathies." McAlexandar pulled a hand from his pocket to shake Randall's. It came out with a bag. "Almost forgot. This was found on him."

Madison gauged the man's reaction as he reached for the pendant and gold chain.

Randall studied it briefly before handing it to Wright. "Put this someplace." He extended a hand to McAlexandar again. "You sure you can't stay for lunch?"

"Maybe another time."

Or maybe at a more appropriate time, was all Madison could think.

CHAPTER SIX

It was two in the afternoon, and Winston was working on paperwork to have Chris Randall's file released. The slamming door made him look up.

Chief McAlexandar dropped into a chair across from him. "She couldn't contain herself." When Winston didn't respond, he continued. "She can't keep her mouth shut." He crossed his legs and ran a hand down the front of his pants.

"I can't fire her because she's doing her job."

"Since when does her job include accusing an innocent man of murdering his own son? Or is that a normal thing for people under your command?"

Winston knew his boss was capable of exaggerating situations, but he also knew enough not to challenge him outright. "What exactly did she do?"

"That's the problem, Winston. The girl doesn't listen."

He noticed how the chief had diverted his question.

"All she does is run off at the mouth. She can't say we didn't warn her." His meaty hands clasped over a knee.

Winston wished he possessed the strength to stand up to his boss. "I'm not sure how we could justify—"

"If you don't have the balls to fire her, suspend her." McAlexandar stood in a brisk movement. "I would have thought more of you." He pushed on the back of the chair. The rear legs came off the floor, and the front ones screeched along the tile.

"I'm not saying no." Winston's words came out too late. His superior was already out the door and no doubt down the hall. Winston never had a chance to say he'd think about it. It wasn't the first time Madison Knight had spoken out of line, and it probably wouldn't be the last. And to be honest, despite her close record, Winston was tiring of the drama she created.

The ride back to the station with McAlexandar had been a quiet one. The air was electric with the words not being spoken. Madison feared this had been a test that she had failed, and one she was set up to fail. She didn't like what the answer equated. He was looking for a good reason to pull her badge.

Madison expected to find her partner stabled behind his desk, but instead found him chatting with a couple of undercover cops. She came up behind him and bobbed her brows at one of the officers and addressed her partner. "Haven't you got work to do?"

The men stopped talking. Terry turned around.

"You're back. I was starting to wonder if—"

"Don't change the subject." She cocked her head, offering a smile to calm her nerves. "I need the file pulled on Chris Randall."

"You know it's locked."

"The criminal aspects, yes. What I'm looking for is his personal background."

"You know where the computer is." Terry smiled at his buddies, whose eyes now avoided his.

"You really want me to kick your ass in front of the guys? Because I will do it."

Terry pressed his lips and enlarged his eyes to the other detectives. "See what I have to work with?" He laughed.

"Later, Grant. The old lady needs you." This from someone Madison knew by the name of Spencer.

"I'm going to pretend I didn't hear that and let you live."

"Ooh…" Spencer shook his hands as if he was scared.

"Go." She smiled. "Come on. We have work to do." She scanned the officers' faces. All their expressions read the same thing: they were glad they weren't her partner. She hated how ambitious women were often regarded as bitchy, while ambitious men were revered. Even so, she softened her approach. "Please."

Spencer started to walk away, stopped, and spoke over a shoulder. "You going to let a woman tell you what to do, Grant?" Spencer chuckled.

"Never gonna live it down. We won't let you," one of the other officers said.

No matter their age, some men never grow up.

With the Hardy Boys gone, she addressed Terry. "We need the name of the vic's mother."

"Just for the record, I looked into woman named on the napkin and found her."

"Good." Before she'd left with McAlexandar, she'd asked Terry to hunt down her down.

"Her full name's Renee Hanover."

"Good." She walked around to her desk and rummaged around in a drawer for a Hershey's bar.

"No gold stars then?"

"Plumb out."

Terry dropped into his chair, clicked some keys on the keyboard. She assumed he was looking into Chris's mother.

"I take it this afternoon didn't go so well." Terry pulled his gaze from his monitor and looked at her.

She walked up behind his chair.

"You spoke, didn't you?" he said. "You always have something to say."

She bit off a huge mouthful and leaned in toward his monitor.

"You're freaking me out here."

"Might as well have not even been there, except—"

"Oh, gross, you're talking with your mouth full again."

"Terry."

Both hands rose in surrender, and he turned serious. "What do you mean?"

"McAlexandar took Randall into another room and told him there."

"Then why bring you along?"

She swallowed a good chunk of chocolate. "Good question. Maybe you could ask him." Her words stalled as data filled the screen. Terry had searched the database for Chris's mother. Looking back at her was the name Martha Cooper. "Guess we can see what the CC engraved on Chris's pendant might have stood for."

"You never got anything out of going? Nothing at all? Nothing about Chris's relationships?"

"Actually, I got plenty. For one, the chief is all buddy-buddy with Randall. The staff knew him, too."

"As you suspected."

She nodded. She wasn't willing to share all her observations with her partner just yet. But one thing she feared was this powerful relationship could make the truth of what happened to Chris that much harder to uncover.

CHAPTER SEVEN

Martha Cooper's current information showed she lived in a village on the outskirts of Stiles, only a twenty-minute drive away.

"How do you know that Randall hasn't told her already?" Terry asked from the passenger seat.

"If you had met this guy, you wouldn't ask that question."

"You're not sharing anything from your visit, so how would I know?"

She tapped a hand on the steering wheel. "The guy didn't even mist."

"You said you weren't in the room."

"Just trust me, okay? He came out with the chief and was more concerned about his household privacy being compromised and the intrusion into his lunch plans."

"Men grieve differently."

"Terry, I realize that, but at the same time, he was just told that…" Her words stalled. She realized she may be letting her feelings for the chief taint her view of Randall—not that she would admit that to Terry.

"You don't like Randall. Seems obvious."

"I don't like the secrecy surrounding him."

She pulled into Cooper's driveway behind a sedan. Terry ran the license plate through the onboard computer.

"It's her car," he said.

"Good, so she should be home."

They got out of the car and walked toward the house. It was Victorian architecture with a wraparound porch. Its brown shingles combined with the light-green trim had Madison craving chocolate-mint ice cream. The idyllic picture was made complete by a white picket fence that surrounded the property.

"I'd say she's doing all right," Terry said.

"Did you have any doubt she would be? Break up with a man like Randall, and I'd be making sure I got a good cut."

Madison rang the doorbell and waited, shivering from the damp chill in the air. The surrounding fields allowed the breeze to gust through, amplifying the dropping temperature.

She waited for what felt like eternity. "No answer. Really?"

Terry rubbed his hands together, blew on them. "Maybe someone picked her up in their car? Or she went for a walk? Either way, she hasn't picked this up yet—" he nudged a plastic-wrapped newspaper with his shoe "—but I guess it could have been delivered after she left."

She hit the doorbell again. A few seconds later, she knocked. She repeated the cycle a few times.

"And since when do you rush to make notification?" Terry matched eyes with her. "You hate it."

He was right there, and it was why they normally kept track of who did it last. Neither of them wanted to be burdened with the task twice in a row.

The door opened to reveal a woman. "Who are you?" She picked up her paper and then answered her own question. "You're cops."

"Detectives Knight and Grant," Madison said. "Martha Cooper?"

"Yes." She dragged out the word, throwing glances between them.

Her record showed her as forty-five, but she didn't appear a day over thirty, with barely a wrinkle on her face. Dressed in black slacks and a gray cashmere sweater adorned by a long string of pearls, she belonged in a magazine spread sitting by a fireplace and reading. She was petite, all of five foot, and kept herself slender. Her brown eyes disclosed intelligence.

"Can we come in?" Madison asked.

She tucked the paper under an arm. "Is this about Marcus Randall?"

Madison found it interesting she assumed Randall was the reason for their visit. "Can we come in?" Madison asked again.

"Fine." The woman let out a deep sigh and eyed them cautiously before moving aside. "It's just that every time law enforcement comes around, it involves that man."

"Do cops come around often?" Madison asked.

Martha didn't answer the question and closed the door behind them, latching both the lock on the knob and the deadbolt.

Madison wiped her boots. "Do you have somewhere we can sit?"

She crossed her arms. "What's going on?"

"We'll get to that."

Martha studied Madison's eyes and rubbed her forearms. "This way then." She directed them to a sofa opposite a chaise lounge she sat on. Perched on the edge, she crossed her legs. Her upper body leaned toward them. A gas fireplace kicked out radiant heat from behind her.

"Unfortunately, we have bad news about your son. He was found dead—"

"What...What do you mean? Does he know?" The last question came out with heat.

"Does *he* know?" Madison prompted, seeking clarification on who *he* was.

"Marcus," she blurted out. "Does he know?"

"He was notified earlier today."

"That bastard." She rose to her feet, paced an oval the width of the room. "He knows everything first. He knew and he didn't have the decency to call me?" She pinched her pearl necklace. Her eyes misted, seemingly fixed on nothing in particular. "My son is dead?" After seconds of silence, Cooper grabbed a tissue from a nearby table, dabbed her nose, and then held it scrunched in her hand. "How?" She twisted the tissue in her fingers. "How did he…"

Madison relayed the basics about where he was found and how, and added, "It seems he may have drowned."

"Was it an accident?" Her tone gave away her dark thoughts.

"The circumstances surrounding Chris's death are being investigated," Madison told her.

An ear-piercing wail hurled from her small frame, and she rocked herself back and forth.

Madison steeled herself emotionally. "We're sorry for your loss, Ms. Cooper."

"Do you have any suspects?" Her gaze froze on Madison's.

"At this point we do not."

"Well, let me give you one." Martha's chin quivered. "Marcus Randall." A hand covered her mouth as she sobbed behind it.

"Marcus Randall?" Madison had to dismiss her personal distaste for the man. "Why do you think that?"

There was another series of deep sobs. They waited it out.

"That man only loves himself and would be completely willing to sacrifice his own son." The intensity in Martha's eyes revealed a struggle.

"You're afraid of him?"

"I was married to that man for five years. Five years I'll never get back. At least I got Chris out of it." She choked back another sob. "Still can't believe it," she added in a whisper.

"If you truly believe Marcus Randall had something to do with your son's death, you need to give us something to go on." Madison had to watch that her own feelings about Randall didn't blind her to other factors in the case. If she reacted prematurely toward Randall, his influence and connection with the chief would likely cost her the thing she loved most—her career. No case was worth that if established on hearsay and unfounded suspicion.

"He had private meetings all the time," Martha began. "Men were in and out of our house, and it wasn't always the same ones."

"That's why you broke up?" Terry asked.

Martha glanced at Terry. "Heavens no. The money was great, the parties too, but after a while it's not enough to make you overlook other transgressions."

Madison took a guess. "Other women?"

"Constantly. That should have been enough, but I accepted it as coming with the territory, so to speak. I just didn't want Chris exposed to him and the men he kept regular company with. It got to the point I couldn't put up with it anymore. I moved out, filed for divorce." She sat on the chaise again and twisted the pearls. "He told me that he'd give me my divorce, a more than fair settlement, as he put it, but I'd have to give up Chris."

"I can't even imagine how that would make you feel." Madison found irony—and some hypocrisy—in the fact Martha had been willing to accept those terms. Her claim was she'd left because she didn't want Chris around his father and his associates, yet in the end, she had abandoned him there.

"Until it happens to you…" She stopped twisting the pearls and held them pinched between two fingers. "I thought maybe Marcus was making a veiled threat, but he wouldn't allow me to see him. But what he didn't know was Chris would come visit me here. He found me at sixteen. At least I had some good years with him." Tears fell, and she dabbed at her nose with a tissue.

"Was Chris ever involved with anything illegal?" Madison asked.

Martha let go of the necklace and picked at the tissue held in the palm of her other hand. "Why would you say such a thing?" Her brows pressed downward into a V. "And wouldn't you have a record of that?"

Madison would temper her response with empathy. "There is a file on your son, but it's locked."

Martha covered her mouth with her hand for a few seconds. "I can't imagine what he did."

"Do you know if he did drugs?" Madison's thoughts were on the bills in Chris's pocket, along with the media rumors.

"I have no idea." Her face hardened. "But with Chris being dead, I'd put Marcus behind it."

Madison nodded slowly. Martha would have every reason to keep pointing a finger at Randall. But with her viewpoint tainted by emotion, she wouldn't be a reliable character witness.

"Was he wearing a necklace when you found him? It would have been a gold chain with a pendant. The letters CC on it." Her misted eyes searched Madison's and caused Madison's stomach to tighten.

"I will look into it," was what she said, but she recalled how Randall had passed off the necklace and pendant to Wright—"*to put someplace*"—as if it was nothing of any consequence.

Minutes later, Madison and Terry offered their condolences and made their exit.

"The necklace was given to Randall, wasn't it?" Terry asked as he got into the car.

"Yeah."

"And how do you propose to get it back?"

"Ask me how I did after I'm fired." She put the car into gear.

His head snapped in her direction. "You can't go there and speak to him."

"That boy was all she had."

"I wouldn't say she looked that hard up."

"From a man about to be a father."

Terry's wife, Annabelle, was about four months pregnant with their first child.

"Don't be like that. A necklace isn't going to bring him home."

"Yet, I'm tagged insensitive? Her only son was taken from her. My sister has three kids, and if she lost one, she'd feel as if she might as well curl up and die herself."

"Fine, just don't take me down with you…if you get fired." He sat back into the seat, eyes on the road.

She knew he was right. She couldn't go storming into the Randall estate and request that the necklace and pendant be returned. And it wasn't worth losing her career to prove a point. She needed to redirect back to the evidence.

"The lady from the napkin—Renee…"

"Hanover," he finished.

"You said you found her. Where does she live?"

CHAPTER EIGHT

The clock on the dash read five thirty when Madison and Terry pulled in front of Renee Hanover's home.

A man answered who could have been singer Marc Anthony's younger brother.

Madison flashed her badge and gestured toward Terry without looking at him. "We'd like to speak with Renee Hanover."

"I'm her husband. What is this about?" He leaned on the edge of the door.

Renee was a married woman. Terry hadn't shared that finding or she hadn't heard him when he had.

"Who is it?" A woman came up beside him. Her hair was dark and reached her jawline. Her eyes were a deep cocoa and held more vitality, blended with a dose of mischievousness, in comparison to the man's eyes. Her focus was on Madison and Terry.

"They're looking for you." The man sidestepped, putting some space between him and his wife.

"Why are you looking for me?"

How did her name and number end up on Chris? Was she having an affair with him, or intending to?

"Can we discuss something with you in private?" Madison asked.

"Sure, I guess so." She put a hand on her husband's shoulder.

He cast them a glance, communicating he didn't trust anyone, even law enforcement.

Renee watched her husband leave and turned to face Madison. The silent inquiry in her eyes read, *What do you want?*

"We're here because we found a napkin with your name and phone number on it."

The woman stepped closer to them, pulling the door in behind her. "Please keep it down." She lowered her voice. "I go to the clubs sometimes, have a few, and get a little flirty. I hand out my number all the time." Her eyes darted between them, to the front lawn past them, back to them. She let out a deep breath. "My husband doesn't know and wouldn't be too happy if he found out."

It made one motive clear. If Renee's husband found out about her flirting, he might have killed Chris out of jealousy.

The smell of cigar escaped from inside the house. Madison looked through the two-inch opening and saw a haze of smoke. "Are you sure he doesn't already know?"

Renee was quiet for a few seconds. "If he does, he's never mentioned it. Please don't say anything." Her eyes went to Terry. "And since when is drinking too much and handing out your number a crime?"

"Your number was found on a dead man. Chris Randall." Madison was tired of playing games and gave it to her straight.

"Found on...dead...Chris..."

"His body washed up this morning," Madison added.

"Washed up..." She traced her wedding band with her right hand.

"We're hoping you can help us with—"

Her eyes widened dramatically. "I didn't kill him! You think I—" She shook her head and stepped back, opening the door wide with the action.

"We're not saying you—"

Her husband returned to her side. A lit cigar was perched in the fingers of one hand. His other arm wrapped protectively around his wife. "What's going on?"

"They think I killed someone." Renee rubbed her arms.

"Why the hell would you think that?" He raised his cigar, took a drag on it, and exhaled the smoke on a slow breath. It lifted as a heavy fog heavenward, but not before brushing across their faces.

Madison steadied the urge to pull the cigar from his fingers and extinguish it on the ground. Instead, she analyzed his reaction to the current situation. He was calm and cool. There was no trace of panic in his eyes, and they seemed to search hers for answers. He took another slow pull on the cigar, this time exhaling the smoke back into the house.

After tangible seconds of silence, Renee turned to her husband. "I'll explain everything to you later."

"Tell me later? You're accused of murder, and you'll tell me later?"

Madison addressed Renee. "When was the last time you saw Chris Randall?"

"How would my wife know him? Isn't he some rich kid? He's always in the tabloids."

"Listen, Mr. Hanover—"

"No," he cut in, "you listen. My wife wouldn't kill anyone." His head slowly pivoted toward Renee. "Chris Randall?"

"We never said she killed anyone, but I am finding it interesting how both of you seem to think we are," Madison said.

He retracted the arm from his wife. "Now I'm confused. She seems to think you're accusing her of it."

Madison took one second too long to formulate a response.

"We're done here." He went to close the door, but Renee stopped it short.

She looked at her husband, licked her top lip, and then turned to them. "It was my birthday—"

"What the hell, Renee?"

"I was out with my girls. We had a few drinks. I met Chris there."

"You sleep with him?"

She refused her husband eye contact.

"You slept with him. I can't believe it. What the fuck?" He slammed the door shut, with him and his wife inside. He yelled at them from there. "Get off my property!"

Madison and Terry stood facing the closed door for a while before leaving and piling into the car.

Terry got into the passenger seat. "That went well."

"Actually, it did. We may have just gotten our timeline. She said she met him on her birthday. Pull up her file and—" Madison's cell phone rang, and she hesitated to answer. Maybe it was the sergeant calling her in for a meeting. It rang again.

"You going to get that?"

She glanced at the caller ID. It was Cynthia. She answered, putting the call on speaker. "Whatcha got for us?"

"I wanted to fill you in before Winston got to you."

Madison's heart sank. *Are the rumors about me getting fired already circulating?*

Cynthia continued. "Remember the bills in the vic's pocket? Well, they turned out to be counterfeit, and they're a very good replicate. It showed up under UV, but to the eye, they would easily pass for the real deal. I reported them to the Secret Service, and they've very interested. It's just a matter of time before they show up."

"The Secret Service," Madison said, and Terry faced her. "Cynthia, the Randalls are worth billions. Why would a rich kid have fake money?"

"Good question for which I don't have the answer. I'm just filling you in. The chief and sarge know, and neither of them looked impressed. Wouldn't be surprised if the Secret Service has already contacted them."

"We'll be back in about half an hour."

"Ah, Maddy…" Cynthia paused as if making sure Madison hadn't hung up yet. "I wanted to tell you that I was able to pull trace from the burn to the vic's—"

"*Chris's* hand." The manual on being a good cop dictated distance from the victim, but Madison hated the label if it could be avoided. She'd let the first reference to the vic pass.

"Yes, *Chris's* hand. When it burnt his flesh, it left behind trace, and I was able to determine the chemical make-up. To start with, it was definitely a cigar, not a cigarette."

"The brand?"

"I'll need a comparison."

Madison knew where to get one.

CHAPTER NINE

"Believe me, I did not kill him." Renee Hanover had tears in her eyes.

When Madison and Terry had returned to the Hanovers' home a second time, they could hear the fighting from halfway up the walk. The couple was now in an interrogation room at the station with Madison and Terry.

"We don't think you did." Madison turned to the husband, whose first name was Miles.

"Why are you looking at me?" he huffed.

"You knew about your wife. It wasn't the first time and wouldn't be the last. When you saw her with someone like Chris, though, you feared she'd actually leave you, so you got rid of him."

"Miles." Renee faced her husband. "You knew?"

He ignored his wife's inquiry.

"Did you see her with Chris Randall?" Madison asked.

"Just say no." Renee tugged on his arm. He shrugged free. "Miles?"

He responded to Madison. "Yes. I saw her."

"Miles, I'm sorry." Renee went to touch him again, but he moved out of reach.

"For the record, you admit to knowledge of your wife's affair?"

"I wasn't having an affair," Renee squeaked.

"Then please clarify your relationship with Chris Randall, Mrs. Hanover," Madison requested.

"I told you. I drink too much sometimes."

The husband pushed his chair back from the table and stood. "*Sometimes?*" he snarled. "It's pretty much a regular occurrence."

Renee's eyes fired and projected blame. "If it wasn't for your cigar habit, we wouldn't even be here."

Miles punched a pointed finger toward his wife. "Ah, correction. If it weren't for your loose nature, we wouldn't be here. This started with you."

Madison had no desire to play marriage counselor. "When did you meet Chris?" she asked Renee.

"My birthday. January tenth."

That date lined up with Richards's estimation that Chris's time of death had been three weeks ago. "Was that the last time you saw him?"

"Yes, and the *only* time." Renee glanced at her husband, who had remained standing and was rubbing at his jaw.

 "And where was that?"

"Caesar's. It's a club."

"What was he wearing?"

Renee worried her bottom lip. "Jeans and a gray hoodie."

Exactly what he'd been found in. Renee could have been the last person to see him alive.

There was a knock on the door.

Terry got up and stepped into the hall. Seconds later, he returned, shaking his head.

Madison could tell from the timing, and her partner's expression, that he'd just received the lab results. The chemical composition of Miles's cigars wasn't a match to the one that had burned Chris's hand. "Guess you're free to go," Madison told the Hanovers.

Terry led them out of the room and then came back to Madison. "Now what?"

She knew by the look in his eyes and the way he'd spoken those words that he was hoping they would call it a day. She wished Miles Hanover would have been found guilty. It would allow her to get her mind off Randall and her suspicions that he knew more than he was willing to share. Her job would remain safely intact. "When I went to Randall's and talked with the cook, there was a box of cigars in a grocery bag."

"Did you see the brand name?"

She shook her head. "Just saw a corner of the box."

"Well, you know we're not getting in there right away."

She cocked her head to the side. "And doesn't it make you wonder why?"

"Hey, every rich man has secrets."

"Fine, but does Marcus Randall's include the murder of his own son?"

Terry left for home, but Madison sat at her computer, thinking about Cole Richards. This case was different to him than other ones. When he'd stood over Chris, talking to Terry and her, his eyes had mostly stayed fixed on the body. Richards, although he was meticulous and cared about finding justice for the victims, knew how to separate himself from the cases. But that wasn't happening here. He seemed personally invested somehow.

She brought up a background on Richards and noted the names of his wife and his birth parents. The latter were still alive, but Richards had been given up for adoption as a young boy and she wondered why.

Her heart beat faster knowing that she was crossing a fine line by digging into the personal history of a colleague, but she was more intrigued than before. She looked up from the computer toward the bullpen, contemplating whether to take a chance on the mud brew. It could take longer to find her answers than she originally thought, so she opted to grab a cup.

The stir stick swirled in the coffee as she raised the mug for a drink. As her eyes fixed back on the screen, she noticed something she hadn't before. Her coffee went down the wrong way, and she worked through a rough coughing fit for a few seconds. Richards had a brother by the name of Shannon, but he had died at the age of six—only months before Richards was put into the foster-care system.

She pulled the death certificate and finally had an understanding why this case would be different to him. Shannon had drowned. And Madison had a sinking feeling that also had to do with why Richards was given up for adoption.

CHAPTER TEN

With a new day came renewed determination. Madison walked into the station and sat across from Terry. "When did you get in?"

"Eight." He took a sip out of a Starbucks cup.

She glanced at the clock. *9:15 AM.*

Next her eyes went to his Starbucks. "Where's mine?"

"You'll have bigger issues to deal with than a lack of caffeine."

"What are you talking about?"

"The Secret Service is here. Two guys are in with McAlexandar and Winston. It's closed door, and the chief doesn't look impressed—at all."

"Surprised he's up this early."

"The sarge didn't look too happy, either. And he came to me for a case update."

"What?" Her heart skipped. He never did that. She was the lead detective, the one he should have come to. Maybe it was just because she was running late.

"Yeah, it was strange. It gave me a bad feeling."

Her stomach tightened with anger and betrayal. "I didn't do anything."

"You told me you talked to Randall's people. The cook, anyway."

She clenched her teeth. "The chief doesn't usually get so involved in our cases. Why now?"

"Hate to break it to you, but McAlexandar's never really liked you."

"Think there's more to it. He's extremely secretive when it comes to his relationship with Randall—and protective. Why? It seems as though he wants me to hold back on the investigation. Normally he wants me diving in, getting answers, solving a case." She was starting to feel like a broken record voicing her curiosity about the chief, but regardless, it was worth mentioning again and again. Maybe at one point it would sink into her partner's thick skull that McAlexandar might be motivated to protect Randall for his own personal interests.

"Just watch yourself."

"Terry, how can't you see it? That man is hiding something. He knew the file number for Chris Randall from memory. He demanded that he be the one to notify Marcus Randall. He obviously has a personal relationship with the man."

"Okay, yeah, him knowing the file number was strange. I'll give you that one." Terry twirled a pen.

"Exactly. There's something going on there, and I don't like it."

"Leave it alone."

"You know every time I'm told that, I just want to push harder." She didn't say as much out loud, but if it took her risking her career to find justice, she would. Although she preferred to figure out how to accomplish that *and* keep her job. But she feared in order to do so, she would have to balance politics with diplomacy—two things she struggled with on their own.

"We demand full access to this case." The Secret Service agent, who was maybe five-four, sat in the conference room chair, with his back straight as if to give the impression of greater height. His hair was the color of a candle flame, and he went by the name of Albert Weiss.

His colleague, Henry Walters, was an older man, probably nearing the age of retirement. The two men sat beside each other across from McAlexandar and Winston.

"How is it you came to be here again?" McAlexandar chose to play naive.

"We were notified of the existence of counterfeit bills."

"Notified how, exactly?"

Weiss's face went serious. "That's not necessary for you to know."

If McAlexandar were to guess, it was that friend of Madison's in the lab who had reported the fake money.

"We need you to hand your file on the Randall case over to us," Weiss said.

McAlexandar jutted out his jaw. "And if I refuse?"

"Not an option." Weiss glanced at his counterpart.

McAlexandar sensed his weakness. He was a rookie, being trained to replace the older agent. "Life is full of options."

"We're not here to get into a pissing contest over territory." The older agent, Walters, stepped in, leaning across the table and lacing his fingers. "We do, however, have a job to do. We understand the case involves a homicide."

"A *possible* homicide," Winston clarified.

McAlexandar glared at his subordinate.

"And we're to understand it involves Chris Randall?" Walters asked.

Apparently that lab rat has a big mouth, like her friend.

"He was the victim," Winston confirmed.

McAlexandar faced Winston again. He would remember this betrayal. In fact, maybe it was time for some restructuring within the Stiles PD. Winston was weak, and a poor leader made for an ineffectual team. The Mouth, Knight, proved the case in point.

The Secret Service men turned to look at each other.

"What am I missing?" McAlexandar asked.

Walters sat back. "We've had our eye on Randall for some time."

McAlexandar ran a flattened hand along his tie. "Yet Chris died on your watch."

"Excuse me?" Walters said.

"I believe you're smart enough to get where I'm going with this."

Weiss cleared his throat. "Who are you to be questioning—"

"We can't be posted on the family every hour of the day," Walters jumped in.

"Apparently," McAlexandar seethed.

"While the death of this young man is regrettable," Walters said, "it is no more the fault of the Secret Service than it is the Stiles PD."

McAlexandar seemed to be fighting a battle that he wouldn't win, but maybe he could turn the conversation on its head and get something useful to take away. "Why were you watching Chris Randall?"

"Oh, not just him. Also Marcus Randall, his father," Weiss answered matter-of-factly.

"And why were they being watched?" McAlexandar felt his heart stall as he waited for the agent's response.

Walters leaned back and rubbed his jaw. "We believe they are running a large counterfeit operation."

"That is ridiculous," McAlexandar spat. But as the implication settled in, he felt relief. It could be the Secret Service investigation that Marcus had wanted his help with and nothing to do with his son's death. Though that didn't explain why Marcus had remained so calm and composed in the face of it.

"We have our reasons," Walters deadpanned.

"And what would they be?" McAlexandar served back.

"We're not under obligation to answer that question." Walters sat back, body stiff, and the eager, young agent mimicked the movement.

"Unbelievable," McAlexandar bellowed.

Weiss cleared his throat but said nothing.

. . .

Madison walked into the lab with Terry. Cynthia was on the phone but hung up when she saw them.

"I was just calling you." Cynthia smiled and adjusted her glasses. "We were able to retrieve the information from the SIM card in the phone and get the number. It was a prepaid dealy and didn't get me too far."

"He probably had more than one." Madison's mind turned to the fake cash he'd had on his person. "Chris had a reputation for drug use. Maybe he used the burner for drug dealing. If he was, it could also explain the fake money."

Terry turned to her. "So you think he was a drug dealer?"

"Suppose it's possible, isn't it?" The idea had just struck her. She wasn't sure if it was sticking.

"I guess, but it's not as if the kid needed the extra income," Terry mumbled.

"He didn't need fake money, either," Madison countered.

Cynthia bobbed her head as the two of them volleyed back and forth.

"Maybe he paid the wrong supplier with the fake cash and it caught up to him?" Madison tossed out another possibility.

"We'll have to wait on tox to see if any drugs were in his system," Cynthia stated.

Madison looked at Terry. "His mother couldn't confirm he even used drugs. It could just be what the media wants us to believe."

Terry shrugged. "A second ago you were making him out to be a drug dealer."

She hitched her shoulders. "Just thinking out loud. Besides dealers often don't use their product."

Cynthia glanced at each of them. "Getting back to the phone… When was Chris last seen alive?"

"January tenth," Terry offered.

"By a Renee Hanover, the woman from the napkin. She met him at a club called Caesar's and confirmed he was wearing a gray hoodie and blue jeans. What he was found in."

"Oh, that place is amazing." Passion sparked in Cynthia's eyes, and the lights in the room seemed to dance across them. "Caesar's," she punched out as if Madison hadn't followed. "The hottest guys go there. It doesn't even get going until about midnight. You and I need to go together some time. Maybe after this case is solved, we—"

"Cyn, focus." The last place Madison wanted to go was some club.

Cynthia narrowed her eyes. "You two can go on and on with your speculations about whether Chris was a user or not, dealer or not, and I make one comment about a nightclub and—"

"Cyn." Madison smiled.

"Oh, you're no fun sometimes, you know that?" She tucked a loose strand of hair behind her ear. "Fine, we'll go back to business. Do you believe her, this Renee?"

"No reason not to at this point," Madison concluded.

Cynthia moved in front of her computer and pulled up a screen full of numbers. "This is a copy of the phone activity on the vic's cell. Sorry, *Chris's* cell." She scrolled down and slid a finger along the edge of the monitor at the same time. "Okay, there are no outgoing calls made after January tenth. There were three incoming on the eleventh, though, and they're from the same number."

"What is the number?" Terry asked.

Cynthia read it off.

"That number belongs to Randall Investments," Terry said immediately, drawing both women's attention.

Madison shook her head. "You and the number thing, that's strange."

"I've told you before, I'm good with numbers," he said. "I had Renee's background long before you got back from Randall's estate, so I started researching Randall's company. I remembered the number from the website header." He paused for a second, looking deep in thought. "The fact it's that number calling Chris's phone is actually in Marcus's favor. I mean, he didn't know Chris was dead or he wouldn't have tried reaching him."

"Randall could have killed his son and called the number the next day so that we'd think he had nothing to do with Chris's death," Madison suggested.

"Touché. Well, we might not ever know for sure," Terry conceded. "That's Randall Investments' main number."

"Anyone from that building could have placed the calls," Cynthia argued, "but Maddy's suggestion is also possible."

"Aw, thanks." Madison smiled at her friend. "So, you believe Marcus might have killed his son?"

Cynthia held up her hands. "I don't even know the guy. I'm not saying that, but you think he was involved, and normally, that's enough for me to be suspicious."

Madison turned to Terry. "Why can't you be more like Cyn?"

"You can't just twist things to fit your theories," Terry grumbled.

Madison let out a deep sigh and addressed Cynthia. "Any voice mails on the phone?"

Cynthia shook her head. "Nope. If there were any, I'd have told you about them already. I do want to point out the tenth to you, though. The last day Chris was seen, there are five incoming calls—four of which were blocked—and one outgoing."

"And what's the outgoing number?" Madison asked.

Cynthia rattled it off, and both women looked at Terry.

"What?"

"You don't know who that one belongs to?" Madison teased with a smile.

"Not this time, smart ass."

"Good thing I do, then," Cynthia said and met Terry's gaze. "I just thought I'd give you another chance to shine, Terry. The number ties back to a Ryan Turner." Cynthia paused, looking at them. "You don't know who that is, do you?"

"Should we?" Madison asked.

Cynthia opened a drawer and pulled out a gossip magazine, flipped through some pages, and pressed one of her manicured fingertips to a photograph. Chris Randall was holding a glass of alcohol up in a toasting gesture to another man about his age. A third guy stood back from them, his face partially obscured by a beer bottle lifted to his mouth. Young women were all around, and the background was blurred out. The caption read, *Partying Randall Style.*

Cynthia pointed to the man Chris was toasting. "Ryan Turner was Chris's best friend."

Excitement laced through Madison's veins. "Do you have an address for us?"

"You want me to do everything for you?" Cynthia scoffed but handed Madison a piece of paper that was sitting in the tray of a nearby printer. "Here. And as it turns out, Turner has a record for drunk and disorderly from a year ago."

Madison read two addresses on the sheet—one personal and one professional. She looked up at Cynthia. "Turner worked for Randall Investments?"

"That's right. He could have been the one who called on the eleventh."

"Good work. What about the incoming number that wasn't blocked? Have you had a chance to track that?"

Cynthia shook her head. She addressed Terry. "She's never happy, is she?" To Madison, she said, "It's on my list of things to do."

CHAPTER ELEVEN

Madison tapped her hands on the steering wheel of the department car. Despite the feeling in the air of early spring, traffic was at a crawl. Normally this type of weather would have people driving with pumping music and feet to their gas pedals.

She and Terry were on their way to Randall Investments, despite her partner's attempts to make her reconsider. She figured, based on the fact it was midmorning and a Tuesday, they would have a better chance of finding Ryan Turner there than at home.

Terry was fidgeting in the passenger seat. "If McAlexandar finds out—"

"We're not going there to speak to Marcus Randall. We'll be speaking with an employee." That was all the justification she needed. "You're not going to lose your job," she tacked on, knowing his real concern.

"I better not. I've got a baby on the way."

"*You* do?" Madison teased with a smile, playing on the way he'd worded things, as if he were carrying it. "How is that going, anyway? Is the morning sickness getting to you? I have noticed the weight change." Complete hyperbole, of course. Terry had a thing with exercise. He actually ran out of choice, though she found it hard to imagine why. Running was the devil's pastime. She glanced over at him in the passenger seat, and he pointed out the windshield.

"Eyes on the road."

She kept her gaze on him for a few more seconds, just to be defiant.

"What are you talking about, anyway? Bah, weight change." He ran a hand down his chest and patted his stomach. "Maybe a couple pounds."

Madison laughed.

"Okay, maybe more. I'm a sympathetic eater. Don't want my wife eating alone."

"She's eating for two. You're eating for one large you," she kicked back, enjoying this little game.

"You're one to talk. When's the last time you hit the gym?"

Ouch. Fun over.

"How is Annabelle, by the way?"

"Nice subject switch. Pretty good. She goes for her second ultrasound and blood testing in a few weeks. She's telling me I must be there with her."

"Not sure if that's—"

"It's not an option or request, Maddy, if you're going to tell me I can't get out of work. I live with her, remember? She can be scarier than you, if you can imagine."

"I'll have to work on that. Say hi to her for me."

"So, no sit-ups, squats, stretching, anything? Boyfriend time doesn't count for exercise."

"Oh, shut up." She reached over and jabbed him in the shoulder.

Housed in a forty-story office building in the center of downtown, Randall Investments gave the impression of grandeur. Inside the front door, Madison felt humbled by the sheer size of the lobby. Sparse with furniture, only a few sitting areas sprinkled the space. The marble flooring gleamed due to a flood of sunlight that streamed in through the walls of windows.

A large desk blocked the hallway leading to the elevators, as did two armed security guards. There were two lanes with swipe machines for employees to scan their access cards and bypass reception.

A male clerk at the desk smiled with a reserved professionalism. "Good morning, welcome to Randall Investments. Please state the last name of the person you have an appointment with and the pass code they would have provided you."

"We're Detectives Madison Knight and Terry Grant. I trust that makes us exempt from a pass code." She pulled out her badge that was on a chain around her neck.

"Unfortunately, without an appointment—"

"I'm sure you've read about the death of Chris Randall."

"Yes, but—"

"We need to speak with Ryan Turner."

Their eyes met in a deadlock, then the clerk eventually said, "One moment." He typed into a computer. "Floor eighteen. Get off the elevator. Go right. I will notify—"

"Do what you must." She went through the unlocked gate with Terry behind her.

"He's picking up the phone," Terry said.

"Pretty much thought he would."

Up on the eighteenth floor, they met with a receptionist who didn't give any visual reaction to seeing them—no smile and no hint of foreknowledge that they were coming up.

Terry leaned over to Madison. "If the guy at the front wasn't calling her, who was he calling?"

Madison wasn't going to share her suspicion with Terry, but she wouldn't be surprised if the man had notified Marcus Randall himself.

"Who do you have an appointment with?" the receptionist asked coolly.

"No appointment," Madison said, "but we need to speak with Ryan Turner."

"I'm sorry, but without an appointment—"

"We're detectives investigating the death of Chris Randall," Madison cut in, providing the same basic information she had downstairs.

"And what does that have to do with Ryan?" Her eyes darkened when she seemed to receive the answer in Madison's eyes. "Right, none of my business." The receptionist picked up her phone. "I'll have to clear it with his supervisor first."

Madison's foot tapped on the floor, and she felt Terry watching her. He never understood her tense nature. Nothing was a rush for him—unless he was panicking about job security.

The receptionist cupped the receiver and addressed Madison. "How long do you think you'll be?"

"As long as it takes," Madison said drily.

The receptionist lowered the receiver but didn't put it back in its cradle. "There's no answer. I'll see if I can page him up here." Before she could, a man of about fifty walked toward them in a gray suit that hung on his frame as if sizes too big. "Mr. Strickland, I was just trying to reach you. These are detectives with the Stiles PD, and they'd like to speak with Ryan Turner."

Strickland turned to Madison and Terry and regarded them skeptically. "Have him paged to the conference room, Loretta."

"Will do." The receptionist proceeded to do as Strickland had directed.

There was no way Strickland just happened upon the front counter. Downstairs must have called him.

"Harvey Strickland, Ryan's supervisor," he said to introduce himself. "This way." He led them through a maze of cubicles until they reached a conference room. A glass-top table sat centered in the space with burgundy leather chairs around it, and one was occupied. "It would seem Ryan beat us here."

Madison regarded the young man who was seated at the far side of the room. He was fair-skinned with dark hair and thick eyebrows, which were bushy enough to be mistaken for caterpillars. He sat slumped forward, one leg casually bent over the other. He wore jeans, an AC/DC T-shirt, and sneakers. Madison noted the attire seemed inconsistent with a prestigious investment firm. She assumed, due to his dress, he worked behind the scenes and wasn't in direct contact with the big investors.

"Ryan Turner," Madison began, then proceeded with formally introducing herself and Terry. As she was speaking, she noted a scab on Turner's top lip.

Madison nodded to the supervisor, implying both a thank-you and a goodbye. Strickland shut the door and took a seat near Ryan.

Looking comfortable, Strickland stated the obvious. "I'll be joining you."

"This is actually a private matter between us and Ryan Turner," Madison said.

Strickland looked between Madison and Terry, then glanced at Ryan, who nodded. Strickland got up and left.

Strange…

Turner was the subordinate and cavalier not only in his appearance, but his attitude as well. Yet, Strickland had looked at him for permission to leave the room. Based on Turner's obvious jittery bloodshot eyes, shifty gaze, and bouncing leg, Madison would guess he was a drug addict in need of a fix. As such, it was surprising he held a job. Maybe the only reason he did was his relationship with the boss's son. She figured it was best to start with the basics. "How did you come to know Chris?"

"Private school. And I can tell what you're thinking by the look in your eyes."

"I'm not thinking anything," she said.

"Heck, you're not. You're probably wondering how a guy like me afforded private school."

Madison shrugged a shoulder. "Sure…"

"It was in no part thanks to my dad. He bailed when I was young, left me and Mom to fend for ourselves. The only way I got to stay in school was because of Chris and Mr. Randall."

"So, you and Chris were quite close?" Madison asked.

"Pretty much brothers. He didn't have anyone, either. His dad—" He stopped talking.

"It's all right. Continue," she prompted.

He shook his head. "Nope, no way."

The subject of Randall was finished before it really began, but for good reason. Turner likely felt a deep sense of loyalty and indebtedness toward the man. "How about you tell us what you—"

"I don't know anything," Turner interrupted.

"You didn't even know what I was going to say."

"I know you're here about Chris. All I know is what the papers are saying, and that I had nothing to do with his death."

"You and Chris were close," Terry commented.

Turner's jaw went askew for a second. His eyes skimmed Terry. "What does that matter?"

"It matters because you could help us in this investigation," Terry said, nonplussed by Turner's cool reception. "When did you last see him?"

"I dunno. A month ago, a few weeks ago." He ran his fingers through his hair.

"How about January tenth?" Madison tossed out.

Turner's eyes went from Terry to Madison. He didn't answer.

"We have another person who said that's when they last saw him," she said in a conversational manner.

"Could have been. I'm not sure."

"Do you know what you were doing on January tenth?"

"Seriously? That's about a month ago."

It was Madison's turn to keep quiet.

Seconds later, he said, "Yeah, that sounds right."

"Where did you see him?" she asked.

"Caesar's."

That was the same club where Renee Hanover had met Chris. "Good club. It's open all night." Madison tried to dredge up the enthusiasm Cynthia had exuded about the place.

"Last call's at two, actually."

Good to know, she thought sarcastically.

"Was he with anyone that night?"

"Chris was always with people, even when he wasn't with people. Everyone crowded around him, wanting to party where he partied."

"Did he get into a fight with anyone?" Terry interjected.

"No more than usual."

Terry leaned forward. "What does that mean exactly?"

"There's always a jealous boyfriend."

Or jealous *husband*. The cigar Miles Hanover had been smoking wasn't a chemical match to what was swabbed from Chris's hand, but it was possible that Miles had switched brands after the murder. "Was there one that stood out from that night?"

"From a month ago?" he spat, then paused and said, "I kind of remember some guy coming at him. Dark features. Short. He was yelling something at Chris about his wife. Told him to back off." Turner shook his head. "Something like that."

That description could match Miles Hanover, but then, it could describe a lot of people. And if it was Miles, where had Renee been? She'd seemed sincerely surprised that Miles even knew about her flirtation with Chris.

Turner went on. "This guy ended up dragging his bitch straight outta there. She was swearing the entire way about how she was her own woman and had the right to party. Some shit like that."

"What did she look like?"

"I don't know. Some short, dark cut." He motioned a line at the base of his jaw and dropped his hand.

That description fit Renee. Were the two of them hiding something?

"Were any punches thrown—between that guy and Chris?" Madison asked.

"No."

"Was he smoking a cigar?" She knew she was reaching. The altercation that had been Chris's last could have happened hours after leaving the club.

"Not that I remember."

"What time did you leave the club—"

The door to the conference room swung open, and Marcus Randall stood in the doorway dressed in an Armani suit and smelling heavily of cologne. "Meeting's over."

Her breathing hitched, but she sat straighter. "We're trying to find out what happened to your son."

"You will do that off company property, off company time. Understood?"

"We're talking about your *son*. You don't want to know who killed—"

"You report to Chief McAlexandar, do you not?" The look in his eyes gave weight to the underlying threat to her job.

She refused to let him detect any weakness. "Sergeant Winston, actually."

"And to whom does he report?"

The fear for her job wrenched her chest, leaving her speechless.

"Just what I thought. And if you need to speak with Ryan Turner, you do it through this man." Randall tossed a business card on the table.

Madison picked it up and handed it to Terry, her attention still on Randall. "You're providing him with a lawyer?"

Randall glanced at Terry. "Sharp one we have here."

This man had a way of making her feel insignificant, and she didn't like it. She worked hard to get where she was, and she couldn't allow him power over her. She owed him nothing. In turn, she owed it to his son to find his killer— assuming there was one was to find.

"I'm not sure why you want to hinder our investigation into the death of your son," she said, finding it hard to keep the accusatory tone out of her voice.

"Who the hell are you to come in here and question me? I can destroy you."

"Is that a threat?" she fired back.

"This nonsense has carried on long enough." Randall snapped his fingers. "Ryan, back to work."

CHAPTER TWELVE

"Every year, our economy is negatively impacted as the result of counterfeiting in a big way. It's not a small accusation."

Walters gave the diplomatic speech, the one designed to elevate the Secret Service above all others. At least, that's how McAlexandar viewed it. He'd been crammed in a room with them and Winston for hours, and it always circled back to a power play.

McAlexandar clenched his jaw. "I'll ask again: what made you suspect the Randalls of counterfeiting?"

"Normally we would not disclose details of our investigation." Weiss glanced at his older counterpart then back to McAlexandar. "But in this case, we've decided to make an exception."

Only because you want our cooperation…

"You're close to Marcus Randall on a personal level. Isn't that true?"

McAlexandar pulled out on the collar of his shirt and stole a sideward glance at Winston.

"He sponsored your election campaign to the office of police chief."

This wisecracking, wet-behind-the-ears agent deserved to find out where he really stood. "I do not know the identity of all of my donors. Many were anonymous." Out of his peripheral vision, he saw Winston turn to face him.

"You had dinner with him about a month ago at the

Fairmont Club," Weiss said.

"How is that relevant?"

"The funds he used to sponsor you may have been counterfeit," Weiss countered.

"Outrageous!" McAlexandar balled his hands into fists, and he could feel his blood pressure rising. "My relationship with Mr. Randall is purely professional. I have no knowledge of the man otherwise."

Walters started, "Has he ever mentioned—"

"How he makes fake money in the basement?" McAlexandar cut him off. "No."

"Given you any reason to question his moral or ethical standing?" Walters asked, seemingly unmoved by McAlexandar's interjection.

"Again, I don't see the relevance." He clasped his hands, tilted out his jaw.

"It is *very* relevant." Weiss paused, assessing him. "The man is in the business of taking other people's money and investing it. Most investment companies have shown a dip in their profits due to the economy. Randall Investments shows growth in the last few years."

"He's a criminal because he's a smart businessman?" McAlexandar scoffed.

"What I'm asking for, Chief, is full disclosure, and I don't feel I'm getting the cooperation—and the respect our office deserves," Walters stamped out.

"I'm telling you all I know." The tie around his neck felt like it was constricting, but he kept his hands clasped.

Weiss stared him down as if he could pry into McAlexandar's thoughts. Seconds later, he broke the eye contact. "We need full disclosure to the murder case, full access—"

"As you've stated already," McAlexandar stated drily. "However, the cause of death hasn't even been confirmed."

"But it is a murder, as you said earlier?" Weiss pressed.

McAlexandar was too angry to speak.

"His death has been deemed suspicious and is being investigated," Winston offered. "Though it appears he was drowned, we have yet to know for sure if that was the cause of death. The manner of death is also unknown. Whether it was an accident, suicide, or murder."

McAlexandar clasped his hands even more tightly, resisting the urge to smack his inferior hard on the back of the head. "Until that can be confirmed and proven—"

"We're not interested in taking over the investigation, nor is it our responsibility or expertise," Weiss said. "We're just asking you—no, *telling* you—should information come to light in your case that is relevant to ours, you are to let us know."

"We will," Winston agreed.

"In accord with such, we're asking for full access to the evidence files. Something may already have come out that will assist us, without you being aware of it," Walters said. "A comment made by someone, perhaps, or something found on his person at the time the body was discovered."

Winston nodded so quickly and agreeably, he reminded McAlexandar of those bobblehead dolls, their heads swaying this way and that at the slightest movement of air. It was time to take control of this meeting. If he was going to help Marcus, he needed more information.

"We share with you, but you don't with us?" McAlexandar angled his head. "Doesn't sound too fair to me."

"We have told you a lot already," Walters replied. "And with your connection to the man, we cannot compromise our case."

"I am an officer of the law, gentlemen. Surely that means something. And as I assured you, my relationship with Randall is strictly professional." He was lying through his teeth, but he'd perfected the skill over the years.

"It doesn't take much to cross from professional to personal." Walters raised his brows. "And we are not willing to take the risk that you'll jeopardize our case."

"However, you expect us to hand over our evidence files in full?" he countered with heat.

"We simply require access to them." He matched eyes with McAlexandar. "Besides, moments ago, you didn't seem too sure it was a murder case." Weiss may have been young, but he was observant.

"Yet it is being investigated as such, if you had been listening, Mr. Weiss." There was no way McAlexandar would address this twerp as *Agent*.

"All right, gentlemen, we'll keep in touch." Walters rose from the table and extended a hand toward him.

McAlexandar gave it a solid shake. As he reached across the table, he heard and felt the vibration of his cell phone in his suit jacket pocket. He had a bad feeling about the caller's identity. He would leave it until later when he had some privacy. Right now, he was just happy to be leaving the company of the Secret Service.

"Can I have a moment of your time?" Winston asked McAlexandar once he reached the hallway.

McAlexandar made a show of consulting his Rolex. "I've actually got something to attend to."

"Only a minute." Winston smiled. "My office?"

After that little exposé in the room, McAlexandar figured his employee would have some questions, but was Winston actually brave enough to call him out?

"For a minute." McAlexandar attempted to return the smile, although he wasn't sure it had formed.

In Winston's office, he sat behind his desk. "I have some concerns," Winston started. "Not exactly sure how to put this."

"By all means, come out with it." McAlexandar was growing impatient. After all, who did Winston think he was, anyway? If it wasn't for McAlexandar, he wouldn't hold the position he did.

"Your conversation with me earlier about Knight."

McAlexandar's shoulders loosened, and the tension in his neck started to melt away. "You will fire her?"

Winston diverted his eyes. "I've given what you said some thought. She does open her mouth too much sometimes—"

"*Sometimes*," he said incredulously. His cell vibrated in his pocket again.

"You want to get that? I can wait."

"Nah." He dismissed the offer with a wave. He knew it would be Randall. Call it a sixth sense, but the man had eyes everywhere. Randall had likely heard about the meeting with the Secret Service and was following up on his pawn's performance.

McAlexandar pulled out his phone, rejected the call, and placed it back in his pocket. "Quite the intrusion at times. Technology is not always our friend."

Winston's features softened, and a smile gave birth. "Tell me about it. Got my daughter a cell phone for Christmas, spent five hundred on it. She racked up a thousand-dollar bill for the first month. Don't even ask me how. And then, yesterday, she comes to me and tells me she wants the latest model. Something about it having more features and the one she has being outdated."

"Kids don't appreciate anything." McAlexandar played along. He never had any of his own for two reasons, apart from simply not being interested. One, the thought of snotty brats sucking his financial well dry didn't hold any appeal, and two, should his marriage ever break up, he didn't want the judge siding with his wife. The law always tended to extend more empathy to the mother.

"I just wanted to discuss what happened in there." With Winston's introduction back to his real purpose for this impromptu meeting, tension thickened the air.

His employee was going to confront him, accuse him of taking fake money to support his election, question his character, and blame him for impeding the investigation into Chris's death. He clasped his hands over a knee. "Thought we were discussing Knight."

"Well, we were. We are. We'll have to let her know what transpired today. Make sure she realizes that every step she takes on this case will need to be accounted for, reviewed, and analyzed."

McAlexandar wagged a finger toward his reporting officer. "You're thinking like a wise man. Establishing solid grounds. Reporting on a case has never been a strong suit for her. I remember that from when I sat in your chair. You're a smarter man than I give you credit for." The vibration of his cell started up again. "I really must be going."

After watching his superior leave, Winston felt he could draw a full breath again. He had come close to confronting the man outright. The small abnormalities were stacking up.

McAlexandar knew the file number for Chris Randall from memory, and he had wanted to be the one to tell the boy's father, on his own. And now the allegations by the Secret Service that Randall had sponsored McAlexandar's election removed any doubt as to a connection between the two men.

In a way, McAlexandar owed Randall, but Winston wondered how deep that debt went and how far he would go to pay it back. Simple questions, with potentially complicated answers. Winston wanted to find out the truth, but then again, maybe it was best he didn't.

CHAPTER THIRTEEN

"Who the hell does that man think he is?" From the entrance to the underground garage, Madison punched a thumb into the key fob to unlock the car doors as if the signal would travel that far.

"He's used to getting his way."

"Well, that's going to stop. I cater to no one, Terry. How am I supposed to do my job when I'm constantly told to keep my mouth shut and turn the other way?"

"Don't know what to say."

"And why wouldn't Randall want us talking to Ryan? Sure, he was friends with Chris, but if Ryan was involved with Chris's death, wouldn't Randall want to know? Wouldn't his son trump the best-friend card?"

"Oh, card talk. I like it."

"Come on. Focus."

They reached the car and both of them got in.

"We haven't made a bet on this case yet," Terry said, settling into the passenger seat.

Normally, at some point during an investigation, they would cast bets on some aspect. "I don't accept credit." The corners of her lips rose.

"Likewise."

"Well, you have nothing to fear. I'll be the one collecting. Then again, maybe I should fear you not making good when you lose."

"Hey, that happened one time." Terry pulled out his seat belt and did it up.

"Maybe we should stop making bets on cases. I mean, making money off someone's death isn't exactly ethical."

"You're only the one making money if you win."

"I usually do."

"Now who's cocky?"

"Just telling you the truth." She laughed.

"Come on. You're in favor of Randall for the murder. You've been suspicious of him from the start."

"But I don't have any real solid ground. Just suspicions, his odd reaction to the news about his son's death, the way he was upstairs just now. He's hiding something."

"And you think that's the murder of his son?"

"He's a powerful man. Maybe he didn't do it with his own hands but had someone else do it."

"Not that you have any real motive. Anyway, I won't hold that technicality against you. Let's make the bet this way. You're in favor of Randall being involved, and I'm not."

"If you feel like throwing your money away, I'll take it. Our regular twenty."

"What happened to not wanting to make any money off a death?"

"Changed my mind. Besides I'll really be earning it by cuffing the killer." Her mind was fixed on Randall, but if he was involved, why was he protecting Ryan? She glanced at Terry. "Call the lawyer on the card Randall gave us, set up an appointment for us to speak to Ryan Turner. If Randall wants to play this game, I'm in." She thought of Ryan's scabbed lip and the apparent altercation Chris had been in prior to his death. Was it with Ryan, and if so, over what? How far did it go?

Terry pulled the card from his pocket. "You sure you want me to do this?"

"Why wouldn't I? And after you do that, we'll call it a day." She needed a bit of distance to obtain a refreshed perspective. And her poor pup, Hershey, was lucky to have seen her a total of eight hours since the start of the week. She had to look into getting him into a day care for dogs. She rolled her eyes. What would people think of next?

Thirty minutes later, Madison was unlocking her apartment door. Hershey barked to be let out of his kennel. She felt badly that he needed to be caged at all, but he couldn't be trusted not to tear the place apart and make "deposits" everywhere.

"Hey, buddy." She unlatched the crate door, and he came out and jumped up against her legs. Her cell rang, and all four paws dropped to the ground, his head cocking to the side.

"It's my phone." She held it out for him to see and realized he probably didn't understand a word she was saying. She looked at the caller's identity, and her stomach tossed at the sight of Sergeant Winston's name.

"Knight," she answered, bracing herself for a fight. Maybe the sergeant had decided to do the chief's bidding and fire her. If so, her next call would be to a lawyer and Internal Affairs. After all, she was guilty of nothing but investigating a case she was assigned.

"There's been a development with the case," he began. "By this point, I assume you know the money found on the boy was counterfeit?"

She let out a breath of air she hadn't even realized she'd been holding. "I do," she admitted. Not that he had informed her of the finding; it had been Cynthia. A double standard that he expected regular updates from her, but he didn't have to reciprocate.

"Then you know the Secret Service is involved," he said. "Well, they have requested full access to the case files."

"That's fine. Makes sense."

"It will require that you update me on the status of the case at regular intervals and that everything is noted, in writing, for them."

"I can do that."

"Knight, you have a hard time keeping me updated on the overall progress of investigations. They will want *details*."

It was just some extra paperwork, more communication. No big deal. At least she still had a job. "As I said, I can do that."

"Get Terry to help you with it. And, Maddy?"

"Yes." He rarely called her by her first name.

"Keep your nose out of trouble. Think before you speak."

"Yeah…yes…of course."

"Night." He ended the call.

Her heart was pounding. She had thought for sure this was the call that would start her down the path of unemployment. But one thing was certain by the way he'd spoken to her, especially his last piece of advice, the chief was hungry for her badge and itching for one good reason to take it from her.

Hershey jumped up on her legs again and started barking. Her phone rang again, and he grounded his paws back on the floor. She answered without a glance at the caller ID.

"Have you given your notice yet?" Blake asked.

"Have I— What?" The last word came out in a near shriek.

"You're moving in with me, aren't you?"

She let out a deep breath. Given her recent musings about her job situation, she had initially taken his question to mean something else entirely. In the context of how he'd meant his question, she hadn't given it a thought since he had asked her. The idea scared her, pure and simple. She preferred to be independent and strong, needing no one.

Hershey pawed her leg, and she looked down into his chocolate eyes.

Bracing the cell between her ear and shoulder, she worked at getting him into his collar and leash to take him out.

"Maddy?"

"Yeah, I'm here."

"You all right?"

She wanted to tell him no, that she was far from it due to the pressure she was under with her current case. Instead, she cleared her throat and said, "I'm fine."

"You sure?"

"Yep."

"Glad to hear it," he said, obviously failing to pick up on the underlying current to her brief responses. "You haven't given moving in with me any thought, have you?"

He isn't totally oblivious...

"Honestly..."

"No," they said in unison.

"Sorry, Blake, I've just been crazy busy with this high-profile case."

"Chris Randall?"

"How did you know?"

"Just a guess. It's all over the papers about his body being found, the cause of death being suspicious."

"It's that elusive cause of death," she grumbled, though it was more the *manner* of death she was interested in.

"You don't know what killed him? Normally, isn't that just a line fed to the media?"

"Sometimes." She wasn't going to lie. Blake would see probably see through that.

"That must make it a tougher case."

"You have no idea."

"Do you think it was suicide or an accident?"

"Not given other factors in the case." Her mind specifically went to the burns on Chris's hand. "I'd say his death, between us, was a homicide. Anyway, I better get going. I've probably said too much already."

"You know what you say stays with me."

"Thanks, Blake."

"No problem. The real reason I called, besides the fact I was missing you, is that I wanted to check in with you, see how things are going. I took a stab that you might have made a decision."

"You know what it's like."

"I do. Call me from time to time during a case, though, would ya? It makes me feel needed."

She laughed. "Who's the woman in this relationship?"

"Oh, you didn't."

"Oh, I did."

Blake broke off their laughter first. "Actually, I also wanted to let you know that I'll be busy for the next while myself. A couple high-profile jobs have come my way."

"That's excellent. I won't feel bad about not being around."

She ended the conversation, promising to consider his proposal for moving in, even though she had made up her mind already. But that wasn't what weighed on her. She had a feeling that she had said too much about the case. She tried to reassure herself it was Blake, and she didn't have to worry with him. What was he going to do with the information, anyway? It wasn't as if he was Randall's lawyer.

CHAPTER FOURTEEN

Madison rarely stepped back from a case and took off early. But she had made that exception yesterday, and now the guilt of doing so pushed her in early this morning. That wasn't the only thing playing on her mind, though. She regretted snooping into Richards's past. She kept trying to convince herself she did it because she cared for him. Her intent hadn't been to dredge up pain, but she wanted to talk to him about what she had found. She sat there glancing at the clock, debating whether she should apologize or explain her motives, then she decided against it. Richards likely wouldn't be in yet, and she had work to do.

She brought up the database to access Chris Randall's file. After keying in his name, she was met with a flashing *Access Denied* spread across her screen. The sergeant was supposed to work on getting a court order to release the file days ago. It should have been resolved by now.

Maybe it was paranoia for her to conclude there was some sort of conspiracy or cover-up, but there were questions that required answers. Was it McAlexandar who had stalled the release of the record, and if so, why?

She cleared the message from her screen, then typed in *Marcus Randall*. She expected to be denied access again, but this time a file came up. She scrolled through it. Nothing was out of place. It would never be that easy.

She brought up the website for Randall Investments and recalled that Tony Medcalf had told her that the company was "worth billions due to their global market share."

Where were they getting these international investors? Medcalf had also mentioned that Chris traveled a lot for business. Had it been for the purpose of signing up clients?

Unlike Medcalf, Jonathan Wright had been tight-lipped— not offering up anything, not even how long he'd been employed by Randall or what his responsibilities included. If Madison was to guess, Wright served in more capacities than a typical bodyguard. She imagined he eliminated any threats against Randall, whether such attacks were physical or defamatory.

"Here, I brought you one." Terry put a Starbucks cup on her desk.

Her eyes slowly came into focus; she'd been so deep into her musings. She looked up from the Randall Investments website still on her monitor. "Thanks." She lifted her drink for a sip.

He leaned over in front of her. "What are you doing?"

"Research."

"On Randall?"

"His company." She doubted he bought the line, but she tried anyhow.

"You're going to have to start focusing somewhere else or you'll get yourself into trouble."

She looked up at him. "I have a job to do, Terry. So do you. That means we have to look at this case from every angle."

"Can you honestly say that's what you're doing?"

She didn't owe Terry an explanation or a defense.

"You just don't like him because the chief does," Terry tossed out.

"We've been through this. Randall makes me suspicious."

"Because he likes to keep his life private?"

Terry's question made her recall something, and she said, "Martha Cooper told us that Randall had numerous closed-door meetings, and that different men would come and go. Who were they? What were they talking about?"

"Who knows? And it might not even matter to our case. I'm not saying Randall doesn't have secrets, but even if he does, that doesn't mean he killed his son."

Yet he seems in a hurry to put Chris's death behind him.

"Madison, are you hearing me?"

"Never mind, Terry." She closed the internet browser. "What time's the appointment with the lawyer and Ryan?"

"They haven't called me back yet."

"Knight. In my office, now!" McAlexandar bellowed across the room.

She glanced at Terry, whose eyes widened. She saw her fear reflecting back in them.

"Okay." She followed McAlexandar's rushed steps to the elevator. They rode it in silence to the fifth floor, where his office was located.

Sandy Taylor, his executive assistant, avoided eye contact. Madison's stomach clenched.

McAlexandar closed the door behind them. Winston rose from a sofa in the corner of the room. His face drooped and appeared heavy with stress. It didn't give her much confidence in her fate.

"I didn't do anything," she said, getting ahead of the attack that was likely coming her way.

"You didn't do anything? You have the gall to come into my office and start with that?" McAlexandar slid behind his desk and settled into his leather chair.

She remained standing. "I'm doing my job." Her voice lost power with the question that followed. "What have I done, exactly?"

"What have you done?" McAlexandar wagged a pointed finger at her. "Let's see."

"Sit, Knight," Winston directed her.

She didn't want to sit. That would imply it would be a longer visit than she wanted. In fact, she was ready to leave now. Both men's eyes were on her. Her legs became jelly and her head faint, but her stubborn nature kept the adrenaline pumping and forced her to keep standing. "You have no grounds to terminate me—none."

McAlexandar leaned over his desk. "I asked you specifically to keep your attention off Randall. You go to his business—"

"It wasn't for him."

"Sit," Winston insisted.

She dropped herself heavily into the chair, crossed her leg away from her boss, and leaned forward. She wasn't going to go down without defending herself.

"Why were you there?" McAlexandar asked.

"To see Ryan Turner."

"Who is he?"

"An employee of his—"

"Relevance to the case, Knight?" Winston asked.

"He was on the victim's—" She was planning to mention the call history on Chris's cell phone, but McAlexandar interrupted her.

"Was Chris Randall even a victim?" he barked, raising his eyebrows. "From what I understand, we're not even one-hundred-percent positive he was murdered." He turned to the sergeant. "At this point, I would like to suspend the investigation into Chris Randall's death."

"That's insane," Madison blurted out. "We have no reason to believe his death was an accident or a suicide. Until we rule out mur—"

McAlexandar held up a hand. "That will be all. It's a waste of taxpayers' money to have you and your monkey gallivanting around the city investigating a murder. A murder that may not even be a murder."

My monkey? She swallowed her rage at him referring to Terry as a primate and directed it to the case. "There's evidence of a struggle. And the bruising on Chris's shoulders can't be dismissed, the burns on his hand—"

"Further insubordination to a superior officer. I move that you be terminated, effective immediately." McAlexandar puffed out his chest.

"But—" Her words stalled when the sergeant placed a hand on her forearm.

McAlexandar's glare bounced from Winston to her a few times. "As I said, I would *like* to suspend the investigation into Chris Randall's death, but Winston has vouched for you and for the need for the investigation to continue. For some reason, he has faith in your abilities." He added the latter sentence begrudgingly.

She didn't need someone backing her up. She stood on her own merit, her own job record.

"With that said, you are aware of the counterfeiting investigation?"

She nodded.

"Guess the girl can keep her mouth shut at times." McAlexandar directed the comment to the sergeant as if Madison wasn't even in the room.

He was such an ignorant ass. Expletives coursed through her mind, but she dared not let any of them come to fruition. It was becoming quite clear, though, that Randall had definite power over McAlexandar.

"With that said, you will be required to document all the steps you take in the investigation moving forward, and everything that you have done to date is to be provided to the Secret Service. Winston will forward you the agent's information."

Most of what he was saying was a reiteration of what Winston had already told her. "*Everything?*" she asked for clarification.

"Until the results come in with a confirmed cause of death—"

"We could be losing precious time—" Her cell rang.

"I want other cases to take front row," McAlexandar trudged on. "Maybe you'll have time to look into that one cold case of yours."

She swallowed the emotion that welled up in her throat. There was nothing else he could have said that would have hurt her more. One case that seemed as if it would haunt her forever. One case that, despite many others being solved, she had a hard time forgiving herself for not closing. This one transgression. One life that would go unaccounted for. She knew the killer, she knew who ordered the hit, but she couldn't get anything to stick.

"Do I make myself clear?" McAlexandar barked as her phone continued to trill.

"Yes." Six rings, and the call would go to voice mail.

"Fine then. You're dismissed." McAlexandar waved her off with a brush of his hand.

CHAPTER FIFTEEN

Madison walked up behind Terry and saw that he was on the Randall Investments website. "Get off the site," she told him.

He spun and followed her with his eyes as she slid behind her desk and took a seat. "What was that about?" he asked.

"Don't bother making an appointment with Ryan Turner and his lawyer." She hadn't answered his question, but it would have to suffice.

"They'd be on their way already."

"What do you mean *on the way*? You didn't have an appointment when I went upstairs." She couldn't make eye contact with her partner, or he'd see through her. She felt so demoralized; she was fighting back tears.

"The office called back. Time's been set for ten."

She glanced at the clock. *9:45 AM.*

"Apologize and turn them away when they get here," Madison said. "Tell them the investigation has taken on another direction."

"Another direction?"

The combined emotions of anger and disappointment in the people she trusted, in the system she devoted her life to, was overwhelming.

"The case has basically been suspended." Her cell rang.

"What do you mean suspended?" Terry asked.

"What do you think I mean?" She matched eyes with Terry, despite knowing hers were misted, and hoped he wouldn't read them. She solidified a wall around herself, refusing to expose her weaker side. Her phone kept ringing, and it only served to enhance her agitation. She answered the call.

"I've been trying to reach you." It was Cynthia on the other end.

"Well, I've been busy."

"Someone's having a bad day."

"The worst."

"It's about to get better. Richards has ruled on manner of death."

Madison walked into the lab with Terry.

"Please just come out and tell me it was murder," she said.

"It wouldn't be any fun if I just came out and said that, would it?" Cynthia smiled at her, but Madison couldn't even find a spark of one in her to return. "You said you were having a bad day."

"*The worst* is how I think I phrased it."

"What's going on?"

"The chief says he wants the Chris Randall case on the back burner, but what he's really saying is it's suspended."

"Why?" Cynthia drew out the word.

"No conclusive evidence it was murder. He said it's too much to ask taxpayers to pay for an investigation when a crime hasn't even been confirmed." Madison glanced at Terry and he gave her this look that said, *Really?*

"But the bruising?" Cynthia said. "The burn? The obvious indication of a struggle?"

"Didn't care."

"Wow." Terry rubbed the back of his neck.

Madison sighed. "I'm beyond the point of caring anymore."

"Yeah, well, I'm not buying that." Cynthia lifted her glasses and placed them on the top of her head.

"It's just, what's the point? I—" She needed to stop talking before she got visibly emotional.

"Oh, come to Cyn." Cynthia pouted and opened her arms, inviting Madison in for a hug.

Madison accepted the offer but kept it brief. She couldn't wallow at any time, let alone in front of Terry. "Okay, enough of that weak shit." She laughed, stifling the overwhelming urge to just cry and let her frustration out. "Let's nail that bastard."

"The chief?" Cynthia flashed a goofy smile. "I'm not into old guys, but he does have money."

Madison cocked her head. "Marcus Randall. Can you help me with that?"

"Again, an older man, but even more loaded. You need help with—"

"Stop, Cyn," Madison said, laughing.

"Oh, you mean give you proof Randall killed his son? Yeah, I can't help you there, but Richards has confirmed Chris's cause of death and ruled on the manner of death in his report." She handed a folder to Madison, which she took without much enthusiasm.

"Just tell me."

"Chris Randall did drown," Cynthia said. "His lungs showed sediment of riverbed, consistent with sampling pulled from the Bradshaw River. Diatoms were also found in his bone marrow and matched those found in the river."

"Richards said if they were found there, he was breathing when he went in the water." Madison pulled from what the ME had told Terry and her during the preliminary. With the thought of Richards, she found it strange Richards wasn't delivering his findings to them himself.

"Correct. Now, his lungs also showed a fairly high concentration of boat gasoline."

Madison's mind went right to Randall's boathouse, but maybe she should try to be more objective. "Boaters frequent Bradshaw River."

"Sure, but not at this time of year. To reach the levels of gasoline found in Chris's lungs, you're likely looking at a relatively isolated section of water, something that isn't churned up much."

"Such as a closed-in boathouse?" She did her best to present her statement as a question.

"Yes, that could do it."

Madison was trying not to let herself get carried away with the notion this result implicated Randall and his boathouse. "Is there any way to figure out where Chris may have gone into the river?"

Cynthia nodded. "Taking into account the flow of currents and the natural process that would have the body sinking then floating again. Also the findings from a forensic climatologist, who advised Richards on recent temperatures in the region—weather affects water flow and decomp," she added as an explanation. "They agreed with what Richards had pegged as Chris's preliminary time-of-death window."

"The girl from the napkin, Renee Hanover, saw Chris on January tenth, and so did Chris's best friend," Terry chimed in.

"Right. Well, that fits with Richards's findings."

"So if you can figure out where Chris went in…" Madison prompted.

"All I can tell you with some certainty is the location of the marina doesn't jibe with the timeline. It's farther upriver from Randall's property."

"Then what you're telling me is Chris could have gone in somewhere around Randall's estate?" Madison asked.

"It's possible."

"And what did Richards say about manner of death? Does he believe we're looking at a homicide?"

"He sure does."

CHAPTER SIXTEEN

Cynthia called out to her and Terry trailed after her, but Madison kept moving and loaded onto an elevator without her partner. She pressed the button for the fifth floor, and her phone rang most of the way up. It was likely Cynthia or Terry, but Madison didn't need either one talking her out of what she was about to do. Some might deem her next step career suicide, but she wasn't about to hide her intentions of investigating the Chris Randall case—as a *priority*. She would tell McAlexandar to his face, and she would accept the consequences. After all, Chris deserved justice, regardless of any pull Randall had with the chief, and she wasn't about to be bullied into looking the other way.

The elevator chimed notice of its arrival, and she walked with confidence toward McAlexandar's office.

Madison stormed past Sandy's desk.

"Stop," Sandy called out. "He's in a—"

Madison swung open McAlexandar's office door.

"We need—" McAlexandar's statement dried on his lips, and his face shot red. "What the hell are you doing in here?"

Randall was sitting across from him and turned to face her. Wright was on the couch. For an instant, she felt faint and wondered if she had acted rashly, but it was too late to back down now.

"We meet again," Randall said. "Wish I could say it was a pleasure."

"Feeling's mutual."

Randall's eyes enlarged as she brushed past him and put the autopsy report on McAlexandar's desk. "There's your cause of death and your manner of death."

McAlexandar picked up the report and read it. "He drowned? You interrupted my meeting for this?" He tossed the file on his desk.

She turned to Randall. "Your son drowned, and based on what the evidence is telling not only me, but also a licensed ME, his death has been deemed a homicide."

Randall remained silent and just held eye contact.

"Someone murdered your son," she laid it out slowly, assuming she might elicit some sort of reaction from him. But he gave her nothing, not even a heavy blinking of an eye.

McAlexandar rose to his feet and pointed a finger at his door. "Get out of my office, Knight!"

"But you're missing the best part. Flip over to the toxicology findings."

"I don't have time for this—"

She turned the papers over to the right spot and pressed her fingertip to the page.

McAlexandar picked up the report, read it, and seconds later, looked at Randall. "Your son had evidence of boat gasoline in his lungs."

"It's a large river, Miss—" Randall looked to McAlexandar for her name as if he'd suddenly developed amnesia, but it was only a play to humiliate her. Not that it was working.

"*Detective* Knight," she stated with confidence. "Your boathouse is at the right location to coincide with—"

"You must be joking," Randall scoffed, seeming to have guessed the direction she was going with her comment. Though she was surprised that he'd bitten so easily.

"I assure you I'm not." She locked eyes with Randall, and seconds tapped off in silence. She finished what she had been going to say before he'd interrupted her. "The location of your boathouse coincides with an established timeline."

"Patrick!" Randall stood and slammed his fist against McAlexandar's desk. "Stop this now."

"We have probable cause to search your property," she said unmoved by Randall's outburst.

"Enough," McAlexandar snarled. "I'm not saying this one more time. Get out of this office."

She held McAlexandar's gaze and fought off a smirk. She took satisfaction in upsetting the man. And she could tell from his eyes he hated the fact she now had the ME's findings to substantiate the reactivation of the investigation.

"You can keep that," she said, pointing at the file on McAlexandar's desk. "I'll get a copy for myself."

She turned for the door and fought off a smug smile. Standing up to the chief and Randall had liberated her from the chains they kept trying to restrain her with. She was now free to get to the truth of what happened to Chris, and if that meant bringing down McAlexandar along with Randall, she would.

With Madison out of his office, McAlexandar had an uneasy feeling. Madison wasn't going to stop until the case was resolved. He saw dogged determination in her eyes. She wasn't afraid of him—or anyone for that matter. She was too committed to finding the truth, no matter what boulders she had to overturn or the ugliness she might uncover. What he hated was her scope included him in her sights this time. He'd be forced to protect his own or risk her jeopardizing everything he had going with Randall. "Just let her search your—"

"Not happening, Patrick."

McAlexandar's mind went to his desk drawer and the bottle of scotch. Today could be a good day to start drinking. "Did you do it?" he pushed out.

"Out in the hall. Now." Randall snapped his fingers to alert his prized stallion it was time to move. When the door closed behind him, Randall continued. "Are you really questioning me? You sit where you are because of me."

"I've worked hard."

"Bullshit! If you worked hard to get to where you are, we wouldn't even be talking."

He hated being reminded of where his power had truly originated. "I've done everything I could to redirect this investigation."

"I want his body released."

"I should be able to arrange that."

"Damn right you'll arrange that. My boy's been subjected to enough dissection."

There was something in his eyes that hadn't been there in prior meetings.

Grief or guilt?

"Legally, she has the right to search your boathouse," he said. "She's just a warrant away."

"Did you not suspend the investigation?" Randall tossed out.

"Yes, pending cause and manner of death."

"Patrick, Patrick. You disappoint me. I don't need any more media attention drawn to me. No matter what they say, all publicity isn't good. Understood?"

McAlexandar put a hand on the pull for the drawer that housed the scotch. He could conjure up the taste of its woody body, the velvet burn as it went down his throat. "Yes."

"Good then. I will arrange for my lawyer to be on-call should she show up at my residence."

McAlexandar loosened his tie. "There's not much I can do, Mark."

"*Marcus*," he spat.

With the look in Randall's eyes, McAlexandar feared more than an end to his career. He had no doubt Randall could make him disappear with the help of his stallion.

It would take time to get everything in order to search Randall's boathouse, but the wait wasn't fazing Madison. Progress was being made—even if slowly. And the fact that Randall happened to be there when she presented the manner of death to McAlexandar was priceless. It gave her an opportunity to see Randall's reaction firsthand. Then when he became defensive, well, it told her she had good reason to be suspicious of him.

Her cell rang and she answered.

"Why haven't you been answering my calls?" It was Cynthia.

"I muted my phone. What's up?"

"Didn't you hear me calling your name? I had more to tell you."

"Had something to take care of."

"Don't tell me you did something stupid."

"We'll wait and see."

"You're making me nervous." Cynthia paused as if waiting for an explanation. When she must have realized Madison wasn't going to provide one, she continued. "I also wanted to let you know that the tox results came back."

"That was quick."

"There was no evidence of drugs or alcohol in his system."

Madison nodded as if Cynthia could see her. "Richards figured it was a long shot."

"I can tell you, though, that last meal your vic had was pheasant."

"Just a guess here, but that doesn't sound like anything they'd serve at a club."

"You'd be right about that. In fact, only one restaurant in the city serves it. Restaurant du François."

She ended the call, and her phone rang again before she put it away. She was getting to the point where she was ready to pitch it into the river. She glanced at the caller's identity, saw Winston's name, and wished she didn't have to answer.

CHAPTER SEVENTEEN

Winston paced behind his desk. "What the hell were you thinking storming into McAlexandar's office like that?"

Madison and Terry sat in the two chairs that faced his desk. As directed, Madison had rounded up Terry for this impromptu meeting, even though it seemed like the purpose was a dressing down intended for her.

Winston held a hand to his forehead as if he was fending off a migraine. "Give me one good reason not to suspend you without pay."

"I'm just doing my job."

Terry jumped in and said, "COD came back drowning, and the bruising—"

"If I hear one more thing about the bruising—" Winston stopped talking and shifted his eyes away from them. "I realize you both have a job to do. McAlexandar wants your focus on the case and for it to be treated as an active murder investigation. He wants the truth as much as we do."

Madison doubted that. "That must please his buddy," she said sarcastically, referring to Randall.

Winston stopped walking, clasped his hands, and leveled a glare on her. "You are to clear everything with me moving forward. Do you understand that?"

She took a deep breath, certain that she had been about to get an earful instead. Winston must not have been fully on board with how McAlexandar was handling this case. "I do."

Terry nodded.

"*Prior* to doing it," Winston clarified. "You have a hard enough time keeping me informed of things after the fact. I need to know you will do this." He stopped beside her and bent over, placing his face next to hers. "Can you do that?"

"Yes."

He stood to full height and walked behind his desk, and she took that as their cue to leave.

"Detective Knight," Winston said, and she turned to face him. She'd almost made it out of his office.

"Yeah?"

"What's your next step?"

Madison mustered a pleasant smile. "I'll let you know as soon as I do."

"Oh, Lord." Winston rolled his eyes and dropped into his chair.

After leaving the sergeant's office, she excused herself from Terry for a few minutes. "There's just one thing I need to do."

He shrugged his shoulders, as if to say *sure* and headed to his desk.

She rapped her knuckles on the door to Richards's office. It was a simple layout—a counter served as a desktop, and filing cabinets were underneath it, except for where two computers sat, allowing the operator room for their legs. Richards sat in front of one of the computers with a report in his hand. He looked up when he heard her.

"I gave Cynthia the autopsy report. Did she—"

Madison nodded. "He drowned. You concluded homicide." She took steps toward him.

"Why are you looking at me like that? I thought *drowning* and *murder* were what you wanted to hear."

"I was just surprised that I didn't hear it from you directly."

"I delegated." His eyes skimmed hers. She sensed he was shutting her out. "There have been more bodies through here in the last week than I care to count," he added, somewhat melancholy.

She slid the chair from the other workstation until it was beside him and sat down. His eyes searched her face;

his expression inquisitive as the lines on his brow drew downward.

"I'm not here so much about the case," she began.

He tossed the report he'd been holding onto the desk. "Why are you be here, then?"

She didn't know how to go about this and was certain it wasn't even her place, but she cared about this man more than she should. Richards was a beautiful person inside and out. His white teeth rivaled those of anyone else she knew. His skin, the color of dark chocolate, was smooth, despite him being her senior by about twenty-five years. She had loved him for years, if only platonically. He was a married man. But he also had a way of caring for the dead that showed he never lost sight of the fact they were loved and missed by people.

"I know this case was different to you," she said, doing so delicately.

He didn't move. He didn't speak.

She went on. "Your brother. I know what—"

His eyes snapped to hers. "How would you know about him?"

"I noticed you were behaving differently…with Chris. You kept your eyes on him during the prep. You had Cynthia tell me your findings. You—"

"You pulled my record," Richards spat.

Put so bluntly, she had taken liberties she shouldn't have taken. She nodded slowly.

"What would make you do that?"

"I was worried about—"

"But it's not your position to worry about me," he said.

She bit in on her bottom lip, not certain what to say.

He got up from his chair and headed for the door.

"I didn't mean to—"

He closed the door and came back to her. He sat down again and faced her. "What do you think you know?"

She studied his face, wondering if he really wanted to know or if there was a veiled challenge wrapped up in the invitation. "You lost your baby brother. He drowned."

"Continue."

"His name was Shannon, and he was only six at the time. His body was never found."

"That's a name I haven't heard for a long time." Richards's voice was wistful. His eyes were distant and hardened over. "Continue."

"You were watching him at the time of the accident." She reached a hand out and rested it on his forearm. "You probably think it was your fault somehow."

"It's time for you to leave."

"Cole, I didn't mean to upset you."

He scowled at her. "I thought we were friends, Knight."

She swallowed hard. He always called her Maddy. And she never recalled him ever being so angry with her.

"I'll go, but—"

"Just go." He gestured to the door. "And close the door behind you."

The pain in Cole Richards's chest was back. The one he'd thought was gone for good, and it had been, until the Randall case.

He balled his hands into fists. His heart beat faster than normal as he felt remorse and grief threaten to seize control over his life again.

He'd never even spoken to his wife about his brother. He had come to accept he was gone, and there was no way to get him back. For years, he punished himself, pushing himself harder, as if doing so would erase the fact he had caused his brother's death. If only he had been more vigilant and not so interested in his friend's trading cards, maybe Shannon would still be here. And maybe then his childhood would have been full of happy memories and not horrid recollections of his cold, impersonal room at the orphanage and feelings of utter abandonment.

Tears fell as he chastised himself with the last words he'd ever heard his father say. *You're no son of mine! You killed my boy!*

CHAPTER EIGHTEEN

Madison drove to Restaurant du François as if she needed to meet a deadline. The interaction with Richards kept replaying in her mind, and she hated that she had to report every step they took in the case.

"I despise being micromanaged," Madison said.

"It's only because the chief hates you."

"I love that you keep pointing that out."

"The way he's letting his personal views affect this case isn't right. Someone on the Randall property could have killed Chris. But until we can prove that beyond a doubt, you have to—"

"Don't say 'cool your jets.'"

"I was going to say 'take it down a notch.'"

"Still. Original." Sometimes clichés bothered the shit out of her.

"Both our asses could be fired, and you're judging the way I talk?"

"I'm under a lot of stress." She refused to tell him about what had happened with Richards. Her heart hurt thinking back to the look on his face and how he had told her to leave his office.

"You're not the only one, Maddy. We're in this together. You fall, I fall."

"I know," she said, appreciating that he had her back. "We need to get in Randall's boathouse."

She ran a traffic light on a yellow to red. A car honked at her, and Terry instinctively reached for the dash. Madison smiled.

"You should let me drive sometimes."

"No way."

"Can't be worse than your driving."

"I haven't killed anyone."

"Yet."

Madison's smile faded, darkened by thoughts of the case and the boathouse. If it were anyone else, they would have already gained access. McAlexandar might have reactivated Chris's case, but he hadn't completely released the reins. It seemed as if he sought Randall's expressed permission first. Until that happened—or hell froze over—she and Terry would have to follow other leads, including this restaurant to see if it was where Chris had eaten his last meal.

"Chris's tox results were negative for drugs," Madison said out of the seeming blue. Sometimes her mind randomly kicked things out. "Could just be as Richards's had said about it being a shot in the dark, but maybe Chris wasn't the hard user the media portrayed."

"Can't believe everything you read," Terry said. "There are still some unexplained items that were on him. The fake money, an unregistered cell phone... Those could make it seem like he was dealing or, at the very least, doing something illegal."

"We need to speak to Ryan Turner again." She glanced over at Terry.

"I'll call the lawyer *again*." Terry pulled out his cell and dialed. After a few seconds, he said, "Yes, I realize we canceled, but... Please... Yes, please reschedule." He ended the call. "They'll be getting back to me. They have to contact Ryan and arrange everything with him. They weren't too impressed the first appointment was canceled."

Madison swerved the car to the curb and came to a stop in front of the trendy French restaurant. It was located on the main street of Stiles. The front face of the building was made up of glass panes with dark-brown framing. *Restaurant du François* was in raised brass lettering above the windows, and five light fixtures illuminated the sign as if it was a piece of artwork. Lights glowed from inside, but there were no patrons.

"Maybe they're not open yet," Terry said as he met up with her on the sidewalk.

Madison walked up to the two etched-glass doors that served as the entrance and looked at the hours of operation posted there.

"Two seatings. Dinner only," she said. "Six and nine." She let out a whistle. "Fancy place." It made her think of Blake with his seemingly unlimited resources and love for the finer things in life. She could imagine Blake frequenting here and being quite comfortable.

A man opened the doors and stared down at them as if they were beneath him. His hands flailed in the air, coming to point in the direction of the listed hours. "*Le restaurant ouvre à six heures et vous devez avoir une* réservation." Not only was he speaking French, he was highly accented.

All Madison understood was *six* and *réservation*. She stepped into the threshold to prevent him from closing the door. "We're not here for dinner."

"Pardon?" He splayed an opened hand on his chest as if that were the greatest tragedy.

She pulled out Chris Randall's driver's license photo. "You see this man at your restaurant before?"

"Dat's Chris, Chris Randall."

"That's correct."

"In da paper." He looked at her leg, trying to get her to move so he could close the doors. "I bid you good day."

"No, wait. Please."

He sighed. Arrogance and impatience sparked in his eyes.

"You serve pheasant here, do you not?" Madison asked.

"*Oui, oui*, of course."

"Did you ever see Chris Randall here before? Say about three weeks ago."

He shook his head.

"January tenth?" Madison just opted to provide the date.

"No. He has never been to my restaurant. I would remember." He curled his long fingers around the door handles, and this time, Madison backed up.

"Bid you good day," he repeated and closed the doors, shutting them out as riffraff.

"Now what?" Terry rubbed his hands together and blew on them.

This case was going nowhere fast. Every time they saw some light, it was snuffed out. Then it occurred to her. "Can't believe I didn't think of this sooner." She turned to face her partner. "Tony Medcalf goes to Hanigan's Market every day."

"Tony Medcalf?"

"Randall's cook."

He nodded. "I don't remember you mentioning his name."

"Well, what if Chris ate at home? Medcalf could have fed him pheasant."

"True, but what I'm going to say next, I say as your friend."

"I know what you're going to say, Terry, and I won't like it."

"You won't like it, but it's for your own good. Before you get fired, please leave Randall, and his household, out of the investigation. Just for a bit even."

She went to talk, but he silenced her with a raised hand.

"We've got to work our way around this case with eyes on *all* the evidence, not narrowed in on one man. One man that, may I add, may be innocent."

She didn't respond.

"If you took him and his estate out of the picture, where would you go next?"

She narrowed her eyes to slits. *What does he expect from me?*

A moment or two passed, then Terry said, "I can't believe you're so focused on Randall, you can't see the rest of the picture."

"Sure I can. I said we should talk to the cook."

Terry let out an exasperated sigh. "There were other calls on Chris's cell on the tenth, were there not?"

"Five incoming, four were blocked, and one outgoing. The latter we know tied back to Ryan Turner." Madison understood Terry's point, though. "Okay, I'll follow up with Cynthia to see if she's gotten anywhere with the blocked numbers or the one that wasn't. In the meantime, we should probably also check out neighboring residences to the Randalls who have boat docks or boathouses."

"And Ryan Turner?"

"Well, we have to wait to hear back from his lawyer." The breeze nipped at Madison's hands, and she burrowed them in her pockets. "But you don't think we should talk to him either, do you? It's just, for a person who claimed to be Chris's best friend, he could have chosen to speak without a lawyer present, but he's not because he's either afraid of or controlled by Randall."

"You're assuming that, and it's based on nothing but your imagination." He paused. "We have to leave Randall alone." He rubbed his hands as if trying to start a fire. "Can we at least get in the car?"

Her cell rang and she answered on speaker. "Knight."

"I processed the bills for prints." It was Cynthia.

Her friend never failed to impress her. "And?"

"They hadn't been in circulation because I only found one print belonging to Chris and a partial— You'll never believe who it came back to." She paused, likely for the sake of drama.

"Cyn?" Madison prompted.

"Ryan Turner."

Madison glanced at Terry but spoke to Cynthia. "Have you told anyone else about this?"

"No."

"Can you just hold off for a bit?"

"For a bit."

"Thanks— Oh, Cyn, you had told us there were five calls made to Chris on January tenth. Did you get anywhere with the four blocked ones?"

"Not yet."

"Okay, and what about the call that wasn't blocked? Can you send me the info on that?"

"Will do."

Madison hung up and looked over at Terry.

His cheeks were flushed red. "You just asked Cynthia to hold back from logging evidence. Are you mad?"

"I'm trying to find out who killed Chris Randall and why."

"You're not going to do that from the streets, as a regular citizen. And that's where you're headed. I certainly don't want to be pulled down with you," he tacked on.

So much for having my back…

"Do you really think we'll be able to get to Ryan Turner if the Secret Service is all over him? That's what's going to happen the minute they find out his partial was on one of the bills," she pleaded her case.

"You must be losing your mind."

"You can get so excitable. Don't worry, leave it with me."

"Why is it whenever you say that, I'm more nervous?"

CHAPTER NINETEEN

There were several turns the investigation could take, but while she decided on their next course of action, Madison pulled in front of a Starbucks and sent Terry in. She used the time to call Hannigan's Market to see if any of the vendors there sold pheasant. At two in the afternoon, they were well beyond the point of showing up and running into Medcalf there as he'd told Madison he went in the mornings.

"Oh, you're too late. It goes fast." The man on the other end spoke quickly, as if in a hurry to get off the phone.

"How early would I have to get there?"

"Market opens at six in the morning."

"Thank you." She hung up.

Terry got into the car and held a cappuccino out to her. "Ten." He pulled out on his seat belt, clicked it into place.

"Excuse me."

"The lawyer called. He'll be downtown with Ryan at nine tomorrow morning."

That could be a tight squeeze to get to the market, look around and corner Medcalf, and then get back downtown for Ryan. Medcalf might have to wait.

"All right, so now what?" Terry looked over at her. "We hit up Randall's neighbors who have boathouses?"

"If I remember right, I think the house just next door to the Randall estate has one, but I'd like to visit a couple houses on the opposite side of the river as well."

"There are mostly docks over there."

"I realize that. But if something happened to Chris, possibly on his property, someone might have seen something." She could tell by the look in her partner's eyes what he was thinking: *Inside a boathouse? Can they see through walls now?* She was being hardheaded about Randall, but she couldn't help it. The man just got her hackles up.

Madison's phone pinged with a text, then another. She looked at them. "Two messages from Cynthia. She hasn't gotten anywhere with the blocked numbers, but the unblocked number that called Chris's cell traces back to a Steven Pickering. Address is twenty-three Breyer Avenue."

"Breyer Avenue? With traffic, that's a good thirty-minute drive from here."

"All right, we better get moving and hope the traffic lights work in our favor." Madison checked the rearview mirrors, pulled out of the parking spot, and cranked the wheel, pulling a tight U-turn.

"What the—"

"Everything's fine, Terry."

"I don't know why you always have to drive."

"Here we go again. Get over yourself. I haven't been in an accident in my entire driving life. Can you say the same?"

Silence.

"All right then, that's why I drive."

"It was nothing major, just a little fender bender. If the idiot hadn't slammed on his brakes at the last second, I would have had time to stop."

"I believe you."

"I'm going to give one of your lines right back at you. Shut up."

She laughed.

He narrowed his eyes at her and took a long draw on his Starbucks. Then, using the onboard computer, he pulled Pickering's background. "Oh, he's got a record. Breaking and entering ten years back, assault with his fists five years ago. A bar fight by the looks of it. At Caesar's," he added.

"Small world."

"Now, Pickering's a bit older than Chris. Twenty-six to Chris's twenty-two."

"He started his criminal career early."

"Sixteen," she said. "Even I can do the math on that one."

Terry smirked and continued. "And graduating from B&E to assault… Who's to say he didn't escalate and kill Chris?"

"Possible I suppose, but going from a fistfight to drowning someone is a bit of a stretch," Madison said. "And five years between his charges? He served little to no time for the B&E?"

Terry shook his head. "He was charged as a juvenile. For the assault, he got two years in jail and one year of community service."

"He had a good lawyer. And no other charges once he got out?"

"No, but still. The fact this guy got heated enough to fight in a public place shows he's fiery. Maybe he and Chris met up, got into a confrontation. It got heated. Out of control."

"If that's the case, they met up at Randall's boathouse, because Pickering's address is nowhere near the river."

"Here we go again."

Steven Pickering lived with his mother in a neighborhood that warranted regular patrol for drug dealing and prostitution. Gangs also had a large presence there, and because of it, no one spoke to the cops.

Pickering's house probably dated back to the 1960s but appeared older than homes twice its age. Its white siding called out for more than a coat of paint; it begged for replacement. Green shutters framed the windows and didn't serve a practical purpose or do anything to enhance the house's appearance. Four concrete steps led the way to the front door, and an iron railing surrounded a four-by-six-foot landing.

The front door swung open, and a man stormed out. Madison jumped to the side to avoid getting barreled over.

"Steven Russell Pickering, get your ass back—" A woman who had been pursuing Pickering stopped in the doorway at the sight of them. "Who the—" She looked Madison and Terry over and curled her lips in disgust. "Boy, get back here now!"

Pickering stopped at the sidewalk and turned around, as if registering Madison and Terry for the first time. He started to run. Terry went after him. Madison followed.

At the next cross street, Madison could still hear the woman's shouts.

Pickering diverted into the back yard of a corner house.

Terry swept in right behind him. "Stiles PD! Stop!"

Curtains were pulled back in neighboring houses; they had an audience. Madison entered the back yard. It was cluttered with rusty grills and lawn furniture—even a dilapidated Chevy sat there with its hood raised, as if screaming for a proper burial.

Madison did her best to keep up with the two men, her breath catching short, her heart pounding. She needed to start taking better care of herself. She'd do something about it starting tomorrow.

"Stiles PD!" Terry yelled, not sounding winded at all, while she was just trying to derive enough oxygen not to pass out.

Pickering reached a chain-link fence that was about four-feet high. He jumped, clearing it a good foot. Terry came to the fence, placed a hand on top, and hopped over in stride. She came to the fence and froze. She wasn't cut out for all this athletic heroism. "Shit," she grumbled.

She took her time lifting her leg and sticking the toe of her boot into an opening to hoist herself over. The other side of the fence backed onto an alleyway lined with garbage cans piled high with waste. Both Terry and Pickering were figures in the distance. Pickering must have been part rabbit, as he leaped over obstacles effortlessly. It was impressive her partner managed to keep up.

She was back into a steady run, the cold air hitting her lungs. She jogged past a parked car with three men inside, and they watched her closely. She sensed they were scheming something criminal, but she didn't have time to deal with them right now. She hoped her presence would at least make them rethink their next step.

"Stiles PD!" Terry shouted again.

Pickering came to a tall, black garbage bin, jumped, but failed to clear it. He crumbled to the ground, a tangle of long legs and arms. He struggled to get to his feet, but it was too late. Terry was right on top of him.

"Hands behind your back!" Terry yanked on Pickering's arms and cuffed him. "You're coming with us."

CHAPTER TWENTY

Steven Pickering was seated across the table from Madison in an interrogation room, his shoulders and spine hunched over. His torso was lean and as long as the trunk of a tree, his legs and arms being skinny twigs. He kept crossing and uncrossing his arms, fidgeting in his seat. "I didn't do it."

"Do what?" Madison asked, passing a curious look over her shoulder at Terry, who was leaning against the back wall. They hadn't told Pickering why they had pulled him in yet.

"That bitch asked for it. Lakisha told me to slap her."

Pickering obviously had other sins to confess. "Who is Lakisha?"

"Just a girl."

"Her last name?" she prompted.

"Hudson." His eyes danced across Madison's face.

"She's saying I raped her now, ain't she?" He sucked in on his bottom lip. "Ain't no way." His hand sliced through the air and hit the table.

"We're not here because of Lakisha," she stated calmly, though now she'd be looking for Lakisha Hudson.

He leaned back in his chair and squinted. "What's we here fo', then?"

Madison studied him, from his eyes that flitted about the room, not focused on anything, to his constant fidgeting. She didn't say anything, playing the power of silence.

He wiped his nose with the back of his arm, sniffed. "Can I go, then?"

Madison leaned toward him. "You a druggie?"

Pickering pulled back and said nothing.

"We're cops," she began. "We can tell when someone's a user."

"I can't go to jail."

"Because you've been there before and you don't like it?"

His arms kept moving, crossing, uncrossing, sitting up, sitting back. "We know your record, Pickering. B&E, assault—"

"Bullshit charges!"

"I'd say not; they stuck to your record. You even served some time. But they are from a while back. So, either you're behaving yourself these days or you're just better at not getting caught." She felt Pickering's uncertain energy. She let the silence hang for thirty seconds before spreading three crime-scene photos on the table. She pointed to one where Chris's deteriorated corpse lay among brown weeds that poked through the mushy riverbank, where puddles had crystallized and crunched beneath your step. "Recognize this man?"

He slapped a hand over his mouth and shook his head.

Even Madison had to admit the man in the photos held little resemblance to what Chris had looked like alive. She placed a celebrity photo of Chris on the table. "What about this man?"

Pickering stopped shaking his head and dropped his hand to his lap.

"Mr. Pickering, do you recognize him?" Madison pressed.

"*Mister*?" Pickering snorted. "Yeah. Sure. It's that famous kid." He snapped his fingers as if trying to conjure a name, but he knew exactly who Chris was—he'd called him, after all. But she would let the show continue for a while. "His name's Chris Randall, I think?"

"You're not sure?" Madison asked, incredulous. She flung an arm over the back of the chair. "He's in the paper, in magazines, on TV."

Pickering crossed his arms. "I don't read. Or watch TV."

It wasn't until now, with the light hitting his face a certain way, that she picked up on a small scab on his left cheek. It was possibly a few weeks old. "I think you're lying."

"I'm not."

"You recognized him right away. Your eyes gave you away." She pulled her arm off the back of the chair, straightening to fully face him. "You see, we're trained to notice those things." Madison glanced at Terry, and Pickering followed the direction of her gaze. Terry pressed his lips together, raised his eyebrows. She continued. "We know you called Chris on the tenth of January."

He pushed the crime-scene photos away. "I ain't do that."

"But you did call him?" she said.

"Yeah."

"What for?"

"Not sayin'."

"Where did you get that?" Madison pointed to the scab on Pickering's cheek.

He touched it.

"Did you get into a fight with Chris Randall?"

Silence.

"You knew Chris, didn't you? Personally?"

Still silent, but she'd wait him out.

A good minute later, Pickering said, "What does that matter?"

"He's dead."

Pickering cocked his head to the side and glanced at the photos. "Not my problem." He'd gone from defensive to cool indifference.

"Might be," Madison said matter-of-factly. "He was murdered."

Pickering's gaze cooled.

Madison continued. "I think you and Chris got into a fight a few weeks back and things got out of hand."

"No!"

Madison crossed her arms. "Then what, Pickering? Tell us what you know, because I can tell you know something."

"I'll be murdered."

"You're afraid of those street punks you call friends? You should be more afraid of withholding information from us. If you killed Chris—"

"I didn't." He let out a deep breath. "But we did get into a fight."

"Over what?"

He shifted his posture, and his eyes roamed the room. "Can't say."

"If you don't say, we'll draw our own conclusions. It will take longer, and in the end, if we find—"

"He offended me," he cut in.

"How?"

"Tried to give me fake paper. That crap don't do me no good."

"You killed him over it," she tossed out nonchalantly.

"No, I told you—"

"What was he buying from you?"

Pickering's gaze seemed to pass right through her.

She took a gamble. "You were his supplier, weren't you? For drugs," she clarified, then waved her hand. "Nah, you don't have to answer that. But our interest lies in the murder of Chris Randall, not your recreational and capital ventures. You tell us what we need to know, and the other stuff can be worked out. Maybe overlooked."

"I ain't buying that shit. A friend helped a pig once, and he's still behind bars…ten years later."

"Must have been the deal he worked out. We might be able to do better."

"*Might.*" Pickering mumbled the single word.

"When did you last see him?"

"Last drop." His arms folded and unfolded. "About four weeks ago."

"Around January tenth?" Technically that was three weeks ago, but Pickering had said it was *about* four weeks ago.

"What day of the week was that?"

"A Saturday."

Pickering hitched his shoulders. "Could be."

"So you showed up with the delivery. Anyone else go with you?"

"Not rattin' anyone out. Bros stick together."

"Sure, I understand that. All right. So, you unloaded, and he paid you. You noticed it was counterfeit cash, threw a punch. But that wasn't enough; he fought back." She motioned to his cheek and the scab again. "You were further angered. You threw him in the water, held him under—"

"No! He was alive when I left him."

"And where was it that you left him that night?"

His face wrinkled up in disgust. "Ain't no way I'm sayin', pig."

CHAPTER TWENTY-ONE

Madison stood with Terry and Winston in the observation room, looking at Pickering in the interrogation room through the one-way mirror. Even without anyone in there, his arms were in constant motion.

"He wants to tell us. Just give me more time, and I'll get it out of him," Madison said.

"Did we find any drugs on his person?" Winston asked.

"No."

"Then our hands are tied. We have nothing to hold him."

"He's a confessed drug supplier," she pleaded.

"I don't make up the law, Knight. Find something solid. Otherwise, we'll have to let him walk."

"He got into a fight with Chris and—"

"*And* he claims to have left him alive. You can't pick pieces of what he says, taking some as truths, others under suspicion. You either believe what he's telling you or you don't."

She could tell by the sergeant's stance this wasn't a battle she was going to win. She had to cut Pickering loose, but that didn't mean she had to stop working the case from the angle of a drug deal gone bad—or that she had to take her sights off Pickering.

After releasing him, she dropped into her chair at her desk. Terry sat across from her at his.

"Pull up a background on that girl Pickering mentioned, Lakisha Hudson," Madison said. "Maybe she can tell us more about this guy and get us something to go on."

"Will do." Terry started clicking on his keyboard, but then paused, looked over at her. "If we're to believe Pickering, Chris Randall was actually using the counterfeit money."

Madison nodded, getting Terry's underlying point. "And if he was using it with his supplier, he was probably using it elsewhere, too."

"That opens up a field of potential suspects."

"It sure does. His murder could just be a case of the wrong person being ripped off. We should probably speak with the Secret Service. Get more information on what prompted their investigation."

"Ideally, but McAlexandar might not like it much, as it puts our focus back on Randall."

"Where it deserves to go—unless he's cleared. Besides, what if Daddy Dearest found out that Chris was using the fake money and got angry? I can't see the purpose for the counterfeit money being to buy drugs. Hard to say what the purpose was at all; Randall's loaded."

"It sounds like you're convinced Marcus Randall is behind the manufacturing of the counterfeit money."

"You aren't?"

"I'm reserving judgment."

"Of course you are," she said drily.

"Fine. Regardless, we need to find out what the real purpose was for that money. Whoever was behind its printing will come out." Terry glanced at his monitor, back at her. "I will give you one thing. This investigation does seem to keep circling back to Randall."

She smiled. "Sounds like you're getting a little suspicious of Randall now. Thought he was innocent?"

"I'm not counting myself out of losing our bet just yet." He typed on his keyboard again. "Okay, so here's Hudson's background." Terry pointed to his screen, and Madison got up and walked behind him.

"No priors," Terry said. "Not so much as a mark on her record— Oh, this isn't good."

"Hey, Knight." It was Toby Sovereign.

She pinched her eyes shut briefly and ignored him. "What isn't good, Terry?"

"You always have a way of ignoring me," Sovereign said. "It humbles me."

She turned and came face-to-face with the man she wished she could just bury in the past, along with their broken engagement. "Sovereign, we're busy here."

"See you're over the flu," Terry said.

"It seems to have finally run its course." He'd responded to Terry, but his eyes hadn't left Madison. "Why do you always get the good cases?"

"Just lucky." She moved to the other side of Terry to put more space between her and the man who had broken her heart and ruined her faith in all men.

"Quite the profile you're building up."

Sovereign wasn't getting the hint, so maybe a more direct approach would do the trick. "Is there something else you need to be doing?" she asked with heat. "Perhaps working a new case of your own, taking care of some paperwork?"

"I got Lou for that."

Lou Stanford was his partner.

"Lucky Lou."

The silence crackled with life, and he was just staring at her.

What the hell?

She clenched her teeth. "We have things to do. If you would be so kind as to—" Her phone rang, and she was quick to answer it. "Knight." She turned her back on Sovereign but instead of hearing him walking away, Terry said something to him, and the two of them started chatting.

Just great…

"Hello…?" she prompted her call to speak.

"It's Blake."

Hearing his voice regurgitated his proposal to move in. "Oh, hey. Didn't think I'd hear from you for a while. Thought you were busy with a big client."

"Well, I still am, but something's come up."

"I've heard that line before." She snickered.

"That can be arranged as well, my dirty-minded woman. But I'm referring to something else."

"Okay, you have my interest."

"I'll try not to take offense that I didn't already have it. But I've been thinking…I've met your family."

"Stop reminding me."

"And I think it's time for you to meet a member of mine."

"You have family…in town?" She felt nauseated. She didn't fare well with her own, let alone someone else's. "Thought they lived hours away."

"My daughter's in the city this afternoon. She just called and wants to meet up for dinner. She also wants to meet the lady I've told her about."

"Don't you think she'll be jealous if she's not invited to go along?" If all else failed, deflect.

"You should watch it with your humor, Maddy. Sometimes you're not quite the funny girl you think you are." She detected the smile in his voice.

"I'm right in the middle of a case." Next, pull out excuses.

"You'll always be in the middle of a case. Piccolo Italia. Eight tonight."

She glanced at the clock and noticed it was after six. "That leaves me less than two hours to get home and cleaned up."

"Then you better get leaving."

She turned around to face Terry and Sovereign, who had stopped talking and were looking at her.

At some point, she had to stop being so afraid of taking chances in her relationships or she'd be a prisoner of her past—and Sovereign—forever. "You know what? Why not?"

"Great. I'll see you soon. Should I send a car?"

"I'll get there myself." She ended the call.

"Someplace you have to be?" Sovereign asked.

"Probably with lover boy," Terry said.

Madison's gaze set on her partner. *Why did he say that in front of Sovereign?* Time to deflect again. She smiled and punched Terry playfully in the shoulder. "Mind your own business, would you?"

When she went to glance at Sovereign, he was gone.

CHAPTER TWENTY-TWO

Two hours later Madison walked into Piccolo Italia, her nerves jumbled and her stomach tossing. She didn't know why the thought of meeting Blake's daughter made her feel so uncomfortable. At least it wasn't his mother. Though it still represented another step in her relationship with Blake.

She looked down at herself and ran her hands along the front of her slacks. She'd decided on a black pantsuit and dressed it up with a creamy silk blouse. She accessorized with a silver chain and the diamond earrings that Blake had given her for Christmas.

As she approached the table, Blake and his daughter were in the middle of an animated conversation accompanied with wild gesturing. They both seemed to notice her at the same time, and they dropped their arms and smiled.

Blake rose to greet her. "Good evening. You look lovely," he said into her ear as he hugged her, then tapped a kiss on her lips. He pulled out a chair for her.

"Thank you," Madison said as she sat down. She looked over at Blake's daughter, who appeared to be midtwenties. That would probably make Blake midforties—not that they ever discussed age before. It had never mattered, she supposed, but now it seemed significant.

His daughter was beautiful and lean with black, shoulder-length hair that contrasted her fair complexion. A fine dusting of cocoa freckles sprinkled the bridge of her nose, and her mouth sat slightly crooked when she smiled, but the expression touched her piercing, green eyes. She made Madison feel somewhat self-conscious, not only about being in her thirties, but also about the extra bit of weight she carried. It might as well have been fifty pounds as opposed to twenty. And recalling how she couldn't keep up in the running pursuit today was of no comfort. Maybe she should have salad for dinner; though in an Italian restaurant, that would be viewed as a crime.

"Dad. Introductions…"

"I was getting there. Not that you gave me much of an oppor—"

"I'm Emily." She extended a hand across the table—long, thin fingers and a slender wrist.

"Madison."

"Emily was the blessed result of a college one-nighter," Blake said, unabashed.

"Quiet, Dad." She affectionately slapped his forearm. "He likes to talk braver than he is. Mom actually dumped him. Didn't think he was going anywhere in life."

"Bet you the woman's sorry now." Blake took a sip of water from the glass that was in front of him.

"She's still my mother."

Blake took Madison's hand. "We haven't ordered anything yet," he said, disregarding Emily's comment. "We were waiting on you." Spoken as if she were late, but Blake considered arriving on time as tardy.

"I was here by eight."

"Oh, don't let him get to you." Emily frowned. "He thinks he owns the world." Her face lightened and she added, "It's just nice to finally meet you."

The waiter, whom Madison had come to know as Mario from previous visits, approached the table and glanced from her to Emily, then back. By the way his eyebrow lifted, Madison suspected his imagination was getting carried away.

"Three of you this evening. How very nice." He smiled uneasily at Madison and addressed her. "What may I get you to drink tonight?"

"A glass of house red," Madison replied.

"Actually, Mario," Blake cut in, "please make that a full bottle."

"Very well." Mario backed away from the table, and Madison assumed rumors would be buzzing around the restaurant staff tonight.

Emily moved her cutlery just slightly more to the left. "Dad told me you work as a homicide detective. You see dead bodies all the time. Must be pretty cool."

Pretty cool? It was possible Emily was younger than twenty-five.

"Told you not to talk shop," Blake said.

"What else am I supposed to talk about, Dad?"

"Anything else, Emily," Blake requested.

Emily clamped her mouth shut, pouted.

"It's all right. I don't mind talking about work," Madison said. "And I'm actually in Major Crimes."

Her eyes widened. "Oh, like *Law & Order: Criminal Intent.*"

Madison smiled. "I don't watch much TV."

"Dad said you're working a big case right now." She leaned across the table and spoke in a lower voice. "Chris Randall."

She looked over at Blake, whose gaze was on the far side of the restaurant, seemingly focused on nothing in particular. "That's right."

"That must be so cool having such a high-profile murder to investigate. So, who do you think did it?" She tossed her hair behind her shoulders. "I'd say it was his father."

"Here's your wine, sir." Mario placed three wineglasses on the table and displayed the bottle for Blake to confirm the label. Once Blake nodded his approval, Mario popped the cork, poured a bit in one glass, and handed it to Blake.

Blake swirled the wine to analyze its legs. Months ago, Madison wouldn't even have connected wine and legs. Blake and she really were from different worlds, with his being more refined than hers.

She watched as Blake continued "the ritual." He inhaled the wine's aroma—known as its bouquet, as he had told her on another occasion—then took a small sip. He let the flavor of the wine fill his mouth and saturate his tongue, something to do with assessing the body of the wine. *Legs, bouquet, body...yikes.*

"Very good." Blake placed the glass on the table, and Mario proceeded to pour for all of them, then took his leave.

Blake turned to his daughter. "You decide what you're having for dinner?"

"Not yet." She put a hand over her menu and looked at Madison. "Chris had everything; his father had nothing. Maybe he was jealous."

"Emily," Blake said firmly, and Madison got the impression he still viewed his grown daughter as a child he could control.

"Oh, fine." Emily perused the menu in a manner suggesting she did so to appease her father, then placed it back on the table. "What made you decide to be a detective?"

"As you can see, she's fascinated by your career choice." Blake sat back with his wineglass and the hint of a smile, though it didn't come close to touching his eyes. He really didn't want to discuss the murder case, and it made Madison wonder why.

"Well, not everyone can do what she does," Emily snapped back. "What was the reason?"

"For going into law enforcement?" Madison took a guess as to what Emily had meant.

Emily nodded. "Yeah."

"A few things, I guess. I wanted to make a bit of a difference, bring answers to people. I never saw myself settling down, getting married, having kids...no offense." Madison smiled at Blake.

"None taken," he assured her.

"My grandfather was a cop." Her thoughts briefly drifted to her grandmother, whom she loved dearly and had lost a couple years ago. She hadn't thought about her in a few days now. Maybe that pain was finally starting to heal.

"Cool."

It was until my grandfather locked up the wrong guy and got shot down in cold blood on the night of his wedding anniversary.

Madison took a sip of her wine to deflect her emotions and looked at Emily. "What about you? What do you see yourself doing?"

"Still sorting that out. I don't want to rush into anything, ya know."

"My girl here is a full-time student," Blake interjected and took a draw on his wine.

"Dad just wishes I'd settle on a major, but one day, he'll be proud of me."

"I already am, sweetie." He put a hand on his daughter's. "I just wish you'd stick with something." For the first time, Madison was witnessing another side to Blake: the father. With that facet came a strong parental pride, and Madison wondered if he had other children she didn't know about.

Blake continued. "Emily here has majored in business, the arts, dabbled a bit in law and accounting. Her education is costing me a fortune."

"As if you can't afford it." Emily laughed and drank some wine. She put her glass down and added with a smile, "Maybe I'll look into criminal investigation next."

Madison was still stuck on her comment *as if you can't afford it.* How wealthy was Blake? He lived in a luxury condo, funded his daughter's vast educational whims, and… Madison's hand went to an ear and traced the diamond earring dangling there.

"Beautiful earrings, Maddy. May I call you Maddy?"

"Sure."

"You can call me Em." She turned to her father. "I really like her. Keep this one."

Blake smiled. "I'll do my best." He reached out a hand to Madison.

"You really won Em over." Blake rolled on his side to face Madison.

They were lying on his thousand-count Egyptian sheets. *Again, how rich is this man?*

"I guess we're even now. I met your family; you met mine," he said.

"Not even close. You can't compare your daughter to my entire family. I don't know who you are." The last sentence slipped out.

"What do you mean?"

Think quick.

"Well, you never talk about your family. How many siblings do you have? Brothers? Sisters? What about your parents? Do you have any other children besides Emily?"

"Wow, that's a lot of questions."

Madison lifted the sheets and looked under them at Blake's naked body. "Don't you think I have the right to know who I'm sleeping with?"

"You should have interrogated me prior to consummation, Detective." He laughed.

She usually loved it when he used her job title, and she would have found amusement in his statement if she wasn't feeling so damn serious all of a sudden. "You want me to move in with you, and I don't even know your mother's first name."

"Sharon."

She smiled. "Father?"

"John." He moved closer to her, snuggling into her. "Enough talk about family. So, are you moving in with me? Because that's all I heard."

"I never said that."

He kissed her nose.

"I said 'you want me to.'"

"I do."

"But why? Things are good as they are."

"You're a chicken shit."

She slapped his chest. "Excuse me?"

"I said it. I'll say it again. You're a chicken shit, Miss Detective Knight." He pulled in closer to her, and she found herself responding to his touch. "Surely there's something I could do to change your mind," he said, flashing a cocky smile and taking her mouth with his. She wanted to sink into the moment, but her chatty mind was killing the mood. She pulled back.

"Why can't we just keep on like we are...having fun?"

"I'm old enough to know what I want, and I know you know what that is." His eyes held intent; his agenda clear. He wanted her to move in just as much as she was against the idea. She couldn't change his mind any more than he could hers. In chess, she believed they'd call this a stalemate. In relationships, it was probably the beginning of the end.

CHAPTER TWENTY-THREE

If digging into Richards's past had taught Madison anything, she wouldn't be doing what she was about to. But her mind kept justifying that she had a right to know everything about Blake Golden. She glanced at the clock on the station's wall and noted it was seven thirty. If she were to really make good use of her time, she'd be down at Hannigan's Market looking for Medcalf. Instead, she was going to pull Blake's background before Terry got in.

She sat at her desk, glancing around, anxious about getting caught. Not so much by a superior to whom she'd have to explain herself, but by Blake somehow. After all, if he wanted her to know certain things, he would tell her himself. She took a deep breath and took the plunge. The report was filling in on the screen—

"Morning."

She looked up, and Cynthia was coming right for her, moving at a quick pace. Madison would never be able to back out of the report in time. She clicked the monitor off.

"Hey." Madison tried to sound as causal as possible.

"What are you up to?" Cynthia moved around to look at the screen. "Your monitor's off."

She had to think fast. "Yeah, having computer problems. I had to reboot."

"Ah." Cynthia glanced over a shoulder as if she was looking for someone, her dark hair swinging in a ponytail with the movement.

"You just get in?" Madison gestured to her friend's wardrobe. She was still wearing her coat and a pair of boots. Maybe if she could get Cynthia talking about something else, she'd let go of the topic of the shut-off monitor.

"Yeah…" Cynthia's gaze lowered and shot back up again to meet Madison's. "Why did you lie to me? Your computer's on." She pointed to the blue light on the CPU.

"Oh?" Madison tried to act surprised, but she never claimed to be a good actress. "It must have booted up already."

"Don't forget to turn the screen on. Not sure why you would have turned it off for a reboot." Cynthia was far too alert for seven thirty in the morning. She reached for the power button on the monitor.

Madison tapped the back of Cynthia's hand. "Don't—"

Too late. The screen came to life.

"Blake Arthur Golden…" Cynthia turned to Madison and cocked her eyebrows. "You're doing a background on your boyfriend?" She laughed.

"Glad you find this so amusing." Madison closed the report.

"Actually I'm surprised you hadn't pulled one long before now."

"Gee, thanks." Madison didn't like how it painted her as an untrusting person. Probably the fact that the shoe fit was what hurt the most.

"No, I don't mean anything insulting by it. You're just normally really careful about relationships."

"How do you—"

"How do I know that? We're friends, Maddy. Just because you project yourself as unbreakable doesn't mean you are."

Am I that easy to see through?

Cynthia continued. "Heck, I screen my men—"

"The system's not intended for personal use."

"Says the woman who just violated that rule." Cynthia dropped her large purse on Madison's desk as if she was settling in for the day. "Is it getting serious between you two?"

"Anyone tell you you're too full of questions for first thing in the day?"

"I wake up ready to ask questions. It's part of the job." The steady eye contact told her Cynthia wasn't leaving until she got her answer.

Madison lifted her Starbucks cup, in desperate need of an escape—and distraction—but it was empty. She put it back down. "He asked me to move in with him."

"What?" Cynthia gasped, and it had Officer Ranson turning to look at them from the front desk.

"Geesh, keep it down," Madison whispered.

Cynthia continued at a slightly lower volume. "When did that happen?"

"The start of the week."

"And you're just telling me now?"

"Hey, sweetie." Detective Stanford came up behind Cynthia and wrapped an arm around her. She squirmed out from under him and cast him a look that could freeze the Caribbean.

Hmm. How interesting…

Madison sat back, smiling. It seemed someone else had secrets of her own.

"Why are you acting like this?" Sandford asked her. He and Cynthia held eye contact for a few seconds before he broke it and addressed Madison. "Hey, Madison."

"Hey." Madison was fighting off a fit of laughter.

Cynthia put a hand on his forearm. "Can we talk later?"

"Of course, baby." He slapped her on the ass and walked away.

"So that's the real reason you're down here." Madison's eyes narrowed to slits. "You're dating Sovereign's partner? Yet you're giving me a hard time about not telling you everything that's going on in my life?" Madison chuckled. Cynthia went serious-faced.

"I'm sorry."

"Why? Because—"

"I thought maybe it would be awkward for you. You were with Sovereign, and he's partners with Lou. Maybe they talked…and maybe Lou talks to me."

Madison didn't want to dwell on how much her friend might know. Her relationship with Sovereign had ended years before Cynthia came on board.

"How long have you two been a thing?"

"About a week. And he's so hot in bed." Cynthia spun to look at his retreating figure—or more specifically his ass, if Madison knew her friend at all.

"You've been seeing him for a week? Yet you didn't say anything about it until now?" For Cynthia, a week was a huge deal.

"Fine, I see where you're going with this. We don't need to give each other a play-by-play of our lives."

"Not exactly what I meant, but, yes."

"Lou and I are just casual, and it means nothing. You and Blake are going to take it to the next level."

"Whoa. I haven't said yes. You know I like my independence."

"I know that's what you say."

Over an hour later, Madison was still thinking about what she'd told Cynthia. Was she just trying to hide behind a claim of liking her independence to save her heart? Maybe, but at the same time, she didn't need a man to complete her, or someone to consult with about everything from what's-for-dinner to which movie to watch on a Friday night. She was perfectly capable of making her own decisions.

"How was the evening with lover boy?" Terry looked across at her from his desk. They were waiting for the lawyer to show with Ryan Turner.

"Be happy I'm not standing next to you, or I'd punch you in the shoulder."

Terry smiled. "Anyway, before you ran off with *lover boy*, I had Lakisha Hudson's background file—"

"I had somewhere to be," she defended herself.

"Yeah, on the top or on the bottom is my question." A flash flickered in his eyes.

"Oh, shut up, Terry. I'm warning you." She jabbed a finger at him, in effect mocking the chief's wagging finger. She had been in such a hurry to get to dinner on time, she never found out what was interesting about the woman's file. By the time she remembered, it had been later at night, though she still had tried to reach Terry. "Did you get my voice mail?"

"This morning. You should know when I walk out that door, the phone's off."

Terry never pretended to be obsessed with his job.

"Ah, so you were on a date with the Missus."

"Now who's fishing?"

"I figured it's fair. You poked into my love life; I can poke into yours."

He flashed a goofy grin. "Oh, it's love."

Madison snarled and pointed a finger at him again.

"At least I'm not living in sin." He laughed.

She rolled her eyes. "Just tell me what you found that was so interesting in the woman's file."

"Just that she's more of a girl. Lakisha Hudson is only fifteen."

"Pickering is twenty-six. He had sex with a minor. That's statutory rape, and it gives us enough reason to bring him in again. That's also why he was so worried when he was pulled in and thought it was about her."

"I think we should talk to Lakisha first. See what she has to say, and maybe she'll be able to shed more light on Pickering's friendship with Chris."

"I know there's a reason I keep you around," she jested.

CHAPTER TWENTY-FOUR

Madison had excused herself for a minute, and when she returned to her desk, Terry told her Ryan Turner and his lawyer were in room one.

She went in, saw the man sitting beside Ryan, then retreated to the hall again, backing into Terry in the process. She closed the door and leveled a glare at her partner. "Why didn't you tell me Blake was Randall's lawyer?"

"You didn't know?"

"No, I didn't know."

"You had his card in your hand. How could I know you hadn't read it?"

She clenched her jaw and shook her head. To think that two nights ago Blake had called her, and she'd opened up about the case. Right from the start, he had known she was assigned; it wasn't just a lucky guess. This deceit probably explained why he was so uncomfortable discussing her line of work and the investigation at dinner last night. Was the introduction to his daughter an elaborate orchestration to increase her vulnerability? To distract her in some way to let her guard down? To make her feel more vested in the relationship?

"I can handle this if you want," Terry offered.

"Nope, I've got this." She swung the door open and sat at the table, across from Turner and Blake. She kept her eyes on Turner, not about to give Blake the satisfaction of acknowledging him. "Just some basic questions. When we spoke last, you said that you and Chris Randall were pretty much brothers."

Turner nodded.

Madison continued. "You also mentioned being at Caesar's with him on January tenth, the last night Chris was alive—"

"Your statement is leading and lends to speculation."

Madison let out a deep breath, refusing to look at the man she shared a bed with just as recently as last night. "Were you at Caesar's with Chris on January tenth?"

"Uh-huh."

"Was that the last place you saw him?"

Turner glanced at Blake as if not sure whether he should answer. Blake gestured for him to go ahead.

"No."

Madison sat up straighter. "Where did you last see Chris?"

"His house."

"The Randall estate?" she asked to clarify.

"You can't feed him a location." Blake tilted out his chin and pulled out on the lapels of his suit jacket.

"I don't see how I *fed* him a location when he offered Chris's house." She chose now to look at Blake. "Mister …?"

A pulse tapped in his cheek. "Golden."

She wrested her gaze from Blake to look at Turner. "And you went to Chris's house after the club?"

"Yes."

"What time did you leave the club?"

"Around two."

"And did you go straight to Chris's house?" Madison was purposely overusing the term *Chris's house* as a dig at Blake.

"We hit a coffee shop first. Chris made me down some first so I could drive. He viewed taxis as common carriers."

"Common carriers?"

"In other words, something commoners used, not someone like him."

It would seem Chris had viewed his wealth as elevating him above the working class, but that outlook didn't seem to bother Turner. In fact, Madison picked up on Turner's eagerness to please Chris. Was that the result of his paid-for education, or something more?

"So you were to sober up and drive," Madison said. "But why not call Chris's father? He could have sent one of his men—"

Turner shook his head. "Nope. Chris hated his father's man-slaves."

"Man-slaves?" Madison repeated, unable to mask her disgust. That was the problem with money: it turned a lot of people into asses. She glanced at Blake, who seemed to be ignoring her now.

Turner shrugged. "That's what Chris called them."

"When he told you the party was over and *made* you down coffee, did that make you mad?" Madison's gaze went to the scab on his lip.

"No."

She motioned to his lip. "No? It would me."

"Inference, Detective. You're alleging that my client had something to do with Chris's death. But you don't even know for certain it was murder, do you? From my understanding, Chris Randall drowned."

Madison felt the anger travel through her, warming her cheeks and earlobes. "Goes to show you're not up-to-date. The medical examiner has concluded the manner of death a homicide."

Seemingly sideswiped, Blake sucked in air through his teeth. "Still, how does one go about proving a drowning was intentional? I believe the media reports said he drowned."

"They stated he was pulled from the river, and that the case was being investigated as suspicious."

"Same thing, is it not, Detective? Again, I return to my earlier inquiry. How can one *prove* intentional drowning? Is it not, in fact, the perfect murder, one that cannot be proven?"

She would be leaving this room viewing Blake differently than she had before. "I assure you, there are ways."

They had a stare down, with neither of them willing to lose.

"You guys know each other?" Turner asked, breaking their concentration.

Blake said nothing, and she wasn't about to answer Turner's question, either.

She held eye contact with Blake for a few more seconds before looking at Turner. "How did you get the cut lip?"

"Relevance?" Blake extended his arm and twisted his wrist to look at his watch.

She could punch him in his big, smug face. "Please answer the question," Madison prompted Turner.

"A fight."

"With Chris Randall?" She held up a hand to silence Blake, and she was surprised that he followed her direction.

Turner's cheeks swelled with air as he exhaled. "I didn't kill him."

"What was the fight over?"

"I didn't even connect with him. Chris moved out of the way, and I ended up hitting a wall." He lifted his hand. His knuckles were scabbed, too.

"There was a lot of anger behind the punch, then."

"Tell me you're not implying anything now." Blake sat back and crossed his arms.

"I didn't kill my friend," Turner pleaded. His gaze darted to the floor then back up to meet hers. "I loved that man like a brother."

Unswayed, she asked, "What was the fight over?"

Turner remained silent.

"You don't have to answer that," Blake said.

"Where was this fight?"

"You don't have to answer that either."

Madison took a few steadying breaths and decided to change course. "Anyone else you know of that might have wanted him dead?"

"His dad," Ryan said quietly.

Blake turned to face him. He wanted to leave—she could feel it oozing from him—but circumstances forced him to stay.

"His dad? Marcus Randall?" Madison asked.

"That's the man." Turner's sardonic tone was well noted. "Seriously, though? I'm not sure." He shrugged, a surefire smirk on his lips.

"This funny to you?" she snapped.

Turner's face fell serious.

"Why would Chris's own father want him dead?"

"He didn't approve of Chris. He'd send him all over to set up new investors. If you ask me, he didn't appreciate his efforts."

That was now two people—Medcalf and Turner—who told her Chris was sent abroad to set up foreign investors. But did that have anything to do with his death?

"What makes you say his father didn't appreciate him?" Madison asked, digging deeper.

"Nothing was enough for that man. You just can't please some people. Well, Chris could tell he wasn't measuring up for Mr. Randall. He thought his old man valued the man-slaves more." He added as a latter thought, "Especially that baboon he carts everywhere."

"His bodyguard, Jonathan Wright," Madison assumed.

"Could be. Chris always called him a baboon."

Yet Medcalf said that Wright was like another son to Randall. Had some sort of sibling rivalry between Wright and Chris led to Chris's murder?

"Chris never got along with either Jonathan Wright or Tony Medcalf?" Madison inquired.

"Who's—"

"Mr. Medcalf is Randall's cook."

Turner looked confused.

"He's also the doorman," Madison added, pulling from one of the other responsibilities Medcalf had rattled off.

"Oh. He didn't really talk about him much other than to say the man was a zero."

"So they didn't get along?"

"I don't know. I'm not even sure the man's existence mattered to Chris."

Maybe Medcalf—who took pride in the Randall family and its affairs—felt slighted by the cavalier attitude projected from *junior* and had "taken care" of him?

"Well, there's one more thing I'd like to discuss," Madison began. "Did you know that Chris made counterfeit money?"

Turner's eyes went straight to Blake, who responded on his client's behalf. "We're here in regard to Chris Randall's murder, not for a discussion about counterfeiting."

Madison noted Blake's referral to Chris's death as a murder now. "Can you tell us why we would have found your prints on bills in Chris's pocket?" She might have exaggerated a little. It was one print—a partial at that—on one bill.

Turner stared at the side of Blake's face.

Blake pulled out on his tie and adjusted his position in the chair. "This meeting has gone on long enough. Should you wish to discuss other charges, i.e. counterfeiting involvement, you may book another appointment. And unless you have factual evidence connecting him to the murder, I suggest you search out other avenues of investigation instead of harassing my client." Blake rose to his feet, and Turner followed his lead.

With them out of the room, Terry turned on her. "You all right?"

"Why wouldn't I be?" She'd just been stabbed in the back again by a man she'd foolishly had started to fall for and trust.

There was a knock on the door, then it opened, and Blake peeked his head in. "Can we talk a minute?"

Terry passed a cursory glance to Blake, then looked at her. "You good?"

"Yeah."

Terry left the room. Blake took a seat beside her.

"I'm not even sure why I came back."

"That makes two of us." She met his gaze, the eyes she'd just peered into last night, the same ones that spoke of love and of moving in together. She must have been crazy to deceive herself into thinking she could make it with a defense attorney. "How the hell are we supposed to make this work? We sit on opposing sides of the table. I do my best to convict the guilty. You work to set them free."

"That is my job. You knew that from the start. As I recall, our first meeting was in an interrogation room."

"I'm just supposed to accept that you're on Mr. Randall's payroll?"

"His money is no different than anyone else's."

She angled her head, not even about to touch on the counterfeit allegations. "It is to me."

"Why? What has he done to you on a personal level? Or is it just because he's a powerful man? Your dislike for them isn't a secret you carry around with you."

Who is he to headshrink me?

"Why didn't you tell me you worked for him, before now? You could have even told me last night."

"I didn't think it would matter. Maybe I even just assumed you knew."

She shook her head. "No, you didn't. Not that it matters."

Blake stiffened. "You don't have to agree with my client choice, and I don't need to defend myself to you."

"Then don't bother."

"Don't get like this—"

"Excuse me?" she snapped.

"You live every day trying to find some reason to end things between us."

"Guess I can stop looking." She left him with his hands raised in the air.

CHAPTER TWENTY-FIVE

"Knight, stop there!"

Madison had just stepped outside the doorway of the interrogation room.

Winston hurried toward her, along with McAlexandar and two other men she didn't recognize in tow. She surmised from their cheap suits that they were Secret Service. Cynthia had given her advanced notice of Ryan Turner's fingerprint being on the money yesterday, and time must have run out.

The group of men came to a standstill in front of her.

The older agent said, "We're looking for Ryan Turner."

Playing stupid, she said, "Why would you—"

McAlexandar and the two agents brushed past her, into the interrogation room. The sergeant stayed back.

"You assured me I would know everything in advance of your doing it." Winston's face was red.

"You knew I would be speaking with Mr. Turner," Madison said.

"But you didn't fill me in as to when, did you? And his involvement in the counterfeiting... did you know about that?" Winston put a hand on his hip.

She wasn't about to throw Cynthia under the bus.

Winston let out a huge sigh. "Your silence tells me all I need to kn—"

"He's not here, just his lawyer," the younger of the Secret Service agents announced as he rejoined her and Winston in the hallway. The chief, the other agent, and Blake also came out of the room.

Blake pulled down on his suit jacket and seemed to avoid looking at Madison. "I represent Mr. Turner. We can book an appoint—"

"Your client is involved in a counterfeit ring," the younger agent interjected. "Did he tell you that? Counterfeiting is a crime against the country."

"I assume you have evidence to back up your allegations? If you do—" Blake extended a business card between his index and middle fingers "—feel free to contact my office and book an appointment. Good day, gentlemen." He looked at her briefly before walking away, and it was there in his eyes, in an unspoken communication; somehow, he knew she'd withheld the tidbit about Turner's print on fake bills from the proper channels.

Thank God he came through for her and didn't voice his suspicions out loud. But was he planning to also keep his thoughts to himself for good, or was he planning to pull it out in the future and use it to bite her in the ass?

"What's going on?" Terry came up beside her.

"Now isn't that a good question," Winston said. "Knight, my office. Stat."

She followed him down the hall, and shut out the Secret Service agents, the chief, and Terry.

Madison remained standing while Winston sat behind his desk.

"I had every right to question Turner."

"You know that's not what this is about," Winston said. "This is about your lack of communication."

"I'm supposed to detail everything to you? And for this case, in advance?"

"That was the deal, unless I misunderstood it." Winston clasped his hands on the desk.

"So, the next time I need to take a drink of water, have a piss—"

"Stop there." He kept his hands laced, but one finger jabbed in her direction. "One more word, Knight, and I will suspend you."

She dropped into the chair facing his desk and gripped the arms until her knuckles went white. "If you were going to, you would have done it already. You want the answers, too." She took a gamble and played to his sense of right and wrong. "

"Not the point."

"It actually is the point. There are a lot of secrets surrounding the Randalls and everyone they're involved with. We need to expose them to get to the truth of what happened to Chris."

Winston's silence was hard to read. Either he agreed with her or he was assessing her loyalty to her superiors. Maybe McAlexandar held more power over him than she realized.

"You have to allow me to do my job," she said, not able to stand the silence any longer.

Time continued to pass slowly, almost as if it had stopped before he spoke. "No more of this, Knight. I mean it this time. McAlexandar wants you fired."

"I know, sir." The last word slipped out much to her surprise.

"This thing is far from over. The Secret Service has requested to meet with you. I told them you were otherwise occupied today. Now get out of my office."

She stopped at the doorway. "Boss."

"What, Knight?" His eyes sagged with fatigue.

"Our plans for this afternoon—" She took a seat again.

CHAPTER TWENTY-SIX

Lakisha Hudson lived with her mother, Dorethea. When she answered the door, Madison could have mistaken her for Aunt Jemima from the pancake syrup bottle. She was a well-rounded woman, big bosom, narrow waist, big hips—*mothering* hips, as Madison's mother would say.

After Madison introduced herself and Terry, Dorethea led them to a living room and set off to fix them a cup of coffee. They could see her over the half wall and through wood spindles that separated the kitchen and living room.

The room was dated with a burnt-orange couch, an old tube television, and a mica coffee table. A beanbag chair sat in one corner.

"I can't say when the girl'll be back." Dorethea came into the room holding two steaming mugs. "You said sugar and cream?" She handed that one to Terry and the other one to Madison.

Madison wasn't exactly excited about the coffee. After her embarrassing running pursuit the other day, she'd requested it black with sweetener—to cut back on calories.

"What's this all about, anyway?" Dorethea slipped back into the kitchen and grabbed a can of Coke that was on the table. She dropped into a chair there and eyed them through the spindles.

"We'd like to speak with your daughter about someone named Steven Pickering," Madison told her.

"What makes youse think Lakisha will know this Pickering kid?" She lifted a can of Coke, slurped back on it.

Right now probably wasn't the best time to point out Pickering wasn't exactly a kid. "We're quite sure they know each other, yes," Madison said.

"Listen, I ain't gonna sit here and tell youse what a good girl I got. I know she gits herself in all sorts of trouble, but what girl her age doesn't? But she doesn't sleep around, take drugs, stuff like that."

The front door opened.

"Lakisha?" Dorethea called out. "Get in here."

"What, Mama?" A young woman came to a standstill in the doorway. Her skin was dark like her mother's, almost black, but her facial features were delicate. "Who are they?"

"Poleece. Say ya know a guy named Pickering."

Lakisha glanced at Madison and Terry, but she said nothing.

"I'm Detective Knight, and this is my partner. We have some questions about—"

"I don't know any Steve Pickering."

"But you know him by first name?" Madison cocked an eyebrow.

Lakisha dropped into the beanbag chair. "Whatev'. I know him. So what?"

Dorethea joined them in the living room area and stood near her daughter. "You lied to the poleece? Haven't I taught ya better than that?"

The girl glanced at her, a defiant teenage smirk lifting the right side of her face. "We got together."

"So you had sex with Pickering?" Madison asked.

Lakisha nodded.

Madison glanced briefly at Doretha, then addressed Lakisha. "You realize he is twenty-six—"

"No." Dorethea's head turned to her daughter. "She must be lying. You wouldn't." Dorethea faced Madison, and she narrowed her eyes. "You said they were friends."

"Mama, don't get mad at them. It's about time you knew." Lakisha shrugged, and she sank deeper into the beanbag chair.

"We'll sue 'im! You're just a baby."

"I'm not a baby! I'm fifteen."

"Still, a man can't—"

"I wanted to." Lakisha stared at her mother. "Some have been my age."

"Lakisha Louise Hudson! How many boys you been with?"

"I don't know."

"You don't know?" Dorethea raged. "How da hell don't you know somethin' like that?"

It was time to refocus this conversation. "Steven Pickering had sex with you," Madison said. "Did you know he was older?"

"Yessss." Lakisha let the word snake off her tongue. "But I wanted to." She crossed her arms.

"Actually, you're too young to consent," Madison said as delicately as possible. Madison remembered what Pickering had said in the interrogation room. *She told me to hit her.* "Did he ever hit you?"

"No."

Dorethea leveled a hot glare on her daughter.

"How long have you known Steven Pickering?" Madison asked.

Lakisha fell quiet, then turned to her mother. "I want to help the police, Mama, to do right. But I'm not telling you everything."

"Lakisha Louise Hudson, you live under my roof!" Dorethea drained back the rest of her soda and set the empty can on the coffee table. "I carried you in ma belly for nine months, not so you could come out and sass me!"

Did every mother give their daughter that line? At least Madison's had, but without the African-American flavor.

"Miss Hudson," Madison started, "I can only imagine it's hard to hear—"

"You a mama, then? You've been in my shoes?"

"No."

"Then you don't know." She threw her hands in the air and walked away.

"What do you need to know 'bout Steve?" Lakisha blinked heavily.

Madison leaned toward Lakisha. "How long have you known him?"

Lakisha reached into her pants pocket, pulled out a pack of gum, popped a piece in her mouth, and proceeded to chew with hard, open-mouth chomps.

Madison waited her out.

"Five minutes," Lakisha tossed out with a grin.

"Five minutes?"

"Pretty much, yeah. The guy wasn't that good. Three of the five were used for foreplay. He was '*Pssfff*, like a bottle rocket.' I believe that's how your generation puts it."

Your *generation? Ouch.*

"You just hooked up the one time?"

"Pretty much."

"What do you mean pretty much?"

"I know Tyrone a lot better."

"Who's Tyrone?"

Lakisha blew a bubble with her gum, snapped it.

"It might be important for us to know," Madison pressed. She was thinking that maybe this Tyrone was involved in the drug world like Pickering.

"Thought you were curious about Steve."

"We are." Madison held eye contact with the girl. "Do you do drugs, Lakisha?"

The gum chewing came to a pause.

"We're not with Narcotics," Madison said. "We're Major Crimes."

Her eyes revealed amusement. "You investigate murders like on TV."

That was the second time she had heard a similar statement in the last twenty-four hours. "Yes, except with *real* dead bodies."

The teen didn't blink. "I think Steve does drugs."

Lakisha seemed more taken with the drug angle than murder. At least she didn't seem to have put together the reason for Madison and Terry's visit. "Why would you say that?"

"Just the crazy look in his eyes, but maybe that's just how he looks." She shrugged a shoulder and resumed chomping down on the gum.

"This other guy, Tyrone," Terry interjected. "You said you know him?"

Lakisha looked at Terry. "Yeah. Pretty much forever. A year? Something like that."

Madison couldn't help but remember how six months in a teenage relationship felt like a lifetime. By that scale, a year would be an eternity.

"Ty intro'd us…me and Steve," Lakisha volunteered.

"Why?" Madison asked.

"Meh. He just thought we'd be good together."

Madison was feeling sick for Lakisha and about how these men were taking advantage of her. "How old is Tyrone?"

Lakisha remained silent.

"Did this Tyrone touch you? Or abuse you in any other way?" She leaned forward. "Is he pimping you out?"

Lakisha shook her head so fast her black hair swished in front of her face. "No! No!"

Madison held up a hand to calm the girl. "It's okay. I believe you, but I need to ask those type of questions."

Lakisha stopped shaking her head, locked eyes with Madison. "I like older guys. Anything wrong with that? I didn't think so."

"How old is Tyrone?" Madison repeated her question.

"Thirty, somethin' like that. Pushing old, anyway."

Based on thirty, Madison was four years past *pushing old*. What did that make her? Ancient? "What's his last name?"

"I'm not telling you that."

"But he lives around here?" Madison was thinking she could track him down in the system if she had some more details.

Lakisha stopped chewing her gum and bit her bottom lip. Her aura of confidence, gone.

"You're afraid of him?" Madison wagered.

Lakisha wouldn't make eye contact.

Not long later, Madison and Terry saw themselves out. Her stride was fast as she headed back to the department car.

"It's so frustrating that they're not pressing charges. Pickering deserves to go away for what he did to her. So does Tyrone…whoever the hell he is."

"You can't make people testify," Terry said.

"Well, whatever… We've got to find this Tyrone guy."

"First time his name's come up. No Tyrones noted in Chris's phone records, although Cynthia wasn't able to get any more info on the blocked numbers."

"Well, thanks to Lakisha, we know Pickering's connected to Tyrone. Maybe they are both drug suppliers."

"Could be. We could grab Pickering and see what he has to say. He doesn't know that Lakisha isn't pressing charges. We could use it to get him to talk."

"We could…" Madison said, but she wanted more before bringing him in again. "Pickering admitted to getting into a fight with Chris, but how far did it go? Did anyone witness the altercation? I think it's time to pay Randall's neighbors a visit, see if they saw something helpful to our investigation."

"Let's do it."

CHAPTER TWENTY-SEVEN

Most of the houses along the Bradshaw River were worth over five million. The ones that had boat docks or boathouses were valued even higher. Randall's estate probably topped them all.

Their first stop was to the house that faced Randall's property from across the river. It was redbrick and sat on a smaller property than Randall's but was immaculate, nonetheless.

She walked around the side of the house and saw there wasn't a boathouse, but there was a dock, a ramp, and a shed designed to mimic the main house. Her eyes went beyond the water to Randall's property.

"I hate that we're forced to dance around while that could be the real scene of the crime." She gestured toward Randall's boathouse. "It's a waste of time."

"That's because you don't open your mind to any other options. You get so damned focused you block everything else out."

"Well, this guy here likely has a boat. He could be the killer," Madison mocked her partner.

"Randall has a boat and smokes cigars, so it really must be him."

She narrowed her eyes. Her effort to jab at Terry had backfired. He was right. She couldn't just run a murder case based on her suspicions and dislike for McAlexandar and anyone who kept company with him. Besides, men mourn in different ways, and Randall could be grieving in silence, behind closed doors. Not that Madison believed he was.

They approached the front door. It was solid-looking and mounted with heavy hardware. It creaked open, and a woman with hair the color of midnight stood in the doorway. Her brown eyes were small in proportion to the rest of her face. Her hair reached past her shoulders, straightened from an iron, and bangs capped off her forehead. She wore yoga pants and a fitted T-shirt, neither of which revealed an ounce of fat, and sweat glistened on her forehead, despite an obvious light layer of makeup. She held a stainless steel water bottle in her left hand.

Madison gave the official introduction, then asked, "Are you Kathleen Klinger?" She had done a reverse-address search and found the property was registered to Kathleen and Ronnie Klinger, ages thirty-six and forty, respectively.

Kathleen eyed Madison and Terry suspiciously. "I am, but why are you here?"

"We'd like to ask you a few questions and look around the yard."

"This about the Randall kid?" A hand dropped to her hip, and she glanced back over her shoulder. She seemed eager to return to her workout. Or something.

"Yes, it is," Madison said.

"We can see their property from here." Kathleen stepped back inside; the unspoken invitation was there for them to follow. She led them to the dining room and pointed out a large bay window.

Randall's boathouse was directly across and plain to see. Madison glanced at Terry, who softly shook his head.

"Did you know Chris Randall?" Madison asked.

"Never talked to him, but we saw him all the time. He was in that boathouse a lot. We'd wave, call out greetings. You know, just being friendly neighbors, but he'd never respond. It was like we were invisible to him."

"You say he was there a lot," Madison started. "Do you have any idea why?"

"Well…" Kathleen pulled out a chair at the table and took a seat. She gestured for them to sit as well, and they did. Kathleen continued. "Ronnie thought I was making too much out of it. I just had a hard time understanding why someone his age spent so much time in a boathouse. I mean, even in the winter."

"That is strange," Madison admitted. "Was he normally there alone?"

Kathleen lifted her water bottle and took a drink. "He'd have people with him most of the time."

"How many are we talking?" Madison asked.

"I'd say around four or five at a time."

"What do you think was going on?" Sometimes you just had to cast the line into the water and see what you caught.

"I think it had something to do with drugs," Kathleen said, "but that's also why Ronnie thinks I'm crazy. There sure were a lot of ins and outs from that place, though."

"Ins and outs?" Terry prompted.

"Just people coming and going. They didn't stay long."

Madison glanced at her partner. That sort of activity could hint at drug trafficking.

"The other week— I guess it was just this week," Kathleen said. "They took a bunch of stuff out of there."

"Chris and his friends?" Madison inquired to clarify.

She shook her head. "Tweedledum and Tweedledee. One of the guys is pretty big. I'm thinking he's Randall's bodyguard?" She shrugged. "But they're definitely in the father's employ and not friends of Chris's. They're older."

Madison glanced across at the boathouse again, and back to Kathleen. "Did you see what they were taking out?"

"No. They were carrying luggage bags. They went in with them and came out." Kathleen swigged back on her water bottle again. "I could tell the bags were heavier when they came out just the way their arms pulled."

It was possible the boathouse served as a storage location for the drugs. And if drugs were in play, then expanding on that assumption, for Randall's men to be there, that would mean Randall knew what his son was into. He'd want to clean up any possible mess to avoid scandal.

"When did you see them do this again?" Madison asked.

"Monday, I believe."

Randall had found out about his son that afternoon. She was struck cold when the thought hit: Randall's men could have been getting rid of evidence in regard to his son's murder. "Do you remember what time Monday?"

"About seven or eight in the evening. I guess it would have been eight. I just got home from kickboxing and came to the kitchen to pour a glass of wine. The light outside the boathouse caught my eye."

"What time of day would you see these people with Chris, the ones you mentioned earlier?" Terry inquired.

"Usually at night."

Terry fixed his gaze on Kathleen. "How do you know it was the father's men who supposedly cleaned out the boathouse?"

Kathleen's grip tightened on her water bottle. "I could tell."

"You've met them before?" Terry hurled out, sounding confrontational.

"No, but I know who—"

"Couldn't it have been pretty much anyone, then? It was nighttime. Even in the moonlight, things get obscure. Especially at this distance." Terry pointed out the window. "And if you never met them…"

"Am I being interrogated here?" Kathleen crossed her arms.

It was feeling like it…

"Of course not, but we need to ask all these questions," Madison stepped in.

Kathleen addressed Terry. "I don't know for certain."

"So, to be clear, the people who cleaned it out might not have been the men who worked for Mr. Randall?" Terry pressed.

"I'm pretty sure it was them. One guy was really tall and built big. The other one was shorter with a smaller build."

Kathleen had pegged Wright and Medcalf by general physical description.

"But you don't know with absolute certainty it was the father's hired men?" Terry kept firing missiles.

Kathleen recoiled. "No, I guess I don't."

"Did you ever see them out at the boathouse before this?"

"Not sure." She got to her feet.

"It's a yes or no question."

A flicker of irritation flashed in Kathleen's eyes. "The bigger guy, yes."

"And you assumed they were moving drugs over there," Terry began. "Did you ever call it in?"

"You must be out of your mind." Kathleen let out a partial laugh, but it faded when neither Madison nor Terry shared her amusement. "Randall is a powerful man. I'm not messing with him or anything to do with him. What is done on his property is his business."

Yet, she has no problem gossiping to cops.

"Do you mind if we look around yours?" Madison asked.

"Go ahead."

Madison stepped outside and zipped up her jacket. The breeze was cold and damp. "She's scared of Randall. The question is why."

"There's enough media coverage about that family to get people's imaginations going."

"But is that all?" Madison was thinking Kathleen might have witnessed something, and Randall had silenced her by either bribery or threat of violence. "You were pretty hard on her in there."

"I'm getting tired of treading lightly around the Randalls myself. If he was involved, I want to make sure everything we have is solid against him."

They both stopped walking once they reached the riverbank. The Klinger dock was simple. The ice on the water here was thin and transparent, exposing a fast-moving current beneath the surface. Here, the water would sweep away spilled gasoline.

Madison turned to Terry. "Are you starting to think Randall killed his son?"

"You sure do. And it's not doing the investigation any favors to ignore the possibility that Randall is somehow involved. But we have to tiptoe around him, and we can't let ourselves fixate on him to the point we miss something important."

She felt the latter comment was more directed at her but appreciated him phrasing it like the caution also applied to him. She smiled, feeling cheeky and closer to winning their bet. "You must admit it seems rather fishy that the boathouse was cleaned out the day he learned about his son."

"Maybe."

So close, yet so far...

Terry went on. "If Randall knew his son was dealing drugs from the boathouse, he'd have other reasons to clean up Chris's mess. He certainly wouldn't want that tarnishing the family name, especially on top of an active counterfeit investigation."

"The way you're saying it would suggest Randall knew about the Secret Service's interest in him and that they would surface with Chris's death. But you're also stating a motive for Randall to kill his son. Here his son had everything but was willing to throw it away, deal drugs on the family property. We're still at a loss as to who exactly was manufacturing the fake cash and why. Like we've said before, I doubt the bills were being manufactured for buying drugs. Hey, I just thought of a few things we should have asked Kathleen." She trudged back to the front door.

When Kathleen answered, she was now wearing a pair of lounge pants and a sweater, which also suited her athletic frame. She had her arms crossed.

"Sorry to bother you again," Madison said.

"I told you all I know."

"Just a few more questions." Madison stepped forward, and Kathleen let them into the entry. "Did you ever see Marcus Randall?"

"Of course."

"See him with Chris?"

"Not often."

"Do you know if they got along very well?"

"I can't comment." Kathleen's eyes pierced Madison's. "Anything else?"

"Just one thing. A month ago, pretty much exactly to the day, did you witness a fight on the Randall property?"

"You're referring to near the boathouse?"

"Sure," Madison said.

Kathleen paled. "The papers say Chris drowned. Was it in there?"

"That's what we're trying to find out."

She could feel Terry's eyes on her.

"I can't help you." Kathleen shrugged her shoulders.

CHAPTER TWENTY-EIGHT

"Can't we just stop for a bite to eat?" Terry made the request as soon as they got back into the department car after speaking with Kathleen.

The plan had been to visit one other home on the riverbank near Randall's. The house was beside the Randall estate and a little farther upriver than the evidence dictated as a point of entry, but it was worth checking out.

Madison glanced over at her partner. "You're always trying to get out of work."

"Seriously, I'm starving. My gut hurts." He rubbed it for emphasis.

She rolled her eyes and laughed. "Fine. We'll do a drive-through."

"Thought you were the health Nazi now?"

"What are you talking about?"

"The coffee at the Hudson house—you had sweetener put in it. I know you've had your cappuccinos made as *skinnies* when you're on a health kick, but I didn't think you messed with your coffee. Trying to cut back on calories?"

Look at who made detective. He needed to direct that laser focus of his to the case and away from her.

"Goes back to the fact I beat you, doesn't it?" Terry nudged.

"Don't know what you're talking about."

"Pickering. You couldn't keep up. But if you're going to cut back for your health, you shouldn't turn to sweetener. It's healthier to have sugar."

She pulled into a drive-through for a burger joint.

"You're serious?" Terry gasped. "Joe's Patties? I'm not this desperate."

Joe's Patties was diner-style fast food, featuring old decor in need of repair and burgers so greasy they slid down the throat.

The voice came out over the speaker. "It's a beautiful day at Joe's. May I take your order?"

"I'll have a Joe's quarter-pounder special. Hold the hot peppers and mayo. Double bacon, double cheese." Madison would have to figure out a way to burn the calories off later. She felt sick just thinking about eating it, but she also felt she had something to prove. She'd hit the department gym in the wee morning hours. Maybe if she repeated it to herself enough times, that would actually happen. *And hell would freeze over.*

"No wonder you couldn't keep up…eating like that."

Madison glared at him.

"Anything else?" came through the speaker, the employee sounding bored to death with her job.

Madison looked at Terry, who shook his head. "I'm not eating this crap."

She put her head back out the window. "Make it two."

Terry sighed loudly.

"Anything to drink with that?"

"Cokes."

"Do you want to make everything a combo? Only two bucks more."

She swallowed hard. She was proud, stubborn, and bent on proving herself, but couldn't inflict that sort of punishment on herself. "No, that's all."

"Your order comes to twelve eighty. Please pull up to the first window."

"Okay. Need money." Madison held her hand, palm up, toward Terry and wriggled her fingers. "Come on."

"I said I wanted food, not crap." He dug into his pocket and handed her a twenty.

"Thanks."

"I never said I'd buy—"

Madison drove up to the window.

A freckle-faced adolescent cursed with bad acne leaned out the window. "That will be twelve—"

Madison handed Terry's money over.

The food started coming out to them.

"You're seriously going to eat this?" Terry eyed the yellow wrapping as if its contents would kill him.

"Why wouldn't I?" Her stomach tossed remembering her last visit here. She had promised herself she'd never put herself through it again.

"How do you think this will help you keep up?"

She pulled the car into a vacant spot. "Just eat your burger."

Madison's stomach was stretched beyond capacity. If she gulped air, she'd be sick. She could feel the grease floating on the top of her stomach. Just walking proved to be almost too much.

"Not sure why you did that to us." Terry followed her up the walkway to Vernon and Margery Silverman's house, which was next door to Randall's property.

"Not really sure what you're talking about." She pressed the doorbell.

"Seriously, that's how you're going to play this? I know you better. You did it to make a point. Everything you do is for a point."

"What point could be made by eating a greasy burger? You were hungry, so we got something to eat." She pushed the doorbell again.

A huge dog came bounding at the door, barking aggressively and eyeing them through the sidelights. She recognized the breed but couldn't remember its name.

"Seems someone's home." Terry bent in front of the window and mocked the dog with a waving hand. "Hey, buddy, hey."

"You're being serious? He's not a beagle or a lab. That dog would eat you if he got ahold of you."

"I don't believe that." Terry's voice took on a higher octave. *Oh Lord.*

Her partner certainly wasn't the stereotypical male cast in Hollywood. He loved the commitment that came with marriage, and he had a more-than-healthy affection for canines.

"What breed is that?" She depressed the doorbell again, hoping a human would answer.

"Rottweiler." Terry moved his fingers up and down at the dog as if he were petting it through the glass.

The dog snarled, drool pasted to the edge of its jowls.

Terry straightened up. "They make good guard dogs."

"I'm starting to get that." She looked around. The house was large, almost comparable to the Randall estate, but without the security gate at the entrance. The lawn and garden beds were expansive and would require lots of manicuring and landscaping during the warmer months.

"Good thing, too," Terry said. "These rich people have these big houses and only the dog's home."

"We caught Mrs. Klinger at home," she countered, her mouth lit in a know-it-all smirk.

"But she didn't have a dog."

"Terry, I'm going to hurt you." She pulled back her arm and was ready to punch him in the shoulder when the door cracked open.

"Don't need religion." The door started to close again.

Do we look like Jehovah's Witnesses?

"Stiles PD!" Madison shouted, hoping she'd be heard through a closed door and over a barking dog.

The door slowly reopened, and a man crested with a full head of white stood there looking at them. His blue eyes were both inquisitive and unfriendly. "What can I do for you?"

The dog kept barking.

"Budweiser!" The man snapped his fingers. "Shh. Sit."

The dog whimpered and obeyed his master.

"Wow, that was amazing," Terry said. "You have excellent control over your animal."

"A dogman here, I see," the man said to Madison and nodded toward Terry. "You have to establish yourself as the alpha right from the beginning. Then from there, a lot of it's in the energy you project."

The man prattled on for a while, and Madison should have been listening, given she had a new bundle at home, but she started to tune him out. She wasn't there to learn how to become the dog whisperer. She did note that for someone who initially had no interest in talking to them, now that they were on the subject of dogs, he was Chatty Cathy. His next pause for breath, she jumped in. "I assume you're Vernon Silverman."

"I am."

"Can we come in?"

"Who are you again?"

You hadn't given us a chance to say... "We're with the Stiles PD—"

"I got that much, Miss, from you yelling at me. But what's your names, and why are you here?"

Madison gave the formal introductions and told him they were there to talk about Chris Randall.

"Now, you may come in." He opened the door wider, bent his head slightly, and extended an arm to invite them in. Once they were inside, he closed the door behind them. "That's really quite the tragedy...what happened to that kid." He was shaking his head, tsking. "He was too young to leave us. Do you think someone killed him?"

"We are investigating his death," Madison admitted that much. "Did you know Chris?"

"Not much. My son's an internet tycoon. He bought me this house. Too gaudy for my liking, but he said it would offend him if I didn't accept it. The only part I love is the boat. Anyway, my son was friends with Chris, even if somewhat casual."

"Does your son live with you?" she squeezed in, hoping to stop Silverman from blabbering.

"Oh, heavens no. Neil met Chris one day at a bar, and that was the turning point for Neil. They were drinking. Heavily. It's something I'm not proud of about my son. But anyway, they got talking. Chris gave him a great idea for an online business. And boom, it took off. Millions later, I live in a castle." Silverman extended his arms and twisted at the hips to display the expanse of the house. "And it's just me and Margery. It's really too much for two people."

A simple answer would have sufficed, but maybe she should be thankful he was open to talking. "How's your son taking the news of Chris's death?"

"Not so well. At least, that's my take on it. Men, we grieve differently."

Madison could feel her partner's eyes on her. It was exactly what he had tried to tell her about Randall. Just because she didn't see the tears didn't mean the man wasn't hurting.

"He's immersing himself in work right now," Silverman said, "but he plans on coming back for the funeral on Saturday."

Madison didn't even know the body had been released. That irritated her. If she was expected to keep everyone else updated as to her next move, shouldn't everyone else be just as accountable? Normally, Richards was good about keeping her informed. He must still be mad at her about digging into his past. She'd have to talk to him again and attempt to reconcile their relationship.

"Where will the service be held?" she asked.

"Received a phone call earlier today from Mark Randall." He massaged his temple. "Although, don't let him hear you call him that. He must always be *Marcus*. The man is so strange."

She found irony in Silverman's statement about someone else being strange. The man had his own issues, top of which was rambling.

"Anyway, his house attendant called."

"Tony Medcalf?" She had a fifty-fifty chance of getting it right. She went with the most likely.

"Yes, that would be him. He said the funeral's this Saturday at one. St. Jude's Catholic Church. It will be a memorial service first, followed by the burial, and a small gravesite eulogy and prayer. Strikes me funny how people get religious when someone dies."

"The Randalls normally aren't?" Terry asked.

Silverman faced Terry. "Heavens no. Marcus thinks of himself as a god. Why would he answer to one? Which I think is just asking for bad things to happen, but to each his own, I guess."

"Do you know what their relationship was like?" Madison asked. She then clarified. "The relationship between Chris and his father."

"Just like any son and his father, moments of tensions, disagreements in point of view, minor stuff."

"Anything specific come to mind?" Madison pressed.

"Marcus never said anything to me, but Chris spoke to Neil. He was tired of traveling to get foreign investors. Apparently, Marcus had him going all the time, and he wasn't home much."

"One would think a young man would love that lifestyle," Terry said.

Silverman looked at Terry. "Maybe if we were talking about seeing the world, spreading his seed."

If that's how he wanted to put it.

Silverman continued. "Despite what you read in the tabloids, Chris wasn't a male whore. Don't get me wrong, the boy liked, even *loved* women, but he didn't need a new one every day."

"Are Neil and Chris still close?" Madison asked, trying to get a solid handle on the relationship.

"They keep in touch, even though Neil lives a few hours from here. He just came home and was going to spend a month with us starting two days before Christmas."

"I sense he left early." Madison made the guess based on a sad glint in Silverman's eyes.

"He left on the eleventh of January, early morning. He apologized profusely, saying something about a crisis with his website. I think he could have handled it from here. Isn't that the appeal of an internet company? His mother's still mad at him."

The skin on the back of Madison's neck pinched. So far, the evidence in the case pointed to Chris being murdered sometime in the wee hours of the eleventh.

"Do you know what this crisis was?" she asked.

"He said something about email confirmations being down. I don't really know much of anything when it comes to computers—or business, for that matter."

"When he was here," Madison said, "did he spend time with Chris Randall?"

"Of course. The boys were inseparable when they were both in town."

"It's great when you have a friend like that." Madison wanted to ask if Silverman knew of an altercation between the two friends, but sensed he'd show them the door. "Do you mind if we look around your property?"

"Why would I? We have nothing to hide." Silverman sat on the arm of a couch. "And don't be entertaining for a second that my boy hurt Chris."

It seemed Silverman wasn't completely naive about what they had to consider, but she still didn't think he'd take kindly to her asking if his son and Chris had gotten into a fight. "We can appreciate your saying that, but we'll still need to take a look around."

"I know you can't take my word. Heck, no one's word is good enough these days. Not even a handshake seals the deal."

Madison pulled out a notepad and a pen. "Could we get Neil's phone number?"

"I'm sure you have ways of finding that for yourself."

So much for having nothing to hide.

Silverman went on. "Now I don't want to seem uncooperative, but he's having a really hard time coping with the news. As I said, he's going to be in town for the funeral Saturday. Maybe you could speak with him there." Silverman reached into a pocket and took out a key. He handed it to Madison. "You'll need it to get into the boathouse."

"Thank you."

Madison and Terry excused themselves and headed toward the Silvermans' boathouse.

"He's quite protective of his son," Terry said.

"Not that I blame him. He has a lot to lose, too." She unlocked the boathouse entrance and they walked inside. "He might not have an attachment to that monster of a house, but you could tell he loves this." Madison gestured around the boathouse. "His eyes lit up when he mentioned it."

The boathouse was compact, and a dock wrapped three sides of the inside perimeter. A motorboat was perched in man-made claws and suspended five feet in the air. The water beneath it was covered with a solid layer of ice.

"I don't see any breaks." Terry got onto his haunches. "And there's no evidence of the ice having been broken and re-formed."

Madison stepped with caution on the deck boards and observed the boating accessories that lined the wall and were hung on hooks. "What would make Neil leave so abruptly?"

"An internet crisis."

Madison cocked her head, raised her eyebrows. "I think Neil had a fight with Chris. The question is, how far did it—" Her eyes fixed on a blue pole with metal tongs on the end.

"It's called a rescue jaw." Terry came over, stood beside her. "The rod extends, I don't know, say ten to twenty feet. The rescuer jabs it into the water. The action opens the J-shaped tongs wide enough to go around a body. When the downward motion stops, the tongs automatically close."

Madison was trying to picture what Terry was telling her and having a little bit of a hard time. "So, the victim is in the tongs, and they don't open?"

"Well, as the victim is being pulled to the surface, the upward movement keeps the tongs shut around them."

"Hmm. What if…" She stared at the contraption. "If it was held out vertically, the closed J-shaped tongs, as you put it, would stay shut? It's easily wide enough in its closed state to slip over someone's head."

Terry's eyes widened. "That could have caused the bruising on Chris's shoulders. The killer extended it, slipped it around his head, pushed down…more on a horizontal angle, and the tongs never opened."

"Instead of being used for its purpose of rescue—"

"It could have been used for murder."

CHAPTER TWENTY-NINE

Vernon Silverman had given them permission to bring in the rescue jaw from his boathouse, and after dropping it off at the lab, Terry had called it a day, but Madison stayed at the station. She did her best to find the Tyrone who Lakisha had mentioned, but with little else to go on but a first name and age range, her search netted fifteen hits. That was too many to justify knocking on doors. If they wanted to get anywhere with Tyrone, they'd have to do it through Pickering. Madison turned to the next person of interest on her list: Neil Silverman.

She started with a Google search to learn more about him and his company. Articles filled the screen on the overnight success of his online business, Overcome It. The site targeted those who had an addiction, whether it was alcohol, drugs, or a hobby. It defined addiction as any endeavor or indulgence that would limit someone's full potential and take them from loved ones.

Madison found irony in the fact that a site established to help people overcome addiction required one to log on and report their activity. Couldn't the site itself, in effect, become an addiction?

She scrolled down to one article on the site entitled, *From Stiles to the World*. Scanning it, she saw Overcome It offered an affordable monthly membership. At the time of the post, which was two years ago, the site had 289,000 paying members. She calculated the math based on the lowest fee.

Her eyes bulged at the result. Four point three million. And that was *per* month. No wonder he could purchase an estate for his father. Apparently, self-help was a large business, and Neil Silverman had tapped into a financial well.

Madison read the article more closely. Neil expressed his gratitude for those who helped him along the way, specifically, "*the prestigious Randall family, also from Stiles, known for their multibillion-dollar investment firm.*"

She backed out to the search results and picked another link. Another piece read:

> Neil Silverman, at the age of twenty-one, retired
> from the world he knew in Stiles and settled in a
> rural town of Hastings, three hours north of his
> hometown.

She brought up Neil's background and discovered he had just turned twenty-three, but more interestingly, he had a record. Five years ago, he was charged with a drunk and disorderly conduct and assaulting an officer.

She looked at Neil's license photo and committed his face to memory. She'd need it if—on the off chance—he did show up at the funeral.

Her eyes landed on Neil's phone number, then she glanced at the phone on her desk. Neil Silverman could know something, and she needed to find out sooner than later. Was there an argument between the friends that had resulted in Neil racing home? Did it go far enough that he had murdered the same man who had helped him start his multimillion-dollar venture?

She dialed, and an automated operator advised that the number was no longer in service. That wasn't making her feel any better about the guy. But before she'd give herself over to paranoia, maybe the number on file was an old one. Just where to find his new one… If Neil Silverman had wanted to keep his new number private, he could have it registered under someone else's name.

Madison went back to the report to see if she could glean any clues. Neil wasn't married, so a number wouldn't be under a spouse's name. She pulled up an online directory, typed in *Vernon Silverman*. Only Neil's father's number came up, showing in Stiles. She tapped her fingers on the desk, staring for a few seconds into space, focused on nothing.

She tried Neil's mother's name, and there was a number tying back to Hastings.

Madison tapped the number into the phone, and with each ring, she knew Terry was going to kill her for going ahead without him. And on top of that, their sergeant, who demanded every step be cataloged in advance, would be unhappy.

"Good evening, you've reached the Silverman residence," a woman answered.

"Hello. May I speak with Neil Silverman, please?"

"Is this a telemarketing call? We're not interested in buying anything."

Madison wasn't going to tell Neil's employee she was a detective unless she had no choice. "Please let him know it's in regard to his friend Chris Randall."

There was silence. Madison thought the woman had hung up on her, until soft music started playing.

"Who is this?" A man asked, sounding strained and agitated.

For a second, she entertained the thought of providing fake identification. "Detective Knight from the Stiles PD."

"What do you want?" Brisk and curt.

"Is this Neil Silverman?"

"Who wants to know?"

I'll take that as a confirmation.

"I've already told you who I am. Can we talk in person?"
Silence.

"I'd like to discuss your relationship with Chris. What kind of a man was—"

"Read the tabloids, Detective. Make your own decision on what to believe."

"I'm sure you can appreciate I need facts, not speculation."
Neil said nothing.

"His funeral is this Saturday. I was hoping we could talk."
Neil hung up.

She held out the receiver and looked at it. The abrupt end
to their conversation left her feeling sick. What if Neil was
the killer and, thanks to her, now knew they were onto him?
He could be clear around the world by Saturday. She'd rushed
in again, blinded by an obsession to get answers yesterday,
and had failed to see how dearly it could cost her—and the
case.

Her mind went to Neil's words: *Read the tabloids,
Detective.* Was there a clue in there somewhere? Why direct
law enforcement there? Then something sparked. The
picture that Cynthia had shown her and Terry of Chris,
Ryan Turner, and another guy.

Madison went up to the lab and into Cynthia's office.
She opened the drawer from which Cynthia had pulled the
gossip magazine the other day. She flipped through the pages
to the picture. And sure enough, the man in the background
drinking the beer was no one other than Neil Silverman.

Hours later, sitting in her apartment, Hershey chomping
down on a helpless stuffed cat with a squeaker in the middle
of it, Madison felt sick about having called Neil. Wasn't
her job already at risk? The dog toy let out a high-pitched
squeak, and she jumped.

She took a sip of wine, and for an instant, her mother's
caution came to her. *Only alcoholics drink alone.*

But she could justify drinking. The case, her empty
apartment—save a four-legged furball—and her failed
relationship with Blake.

It was over, right?

Sometimes it didn't feel like she'd made a clean break,
but there was no way she could continue seeing him. Just
finding out that he was on Randall's payroll was tantamount
to betrayal. Or maybe she was reacting like a controlling

drama queen. He had made a valid point when he told her she knew he was a defense attorney from the start. It's just until now she hadn't thought about the type of people he could represent. The accused were one thing, but people like Randall were another.

She moved from the couch to her desk, taking along her plate with a cold slice of pizza on it. She had already eaten three pieces—so much for her diet and eating lower calories. Though she'd really blown that with the greasy burger. Ah, tomorrow was a new day.

She turned her monitor on; the computer she always left on standby. Not that she went on it much. She'd be fine to live life without a computer—in a society becoming too dependent on them—but they did serve a purpose.

She clicked the button for the internet, waiting for the CPU to execute her command. It took a good minute to bring up Google, given the cheap internet package she had. When the page loaded, she typed in *Blake Golden*.

Hershey came over and barked at her feet as if reprimanding her.

She held up her glass. "The wine's making me do it." She had almost polished off an entire bottle.

Hershey whined and whimpered now, and she clued in.

"Ah, you need to do the deed." She glanced at the screen, and the spinning wheel was turning at the top of the browser while the page itself was blank. "All right, let's go." Madison got up, worked Hershey into his collar and leash, and headed down the elevator.

She'd just stepped out the front of her building and her cell phone rang, and she answered.

"What do you know? You answered."

"Chels?" The sound of her sister's voice transported her back to the get-together at her sister's this past Sunday— only four days ago, but it felt longer than that. She had promised to get back before their parents had left town, but that hadn't happened yet. They might even be home by now. Honestly, she'd been so preoccupied with the case, she couldn't remember when they were flying out.

"I told myself I wouldn't ask this," Chelsea started, "but why haven't you called?"

"Let's not get into it." Madison watched Hershey sniffing the sidewalk and scraggly bushes, searching out the perfect spot.

"I held off calling until now, thinking you'd make the first step. You were the one that left the dinner at my house, remember?"

"I was called to a murder scene. One I'm still working on." Madison ran a hand through her hair. "Listen, I've had a long day. Can we do this another time?"

"That's your answer for everything. Another time, not right now, later. Well, too bad. I want to talk about this now."

Madison snapped her mouth shut, angry. She didn't need this right now.

Hershey finished his pee and was sniffing around again. Madison could tell he was getting ready to do a number two.

After a minute or so, Chelsea said, "Please talk to me."

"What do you want me to say?"

"Mom's heading home tomorrow."

Madison must have had her dates mixed up. "And Dad's not?"

"Why do you have to be like that?"

"Be like what?" If anyone had a problem, it was their mother. When Madison went to leave Chelsea's, she'd bent down to kiss her nieces in the entry, and when she rose, she'd met her mother's eyes. Her mother just stood there, said nothing, and *did* nothing to close the distance between them. She just crossed her arms and scowled.

"I'm going to hang up if you don't start talking to me."

Tears stung the corners of Madison's eyes. She fought for strength to speak. "Mom had her chance to say goodbye; she chose not to."

"You're going to have to grow up some day, M."

"You're younger than I am."

"Why do I feel like the older one some days?" Chelsea paused, and the line remained silent for a few seconds. "She's not going to be around forever."

"I know." Their mother was only sixty-five. There was still time to reconcile matters between them.

"How's Blake?" Her sister shifted direction but didn't know she'd gone from one sore subject to another.

When Madison didn't say anything, Chelsea added, "He's a great guy. You should hold on to him."

"How are the girls?" Deflection: something she was good at.

"You guys still okay?"

"Well, you switched from Mom to Blake, so I—"

"It's not the same thing. Mom was becoming a source of conflict. I was trying to lighten our conversation."

Madison watched Hershey make a tight circle, hunch up and— *Whoa! That is ripe!*

Madison gagged.

"You okay over there?" Chelsea asked.

"I'm fine." *Blech.* "Just a second."

"I have to get going. Just stay in touch, okay? We're in the same city, and it would be nice if you could get by to say goodbye tomorrow. Two o'clock at the airport, before they go through security."

"I'll see what I can do." She'd find a way to keep herself busy and otherwise engaged. Given her current workload, that shouldn't be difficult.

"Guess that's all I can ask for. Night."

"Ni—" The line was already dead. Her sister was always quick when it came to hanging up.

Maybe her sister was right, and it was time for her to grow up, face the decisions she'd made in life, and stop allowing her mother so much power over her. Her mother wanted grandchildren. Chelsea's three weren't enough, apparently. Her mother felt that Madison needed a husband to find true happiness in life. She wondered if her mother was blind to the studies that showed one in two marriages ended in divorce. That certainly didn't sound like happily-ever-after. It sounded like a headache—an *expensive* headache once lawyers got involved. Besides, what need did she have for a husband and kids when she had a mess to clean up right here?

"Wow, buddy, you sure know how to bake 'em." She bagged Hershey's shit and dropped it in a garbage can outside her building on the way back inside.

Upstairs, she unleashed Hershey and took the last sip of her wine, depressed by the fact she'd have to hit the liquor store for more.

Moving back to her computer, she saw that the results were up for Blake Golden. The first site was Golden, Broderick, and Maine, where he worked. She looked farther down, clicked on the link, and waited for it to respond.

She read the screen as the pieces filled in. A snippet of an article from twenty years ago read:

> *Blake Golden, son of John and Sharon Golden, announced his engagement to Broadway actress Karen Scott yesterday.*

Engagement? Maybe his daughter wasn't the result of a one-night stand, after all.

> *The wedding date is still being decided upon, but we can prepare ourselves for the wedding of the century.*

"Wedding of the century?" she said out loud.

She Googled the names of Blake's parents. As the screen filled in and she read, her heart took pause. "Now that would explain a lot."

CHAPTER THIRTY

Madison and Terry parked outside Hanigan's Market. If everything worked according to plan, they'd run into Medcalf and be able to find out the answers to a couple of questions. One, did he serve pheasant for dinner on January tenth? Two, what brand of cigar did Randall smoke? All she had seen at the house was the corner of a box, enough to know they were cigars, but that's about it.

"I still think we should stay away from the guy, Maddy."

She turned to Terry. "We have to follow whatever leads we have."

"If that's the case, are you forgetting about the potential murder weapon in Silverman's boathouse and the fact that Neil was in a hurry to go home earlier than planned? And what about Pickering and his buddy Tyrone, who probably sold drugs to Chris?"

Terry wasn't prone to rage, but if he found out she had already reached Neil, there'd be hell to pay. "We'll get to those things."

"Don't you think those are important things to get to *now*?"

"They are, but—"

"But nothing. I can't lose my job."

"I know. You have a baby on the way."

"Don't mock it."

She looked at him. "Sorry."

"You have no idea what responsibility is."

Madison wasn't even going to dignify his accusation with a response. "There he is." She sat up straighter and pointed toward Medcalf. His dark hair bushed out from under a black beret. His arms were loaded with cloth grocery bags.

"Nice choice of hat. And the guy is heterosexual?"

She remembered the way Medcalf smiled at her the first time they met. "Definitely."

"Hmm."

As she reached to unfasten her seat belt, her phone rang, and the ID showed Winston. "Knight."

"I need you downtown ASAP."

She looked at the dash. It was only seven in the morning. "We're in the middle of—"

"The Secret Service wants to meet with you and Terry now."

"Fine, we'll be right there."

Thirty minutes later, Madison and Terry were in a conference room shaking hands with the two suits that had been on her after speaking with Ryan Turner yesterday morning. She remembered the younger agent with the reddish-orange hair. He made Madison think of a famous clown associated with a worldwide fast-food chain. If the hair color wasn't enough, genetics hadn't blessed him with height, either. She could see over the agent's head.

"How nice to meet you, Detective Knight." His shake was solid and eager. "Grant." He pressed down on the front of his suit. "I'm Agent Albert Weiss, and this is Agent Henry Walters."

Walters was an older man with a pleasant face and grandfatherly eyes. He smiled at them.

Madison dropped into a chair, and Terry sat beside her.

Winston kept his eyes trained on her from the far end of the table, where he was seated. Madison was surprised McAlexandar wasn't there.

"I apologize I'm late, gentlemen." McAlexandar opened the door and took position beside the sergeant.

She let out a deep breath and avoided looking directly at him. Both Secret Service agents sat down, and Weiss took the lead.

"We've been reading over your interview notes and have come across some interesting tidbits." Weiss opened a briefcase, took out some folders, spread them on the table, and rooted through them. He took out a few papers that were clipped together. "Here it is. Your interview with Steven Pickering." Weiss kept his eyes on the report. "He said that Chris tried to hand him fake cash."

McAlexandar glanced at Madison, then directed his words to Weiss. "From what I understand, Pickering is a drug dealer and raped a minor. Surely, we're not going to take the word of a lowlife over that of the established Randall family. Add to that, you're pointing a finger at a dead man, someone who can't defend himself. That's a new low even for the Secret Service."

Weiss didn't so much as look at McAlexandar, and he leveled his gaze on Madison. "Do you believe Pickering was telling the truth, Detective?"

Madison was fully aware that McAlexandar was staring at her, and any other day, she'd be ready to fight. Today, her mood was different. She felt more reserved. She tried to tell herself it had nothing to do with her hurting heart, which was wounded by the words of both Terry and her sister about needing to grow up and accept responsibility. "Yes, I do."

Weiss nodded. "That is good enough for me." He placed that report back into the folder and pulled out another bunch of papers. "Now, Ryan Turner. His partial print was on one of the counterfeit bills. Were you attempting to hide this from us?"

Her heart sank. "I'm not sure why you would think that's the case."

Weiss held eye contact with her. But there was no way she'd tell anyone Cynthia held off on informing everyone else—when Madison had been the one to make that request of her.

"Do you want to think harder about your answer, Detective?" Weiss pressed.

Her chest heaved, and she let out a long, steady breath. Maybe a little white lie wouldn't hurt. "I got a text just yesterday morning."

Terry shifted beside her.

"I would have found out with everyone else," she added.

"By text?" Skeptical, with a raised eyebrow.

"Yes, during the interview with Ryan Turner, not before."

"Can we see that?"

Madison went for her cell phone and feigned absentmindedness. "I'm not the best with technology, but one thing I am is clean. After I read a text, I delete it."

"Then there shouldn't be any on your phone." Weiss extended his hand. "Would you mind if I had a look?"

She moved her fingers over the keys, thankful she knew the quick keys to access the menus. Hopefully, she had remembered correctly. She smiled as she passed her phone to the agent.

Weiss moved his fingertip across the screen. After a few seconds, he stretched his neck left then right and placed the phone on the table. "Who sent the text to you?"

"The lab."

"The *lab*?" Weiss dragged out. "Specifically?"

"Cynthia Baxter."

"Does she make a habit of informing you by text message, Detective?"

"Sometimes." She had to redirect their attention from Cynthia. She also had to remember to let Cynthia know they'd be asking about a nonexistent text message. "Do you believe Ryan Turner is involved in the counterfeiting?" Deflect again.

Weiss sat back in the chair. His eyes were noncommittal.

"I mean, if you really did, we wouldn't be having this conversation," she said. "You'd be hunting him down."

"A partial print is not enough to prove Mr. Turner was involved."

"But you want to speak with him, correct? I mean, that's why you stormed up to the interrogation room. You weren't there to chat about the weather." Her regular fight was coming back. They were making her feel as if she had messed something up, and she didn't care for it—one bit. "I'm just curious how your investigation got started in the first place. No one's filled us in." She gestured to Terry and herself. "We're left to partially operate in the dark when it comes to what you're looking for. You either think that the Randalls were the counterfeiters or you believe Ryan Turner is. Correct me if I'm wrong. Sometimes I see things in black and white."

McAlexandar sat there with his arms crossed, his lips tightly pressed together. He actually looked pleased by her comment.

The room fell silent except for the soft ticking of the clock on the wall and the honking of horns from outside.

"What started all of this in the first place?" Madison repeated her question. "We're trying to solve a homicide, and we need any leads we can get. It's possible someone Chris tried to pass the fake money to took revenge."

McAlexandar's eyes narrowed, and he scowled at her. He wasn't pleased anymore—not with her underlying acceptance that the Randalls were guilty of fraud.

Weiss pinched his lips with his right hand and acknowledged his older counterpart, who nodded at him. "A few years back, Randall Investments were audited by the Internal Revenue Service. There were seeming inconsistencies, things that caught their attention."

"Like what?" Madison asked.

"Mostly the turnaround with accounts. There were a lot of new ones, but then the same ones would close out a few years later. This happened on a large scale. I'm talking millions of dollars."

"I'm not sure I fully understand," she said.

"Every time someone makes an investment with a firm like Randall's, there's a commission fee that the investee makes off the investment," Walters stepped in. "Every time investments are changed, there are also fees associated with that."

"I'm still not sure if I get how that led the Secret Service to suspect counterfeiting."

"The IRS passed their findings on to fraud-investigation services, but the accounts in question were all from overseas. They started looking at their origins and realized that all accounts were corporate in origin. A background on all the businesses showed each of them went bankrupt. Really, what are the chances? One day hundreds of thousands are invested, the next, they close their doors?"

"Dummy companies," Madison surmised.

Weiss and Walters nodded.

"With the state of the economy, failing businesses are on the rise," McAlexandar interjected. "Doesn't mean anything illegal is going on."

"For a while we had to release the freeze on Randall Investments' assets and let them get back to business," Weiss said. "At first it seemed the dummy companies were legitimate. Their paperwork was in order."

"Because it was, perhaps." McAlexandar wiped at the sleeve of his suit jacket, as if flicking off lint.

"I'm still curious how the counterfeiting investigation came into play," Madison said, wondering why the Secret Service was dancing around the question.

"This is where things get somewhat brilliant," Weiss said. "We believe that money was generated here, taken to the Cayman Islands, deposited into a numbered account, and then withdrawn only days later. But that's where we lose the trail."

McAlexandar pulled out on his necktie and clenched his jaw.

Madison addressed the agents. "So, they deposited fake money and withdrew real money?"

"Exactly," Walters replied. "Then they took the real money, established dummy companies, and invested it with their firm. Now, the bank in the Cayman Islands takes the matter very seriously and has set new measures in place to avoid this happening in the future. For example, working cameras to catch their customers, and new counterfeit detection machines, but it's a case of too little too late. And even with the new precautions, it's unlikely to stop people as talented as the Randalls."

McAlexandar scowled. "What are you saying?"

"Their bills are a near-perfect replica of the real thing, including weight and texture," Weiss said calmly and with authority. If McAlexandar was getting to him, he didn't show it. "They even have tiny red and blue fibers embedded like the real thing. Basically, the only ways to spot they're fake is with the aid of a UV counterfeit detector or if you magnify the bills. The microprinting that exists with legitimate currency is not present on their bills."

"But wouldn't the banks in the Caymans check the bills, especially when they were making such a large, physical deposit?" Madison asked.

"Surely they'd have a UV machine," Terry interjected.

Weiss nodded. "They did, but it turns out they had someone on the inside, and that former bank employee is now serving time in his own country for fraud."

Terry rubbed the back of his neck. "So what brought the counterfeit money to light?"

"Customers of the bank in the Caymans started reporting that vendors weren't accepting the money they'd withdrawn, telling them it was counterfeit. These were people trying to spend the money at stores with UV detectors," Weiss started. "The bank made a record of these complaints, though they weren't taken seriously at first. After all, what was to say these people weren't in fact the criminals, trying to make an exchange—fake for the real thing? It wasn't until several complaints piled up that it became apparent something was wrong."

"And how precisely did you connect this back to Randall Investments, before this bank employee was discovered?" McAlexandar asked.

"It took time, but eventually, as the bank monitored its deposits in a stricter fashion, the scam came to light," Walters said. "Their video captured a grainy photo of a young man entering with two stuffed duffel bags. He deposited the funds into a numbered account and provided the name of Weston Baker. The funds were later wired to another bank in Germany, where someone withdrew it and closed the account. No leads there." The faces in the room asked the question without words. "We still don't know the meaning of the name he used or if there even was a reason. It's not really the point. Anyway, all we had was the crappy video from the Cayman bank, but it showed a man who was six foot even, approximately one hundred eighty pounds, and that isn't the only coincidence we have. Flight logs put Chris Randall in the Caymans that day."

McAlexandar sat back, puffed out his chest. "How did you find that out?"

"We're the Secret Service." Weiss gave a smug smile. "We spoke with the pilot at the time." He sorted through some papers. "A Bobby Longwell. Randall has since dismissed his services. A few years back, I understand."

"So that's all you have? A trip to the Caymans and a man the same height as Chris Randall?" McAlexandar smirked. "This is ludicrous."

Neither agent said a word.

"You're viewing the videos with prejudice," McAlexandar tacked on.

Weiss's jaw twitched. "This situation is like an onion. And I, *we*—" he gestured toward the older agent "—have only peeled back a few layers."

McAlexandar made a dramatic show of looking at his watch.

"We also believe it's more than a coincidence that surveillance on Chris Randall showed him carrying two duffel bags pretty near identical to the ones in the video."

"You've got to be kidding me," McAlexandar scoffed. "Surely, thousands of them were sold. And you know what you can do with your shitty photo of a man the same stature as Chris Randall…" McAlexandar's ground his teeth.

"There's no need to get so hostile," Walters said.

"When the Secret Service comes to me, I expect there to be solid evidence, not suspicions and coincidences." A vein bulged in McAlexandar's forehead, and he jabbed a finger onto the table.

Weiss tilted out his chin. "Then how about this: can you explain why all the global accounts were signed by Chris Randall? Also, why is it Randall Investments' bank accounts always grew when the investments were withdrawn by the failed dummy companies?"

CHAPTER THIRTY-ONE

Terry took off from the meeting room at a fast pace.

Madison hurried to catch up. "Can we talk a minute?"

He stopped walking and spun. His eyes were daggers. "You lied to the Secret Service."

She had a feeling her partner might be upset with her about that. "I didn't feel I had a choice. Cynthia would be in—"

"Since when do you care how your actions affect other people?"

"That's a little harsh," she snapped back; the comment hitting a little hard given she had been planning to miss seeing her parents off at the airport.

"But true."

She didn't say anything. She was too angry, too hurt.

"Lord, Maddy." He threw his hands in the air. "How can I continue to work with a partner like you?"

"Listen, please calm—" She went to place a hand on his shoulder. He stepped back.

"Don't try and calm me down, okay? I'm mad."

"Please just listen to me." She moved in front of him and tried to get him to look at her. "If Chris was the counterfeit runner, maybe he messed up along the way, got greedy, and started using it for his own endeavors. We already know he tried to buy drugs with it. Maybe Marcus Randall found out. He knew it would only cast more suspicion and further the Secret Service's investigation. The business was already being monitored. He could have decided to take out his own son."

"You're kidding me." Terry sighed and took a few steps. "Whatever you can say to take the conversation off you. I'm going to talk to Pickering. You can come with me or not. I don't really care."

Could stubbornness be a fault? Madison considered that question the entire way to the east end of the city. Terry didn't say one word to her, and she refused to speak to him.

At the Pickering residence, the same woman who had been yelling at Steven the first time they were there braced herself in the doorway. Her bosom spilled over the top of her low-cut shirt, but she didn't seem to care.

"Steven's out."

"Do you know when he'll be back?" Madison asked.

"He's a grown adult. No idea." Her speech was slurred through crooked teeth and plump lips.

"What is your relationship with Steven?" Madison would guess she was his mother, but these days it was best not to assume.

"His mam. Cheri Pickering. Thinks we've seen each other before, though, I could be wrong. All you white people look alike."

As if she doesn't remember. "Yes, we've been here before."

"Can we come in for a few moments?" Terry asked.

Madison felt her skin prickle. They were being watched.

"No poleece are comin' in here. Na-nah, not in my home. Not now, not ever." She shook her head rapidly.

Madison stepped closer to the threshold. "It might be safer if you let us—"

"It might be safer if you left." Cheri pointed to the road behind them and scurried behind the door. The deadbolt latched shut.

"Hey, pigs! Oink, oink!" Teens chorused from the other side of the street.

To hell with this!

Madison stomped off toward the group.

Terry caught her arm on a backswing. "Don't do it."

She shook free of Terry's grip. "We have a job to do. And if Steven's not here to talk to, maybe one of these punks will know something."

"Wait! They're not going to talk to—"

"Whoa, looky what we have here." Catcalls and whistles filled the area. "Cuff me! Cuff me!"

More catcalls and whistles. There were six guys. Five were leaning against a car, and one was sitting behind the driver's seat. The largest of them bashed his fists together as she got closer.

"I want her first," the large one said.

The group of five circled her, and for a few seconds, her pride, her arrogance, and her stubborn nature that told her she was afraid of nothing failed her. She was scared.

"That's enough! Back up!" Terry came over with his gun readied.

"Why? What's ya gonna do? Shoot us?" the large one mocked, and his cronies cackled.

Not a bad idea, was what Madison thought.

"Back away!" Terry shouted again. "You don't want to go down for injuring or killing a cop."

Whoa! Don't give them any ideas!

"And why not?" The large one scrunched up his face in disgust and hurled a wad of spit through the air. It landed with a *splat* on the road.

The rest of his little gang started moving in closer to Madison, and she felt panic rising in her chest.

"I said, back up!" Terry swung his gun in front of them, making his message clear: he wouldn't be repeating himself a third time.

More whistles.

"Just shut the fuck up!" Madison summoned her strength. She would thank Terry later for stepping in, if her pride would let her. Three of them moved back in around her and started circling again. Madison put a hand to her holster, ready to draw her weapon if needed, and to protect it from them snatching it from her.

One of the guys waved his hands as if in mock fright. "Oh, both pigs mean business."

Two of the five left Madison and moved in on Terry.

Her heart was beating so fast, and she was riding an adrenaline rush. She couldn't allow them to sense her fear. She jutted out her chin. "Any of you know Steven Pickering?"

The large one put his face to within inches of hers. "What's it to ya?"

"Do you know of a man named Tyrone?" She just kept the questions going.

"Anyone—" the large one turned to his associates and snapped the fingers of his left hand "—a Tyrone?"

"Leave the neighborhood, pigs!" the guy from the car called out.

"He's right. Leave or we'll mess you up real good, *pigs*." The large one bashed his fists again and glanced briefly at Terry.

"We're not going anywhere until you talk to us—" She stopped speaking at the feel of the large one's breath on her face and neck. She couldn't draw her gun now if she wanted to. Even if she managed to pull it, it could easily be turned on her. "Tyrone—"

The large one reached out and stroked her hair.

What happened from there was a blur. She swung her arm back and hooked his torso, then dive-bombed him to the concrete, laying him out flat. She ground the heel of her boot in his abdomen and drew her gun. It had all taken only seconds.

The other two men who had swarmed her now backed away, as did the two who had moved in on Terry.

"I'm not going to ask you one more fuckin' time!" She pointed her gun on them.

Hands slowly rose in surrender.

"He dead." The voice came from the guy in the car.

Madison turned to him, still cognizant of the men closer to her. "He's dead?"

"If he's not, he should be."

The large one offered through grunts from the ground, "The bitch fucked us up real bad—"

"Why the hell you tellin' 'em this?" the guy from the car asked.

"We ain't afraid of nothin'."

"Looks to me you should be. Some damn female pig laid you out flat." The guy in the car laughed and so did the two of the four other guys. The large one wasn't amused. And neither was another punk, who was about five-four, tops.

He rushed to the car and decked the guy behind the wheel, and the guy in the car just took the hit.

So there's the pecking order… And the large one isn't the leader.

Madison eyed Five-Four. "You kill Tyrone?"

"Didn't say that, bitch," Five-Four hissed.

"What are you saying, then?" She squared her shoulders.

"I'm saying he's as good as."

"You beat him?"

The gang cackled, and the sound sent shivers snaking down Madison's spine.

"Not too bright, are ya?" Five-Four said. "Surprised you're down squealing in our hood when Tyrone is downtown turning on his brothers."

Madison hoisted up the guy from the ground and snapped cuffs on him. "Terry, call for backup. Let's bring 'em all in."

After backup arrived and carted off *the catch*, Madison drove her and Terry back to the station. She called the department's front desk on the way. "Officer Ranson, please connect me to Detective Commons."

Alex Commons was a veteran narcotics detective.

"I'm sorry, but Commons is in interrogation right now," Ranson told her.

"Who's he in with?"

"He didn't say. There's no record."

"No record? We always log in who we're talking to."

"I'm sorry, but he didn't this time."

"Can you interrupt and let him know I need to speak with him? It's urgent."

"Unless you know for a fact it will help his case, I can't. I'm sorry. Last time I did that to him, he wasn't too hap—"

"It has to do with a murder case," Madison rushed out.

"I'm sor—"

Madison hung up. Apologies meant nothing. She gunned the accelerator and turned on the lights.

"I hate it when you light us up," Terry grumbled.

"You always find something to whine about, don't you?"

Madison stormed by the front desk, ignoring the hound eyes of Officer Ranson. "Which room?"

"He just got fin—"

She kept moving. The blinds to the room were closed, and the door was shut. She knocked before opening the door. The room was empty.

"Knight, you were looking for me?" Detective Commons hitched a thumb over his shoulder. "Ranson told me."

"Tyrone," she spat.

"I'm missing something here."

"You had someone in for questioning. A Tyrone somebody?"

"I'm in the process of booking some guy known on the street as Thor. He's in holding. Charges will be for drug trafficking to minors. Found him dealing dope outside a high school."

"Thor?" She'd admit her listening had drifted a bit after that name drop.

"Well, that's the thing. He's not cooperating and telling us his real name. Won't take us long, though, and we'll have it. I'm sure it will just take his prints to be run through the system."

"We might have a first name for you. Let us talk to him."

"You could just—"

"He may have something to offer our murder investigation."

"Fine. Just no cutting any deals."

No worries there!

CHAPTER THIRTY-TWO

"Not what you'd expect, am I?" The man known as Thor was of average build with light, creamy skin. "Probably thought I'd be a black guy."

Madison took a seat across from him. She'd shut Commons out of the room along with her partner. They'd be watching from the observation room next door.

"You guys don't know what you're doing around here, do you?" He traced his upper lip with his tongue, showing off a gold stud. "First, I get dragged in on bogus allegations, and now this, a female cop on a power trip. I find that kind of hot, actually."

"Steven Pickering." She wasn't going to waste words on this guy.

He leaned across the table. "Oh, we're playing hard to get, baby?"

She clenched her hands into fists beneath the table. "You know him?"

"Is this a pop quiz?" He laughed and rolled his head back. "'Course I know him."

Huh, that was easier than I thought. "You openly admit that?"

"And why wouldn't I? The man's a"—he formed a circle with his thumb and index finger—"zero."

Thor at least thought of himself as a leader. "Lakisha Hudson?" Dropping a name or question at the sight of vulnerability or arrogance was often an effective interrogation tactic. It threw the perp off balance and usually prompted them to speak.

He slouched in his chair. "What about her?"

"You introduced her to Steven Pickering," Madison said, running with the assumption she was looking at the Tyrone whom Lakisha had mentioned.

"So what if I did?"

Madison smirked. "You're Tyrone."

His eyes snapped to hers. "How did ya know that name?"

She stood up, walked up next to him, and perched herself on the edge of the table. "You know what I hate almost as much as drug dealers? White people pretending they're black."

He balled up a wad of spit, projected it across the room. It just missed her.

"I'll assume you missed on purpose."

"Assume what you want, bitch."

"What's your last name, Tyrone?"

"You know everything. You tell me."

"I bet Tyrone isn't even your real name."

Silence.

"Did you know Chris Randall?"

More silence.

"Steven Pickering said you two made a delivery to him—"

"Bullshit, he'd never say that." He lowered his head, matched eyes with her. "He knows better."

"Now you're threatening his life…in front of a police officer?"

Tyrone didn't say anything.

"Were you ever at the Randall estate?" She started to pace the room with a deliberate rhythm: three steps, stop, two steps, stop. Tyrone's silence told Madison that the deal had taken place on Randall's property. She continued. "I'm sure his daddy would be happy to hear about it. How you provided drugs to his son so he could keep up his habit and deal to others." She was trying to put some fear into him, and it seemed to be working. His body language stiffened. "But something went wrong, didn't it? He tried to pay for your hard work, risking your neck, with fake money. That must have made you mad."

"I ain't sayin' nothing."

"Steven stood up for you, though, didn't he?"

His eyes bounced to hers. "He did it."

She stopped walking, angled her head. "Did what?"

"Killed Chris."

Madison looked at the one-way mirror and then back to Tyrone. "Steven Pickering killed Chris Randall?"

"Yeah."

Madison bent over, putting her face to within inches of his. "How did he do it? I'm just curious."

"Drowned him."

He could have read that in any newspaper. "How did he drown him? *Where* did he drown him?"

"I want to talk a deal. I'll speak, and in exchange, the drug-dealing charges against me will be dropped." Tyrone sniffed, sat back in the chair, and tapped his forearm. "That's all I'm saying."

"We'll need your last name."

Madison joined Terry and Detective Commons in the observation room. "He didn't deny dropping the drugs off to the Randall estate," Madison said.

Commons looked in on Tyrone, and Madison followed the direction of his gaze. Tyrone was sitting there, slumped over and picking at his teeth.

"He didn't admit to it either," Commons said. "And you fed him the location. And I remember specifically telling you no deal."

And she hadn't made one, though she was prepared to do so—*if* Tyrone had cooperated and provided his last name. "We know Pickering confirmed being there."

Commons shook his head, and she felt the judgment in his glare.

She arched her brows. "Do you know my closed-case record?"

"I don't care about your—"

"He could have killed Chris Randall," she shot back. "It's my job to find out if he did, or if he knows who did."

"Just don't mess up my case because you're eager to whitewash drug-dealing charges in exchange for the identity of a killer."

"I believe murder is a little more severe than some drug dealing—"

"Then you fail to see the larger picture. That man there is a serial killer. A mass murderer, really." He flailed a hand toward Tyrone. "You've never been there when the news about a drug overdose is given to the parents."

"Listen, I'm not underestimating what you're doing here," she said.

"Of course you are." Commons walked off.

Madison went back into the interrogation room. "Tyrone—"

"Please," he interrupted, "just call me Thor. We've come to know each other a bit." A corner of his mouth lifted in a sly manner.

"Did you witness Steven Pickering kill Chris Randall?" She was tired of dancing around what she wanted to know.

His eyes darted away, then met hers.

"Please answer the question," she said firmly.

"Yeeesss." He dragged out the word.

"How did he hold Chris under the water?" she asked.

"This a trick question?"

Could be.

"With his hands," he huffed out.

She stood.

"Hey, where are you going?"

She kept walking to the hallway and ran into McAlexandar. He was clapping.

"Bravo," he said. "You finally focused your attention on a worthwhile candidate, Knight."

"Excuse me?" she croaked out.

Randall came up behind McAlexandar as did Terry. Her partner made eye contact with her and enlarged his eyes as if saying, *This is going to be fun.*

"I can't begin to thank you enough, Miss Knight." Randall extended a hand toward her. Her instinct was to pull back, but McAlexandar's eyes directed her to reciprocate. "I know my son was involved with the darker side of life. He thought partying and drugs were the way of real living. He'd never listen to me. It ended up being what killed him."

"Our investigation hasn't been concluded."

"Knight, we both know lowlife addicts like Tyrone are not credible characters," McAlexandar said.

Terry jingled the change in his pockets. Everyone looked at him, and he took his hands out of his pockets.

"He said that Steven Pickering did it," Randall said. He gestured toward the closed door to the interrogation room. "We all heard it."

"Now, that I do believe." McAlexandar smiled at his companion, and Randall nodded.

Whenever it suits your purpose.

Madison narrowed her eyes. "But he didn't know how."

McAlexandar's smile faded at her objection. "We were standing right here. He said he held him under the water."

Madison studied Randall's facial reactions and his body language. They were discussing the murder of his son in a somewhat casual manner, and he didn't give the impression it even affected him.

"Bring in that Steven Pickering fella." McAlexandar pointed a wagging finger at her. "In the meantime, send this guy back to lockup." He made a sweeping motion with his hand toward the room, referring to Tyrone as if he were rubbish to discard. Madison supposed, to McAlexandar, he was.

"How can they expect us to work like this?" Madison and Terry were headed back to the Pickering residence. "Can't you see something's not right?" Terry didn't answer, and she glanced over at him in the passenger seat. "Shit, Terry. Come on, admit it."

"What do you want me to say? McAlexandar and Randall are covering up Chris's murder together?"

"You could start there."

"Just because there's something there doesn't—"

"So you see it?"

"I said *something*. You can't read more into it than there is."

"But we've talked about it before. Randall finds out his son is pocketing some of the fake money for his own purpose, is careless with it. He got angry and decided to put an end to it."

"Good story." He turned to face her. "Now prove it."

She was quiet for a few seconds. "Can't quite yet. But how do you feel about Steven Pickering or this Tyrone guy?"

"Not sure. And we never have spoken with Neil Silverman."

She took a deep breath, doing her best to hide it. Her amateur move of calling him—and possibly tipping him off—caused an ill feeling in the base of her stomach.

"I'm going to look him up once we get back, hunt him down. I think it's a good idea we speak with him. Probably before Saturday," Terry said.

She had to think quickly. "That's just tomorrow. Think that's necessary?"

"Ah, yeah, or I wouldn't have said it."

"Think of it this way. You find Neil. What if he is the killer? As it stands, Vernon Silverman says he plans on coming back for the funeral. You might scare him off." Her gut tossed.

Terry lifted his shoulders. "Never really thought of that."

That makes me feel a little better…

"But you're assuming he'll actually come." Terry turned to her and pressed his lips together.

She put a hand on her poor stomach. *Or maybe not.*

CHAPTER THIRTY-THREE

"The brass is looking at the drug dealers. Big surprise." Cynthia tucked a strand of hair behind an ear and shrugged a shoulder at Madison. "News travels."

At this point, Madison was in the lab. Terry had passed in favor of hunting down Neil Silverman. She still hadn't found the courage to confess what she had done.

They'd managed to finally bring in Pickering. His mother tried to serve as a blockade, but she moved to the side after Madison threatened to take her downtown for obstruction of justice. When they had searched him, they found a baggie of coke. Pickering requested a state-appointed attorney, and it would take a couple hours for one to show up, so Madison decided to visit Cynthia in the lab.

"McAlexandar wants me to nail them for the murder." Madison leaned a hip against the table.

"Well, then there must be some proof," Cynthia said.

"Yeah right. The chief just wants to look good to his buddy Randall. There isn't any concrete evidence against Pickering or this Thor/Tyrone character. All we have right now is the fact there was a delivery of drugs, which we assume was dropped at the Randall boathouse. This is based on the fact one guy doesn't deny the location and the fact someone else saw a bunch of stuff being unloaded from the boathouse." She thought back to the exercise guru across the river from the Randall estate.

"Huh. But now you have this." Cynthia put a gloved hand on the rescue jaw they'd brought in from the Silvermans' boathouse.

"Please tell me you found something on it we can use."

"Well, its size is consistent with the bruising on Chris Randall's shoulders. It's not a perfect match, but it shouldn't be exact." Cynthia snuffed out a laugh. "You have to love those TV crime dramas that match bruises perfectly to an implement. A bruise is always bigger than what caused the damage."

Madison smiled, but doubted the expression touched her eyes. "Did you find any blood on the rescue jaw?"

"These are designed in such a way that the aluminum jaws are blunt, so they don't puncture skin."

"True, and come to think of it, Chris's skin wasn't cut. What about prints? Placement would likely be on the rod end."

Cynthia lifted her glasses and rested them on her head. "Assuming the killer wasn't intelligent enough to wear gloves."

"I'd surmise a heat-of-the-moment kill, no planning, no gloves."

"Don't worry. I'll be working this thing over and should have all the answers for you in twenty-four hours."

"Please hurry, before I'm forced to press charges on someone who's innocent."

"You don't know they didn't do it. Besides, Randall's boathouse likely has the same style of rescue jaw. And, lady, you have no right to rush me after what I did for you."

"What you did for—" Madison's mind went blank.

"Letting you know about Ryan's print on the bill *before* logging it. I gave you a head start. Please tell me it did you some good."

"Not really." Madison cringed and steeled herself for what she had to say next. "I'm going to really end up owing you."

Cynthia replaced her glasses on her nose. "And why's that?"

She winced. "Because the Secret Service suspects that I knew in advance…"

"From me?" Cynthia put a hand to her chest. "Shit! Madison, I could lose my job."

"It's all right. I've got your back. I told them I got a text message from you the same morning everyone else found out. It just came to me at a convenient time."

"Uh-huh. And they bought that? Did you even consider the consequences beforehand? They can come here, check my outgoing."

"Not really. Not without a warrant, and it wouldn't be worth it to them. Technically, I didn't need to allow them to see my cell phone."

"But you did? I'm confused?"

"I told them I delete my messages after I read them."

"They fell for that?"

"Well, I quickly deleted all the messages I had before handing it over."

"Impressive. You're not exactly a technical wizard."

"Hey, I know some things."

"Speaking of…" Cynthia's face fell serious.

Madison sensed the energy in the room change, the tone directing to the personal.

"How are you and Blake these days?"

"Why?"

"He's Randall's lawyer." Cynthia paused, searching Madison's eyes. "You all right with that? I mean, it's great if you—"

"Of course I'm not. I mean, what does it tell me about a guy when he's on Randall's payroll?"

"You haven't proven anything against Randall. You just don't like him."

"And my gut feelings are normally right."

Cynthia raised her eyebrows. "Not always. I can think of a few occasions."

"This is different. There's something going on between him and the chief. Come to think of it…I wonder if the kid's file has even been unlocked." Madison headed to Cynthia's computer.

Cynthia blocked access. "No, I'm not going to let you change the subject."

"Why is it everyone else can?" She looked away, frustrated, and caught the time on the clock on the wall. If she was going to see her parents off at the airport, she had to leave now. "I've gotta go."

"No, you're not—"

"I mean it. I do." She could cling to her stubbornness and not say goodbye to them, but she was confident it would leave her with regrets.

"You knew he was a defense attorney when you started seeing each other," Cynthia said, not letting the topic of Blake go. "I just wouldn't want you to throw something away that could be great just because of what he does for a living."

"Too late. Besides the man is the enemy, Cyn. We fight for opposite sides. I fight to build a case; he fights to tear it down." Madison's gaze drifted to the clock again.

"I Googled him the other night."

"You what? Blake?"

"Uh-huh." Cynthia bobbed her head.

"I thought you were busy with what's-his-name, Sovereign's partner." Madison knew his name was Lou but played indifferent. She really had to go.

"We can't be going at it all the time." Cynthia smiled and narrowed her eyes. "We even talk sometimes."

"Surprising."

Cynthia went on. "He loves you, Maddy. He wants you to move in with him. That's rare these days. Other than his career, the relationship seems to be going great, doesn't it?"

"Other than his career? Too bad it's such a glaring *other than*."

"He's rich."

"Doesn't impress me."

"Not even a little?"

"Not in light of other things, that's for sure."

"But you do realize how rich, right? As in, he could have a hundred children and they could have a hundred and all of them would be set for life."

"I remember reading something about it on Google," Madison said, feigning little interest.

"You Googled him too." Cynthia smiled.

"I'm not proud of it."

"But you looked him up, right? In addition to pulling his background." Cynthia fell quiet for a few seconds. "A minute ago, you said 'too late.' You break up with him already?"

"I think so."

"Maybe you should think about giving him another chance and working it out."

Madison shrugged. She wasn't so sure. She'd been happy single, and it was far less complicated.

"Maddy, his parents own WorldTrek, the world's largest distribution center for online purchases. They're worth two hundred billion." The last word came off Cynthia's tongue as bubbly champagne.

Madison had discovered that last night, but hearing Cynthia say it made something clear. Maybe most women would be thrilled that the man who loved them was loaded. She just wasn't one of them. "Sorry, but I really have to go."

Madison called Terry from the road to let him know she had to take care of something. She took a department car and put the lights on to cut through traffic. Her eyes kept going to the clock on the dash. It was one fifty now.

She wasn't going to make it to the airport before her parents went through security. She pulled into the lot and parked in the loading zone. An overeager employee rushed over.

"You can't park there unless—"

She flashed her badge.

He looked at the unmarked sedan and nodded.

She ran into the airport and looked around. She couldn't remember the airline her parents were using, but in her favor, this airport was rather small. One more scan of the space, and she spotted her family. She closed the distance and watched Chelsea and their mother hugging. Their father was standing back, frowning—until he saw Madison. Then he lit up.

"She came." Her father nudged her mother's arm. "Maddy," he said as he headed toward her.

Chelsea and their mother backed out of their embrace, looking in Madison's direction. Their faces registered surprise. Seconds passed before her sister smiled at her. Their mother never did.

"Yay, Auntie Maddy." Brie, Chelsea's youngest at the age of four, came running out from behind Chelsea and wrapped her arms around Madison's legs.

Her father reached her second and hugged her, maneuvering around the youngster. He kissed her on the cheek and whispered in her ear. "I'm glad you made it, sweetie."

Madison touched her dad's face. "Me too."

"We didn't think you were going to show," her mother said coolly. "Your own parents…and you couldn't even make it over to Chelsea's again."

"I have a job to do, Mom," Madison snapped back.

"Sometimes I forget that you're too busy with that life of yours to worry about us old folks."

Chelsea wedged between Madison and their mother and hugged Madison. Chelsea whispered into Madison's ear, "Don't let her get to you. She does love you."

She has a funny way of showing it.

Madison pulled back. She'd told herself on the way over that she wasn't going to let their mother get to her, but the execution was proving to be tougher. Her emotions were threatening to surface. She needed a distraction, so she focused on Brie, who still had her arms around her legs. Madison put a hand on her head. "Where are your sisters?"

She stopped hugging Madison and looked up. "They are at stool, silly. And Daddy's at work."

"Oh, they're at *school*." Madison corrected her with a smile. The young girl was nodding and smiling back.

There were a few awkward seconds of silence.

"Well, I came." Madison jacked a thumb over her shoulder. "I probably should be going. I'm in the middle of a—" Her eyes met her mother's.

She tilted out her chin. "I sure hope you're going to hug your own mother before you go." Her voice was gruff.

"Yeah, of course."

They hugged awkwardly, and Madison patted her mother's back. Before Madison drew back, her mother planted a kiss on Madison's lips and squeezed her hand. She said nothing as she looked in Madison's eyes.

What does she want from me?

It felt so uncomfortable standing there, having her mother trying to read her mind. Madison even got the feeling the woman actually cared about her. Madison felt tears burn her eyes.

"It would have been nice to see more of you, sweetie, but we'll be back again," her dad said.

"Or maybe you could come our way," her mother said. "We have a lot of good-looking men in Florida. That's if you and Blake don't work out." The softness in her mother's gaze surprised Madison and diminished her defensive instinct.

"Maybe," she consented.

Chelsea stood behind their parents and smiled at Madison.

Madison acknowledged her with a prolonged blink. As she did so, she feared the tears that lingered there would squeeze out. It had felt so good to be hugged by her parents and to feel loved by her mother. It had been far too long.

CHAPTER THIRTY-FOUR

Pickering stretched out his long legs and lifted one onto the corner of the interrogation table. His court-appointed lawyer stood behind him.

The defense, who went by the name of Victor Carling, had more facial hair than he had on the top of his head. The fluorescent lights danced on his bald head, and Madison had to fight not to look at it.

When she was on the way back from the airport, Terry had called and told her the news: Tyrone's print got a hit, and his real name was Jayson Coates. Like Pickering, Coates had a criminal record.

Madison slapped a folder on the table and sat across from Pickering. "Jayson Coates. Breaking and entering. Assault. Rape allegations."

Pickering avoided sustained eye contact, even though the mention of Tyrone's real name had him glancing at her quickly.

Madison continued. "The other day you said you delivered drugs to Chris Randall."

His lawyer studied his hands and picked at his fingernails. Pickering gave an exaggerated shrug of the right shoulder.

"You said Chris was alive when you left him," Madison said. "But we have someone else who was there. Someone who says differently."

Pickering pulled his leg down, leaned forward. "Then they're lying."

"The drug deal went down on the Randalls' property. Maybe near the boathouse." She laid the trap, hoping to catch an admission.

"You have nothing on me."

"We have a witness who says you held him under with your hands." If it took pitting Coates and Pickering against each other to expose the truth, so be it. But by not coming out and saying Coates was the witness, it would mess with Pickering's mind, throw him off his game.

He peered into her eyes as if he were a jungle cat sizing up his prey before pouncing. "Who? Jay? That's why you said his name when you came in?"

The lawyer placed a hand on Pickering's shoulder.

Pickering was on his feet in a flash, staring his lawyer in the face, with both fists pumped. "Don't touch me again."

Terry hurried over and pulled Pickering back. "Sit down!"

"I sit 'cause I want to, you pig. Not because you tell me to." He slumped back into the chair.

"Seems you have about as much charm as your friend does," Madison said.

"And who is that? Just come out and say it to me."

"I think you know."

Pickering slammed his fist on the table.

"Whoa. You've got quite the temper."

"Doesn't mean I killed Chris," he hissed.

"Yet you go right there. And you did admit to a fight with him." Madison glanced at the lawyer, expecting him to interrupt, but it was Pickering who spoke.

"'Course I did. The bitch did this to my face—" he pointed to the scab on his cheek "—and it bled like I had been capped. And the fucker did this after trying to pawn off crap as money."

"That must have made you mad—"

"It is Jay, isn't it? Jay's the rat." He leaned back in his chair, slammed a palm on the table. "Should have known better. Can't trust nobody."

"Known better—*what?*"

Pickering bowed his head and shook it. "Too good to be true."

She let the silence in the room have the power. Most times, it would drive someone to the point where they would have to speak to fill the void. After a few seconds, it seemed to work.

"Jay said I could go along."

Terry paced to the door and stood there with his hands in his pockets, jingling change. "So he's the one in charge?"

Pickering and the lawyer glanced at him.

"Of that drop, anyway," Pickering said.

"Jayson was there when you were dropping off the drugs, and got into the fight with Chris?"

"Uh-huh."

"Originally, you never confirmed anyone else was there with you, even though I had asked," Madison said.

"I said, I wasn't ratting anybody out."

"Huh. So I'm to assume you weren't alone based on that statement?" She had but she was toying with Pickering right now, trying to rile him up. "If we can't trust you in a small matter, how can we believe anything you say?"

"I don't want to go back to prison," he mumbled.

"Not sure I can do much about that. You had coke on your person when you were brought in. That's not even touching on the fact you raped a teenage girl." Like Terry had mentioned yesterday, Pickering didn't need to know that the Hudsons weren't legally pursuing the matter.

"She's...she's saying that I—" Pickering gulped. "I want a deal."

Madison sat back. "We don't give deals to people who have nothing to offer."

"What if I said I did?"

"Tell us what you've got, and we'll go from there."

Pickering looked at his lawyer, who nodded consent.

What a joke. Madison wanted to roll her eyes.

Pickering took a deep breath. "He's a white guy…Jay. If my bros even knew I hung out with him, they'd kill me. And I mean fo' sure. No way around it."

She sat back and banged the table. "He's a part of this group you hang out with. We know because they've all been brought in."

Pickering's eyes widened.

"Talk to us," she pressed. "And tell us the truth. Don't waste any more of my time."

"Fine," he eventually said. "We showed up at Chris's place."

And there was one confirmation she'd been waiting to hear, but she wanted to narrow that down even further. "His house? The boathouse?"

"The boathouse."

"What happened next?"

"Chris is there, ready to take possession of the shipment. He had us load the coke up on the cruiser, like he did every other time."

"The cruiser?"

"A boat," he said, seeming surprised she didn't know that. "Anyway, that's when Chris paid us with fake cash."

"Then you got into a fight?"

"Yep."

As Madison sat there watching him, she remembered that the Secret Service had told them the bills were hard to spot from the real thing, and next to impossible with the naked eye. "And that's what the fight was about…the fake money?"

"Uh-huh."

"So, you're a human UV machine that can scan bills?" she said with impatience. She detested liars.

Pickering's face scrunched up. "What are you talking about?"

She took a few deep breaths, tried to calm herself. "How did you know it was fake money?"

"You could tell."

"Try again."

Pickering remained silent.

"Unless you start talking, I'll have no choice but to lock you up and see if you're talkative in a few hours. Then again, I might not bother to come back for you."

Pickering glared at her, but he stayed quiet.

Madison put a palm on the table and went to stand up. "All right, then. You leave me no choice. I'll get a narcotics detective in here."

"Stop. *Stop*, okay?"

"We don't have time for games." She pushed her chair in.

"The fight wasn't about money," he rushed out. "Well, it was, but it wasn't."

Madison sat back down.

Pickering rubbed his left cheek on his shoulder. "He wanted a deal. A volume discount, as he called it. We don't, Jay don't, give no deals to anybody. One price for everybody."

"Did Chris Randall do a lot of volume with you?" she asked.

"Regular drop. Every Saturday. Payments on delivery."

"And you always delivered to the boathouse?"

"Always."

"How did you get through the front gate of the estate?"

"He just told *Freddy*"—he put finger quotes around the name—"we were his friends."

She figured Freddy must have been a nickname for the guard. Thinking back, she remembered he had a round body and black hair. He somewhat resembled a real-life Fred Flintstone. Then again, would a twentysomething even know who Fred Flintstone was?

"Getting back to that night. January tenth, when you didn't offer Chris a discount, who started the fight?"

"Chris hit me square in the face." Pickering turned his head to the side, showcasing the small remnant of what had been a blow to the cheek. "Probably going to scar."

"It adds character," Madison deadpanned. "So Chris threw the first punch? You fought back, but you were so mad at his lack of respect and trying to gain the respect of Jay, you had to show Chris who was boss."

Silence. And still no word from the lawyer.

"You pushed him in the water," Madison went on. "You held him under—"

"I did not!"

"While he battled to stay above the icy water, doing his best to reach the dock, you held him under." She applied pressure to Coates's claim that Pickering had simply held Chris under the water.

Pickering turned to his lawyer, who awoke from his partial coma and came to his defense. "Detective Knight, is there any proof to your speculations?"

Weak rebuttal. Redirecting back to Pickering, she said, "Have you ever been to any other boathouses in the area?"

"No."

"You sure you don't want to think about that?"

"Nothin' to think 'bout."

"When you got into this fight, how far did things go?"

"I told you before. He was alive when we left."

She shook her head. "You're not giving us enough to cut you any deal. Do you know who murdered Chris Randall?"

"Jay did it."

"Jayson Coates?" Madison leaned down beside him.

"Yes."

"Yet he's saying you did it."

Silence, followed by a rough swallow.

"You saw him kill Chris?" Madison pressed.

"Not exactly."

"You're wasting my time." Madison resumed full height.

"Please, I know he did it. He bragged about it later. He said that the bitch deserved to die, trying to con him into a discount."

She slapped the table, and Pickering flinched. "I'm going to need more."

"I think he went back and took care of it. I couldn't reach Jay until later that night. And he always answers his phone."

"So because he didn't answer his phone…" *This guy is unbelievable.* "So you don't know anything for certain?"

"He said he'd drown him, harder to prove murder."

Madison studied his eyes. "People say things all the time. Doesn't necessarily mean anything."

Outside of the interrogation room, Terry excused himself to use the washroom, and Madison headed back to their desks. They had spent hours in the room with Pickering, and she didn't think she was going to get anything else from him. She passed the observation room as McAlexandar was coming out. She hadn't even known he'd been watching.

"Don't tell me you're cutting this kid loose," he accused.

"Of course not. He'll be doing time for possession."

The chief put his hands on his hips and huffed out a breath. "Don't get smart with me, Knight. You know what I'm talking about."

"I really don't think he killed Chris."

"You've only gotten started with this kid. You've got that rescue jaw."

"That came from a neighbor's house, not the Randalls'. He claims not to have been in any other boathouses in the area."

"And you're taking the word of a druggie who had already misled you?"

"Unless I have evidence, I can't charge him based on his lot in life and recreational habits."

McAlexandar scowled. "The kid has openly confessed to dealing cocaine in large quant—"

"That doesn't make him a killer." She took a few steps down the hall. "I know you don't want the blame to go to Marcus Randall but—"

"What the hell is that supposed to mean?" McAlexandar roared. His face shot bright red, and his nostrils flared.

Madison stepped back but crossed her arms. "Just as it came out, I suppose. It's no secret there's a personal connection between you and Randall, but it can't be allowed to affect your judg—"

"Who do you think you are?" he snarled.

She took a deep breath, trying to muster up some diplomacy. "We took an oath to protect and serve. How can we carry that out when we're ready to convict an innocent civilian?"

"Hardly innocent. He's a drug dealer."

And a rapist... Not that she was going to add more in favor of his argument.

"I don't need you to lecture me on the principles I stand for," he added.

"I'm not intending to. But I'm not going to press murder charges without proof, either," she stamped out.

About thirty seconds later, he said, "What do you need?"

She'd expected him to rebut with a threat that he'd get someone who would. She shook that aside and answered his question. "Access to Randall's boathouse would be a good start."

He rubbed the back of his neck. "I'll see what I can do, but until then, you keep that shit in lockup!"

Ah, no problem there.

CHAPTER THIRTY-FIVE

Why do I even care? It's not like I need her.

Blake was having a hard time getting Madison off his mind. He hated any feelings that hinted at dependency. They were evidence of a weakness, and he needed to root them out before they took hold. After all, in his line of work there wasn't room for vulnerability.

He preferred being the pursuer, not the pursued. And that's why their relationship had worked out so well until now. Madison was the right amount of stubborn and fiercely independent. She was as involved in her career as he was in his. In the past, when they had their differences, she had allowed him to make the first move back. He liked that about her. And in that way, he and Madison were a perfect fit.

He sat behind his desk at his law firm, Golden, Broderick, and Maine, which was located on the outskirts of Stiles. He had accomplished a lot in his career and being the majority partner allowed him flexibility.

With a reputation established on repeated courtroom successes, including some of the most high-profile cases the area had seen, they didn't take on work pro bono, and their clients had to be of a certain income level. But for every standard, there was an exception.

Blake had taken on the odd case for free or at a substantial discount. At times like those, seeing as they were so rare, he allowed himself a pass—and no one needed to know, not even the other managing partners. He always paid the equivalence of the regular fees from his own pocket.

Psychobabble would have him believe it was philanthropy, but everything Blake did was for a reason, and one way or another, he always ended up coming out ahead. It was while working one case pro bono that he'd met Madison.

Before her, his relationships were brief affairs and rather meaningless, even if sexually gratifying. The women he aligned himself with were cool and distant and that had worked out for him in the past. But with Madison, her independence—one of the very things he admired about her—was costing him.

The judgment that had been in her eyes, and the accusations that hurled from her mouth cut him. And like the wounded, he felt embittered and found himself starting to swallow the feelings he had for her.

She knew who I was when we started seeing each other!

I don't need to explain myself to her—or anyone, for that matter!

Too bad he didn't buy his own defense. Rather, he was slowly being torn apart. He'd even lost sleep over their confrontation last night.

Pathetic!

He was a powerful, rich man, with above-average looks. Why was he wasting his energy fretting about this? Did he really love her?

He glanced at the phone on his desk, actually contemplating whether he should call her, when it buzzed.

"Mr. Golden, your four o'clock is here," Sarah Fairchild, his assistant of seven years, said over the intercom.

"Thank you." He continued staring at the phone, feeling like he'd been "saved by the bell." What the hell had he been thinking? If anyone should be calling anyone, it should be Madison making that move. After all, she was the one in the wrong.

Blake gestured for Weiss from the Secret Service to sit in the leather chair across from him and Ryan Turner. There was no sign of the older agent who had been at the station the other day.

"This meeting will be brief," Weiss said. "My concern is Mr. Randall will be increasing a bill only the country will be forced to cover."

The agent certainly had a flair for the dramatic. Blake tugged out on his jacket. "This meeting was set for you to meet with Ryan Turner. Should you wish to speak with one of my other clients, Ms. Fairchild can book you an appointment." Blake extended his arms, latched hands, and twisted his wrist to look at his watch.

Turner sat to Blake's right, and his feet tapped a constant rhythm on the hardwood floor. He was a weak person, and if Blake made that observation, it wouldn't have been lost on the Randalls or this Secret Service agent. Ryan had expressed in private meetings that he and Chris were like brothers. Blake knew better. The Randalls didn't let anyone in unless it served their purposes.

"Very well." Weiss set his gaze on Turner. "Your print was found on a counterfeit twenty, can you explain that?"

"No."

Blake fought a smirk. He'd trained his client well, telling him the importance of keeping answers brief—and to one word whenever possible.

"Are you aware of every bill you touch, Mr. Weiss?" Blake asked.

"*Agent* Weiss." He looked at Turner. "Did you know that Chris Randall was making counterfeit money?"

"No."

"Any suspicions?"

"None."

"All right, let me redirect this way, then. Are you aware of anyone in the Randall household making counterfeit money?"

"No."

Blake was smirking; he couldn't help it. Turner was doing fantastic.

"Mr. Turner, it is in your best interest to cooperate with us."

"Don't try to intimidate my client with transparent threats. He is cooperating. He's answered every question you've asked him, so if that is all..."

"He's answered them with one word."

"One word has been all that's needed."

Turner's foot stopped tapping, and Blake took that as a bad sign.

Blake stood. "My client has not admitted to knowing anything regarding the counterfeiting. This meeting's over."

"Actually, it's not." Weiss settled back into his chair. "You do realize the Secret Service is a direct branch of the government, Mr. Golden? With that being said, as an agent of that organization, I have the right and the authority, to say when it's over." Weiss focused his eyes on Ryan. "Was Chris making the money? Why? For who?"

Turner faced Blake and worried his lip. In this case, a yes or no answer wouldn't work. Blake gestured for Turner to answer.

Turner sniffled and pinched the tip of his nose.

"Mr. Turner has just lost a good friend," Blake started. "A man he thought of as a brother. We'll do this another time."

"This isn't a sporting event you can record and watch later. Regardless of whether it's convenient at this time or not is inconsequential." Weiss put his attention on Turner. "Who was he doing it for?"

"I told you, Chris didn't," Turner said.

"And you know this for a fact?"

"Yes."

Blake smirked. Back on track with one-worded responses.

Weiss scowled. "If you know Chris was counterfeiting, it is your civic duty to speak up. Is the counterfeiting still going on?"

"My client has already told you he had no idea about the counterfeiting. What you're doing now is nothing short of badgering him." Blake walked to the door and swung it open. "This meeting has reached its end."

"Here is my card." Weiss extended it across the table to Turner. "Should you wish to discuss this matter further with or without council, this is how to reach me. If you know something and don't tell me, and I find out, you'll be considered an accomplice—"

"Spewing threats now. Besides, this path you're on has you chasing down a ghost. Chris Randall has been dead for weeks." Blake stared at the agent.

"But it wasn't just Chris involved with it, was it, Ryan?"

"I don't like your implication, *Agent*," Blake said.

"Whether you do or don't makes no difference to me," Weiss said. "He got you involved, Ryan, didn't he? Who were you doing it for?"

"No, no…" Turner shook his head. "I'm not doing this."

Weiss leaned across the table. "Chris was forced into the situation by his fath—"

"Stop it immediately!" Blake snarled.

"You were his brother, as Mr. Blake here pointed out. It makes sense you went along."

Blake felt heat blanket the back of his neck. "Here is the door, Mr. Weiss. I suggest you use it and leave now, before I file harassment charges."

CHAPTER THIRTY-SIX

McAlexandar stomped off, and Terry was walking down the hall toward her. "Do you believe what Pickering told us?" Madison asked.

"He's not exactly the most honest and forthcoming person. Think he's just trying to get the focus off him. He knows he's going to be charged with possession already."

"I'm starting to think this whole thing is a waste of time. Coates is pointing at Pickering. Pickering's pointing at Coates. McAlexandar would be happy to charge either one. Whatever it takes to get our focus off Marcus Randall. How he feels, not how I feel," she clarified.

"We still don't have any hard proof Mr. Randall is involved," Terry said.

"No more than the chief has on Pickering and his buddy."

Terry looked like he was concentrating deeply. "Speaking of he said/he said, I'd like to talk to Coates…alone. Let's see what he has to say when we tell him Pickering told us he's the one who killed Chris."

"Couldn't hurt." Madison settled into the observation room attached to another interrogation room. They had Coates brought up from holding and Madison watched Terry go to work through the one-way mirror.

"Your real name is Jayson Coates," Terry said, pacing the perimeter of the room.

"Am I supposed to be impressed?" Coates sat back.

"I don't care if you are or you aren't. You've been a guest of the city before."

A shoulder shrug dismissed Terry's comment.

"Did you kill Chris Randall?"

Coates's eyes blinked heavily, deliberately, and he let out a deep-throated laugh. "I told you who did it."

"Well, he's saying you killed him."

"That son of a bitch!"

"You said that Steven held Chris under with his hands." Terry stopped walking. "But there was more to Chris's murder. He didn't go like that."

Coates picked between his front teeth with a fingernail.

"I'm going to lay out what I know," Terry said.

"Story time is it?"

Terry went on. "Chris wanted a discount on your fine merchandise. You got angry and taught him a lesson."

"Bullshit!"

"Truth hurts." Terry jingled the change in his pocket.

"If it *were* the truth." He paused. "I didn't do it."

"So you stand by your earlier comment that Steven did it…with his bare hands?"

Coates's face hardened. "Steven's the one who started everything. He threw the punches." He balled up his fists, punched them against the table. "He's dead."

"*He's dead*? You're threatening Steven's life to a cop? Not hard to imagine you meting out your own revenge on Chris. I'm seeing quite the temper."

"It's a figure of speech."

Terry remained silent.

"You've got to believe me." Coates's eyes narrowed.

"I don't have to believe a word you say." Terry went for the door. "And for the record I don't."

Terry slammed the door behind him, and Madison could hear his footsteps coming down the hall to her.

"I've had enough of this tonight. I don't think either of them did it. A drug deal gone bad or not, I think the worst it got was a fistfight. I think it was about pricing before it was about the fake cash."

Madison nodded. They'd spent hours trying to ignite the flames of a confession, but nothing had resulted besides transparent allegations flinging between the two men. "We need more to go on here."

"We'll pick it up in the morning."

"Fine," she consented, "but tomorrow's going to be a busy day. It's Chris's funeral, and I've asked McAlexandar to get us access to Randall's boat—"

"You what? Do you want to commit career suicide? We don't have anything solid against him yet."

"What I want is to find the truth, and if Randall doesn't have anything to hide, this charade has gone on long enough."

"How did he take it? McAlexandar?"

"Not so good at first."

"Great."

"You say that like you've lost your job and it's my fault."

"Well…"

"He ended up saying he'd see what he could do."

"He really meant he needed time to discuss your attitude with Winston and get you fired. Me too, probably."

"You're so paranoid."

"Wonder why."

"Trust me."

"Every time you say that, my faith decreases."

"As you've said before," Madison mumbled, but Terry was already a ways down the hall.

Madison wished she had someone to go home to. Not that she needed a family, or even a husband. She blamed the inner reflection on her mother's comment this afternoon about there being a lot of handsome men in Florida. She let the melancholy thoughts go, as she remembered Hershey. He'd likely be the only stable male in her life besides Terry and her father. At least neither of them would let her down. It brought to mind someone else who fit that bill. She had to set things right with Richards.

. . .

Madison knocked on Richards's office door, and he shouted, "Enter."

When he saw it was her, his face fell.

"I'm sorry for looking into your private life," she said.

He unbuttoned his lab coat and draped it over the back of a chair without looking at her or saying a word.

"It was none of my business," she went on. "It's just the way that you looked at Chris, I knew there was more there."

"But like you said, *none of your business.*"

She reached out a hand to touch his forearm, and he didn't move back to avoid the contact. "I never meant to bring up the pain again. That wasn't my intention."

"Next time, if you wonder about something, ask." His eyes met hers now and radiated pain.

She nodded slowly. "I promise."

"All right, then."

"Are we good?"

"We will be."

She supposed that was all she could ask for. "I understand. Again, for what's it's worth, I'm sorry." She turned to walk away.

"Maddy."

"Yeah." She spun around.

"Please don't tell anyone else about this, about what happened with my brother. It was a long time ago, but…" His words stalled there.

"I understand." She squeezed his shoulder and left to call it a night.

CHAPTER THIRTY-SEVEN

"I found Neil Silverman. He lives in a town called Hastings about three hours north of here." Terry announced his finding with such pride Madison couldn't confess she'd already contacted him.

It was Saturday morning, and they were at the desks down at the station waiting on word from McAlexandar as to whether they had permission to go into the Randall boathouse.

"Neil's supposed to be here today for the funeral," she said, "so we should be able to catch up with him there."

"Well, if he doesn't show, we know where to find him."

Madison didn't have anything to add. She had lost sleep thinking Silverman might not show.

"There's no way we're getting in…to Randall's boathouse. Hope you know that," Terry said. "We could be sitting around waiting for something that might never come."

Madison's phone rang. "That could be him now." She said the words and felt like she'd popped into an alternative reality; she'd never been eager to hear from the chef before. She answered without consulting the caller ID. "Knight… Okay… Great." She hung up.

"We're in?"

"Actually, that was Cynthia, and she has some findings related to the rescue jaw. Neil Silverman's prints are all over it." Madison remembered Neil's brush with the law five years ago, and that must have gotten his fingerprints put in the system.

"That could take Randall and the drug dealers out of the picture."

"*Could?* I thought we were already doubting their involvement anyway." Madison felt nauseated knowing she could have scared off the killer, but she had to reel in her emotions.

Terry shrugged. "Neil's prints on the rescue jaw doesn't get us that far either, though. They could have gotten on there at any time. It was his father's. Did Cyn pull any epithelial off it that belonged to Chris?"

"Not that she said." Madison wished the absence of epithelial would be enough to cement Neil's innocence. It would ease her conscience. "I don't know. Why would Neil be in his father's boathouse touching the rescue jaw? We'll certainly ask him. We do know that Chris didn't go into the water inside the Silverman boathouse because the ice was intact."

"Well, I was still curious about Neil and his rush to leave. So I pulled his background, and it's clean except for one incident about five years back."

Madison nodded for Terry to go, not about to admit that she'd already looked into Neil's background.

"He was charged with drunk and disorderly conduct, assaulting an officer... Both counts were on the same date so I took a closer look. Neil was pulled over for erratic driving. Neil exited a vehicle and assaulted the officer."

"His father mentioned he drinks too much sometimes," Madison interjected.

"Sure. But there's no record of drunk driving, just drunk conduct."

"Maybe he was the passenger?" She wasn't sure where Terry was going with this.

"He could have fought to defend the driver."

"You don't think that was..." There was that feeling that would whelm in her chest, taking her to the point of following intuition and instinct without reason or proof. She went to her desk and typed *Chris Randall* into the system and waited for the results. "The file's still locked. Why the hell is it still—"

"I don't think it's ever going to be unlocked." Terry's eyes said it all. It would have cost a lot of bribery money to seal the record, and it would take a lot more than a requisition to have it reopened—assuming one had even gone through. "Let's say that Neil and Chris were partying, drank too much. What if Chris was the driver? Neil came to his defense, mostly emboldened by alcohol himself, and assaulted the officer to keep him from Chris."

"Chris would have been charged with DUI, but his father's a very powerful man." Madison recognized the story as a mere fabrication, but kept it going. "And based on the date, Chris and Neil would have only been seventeen. Underage."

"And for his loyalty, Silverman gets a record. Charges had to be laid on someone."

Madison found it sad that two teenagers were even served alcohol to start with, but she carried on with their theorizing. "This could just be the beginning. Maybe Chris took advantage of Silverman all the time, and Silverman finally got tired of it. It could be motive."

"The incident we're talking about was five years ago, though, and Chris made Neil a rich man. Neil has Chris to thank for his internet company... Bring up Neil's website," he said and told her where to go.

She acted as if she'd never visited the site before.

"Look at the banner," Terry said.

She looked at him, not sure what he meant.

"The ads along the top. That's what they call it." He rolled his eyes.

She thought about punching him in the shoulder. "Randall Investments." She clicked around some of the pages and signed up for a free trial. "All the pages showcase Randall Investments. There are some ads for other things, but the majority are for Randall Investments."

"So Chris gives Neil the internet company idea and pretty much buys it for him through sponsorship to start."

"But why would someone do that?"

"Very good question. Internet advertising isn't the most affordable means. Usually, there's a premium attached to it, especially as the website grows." Terry rubbed the back of his neck.

"Maybe Neil approached Chris about raising the cost of the advertising space. He could have gotten more from someone else. Chris took offense. After all, the whole thing started from his idea."

"They got into an argument, and it got heated." Madison continued clicking on different pages of the website.

"Possibly they were sampling some of Chris's *goods*. Weren't in their right minds."

"But Chris didn't have drugs in his system, remember? And the rescue jaw was in the Silvermans' boathouse." Madison turned to face her partner. She felt as if they were spinning in a circle.

"That doesn't mean it belonged to the Silvermans."

"Oh…okay, now we're talking. Given this theory amounts to anything, we're still forgetting one thing. Does Neil smoke cigars?" Madison's cell rang, and she answered. "Knight… Okay… Yes, I understand." She hung up, rose from her chair, and grabbed her jacket from the back of it. "We're in."

CHAPTER THIRTY-EIGHT

"So, what do you understand?" Terry asked Madison as they drove to the Randall estate.

His question caught her out of the blue. "What are you talking about?"

"When you were talking to the chief, you said 'I understand.' Understand what?"

Terry didn't need to know she was responding to McAlexandar's direction that this was only to be a look-see, and even if they found something, they weren't to collect it. "It's nothing," she said.

"Why do I get the feeling it's more than nothing?"

"He just reminded me that it's his son's funeral today and to be diplomatic." Not entirely a lie, as he had said that, too.

"That's like telling an ambulance-chasing lawyer to stop. They make their living off it. Ride the rush that comes with it."

"I'm nowhere near that bad," she said, taking offense, though she might be a bit of a conflict junkie.

Terry tucked in his chin and regarded her with skepticism. "A matter of opinion, but there's more you're not telling me. What is it?"

"Look at that. We're here." She pulled into the driveway of Randall's estate.

"Nice subject switch."

"I thought so." She smiled but let the expression fade for "Freddy," the guard at the gate. "We're Detectives Knight and—"

"Yes, Mr. Randall's expecting you," Freddy interrupted. "Take the drive that splits left toward the river. The boathouse is right there." The bar lifted, and Madison drove through.

"This place is huge," Terry commented with a sense of awe.

She glanced over at her wide-eyed partner and could imagine drool dripping from the edges of his mouth. "You haven't seen anything yet," she said. "The kitchen is larger than my entire apartment. There's also a large indoor pool."

"All for one man...well, now."

She could tell she was losing her partner to some sort of daydream, but let him live there for the moment.

She rounded the bend, and the boathouse came into view. The paved drive stopped about fifty feet shy but continued as a pathway to the boathouse. Chief McAlexandar stood at the mouth of the path, his hands clasped in front of him.

Terry snapped his head toward her. "You never said the chief would be here."

"I thought that went without saying."

They got out of the car, and McAlexandar rushed over.

"We must make this quick. The service is at one," he said.

She nodded to give acknowledgment not agreement. Her priority was uncovering any truths this boathouse may contain. And that would take the time it took.

Her heart beat fast as she walked toward the building she had anticipated being in for so long. She studied the structure. Lights were mounted in the two front corners, and there was a security camera over the door. She pointed it out to Terry.

McAlexandar stopped just outside the door. "I'm going to let you go in alone. Do your thing, and then get out."

"Yes, sir." The salutation came easier than normal and was even *somewhat* sincere. After all, her respect for him had increased a notch based on the fact he had gained access to the boathouse—even if his one disclaimer soured the deed.

McAlexandar, who had his mouth open, likely ready to retort, snapped it shut, dipped his head, and walked away.

Madison led the way inside the boathouse. It was certainly larger and fancier than the one on the Silverman property. The walls were galvanized steel, and the structure was supported by iron beams that ran down the middle into the bed of the river, giving room for two boat slips. There was a wooden dock along the outskirts, but none was between the two boats that were suspended over the water about five feet. One was some sort of party boat. It had a deck with a railing around the perimeter, and there was a covered barbecue sitting on it. The other one was two stories with a main level and bunker room underneath. Madison pointed to it, and Terry nodded. He read her mind. The cruiser Pickering had mentioned; the boat where the drugs were stored.

"Hmm, that's interesting." Terry crouched down and pointed to an area of ice that had been re-formed. Shards fanned out from a thinner layer of ice, like sunflower petals.

Madison moved closer to the edge of the dock. "Chris could have gone in there."

Terry gave her a warning look. "Or something."

She narrowed her eyes at him. "You're such a skeptic."

"One of us has to be."

Usually he was telling her she was too cynical, but she let his comment go. "So even with that sort of evidence—" she gestured to the re-formed ice "—you don't think Chris went in here?"

"Not what I said. I think it's quite possible. Still doesn't prove Randall killed his son. This place was a regular hangout for drug dealers."

"At least we still have the two delivery boys in lockup," she said.

"Don't hate me for saying this—" he held up his hands "—and I'm not siding with the sarge and chief, but circumstantial evidence doesn't look good for them. They had possible motive."

"But they don't know how Chris was drowned," she countered. "Not to mention that by pointing the finger at each other, they've established reasonable doubt for any defense attorney to get charges against either of them dropped."

"They could have conspired and are withholding the true method."

"Sure, but any case against them isn't going anywhere right now, and I really don't think they did it." She walked around the U-shaped dock toward the party boat. "Did you notice the camera outside? We need to get our hands on that footage and see if it gives us something."

"Good luck getting that."

"Well, I got us in here, didn't I?" She knew the only reason was to build a case against the dealers. That's all McAlexandar was truly interested in, not the truth. She spotted a white chest against the far wall and walked toward it. She opened the lid and found some fishing gear and a tackle box inside. She looked at the walls. "I don't see any rescue jaw."

"It's possible they keep those on the boats."

"You said *those*, as in plural."

"Well, if Randall is serious about boating safety, there should be one to go with each boat."

"Hmm." She stood on the toes of her boots, as if that was going to give her enough height to look inside. "They must have used a ladder to get onto the boat."

"Unless they are exceptionally good jumpers." Terry laughed.

"Ha, ha." She looked around and found an A-frame ladder, brought it over, climbed up. "Oh."

"You see one?" Terry asked.

"I see a life preserver and what almost looks like a rescue jaw. But it has a rope hoop on the end of the pole instead of aluminum jaws."

"Oh."

"*Oh?*"

"The chances he would have both types of rescue jaws are rare, not improbable, but more unlikely. Of course, I could be wrong, depending on how serious Randall is about boating safety."

"They do the same thing?"

"Not really. The hoop is for someone who is struggling in the water to loop their arm into so they can be pulled into the boat. The jaw is for—"

"Retrieval from under the water."

Terry nodded.

"Okay, so he could have both. Maybe the killer disposed of the one used to drown Chris in the river?" Her proposition completely discredited the one they had with Neil Silverman's prints on it, and for the moment, it eased up the tension in her gut.

The door cracked open and sunlight streamed in. McAlexandar stood in the opening as a blackened shadow. "You have two more minutes." He closed the door again, leaving himself on the outside.

"Two minutes?" Terry looked at her. "Why is he rushing us?"

"You still don't really get it, do you? While he wants us to find evidence, he just doesn't want it to be against Randall."

"But what if he did it?"

"What if?" They had stood there face-to-face before Terry headed to the door. She thought he was going to leave until he stopped walking. His attention was on the deck boards. "Terry?"

"I found something." He pulled a plastic evidence bag from his back pocket, slipped on a pair of gloves, and bent down.

"What is it?"

He resumed full height, the bag with his find pinched between two fingers. "I'd say it looks like a cigar. The one that burned Chris?"

"Time's up." The door flung open to McAlexandar, who was ready to escort them off the property.

Madison snatched the bag from Terry and stuffed it into her coat pocket. "We're leaving." She established brief eye contact with Terry, who looked a little confused by her whole grab-and-dash move.

In the car, Terry asked, "What was all that about?"

"If I tell you, you promise you're not going to shriek like a little girl, then start ranting on about the unemployment line and food stamps?"

"What did you do?"

She tapped a hand on the steering wheel, debating whether to tell him. "We weren't supposed to collect anything."

"That doesn't even make sense."

"Tell me about it, but that was the order that came along with the search."

Terry held eye contact with her. "That's really what the whole 'I understand' thing was about. Then why even let us look around?"

"Good question. Two other questions are: what is Randall hiding from us and why is the chief helping him?"

Terry shook his head quickly. "I'm just going to pretend I didn't hear that—again."

"Why avoid those questions? They have merit and deserve answers."

He turned to face her. "Why? Let's see… I like my job?"

"So, for that, you're willing to turn the other way when a superior turns his back on the law?"

"I didn't say that."

"Pretty much sounds to me like that's what you're saying."

"Maddy, you're so black and white. There's no in between for you. You need to learn to find the shades of gray, or you'll have all sorts of problems in life."

"Shades of gray? Who are you?"

"Never mind. It's like talking to a concrete block."

"Concrete block? People normally say it's like talking to a *wall*."

"Normally."

Anger pulsed through her. First, he'd told her she needed to be more responsible, and now she failed to see *shades of gray*. What was with all the criticism lately?

CHAPTER THIRTY-NINE

Madison and Terry went home and changed for Chris's funeral. They'd staked out at St. Jude's Catholic Church, hoping to find Neil, but there was no sign of him. Now they were following a long procession of cars to the cemetery. She was wishing their luck would change and Neil would make an appearance.

"We're going to have to put a BOLO out on him if he doesn't show here," Terry said.

A be-on-the-lookout bulletin.

"Let's not jump to any conclusions yet." *God, let Neil come.*

"Since when do you make excuses for a suspect?"

Since I might have spooked him...

"Well, he might not be a religious person," she said, recalling Vernon's words: *people get religious after a loss.*

"Going to church for a funeral service has nothing to do with being religious."

She looked over at him. "I'd disagree with that."

"Hey, there's a lot more to being religious than filling a pew."

"Fine. I'll give you that." Not that she had too much experience with religion herself. But she'd be lying if she said that standing beneath the towering steeples of the church hadn't had her pondering the deeper things in life. She felt Terry staring at her. "What?" Slightly abrupt, but his gaze was making her uncomfortable and giving her the feeling he was judging her. She might be feeling a little guilty and paranoid about Neil's no-show.

"I don't know... It's just every time the subject of Neil Silverman comes up, you get weird."

"I don't think I—"

"No, you do. And normally you'd be all over hunting him down. You're not this time. What did you do?"

She kept her eyes on the road, avoided eye contact with her partner. "We have two suspects in holding, or don't you remember?"

"Don't try to redirect the conversation." He shifted his body more toward her. "Come on, spill it."

She glanced at him, and everything from his body language to his eyes told her he wasn't going to drop the subject until he received a satisfactory reply. "I called him," she said.

"You what?" he spat. "You tipped him off! No wonder he didn't show."

"I didn't— That wasn't my intention."

"Well, you might want to start praying he shows up, because if he is the killer and doesn't, you're going to be in deep shit."

Just the fact Terry swore told her just how pissed off he was. But she was angry enough at herself for both of them.

"You better hope he shows up," he repeated.

"I know."

She pulled into the cemetery, marked with an elaborate sign that read *Eternal Acres*. It was one of the largest graveyards in Stiles and was situated on acres of manicured lawns—in the warm seasons—and mature trees.

Everyone in the procession parked and then walked to the burial site, but Madison and Terry held back. If it hadn't been for the break in the weather, Chris's internment would have needed to wait for spring.

"Neil Silverman could be across the globe by now," Terry hissed. "What did you do exactly? Call him up and start asking why he had left his parents' place in such a hurry? Or did you just come out and ask if he killed Chris?"

"I'm not even justifying that with a response." Her eyes followed a silver BMW that pulled in and parked at the base of the hill.

"What do you know? This could be him." Terry started walking toward the car but stopped short when the driver got out and it was an Asian man. Terry set his gaze on Madison. "We have to issue a BOLO for Neil Silverman and his car."

"Just give it time." She tried to sound confident, but she was flaking apart inside. It was quite likely Neil wouldn't make an appearance.

She and Terry remained for the eulogy, which was thankfully brief—as Vernon Silverman had said it would be—and the coffin was lowered into the ground. Martha Cooper cried into tissues the entire time. Her world had truly been flipped on its head, and returning to any semblance of a normal life would be a ways off in the future.

As the crowds filtered out, Madison and Terry continued to hold back.

"I screwed up," she eventually said, filling the silence between her and Terry.

He said nothing.

"I screwed up," she repeated. "And I admit it."

"I'm not hard of hearing." Terry walked to the department-issued car.

"That's all you're going to say?"

He stopped, turned around. "There's not much else to—"

Another silver BMW pulled in.

She held her breath, hoping this was their guy. "Just that Asian man again?"

"Nope. This one is the current year's model. This could be Neil."

A dark-haired man got out and headed to the gravesite.

"*Is* Neil," she said.

Neil stood by the fresh mound of dirt and signed the cross.

"Guess we might have an answer as to whether or not he's religious, too," Terry said. "So, why wasn't he at the church?"

"Let's find out."

They gave Neil some distance while he spoke to his deceased friend. Neil was just loud enough to know he was talking, but she couldn't discern what was being said.

After a few minutes, Madison approached him. "Neil Silverman?"

The man turned to face her. "Who wants to know?" He brushed a hand to his cheek, his eyes revealing shame at his sorrow.

"I'm Detective Knight. We spoke on the phone."

"This isn't a good time." His gaze returned to the fresh grave.

"You were close with Chris."

"Why should I talk to you?"

"We have your prints on the murder weapon." Madison was tired of tiptoeing around this case, and she may have exaggerated the details. They had his prints on a rescue jaw, yet it wasn't tied back to Chris Randall.

"The murder weapon?" Neil glanced at Terry. "I'm confused. I thought Chris drowned." He took a few steps toward his BMW. "I have to be with my family now."

"Why weren't you at the church?" Madison asked. "Why wait until everyone left to show up here?"

He stopped walking but didn't turn around. A hand went to his face, and Madison guessed he was wiping away tears.

"The last time you saw Chris, you got into a fight, things got out of—"

"That's not entirely correct." Neil turned now, his eyes containing a fire. "We got into a fight. I'm not going to lie. It wasn't pretty, but it didn't end the way you're trying to imply here. I didn't kill Chris. I loved Chris." His voice cracked.

"You were going to spend the entire month with your family," Madison started, "but the fight led to your going home early, didn't it?"

"I'm leaving now."

"You fought in the wee hours of January eleventh or thereabouts?"

Neil's gaze met Madison's. "Are you arresting me?"

"The eleventh is the day Chris was killed."

Neil's face darkened and he sniffled. "Unless you are going to arrest me, I'm leav—"

"Right now, we just need to talk. We have questions we need answers to."

"And what makes you think I have them?"

"Let's give it a try."

CHAPTER FORTY

"I've cooperated with you. I'm not sure what more you could want." In the harsh light of the interrogation room, Neil Silverman looked older than his age, but certainly in close image to his father except for a more rounded jawline.

"We appreciate that you came downtown to speak with us, but we still don't know the answers to a lot of our questions."

"Haven't I been through enough already?" Neil's brows compressed downward, frown lines manifesting themselves. He might have money, but Madison sensed his life was a lonely one.

"Your record shows an assault on an officer," she said.

"What does that have to do with anything?"

"What prompted the assault?" she asked.

Neil stretched out his legs. "I don't have to answer that."

"You're going to stop cooperating now?"

"I never said that." He ran a hand down his face. "I just don't see what that has to do with Chris's death."

"Chris's *murder*," Madison stamped out.

Neil rubbed his arms.

"Was Chris driving the car that night?"

Neil clenched his jaw but said nothing.

Earlier that morning while waiting on McAlexandar's call, Madison and Terry had talked to the officer who had booked the charges. He said he prided himself on his memory and was positive there were two younger men in the car when he pulled it over. Neil Silverman was in the passenger seat. When they asked about the identity of the driver, the officer's recall got fuzzy. Madison suspected the driver was no one other than Chris Randall and the officer's silence had been bought. If she could get Neil to admit that Chris had been the one driving drunk, it could establish motive for Neil to want to kill him. After all, Neil took the hit with a permanent record while Chris walked away scot-free.

"Did you take the fall for him five years ago?" *And more times since*, Madison thought but left unsaid.

"Check your records. You'll see that I was the only one charged." Spoken matter-of-factly but also evasive.

Still, Madison didn't detect any bitterness, though Neil could be a good actor. "How long did you know Chris?"

"Since I was a teenager."

"Thirteen? Fourteen? Fif—"

"Fifteen. Second year of high school."

"So you met at school?"

"No. At a club."

Vernon Silverman had said that Neil met Chris at a bar and was drinking heavily, something Vernon wasn't proud of about his son. Madison wondered if Neil had kept his father in the dark about when that happened exactly— teenagers hardly told their parents anything. But Neil had been seventeen at the time of the charges against him, and it would be logical Vernon knew about them, but he hadn't volunteered anything on that subject.

"You were kids," Madison said.

"Good fake IDs and the fact Chris was a Randall. No one would turn him away. Chris and I just connected… eventually. It started out with me stalking him."

"You stalked him," Madison said.

"Yeah, harmless. We'd always have a lot of fun when we were together, though at first, we'd just *run into each other*. Chris had girls around him all the time, real pretty ones, too. I'd find out which clubs he was going to, and I'd go as well."

"So, eventually you grew on Chris?"

"He never even suspected I was trailing him. He just thought it was great how we always ended up bumping into each other. He thought fate intended us to be friends." Neil laughed. "I'd laugh at him for saying such BS. Wasn't long before he'd come pick me up, and we'd go clubbing together."

Madison thought of Ryan Turner and wondered where he was in all this. Was he possibly jealous of the new friend in his *brother's* life, enough so that he killed Chris?

"When was the last time you saw Chris?" She'd asked when their fight had taken place at the cemetery, but she'd been the one to provide the date. And Neil hadn't confirmed or denied.

"January tenth…eleventh? It could have been past midnight."

"So you would have been one of the last people to see him alive."

"I've always been lucky." His sentiment could have been genuine if not for the undercurrent of sarcasm.

"Why were you in such a hurry to get home?" Madison began. "We were told you left early on the eleventh."

"There was a problem with my website."

"Specifically?"

"New account log-ins."

Madison consulted some notes. "Your father mentioned it was email confirmations."

"Same thing."

She held eye contact with him.

Neil continued. "When someone signs up for a new account, they fill in their information, including their credit card. They get an email confirmation where they have to click the link to activate the account. That part was down."

"Couldn't you fix that from your parents' place or have someone else take care of the problem back home? Isn't that a perk of running an internet company? You don't have to be fixed to an address."

"You don't understand."

Madison clasped her hands on the table, leaned forward slightly. "Then enlighten me."

"The servers needed to be reset, and the programming had a small glitch that I needed to fix. I don't let anyone else touch that."

"Again, you couldn't do that from anywhere?"

Silence.

"Mr. Silverman, please answer Detective Knight's question," Terry prompted.

"I could have, yeah, okay. Is that what you want me to say? How about I killed my best friend, too?"

"Is that a confession?"

"Of course it's not." He reached for the cup in front of him but placed it back on the table after noticing it was empty. "Listen, I'm just sort of hands-on. I'm not a real computer geek."

Terry got up. "That contradicts what you just said about not letting anyone else touch your programming."

"Whatever."

Madison shrugged her shoulders. "Fine, you left, but why not fix the problem and then come back? You had been planning to stay with your parents until the twenty-third of January."

Neil slumped in his chair. "I feel like I'm being accused of Chris's murder."

"Should you be?" Madison stamped out.

Neil waved his hand, reached for the cup again, and this time pushed it away. He rubbed a hand to his throat. "I— Okay, this can't get back to my mother." He paused, and Madison nodded. "I'm not into the family thing, Christmas, the gifts, the ceremony. I'm more of a simple person. But I did all that for her. I was just tired of being around them. I love my parents, but I prefer my independence."

Madison settled back in her chair now, but kept her back straight. "A simple person doesn't buy his father a mansion and insist he accept the offer."

"Listen, I know it might sound stupid, but it's the truth. My home in Hastings is large, too, but it's what society expects. I have money, so I have to flaunt it. Isn't that what this world's about?"

"Tell us about your fight with Chris," she requested.

"It was just words. It never came to blows."

"Why did you fight?"

"We just never saw things the same way anymore." His voice cracked, and he sniffled, but mostly Madison picked up on the pain in his eyes. It was just a gut feeling, but it made her suspect they might have been more than close friends.

"You were lovers," she concluded, and Neil's gaze jumped to hers. "But Chris didn't want to continue?"

Neil's eyes beaded with tears. "He said it didn't mean anything to him. He'd been high when we started out. He was curious. He said he'd been with a lot of women, and believe me, he had. He was just all about living life to the fullest, living in the now, you know? I didn't even think it would go as far as it did."

"You loved him," Terry interjected.

Neil glanced at Terry, back to Madison. "Yeah, I did. And I still do."

"When did you and Chris begin seeing each other as a couple?" Madison asked.

"As teenagers. It was nothing serious, at first. Even to me. But we'd keep falling into bed together...and I thought it was starting to mean something to him, too."

Madison relaxed her posture to encourage Neil to keep speaking. "But it wasn't?"

Neil shook his head.

"When was the last time you got together?"

"When I was down for the holidays."

Madison tried to contain her surprise and spike in adrenaline. She wanted to revisit the reason for the fight between Neil and Chris. "So your relationship did have something to do with the fight, then?" she broached with caution. "As you said you never saw things the same way anymore."

Neil's eyes drifted to the table, and for the first time, Madison sensed shame mingled with anger and hurt.

"There was more to it," she concluded. "You loved Chris, but you weren't at his funeral or gravesite eulogy. Why?"

Neil met her gaze and the blanks filled in.

"It was because of Marcus Randall."

"He hated me, for what I did to his son. 'Turned him into a faggot,' he said."

"When was this?"

"He walked in, not when we were…you know, but we were holding each other," Neil relayed, not answering Madison's question. "I'd just kissed Chris's cheek. If he'd come in a second later, he wouldn't have seen anything. Again, chalk it up to my luck. And now, I'm not the same person because of all this. Before, I considered myself a straight arrow, as my dad likes to put it. My mother, she doesn't know. It would devastate her. She wants grandchildren."

"So Mr. Randall spoke those hateful words, but did he do anything?" Madison pressed.

Neil sighed deeply. "He told me to get off his property and told me not to come back. Ever."

"That's all?" Madison said. "He didn't make you leave?"

Neil shook his head.

Madison found that hard to believe but was going to let the matter go for now. "What happened after he told you to leave?"

"I'd never seen Mr. Randall so angry. His face was a bright red. He had a pulse tapping in his cheek. His nostrils were flaring. I thought he was going to beat me. But Chris stood in front of me as a barrier. Randall yelled at him, told him he was disappointed in him, that he would never amount to anything because he was a queer."

"Do you think Marcus Randall knew about you and him before that night?"

A shoulder lifted, fell. "He must have to say I made Chris a…faggot. I'm surprised he never had me killed."

"Had you killed? You believe Mr. Randall could be a murderer?"

His gaze diverted any attempts she made at reestablishing eye contact. "Mr. Randall is a man who takes care of business, if you know what I mean. That's all I'm saying."

"What happened after Chris stood in front of you?"

Neil shook his head. "I've said too much already."

"Did he hit Chris?"

Silence.

"We can protect you from Randall."

"I have a business I have to get back to, Detective." Neil went to stand.

"Sit down," she barked. "Answer the question."

He laid both of his hands flat on the table. "He— I don't want to get killed. My parents, they still live beside Randall. If he finds out, he might hurt them."

"If Randall does, we'll be all over him. You've stated your concerns on record."

"Wow, thanks. That would bring them back." He paused. "He came in, smoking a cigar, not like the ones I smoke, but I remember the smell of it. They always smell so sweet."

The mention of the burn to Chris's hand had never been disclosed to the media. That would imply that Neil was, in fact, with Chris around the time of his death. Madison could hear herself breathing.

Neil went on. "He flipped out that Chris would attempt to protect me. Chris had taken a hit already."

"A hit?" Madison wasn't sure if he meant drugs or a physical blow.

"He had done some coke," Neil clarified. "He went to push his father away. All I remember then was Chris screaming."

"He was burned by the cigar?"

"Yeah, I think so."

"Then what happened?"

"Mr. Randall left."

And they had circled back to that: Randall just leaving. Is that really how everything had taken place? Madison also had this sinking feeling that she and Terry may have placed too much emphasis on the burn to Chris's hand. They'd run with the assumption Chris's killer had done it, but it was just as possible that it had happened in an altercation apart from his murder—like the one Neil had just mentioned. Maybe they'd been too narrow-minded. That thought made her sick.

CHAPTER FORTY-ONE

Madison settled into her chair and tried to push aside her uneasy feelings. "What happened after...when you were left alone with Chris?"

Neil went on. "Chris said he had his fun, and we were over for good."

"That would have really hurt. Probably made you angry, too."

"Not enough to kill him, if that's what you're getting at," Neil countered with some heat.

"You gave us the impression your romantic relationship with Chris was rather casual. The last time you got together had been over the holidays. What about before that?"

"It had been a year, at least. I met someone, and we hit it off—until we didn't. When I came back here for the holidays, I tried to reinitiate things with Chris. Told him I was coming off a bad breakup. Maybe I should have known he only got together with me one more time as a favor to me, not that it actually meant anything to him." Neil stopped speaking and licked his lips. His chin quivered from holding his emotions at bay. "Before I left...that night...morning...Chris called me a faggot. I could take that from Mr. Randall, but Chris... Though that didn't hurt as much as him telling me to leave."

"What did you do?"

"I left," he spat. "It was clear he didn't even want to be friends anymore." Neil's eyes were watery, unfocused. "I like to think he would have come around." He toyed with the empty cup. "Have you spoken with Ryan Turner?" When she didn't say anything, he continued. "They were childhood buddies. Like this." He linked his fingers together like a chain.

"Were Ryan and Chris ever lovers?" Terry asked, maybe trying to figure out the correlation and why Neil had brought him up. Madison was a little thrown by the new direction that Neil had laid out.

Neil sat back and looked at Terry. "You're kidding me, right? Nah, Ryan would never do anything like that. Straight as they come. He smells a chick, and he's hounding up her skirt, down her pants, you name it."

"So there was no way he was jealous of your relationship," Madison said. "At least the way he perceived it to be?"

"Absolutely no way."

"Do you like boating?" Madison tossed out there, bringing the conversation back to where she wanted it to go.

"My dad does." Neil furrowed his brow. "What does this have to do with anything?"

"Did you ever go in your father's boathouse?"

"No."

"So you'd have no reason to touch a rescue jaw that we found in there?"

"A *what*?"

"It's a long pole with metal tongs on the end, used for rescuing people from drowning."

"Don't remember touching one of those."

Madison's insides fluttered. She had caught him in a lie, but did that mean Neil was their killer? "Your prints say otherwise."

"And how do you have my prints?"

"That lovely assault charge from five years ago."

Neil crossed his arms. "Maybe I want a lawyer."

"Is that a request?"

He uncrossed his arms. "I really have nothing to hide, but if you keep implying things that are not there, I won't be left with much of a choice, will I?"

Madison studied his body language, his eyes, his face, the way his arms were folding and unfolding. He was uncomfortable. He was hiding something, and they needed to figure out what. "You mentioned that Mr. Randall's cigars smell different from yours. So, you smoke them?"

"Yes, I do."

"Brand?"

Neil reached inside his suit jacket, pulled out a cigar, and held it up.

"Would you mind if…" Madison reached for the cigar.

"No, go ahead. Though I don't understand why you're interested."

"It's not for you to worry about," Madison said, but if his cigar matched the composition of the one that burned Chris's hand, he might need to do some explaining—he'd just told them that Marcus Randall had burned Chris.

He shared glances between them. "You're not letting me go, are you? I can see it written all over your faces."

"Until we can get some things clarified, we'll need to hold you. We'll also need your DNA." By a reach, it might match up to the piece of cigar that Terry collected from Randall's boathouse—assuming there was DNA on it to cross-reference.

"I didn't do anything."

"If that's the case, you have nothing to worry about. But do yourself another favor and answer this question: were you smoking a cigar in the boathouse that night?"

"No. Now can I go?"

"As soon as we process your DNA and get some results."

"Great, and how long will that take?"

"At least twenty-four hours."

"You're kidding me. I can't grieve him like this."

"Listen, the results might come back sooner than later. If they do, we'll get you out of here."

Madison got up and left the room. Once Terry joined her in the hall, she turned to him. "Do you think Silverman did it?"

"I'm not too sure, but he's obviously a liar. He said he didn't touch the rescue jaw, but he obviously had."

"Okay, so just listen to me."

"Oh, lord, is it going to be more about Randall?"

"Well, wouldn't he have good motive?"

"Except for the fact he's Chris's father."

She gave him a blank stare. "Yes, besides that." Terry went to walk away. "Just one minute. What if Randall couldn't handle it anymore? His son was good for business in the sense he traveled, set up foreign accounts, and we'll assume was at the heart of his counterfeiting ring. He's the one who made it work. But beyond that, he betrayed his father and let him down in every other way. He had everything, yet chose to deal drugs, and on top of it, was an acting gay man for some time. For someone like Randall, who prided himself on his reputation, that could have been the final straw."

Terry sighed deeply. "I hate to agree with you."

"Geez, thanks."

"But, yeah, it could have been. Though there's something that's not sitting perfectly well with me. He said that Mr. Randall just left after his outburst. Mr. Randall doesn't strike me as the kind to just leave. He would have seen Neil tossed off his property."

"I was thinking the same thing." She glanced back toward the interrogation room. She hesitated to admit to something else she'd thought of, but it was probably best to get ahead of things. "All along we've assumed that the cigar burn was part of Chris's struggle that ended up resulting in his death, but maybe we've been narrow-minded in that regard. The burn could have happened, then the murder. Two separate acts, two incidents."

"Could have been two different people involved, too."

"Sure. What we have is a witness who just said that Randall burnt his son with a cigar."

"Actually, you said that. He agreed," Terry interjected. "And who knows what to believe that comes out of his mouth."

"Fine, but if Mr. Randall did burn Chris, it would only demonstrate how angry he had been."

"It sounded like a push-and-shove match—again running with the assumption Neil told us the truth. But the cigar burn could have been an accident. As you just said, two separate things: the burn and the murder."

"But what if Mr. Randall returned after Neil left and killed his own son?"

"And that's a crapshoot to prove."

He was right, and she hated it. "Well, we should still find out if the piece of cigar you found in the boathouse can confirm or discredit Neil's account of what happened there."

They had dropped it off at the lab before getting to the church that afternoon.

"Even if Chris's DNA is present, we might not know if Mr. Randall smoked it. And so what if we do? You just said—"

"I know…about the burn and the murder being two different incidents."

"Right. Then why so much emphasis on who burned Chris at this point? It won't necessarily get us closer to his killer."

"But it might."

Terry shook his head. "You've lost me."

"It could tell us if Neil Silverman is a big, fat liar and possibly hiding a murder." Her phone rang and she answered. She listened to her caller's message, finding it hard to believe who it was and what was being said. When the call ended, she stared at Terry. "You're not going to believe this."

"Hit me."

"That was Ryan Turner, and he's ready to talk. Without a lawyer."

CHAPTER FORTY-TWO

It was dark when Madison and Terry stepped outside of the station, and she dropped by her apartment to see to Hershey on the way to Turner's house. Her little furball needed some love, food, and time to sniff the wind and take care of business. Terry made a huge fuss over the chocolate lab, but eventually she pried him away.

"What's Randall going to think when Ryan speaks to us without a lawyer?" Madison asked once they were back in the car.

"He won't be too thr…illed…that's…for…sure." Terry's words were torn apart by a yawn.

"You going to make it?"

"Not really sure. It wasn't a good night last night. Annabelle kept getting up to use the bathroom. She blames it on the baby."

"Guess the blame game starts early." Madison laughed. She had noticed that with parents a long time ago.

"What do you mean?"

"Parents use their children as excuses for everything from running late, to having a headache, to not sleeping." Those *side effects* only cemented her desire not to have any children.

"Sounds as though they're probably to blame."

"But yours hasn't even entered the world yet. How can it already be guilty of something?" She reached over, slapped her partner's arm. "Seriously."

Terry scratched the back of his neck. "Just a license you get, I guess." He laughed.

Madison pulled to a stop in front of the address provided. The house was in a nice neighborhood. Stonework landscaped the front lawn and probably cost more than her rent for five years. "This is the right address?"

"Number 5233?" Terry leaned forward, looking out the windshield. "Yep, this is the place."

"Randall must take care of him personally as well."

"Well, he didn't find him making a move on his son." Terry spoke over his shoulder as he went to get out of the car.

She grimaced. "Not exactly a joke told in good taste, Terry."

"Hey." He held up his hands. "I can't say I'd be happy about that."

She slammed her door. "Within five minutes, your unborn child has been blamed for keeping you and Annabelle up last night, and now you're prejudging his or her sexuality preference."

"No, I'm just saying, I'm not sure I could handle…walking in on…"

"You should love them no matter what."

"I will. It's just that—"

"Maybe you're not ready to be a parent."

"Says the girl who didn't even have a goldfish before I got her Hershey for Christmas."

"Oh, shut up." She punched him in the shoulder. He rubbed the area.

"I've missed the abuse lately. Bring it." He started laughing, but it stopped short when the front door opened. No one was there.

They walked inside, and the door shut behind them. It was starting to feel like they'd entered a haunted house until she saw Turner standing there.

"Follow me," he said, and led them down a narrow hallway toward the back of the house. The curtains were drawn on every window they passed. Turner took them into a sitting room that was furnished as if everything had been touched by the magic of a professional interior designer.

Turner went straight to a bar cart and poured himself a glass of whiskey. He swigged it back in a couple large mouthfuls, pinched the tip of his nose, dragged his hand down his face, then poured a couple more fingers' worth and took the drink with him. "Let's sit." He plopped down on a burgundy-upholstered chair, and Madison and Terry took seats in two others.

"You know who Chris's killer is?" Madison asked, getting right to the point.

Turner nodded.

"Why not come to us before now?"

"I wasn't in my right state of mind."

Like now? is what Madison wanted to say. His eyes were dodgy and very glossy. The booze was hitting him hard, and if his dilated pupils were any indication, he was also on drugs.

"And…and I have things to confess." He slurped back some alcohol. "We were partners."

"Partners?" Maybe Neil had been wrong about Chris and Ryan's relationship…or in denial.

"I guess more like brothers," he slurred.

"No, you mentioned that before," Madison said. "Why say partners now?" Then she pieced it together. "You helped make the counterfeit money. That's why your partial print was found on a bill. You got careless."

"I wasn't careless. It's just that Chris was spending it on his own things, and I wanted some for myself." He rolled his eyes. "It's not even like he needed fake money."

Madison gestured around the space. "Doesn't look like you do, either."

"He took care of me."

"But he didn't want to anymore?" She was just tossing things out to see what sort of reactions she could elicit.

"He said he was protecting me from myself. He said I got myself in too deep already." Turner's voice cracked, and he sobbed into his hands.

"Listen, we don't care about the counterfeiting. Our job is to find out who killed Chris." Madison leaned forward. "Did he turn his back on you, then you killed him for it? You grabbed the rescue jaw and—"

"A what?" His forehead pinched like he had a headache.

"A rescue jaw is a long pole with a metal tong at the end," Terry interjected.

"Oh my god, that's what killed him?" Uncontrolled sobbing mingled with one outcry. "Why the fuck?"

Madison could feel Terry shrink beside her. He detested swearing, and every time this word was pulled out, he responded the same way.

After a while, Turner seemed to compose himself enough to talk. He swallowed hard and loud. "I've seen that…that thing you described in the boathouse."

He just confirmed the existence of one. Why didn't they see it when they looked around? Maybe the killer let it go into the river with Chris?

"Where is it kept?" Madison asked, careful to word her question in the present tense.

"Uh…" He spaced out on them for a few seconds, his mouth gaping open and shut, open and shut, open and shut. "On the wall, held up by brackets."

"We never found one there," she admitted.

"It's there! That's where it goes."

Madison remained quiet, another possibility striking her. The killer could have drowned Chris with Randall's rescue jaw and then stowed it in the Silverman boathouse, but if that was the case, the killer would need a key. This wasn't looking good for Neil Silverman. "What was the color of the rescue jaw?" she asked.

"I think it was blue."

Color-wise, that was a match to the one found in the Silverman boathouse. Was that just a coincidence?

Madison leaned forward and said her next words gently. "Do you know who killed Chris?"

Turner threw his glass into the nearby fireplace, where it shattered. Madison jumped.

"That lawyer's on Randall's payroll," Turner said. "I can't trust him."

Madison swallowed deeply. *That lawyer* was the man she'd been sleeping with for months. But what did Blake have to do with her question?

"Did Mr. Golden kill Chris?" she squeaked out.

Turner's legs bounced up and down, and his eyes fixed on the fireplace. "Things I know…" He swallowed hard. "They could destroy Mr. R."

Madison let out a breath, grateful Turner's focus had turned away from Blake.

"He had Chris do things for him. Illegal things." Turner's gaze drifted to the bar cart.

Madison reentered the conversation. "Like deposit counterfeit money, transfer it, and set up dummy companies?" She'd already asked outright if Turner and Chris were partners in the counterfeiting, but he hadn't come out and fully admitted to it.

He glanced at her. "I'm not saying anything."

"You were involved with it. That's how you and Chris were partners," Madison said.

Turner visibly trembled and shook his head. "We got ourselves into trouble, and now they're going to kill me."

It could be a challenge to interview people when they were sober. When they were hopped up on drugs and alcohol, it was exasperating. Ryan just kept jumping all over the place. Madison stood. "If you're wasting our time here, that might be the least of your worries. Now, speak."

Turner met her eyes. "I owed money to…Mafia-type people." He snorted, partially laughed. "You'll think I made this up, and I don't give a shit if you do. Ever hear of Dimitre Petrov?"

Do I know him?

She sat back down.

Because of her, the Russian Mafia don was serving time in prison. Sadly, she could only get one murder charge to stick, but she'd take what she could—not that his incarceration in any way impeded his organization. Dimitre wielded power from behind bars. She was also quite sure that Dimitre was responsible for the death of a young defense attorney—her one cold case that would haunt her until she got closure.

"Yes. I know him," she eventually said. "But I'm not sure where you're going with this. Did you do something to him?" *Does it have anything to do with Chris's murder*, she screamed in her head.

"I stole from him. And I'm talking hundreds of thousands."

"And yet you're alive to talk about it?" Madison scoffed. "I don't think so."

"But Chris isn't," Turner punched out, and she took the hit to the gut. "He paid them back for me. Every penny…" His words faded.

Madison was starting to put the pieces together in her mind. "He paid off the Russian Mafia with counterfeit money?"

Turner shook as if tremors rocked his body. "I know he did. He bragged about getting away with it, too." His eyes glazed over, full of fear. "Fuck, I'm dead! They're going to kill me, too!" He rose to his feet, paced in a circle. "You've got to get me out of here. They probably know I brought them into this already. Shit!"

Madison put a hand on Turner's shoulder. "Calm down."

He moved out from under her touch. "*Calm down*? They're going to kill me. How am I supposed to calm down?"

The lawyer's dead body…bullet wounds…blood…

She shook aside the onslaught of images from her cold case.

"How do you know that they didn't off Chris?" Turner's voice reached a higher octave.

"Well, if they wanted to make a statement, his body would have been displayed. If they didn't want him found, he wouldn't have been."

"Maybe they didn't think it through."

"They always think it through. They never mess up." *Or rarely...* She should be content she had been able to pin one murder charge on Dimitre.

Turner swallowed audibly. Fear swept over his expression as his face paled. "That's reassuring, coming from a cop."

"Listen. Chris would have had one to three bullets in him, or there would have been evidence of torture." One burn mark on the back of Chris's hand didn't qualify.

"Please go, please. They're going to kill me."

"You asked us to come here. Why?" Madison couldn't contain her frustration any longer.

"To confess. To let you know it might be my fault Chris is dead."

"Unless you held him und—"

"You don't get it. He paid back my debt in fake cash," he punched out.

"Come on, let's go."

"Where?"

"Downtown."

Turner's face became a mask of panic, and he looked at Terry. "Why the—"

"If the Russians are after you, you'll be safer with us," Madison cut in. "You also confessed to having knowledge of the counterfeiting ring and didn't deny involvement. The Secret Service will want to talk to you."

"I've already talked to them. And what do you care... about the money part? You investigate murder—that's what you said."

"We don't have a choice. I'm sorry."

Madison and Terry escorted Turner out of the house. She knew they were betraying Turner's trust by taking him in, but she didn't see any way around it. And she hadn't been lying when she'd told Turner he'd be safer with them than on his own.

Terry guided Turner to the back seat, and Madison stood outside the driver's door, the hairs standing up on her arms and the back of her neck. She felt eyes on them.

After Turner was in the car, she whispered to Terry, "We're being watched."

"I feel it, too." He looked around, careful not to alert Turner to their concerns, while she was more obvious. She scanned the street, left and right, but saw nothing.

Madison and Terry got into the car.

"They're going to kill me. They will," Turner said from the back seat. He must have sensed something wasn't right.

"Just stay calm and keep it down." Madison hated the unsettled feeling of being watched without being able to see who was doing the watching.

"Forget it. I changed my—"

An SUV's high beams came on across the street. It was nearly impossible to discern the make and model. She pulled to the mouth of Turner's driveway, hoping to get a better look.

"It's a Lincoln Navigator, recent model," she said.

"Too bad front plates aren't required. Maybe we could ID the driver."

"Assuming we could make it out."

She turned onto the street, and the Navigator followed her lead and crawled along in the lane beside them. The windows were darkly tinted, but the passenger's window was cracked open, and a cigarette butt was flicked out.

Sergey, one of Dimitre Petrov's right-hand men, was a chain-smoker. Could it be him and Anatolli in the Lincoln?

Madison glanced at Terry and remained silent. She still didn't think the Russians were involved with Chris's death, but she did wonder if that was just because someone else had gotten to him first. She spoke over her shoulder to Ryan. "We're probably the only reason you're still alive."

CHAPTER FORTY-THREE

"Let me get this straight. You have three people in holding for one murder?" Winston didn't look impressed. She wondered why he was even at the station this time of night, and on a Saturday to boot.

"Two of them are being charged with drug possession and dealing. One's waiting for lab results. This guy's just come in to talk some more." Madison didn't mention anything about the counterfeit money and Turner's knowledge of it. Although it would have to come out. She just preferred it to be after she'd had her time with him.

"Came in to talk some more? Who?" Winston moved farther into the observation room and looked through the one-way mirror. His head snapped to Madison. "Ryan Turner? Where is his lawyer? You won't be able to use anything he says."

"He's waived his right to counsel, in writing." They'd gotten that just after parking him in an interrogation room.

"I don't know what you're up to, but—"

Terry walked in with two cups full of mud brew from the coffee machine in the bullpen. He handed one to Madison.

"Seriously, I'm not sure what you two are up to, but it better mean this case is coming to a close soon."

"Well, I sure hope so."

"Do I have all your updated paperwork on my desk?"

"You will."

"Damn right I will. I want that waiting for me when I come in. And I'll be here early, so you best complete it before leaving tonight." He left the room.

First a Saturday, now a Sunday. Madison might start to believe in unicorns.

"I'm never gonna get home," Terry said.

Madison eyed the coffee, steeling herself before braving a sip. "Listen, it's the job. You know that by now."

He took a large sip of his coffee as if the flavor didn't affect him at all. "I know what the job is, Maddy, but this case is a mess. The sarge is right."

"And whose fault is that? Is it mine? If it were anyone other than a friend of the chief, we'd be in that boathouse without prejudice. We'd be able to do our jobs the proper way. We'd have a warrant by now."

"Based on what?"

"You know the answer to that question," she said, but she went on to spell it out anyway. "If the scene of the crime is uncertain, you start with the victim's house. With our case, the boathouse is in the right location upriver to account for currents and when Chris surfaced. As well as the fact he had gasoline in his lungs. If it were anyone else and the right to search the property was withheld, it would be deemed suspicious or even obstruction." She looked down into the cup again, prepared for another sip. "This stuff tastes like crap."

"What doesn't kill you makes you stronger," Terry lamented. He held his cup in a toast gesture toward the one-way mirror. "Shall we?"

"Let's do." Madison led the way into the interrogation room.

"The Secret Service is on their way yet?" Turner looked uncomfortable under the buzzing fluorescent lights.

Madison walked around the table, sat on the edge facing him. "Not yet. We still have some questions."

Terry stood by the door, leaned against it with his cup held tightly in his hand. Steam rose from it.

"That was the Russians…in the car next to us, wasn't it? They're going to kill me," Turner said.

She didn't want to scare the kid, but the profile fit: surveilling large, black SUV, dark-tinted windows. That could have fit the stereotypical image of any shady criminal, but given the fact Turner had gotten himself entangled with the Russians, the vehicle scored high in favor of it belonging to the mob.

"I think so," she said gently, then took a seat across from him. "I'd say you have their interest."

"Which, for the Russian Mafia, means that I'm dead."

"Not if I can help it."

"Oh, God, you can't let me out of here." He shrunk into himself and clenched his fists.

"Just calm down. Breathe." Terry put his cup on the table.

"How the hell am I supposed to do that?" Turner tried to steady his gaze on Terry, but his pupils were dilated and unfocused.

"Just tell us how you stole money from Dimitre Petrov in the first place," Madison told Turner. It might be a detour from getting to Chris's murder, but sometimes you had to pull on every string to solve a case.

"How does that help Chris?"

"It helps you."

Turner shook, his nerves dialing in again. "I'm not as dumb as I look. I know that I come across like some cokehead that's just waiting around for his next high, who's killed off all his brain cells." He shook his head. "But that's not who I am. That's how I choose to be perceived."

"Why?" she asked.

"If I come across like that, people don't expect anything from me. I'm not a threat." He shrugged his shoulders. "It's rather genius of me, actually."

"Genius of you to take drugs?" Madison pressed her lips together and shook her head. "Don't think so."

"I don't give a shit what you believe," he spat. "And all I have to do is scream for a lawyer, and this show of yours is over."

"And all we have to do is put you back on the street."

A small pulse started in his cheek, and his eyes darkened.

"How did you come to owe the Mafia money in the first place?" Madison said coolly. She was tiring quickly of this kid.

Turner rolled his eyes. "I can count cards."

"I'm not following."

"Then just shut up and listen," Turner snapped. "I counted cards at Fostrich Casino."

"Not too genius," Madison said, taking another jab at Turner's claim of being intelligent. "The Russians run that place."

"I know that *now*." Turner paused, stared at the table for a few seconds. "They found out and demanded I pay back my winnings, but the money was gone."

"How much are we talking about?" Madison was truly starting to fear for the kid's life.

"Close to a couple hundred thousand. And before you ask, a fast car and loose women."

"That's a lot of women."

"If you're not factoring in a decent car and sweet pu—"

"You say that P-word, I'll deliver you to the Russians myself."

Turner's brows shot down. "You're a cop."

"I'm also a woman, and that word is beyond offensive."

Turner went on. "I bought a Corvette Grand Sport. I offered it as repayment, but they wanted the cash. I went to Chris, and he told me he'd take care of it. Well, he took care of it all right. He came back later, laughing and telling me how gullible they were."

Madison addressed Terry. "Because the replicas were so close to the real thing." She turned to Turner. "When did this repayment happen?"

"Around the start of January, I guess, maybe a little later."

"Your friend goes missing on January tenth and you didn't think this was pertinent information?" Madison rose to her feet.

"Even you didn't think it was the Russians when I first brought them up."

I'm going to strangle this guy!

"That's still not answering my question." Madison took a few deep breaths. Trying to talk with Turner was comparable to banging one's head on a wall. "Listen, it might not be them behind Chris's death, but that doesn't mean they won't come for you. The particular Russians you got yourselves involved with are some of the most dangerous men on the planet. They would think nothing of ripping out your spleen and serving it to their boss on a silver platter with a glass of merlot." Madison got up and paced, a hand to her forehead.

The door opened to the interrogation room, and Blake stormed in, McAlexandar behind him. "What the hell are you doing speaking to my client without my presence?" His brown eyes accused her along with his words.

She bristled. "He waived his rights."

"He is in no mental state to provide such approval. He is grieving the loss of a friend who was put in the ground today." Blake studied Turner. "He is also under the influence." He motioned with his hand for Turner to get up, and he did.

"Knight, what the hell are you doing?" McAlexandar barked.

All she could think about was Turner's safety. If they released him now, he was as good as dead. He probably wouldn't make it through the night. "He knows about the counterfeiting," she rushed out.

"You told me you didn't care about that!" Turner spat.

"I lied." She stood her ground, even though she was quaking inside. She attributed it to a couple factors. One, Blake's betrayal for working for a man who stood against everything she was; and second, she feared Turner's fate if he left the station. She could have alluded to Turner's participation in the counterfeiting ring, but she had only said he had knowledge of it.

"Ah, shit." McAlexandar put a hand to his forehead.

Blake stood in front of Turner, his back toward him, and said to Madison, "Everything he told you is to be taken off the record. *Everything.*"

McAlexandar kept shaking his head.

"He waived his rights." Her chest tightened at the sinking feeling she was losing this battle.

"You coerced a man under the influence of drugs and alcohol, who is in no emotional state to waive his rights." Blake held steady eye contact with her.

"I didn't coerce anyone."

"Is that what he'll remember in the morning?"

Emotion churned within her, bringing the urge to cry, but anger fueled her more, leaving her speechless.

"We'll be leaving." Blake left the room with Turner.

"You're making a mistake." The words managed to escape her closing throat.

He kept walking. She was sure he heard her.

"Detective Knight, you've crossed the line this time. We'll be meeting with Sergeant Winston first thing Monday morning. I'm giving you a day to get your story straight." McAlexandar stood there like an ox, solid and unmovable, stubborn and unyielding.

"Turner's dead. We just signed that kid's death certificate!"

"Everything's so dramatic with you, Knight."

"Chris went into the water inside the Randall boathouse." She was now in the mood to fight.

"Excuse me?"

"You heard me. The ice in there had been broken and has re-formed."

"You're saying that Marcus Randall killed his son? We're back to that?" McAlexandar scoffed laughter toward the ceiling.

"That's not what I'm saying. What I am saying is, Chris was killed in that boathouse. The timeline, the ice breakage, the—" She stopped talking. She was so worked up she almost mentioned the piece of cigar they'd collected from Randall's boathouse just to spite him, but that would get Terry in trouble. There was no sense dragging him down with her.

"The *what*? Don't stop there. By all means, continue running off at the mouth. I'm rather enjoying it." He crossed his arms.

"Why are you so protective of Marcus Randall?" she shot back.

McAlexandar's hardened face cracked in lighthearted laughter. "You've got some nerve, I'll give you that, but there's one thing you lack, and that's rational thinking. You always blow it right there." He tapped a finger to his forehead.

She was so angry it was hard to form words. "If you have nothing to hide—you or Randall—then give Terry and me access to the surveillance footage from the camera outside of Randall's boathouse."

He blinked, squeezing his eyes shut. "You hard of hearing?"

She was already in trouble; she might as well keep going. "The footage from that camera might help us."

"Let me get this straight." He shifted his weight from one leg to the other. "You want my cooperation?" He laughed. "You do have nerve."

The energy in the room was tangible. He'd have her badge pulled tonight if he could.

"Chief," Terry began, finally getting involved, "I'm sure Marcus Randall wants to know who killed his son. That video might help us figure that out."

He stood there looking between them, not speaking a word for what seemed like a long time.

"You seem to think Randall's innocent. Let us prove it," she said, approaching the matter from another direction.

"You should keep quiet and let your partner here do the talking." McAlexandar pointed a finger at Terry. "I will talk to him and see what he says. No promises. And…I hope you're listening, Knight." He glanced at her, then back to Terry. "If Randall lets us have access to the camera footage, I want you in charge of it."

Madison protested, "You can't do that. I'm the lead on this case."

"You'd be surprised by what I can do." He left the room.

"Urgh." She let out a loud sigh. "I can't believe that guy."

"Well, you best start because I don't want a new partner. Although it might be easier to break in a new one than to patch this one up."

She was about to lash out at him verbally and physically, but there was the hint of a smile on his lips. Only Terry could make her feel remotely better after a confrontation like the one she'd just had with McAlexandar.

CHAPTER FORTY-FOUR

McAlexandar had let the matter rest for the night. He wasn't going to approach his greatest ally with more about his son on the day he was put in the ground. But with a new day came strong hesitation. What if his asking Marcus for the camera footage made him question his loyalty?

"Go ahead, Chief. I'll let him know you're coming in." The man at the gatehouse opened the barrier, allowing him access to the estate.

It was ten thirty Sunday morning when he made his way through the winding drive to Marcus's front door.

Tony Medcalf stood there, motioning for him to enter the home. "He's in his office."

Marcus's prized stallion was stationed outside the office, as usual. He grabbed the door for McAlexandar and shut him inside.

Marcus's back was to the door, and he was looking out the window. "The grounds never look the same this time of year. It's winter, and everything dies." It was possible yesterday had changed his friend in ways McAlexandar couldn't understand.

Marcus swiveled to face McAlexandar. His arms rested on the arms of the chair. His one hand held a rocks glass with a couple of ice cubes; very little amber liquid remained. His eyes were bloodshot. McAlexandar sensed the grief as a darkness that comes with the acceptance that a loved one has died.

"Maybe I should go," McAlexandar offered.

"You're here now. But I have learned something this week. Life for people like us...it seems so certain." His lips curled downward and pressed together, if only for a second. "It's not." He inhaled deeply through his nose, out through his mouth. "But we have to move on."

McAlexandar was starting to feel extremely uncomfortable. He wasn't the supportive, brotherly figure, the shoulder to cry on. He was more a friend during the good times. Randall sat before him a broken man, only one who was in denial. And that was worse. His tongue was dry for words as his mind raced with thoughts. The only reason he had stayed seated is because this broken man still had the power to make him mayor. And until he saw evidence that was in jeopardy, he would stick around. After all, he was in politics, and playing a part went along with that. "My symp—"

"I'll stop you there. I've heard too much of that." Marcus held up his glass. "Scotch?" He asked as he walked across the room.

Based on his unsteady steps, it was clear he'd had a few already. Maybe the alcohol was to blame for Marcus's behavior.

"That's right, you don't drink, do you?" Marcus laughed. "Perrier water, then? Straight up or with a twist of lime?" He placed a crystal glass hard on the bar cart. "This life is ridiculous."

He had to find a way to get out of here; he couldn't subject himself to witnessing any more of this. Possibly if he just said what he came here to say and went on about his day? "The detectives searched the boathouse, and—"

"Did they find anything?" He was still at the bar cart, his back to McAlexandar.

He hesitated. "They did."

Marcus returned with a drink and directed McAlexandar to a plush, green leather sofa with brass pins. "Please forgive me, I forgot your water over there." He made a motion to go to the bar cart.

McAlexandar held out a hand to stop him. The man before him had truly changed, at least for the time being. "They found evidence that the ice was broken, like something or someone—"

"Chris."

McAlexandar nodded. "Possible."

"Is that all they found?"

McAlexandar was placed in another tough spot. How was he supposed to answer that? Marcus could change moods on a whim, but today's display of weakness was new. Based on disrespect of that feature, he proceeded with the truth. "Part of a cigar."

Marcus took a long draw on the scotch, and just watching him made the craving bite McAlexandar. He conjured up the flavor, its woody texture coating his tongue… He took a deep breath.

"You don't have control of your people." Marcus placed the scotch down and twisted a gold ring on one of his thick fingers. "Not attractive, Patrick."

I'll tell you what's not attractive… He bit down the urge to say that out loud.

"I would have expected more of you," Marcus added. Seconds passed, then he said, "But I tell you what." He reached out his arm, extending it along the back of the sofa. "I'll allow it to be reviewed as evidence, but this is extended with one stipulation."

McAlexandar felt the back of his neck pinching from anger. The man he knew was starting to resurface; he could see it in his eyes. "By all means."

"I'll allow the testing on the cigar; however, if it in any way makes me look guilty of killing my son, you better fix it or I'll have it dismissed. Do you hear me? I'll fight it. Your people were given access to the boathouse for a look-see; there was no authorization given for probing around, collecting items from my property."

McAlexandar nodded his agreement. He knew enough that for normal people, that defense wouldn't stand. With the cigar in plain sight, the detectives had a right to collect it, but with powerful lawyers and judges in his corner, Marcus could get away with it. He'd claim not to have authorized access to the boathouse in the first place.

"Now, is that all you came for?" The words carried impatience.

"There is one more thing, actually."

"By all means, Patrick." Marcus made an obvious glance at the grandfather clock.

"Can we have the video footage from the boathouse camera?"

Marcus laughed, hard and from deep within. McAlexandar didn't join him. "You're serious?" When he didn't say anything, Marcus leaned forward. "Seeing as we're talking favors, how's mine coming along?"

CHAPTER FORTY-FIVE

Madison played with Hershey for a bit before heading into the station. She was actually sad to leave him, even though pouring herself into the investigation today was the best thing she could do for her mental and emotional health. She'd barely slept last night as thoughts of the case and her personal life mingled. The way Blake had looked yesterday was seared into her memory. Their relationship was over, and there was no doubt in her mind he was in agreement.

Terry was taking the day to be with his wife, unless any major developments came about, but Madison had called Cynthia and roped her into coming in. Madison met up with her in the lab.

"There wasn't any DNA to pull from the cigar."

"Which one?"

"Oh, the piece of one, from the boathouse."

Madison nodded. It had been a long shot anyway, but it would have been nice to at least forensically put someone else in that boathouse with Chris—whether that was Mr. Randall or Neil Silverman. Not that it meant the person smoking a cigar had killed Chris. Sometimes it was easier to stay locked in on something than let it go, adopt a broader perspective. She took a deep breath. "What about the cigar type itself? Is its composition a match to what you pulled from Chris's burnt hand?" Not that they knew what brand Randall smoked yet.

"Negative."

"What about the cigar I got from Neil Silverman?"

"Well, you know its source, and it was unsmoked, but its makeup wasn't a match to what burned Chris, either."

"That would be too easy." It was feeling like a case of déjà vu, just like how they had Neil's prints on the rescue jaw but couldn't tie it back to Chris Randall. *Guess Neil Silverman just got his golden ticket out of here.*

"What about the two drug dealers? Are you getting anywhere there?"

Madison shook her head. "They admit to an altercation, as does Ryan Turner, Chris's supposed best friend. Apparently, even Marcus Randall got into a round with his son the night he went into the river."

"Who told you that?"

"Neil Silverman, not that it matters. He'll have to be released. Guess I'll have to go sign the paperwork for that before I leave."

"Wait. Maddy?"

"Yeah." Turning around to face her friend, she realized how tired this case was making her.

"How are things?"

"What do you mean?"

"Between you and Blake?"

"What is it with you mixing business with pleasure? Don't you have some samples to match or something?" Madison smiled on the outside. Inside, she didn't feel like smiling at all.

Madison set things in motion to get Neil Silverman released and called Terry to let him know the latest developments— if she could call them that. She was back at home with her sweet pooch, but her apartment still felt lonely and like the walls were closing in on her.

She took Hershey out for some fresh air and figured it would be a good opportunity to burn off some calories, chip away at those extra pounds.

They walked for half an hour, and she thought of turning back, but she didn't. She kept going as her mind raced. She thought about Richards and how she hoped their friendship would return to normal over time. She also replayed the facts of her cold case in her head. She should be working on that, but she couldn't seem to keep her focus on any one thing right now.

An hour passed, and she hadn't intended to go as far as she had, nor in the direction she had. Blake's building looked taller than the last time she was there, which was a week ago. It felt so much longer than that.

"Detective Knight. You coming in?" The doorman eyed Hershey as if he was an abomination.

"Oh, no." *Hell no!* "Not today." She gave him a pressed-lipped smile and started walking again.

It felt good to move, to breathe in the cool air. In a way, it cleansed her soul of the torment that festered there. Life wasn't fair. There was no getting around it, and just when one thought they had it figured out, things would change. It wasn't evil people and those guilty of many sins who caught the life-threatening diseases or succumbed to tragedy; it was innocent people with loads of loved ones. Young people who hadn't even started out in life, people who had everything going for them. The one certainty in life was nothing was certain.

She lived that truth repeatedly. Whenever things seemed to be going well, they eventually blew up in her face. That's probably why, after getting her heart broken the first time, she had sworn off dating. Who needed a man, anyway?

Really, her relationship with Blake had been doomed from the moment they started speaking of love. That simple word complicated everything.

She needed to pull herself together, forget all about Blake and relationships and focus on the case. After all, hadn't her failed relationship with Sovereign taught her the valuable lesson that nothing was forever? She could relate to the romantically tortured. And thinking of such, her mind turned to Neil Silverman.

He had sacrificed a lot for Chris without any appreciation in return—or so it seemed. He had apparently just left Chris after being humiliated; that was hard to accept. She just wished there was something she could do right now, but her hands felt tied.

CHAPTER FORTY-SIX

Madison woke up ready to deal with whatever malicious attacks came her way from McAlexandar and Winston. She was going to defend herself, and after replaying the scenario many times in her mind, she had an idea how she was going to handle it.

"The chief's in Winston's office. They're waiting for you." Officer Ranson gave her an empathic look.

Madison tapped the counter. "Don't count me out yet."

"Working the front counter isn't all that bad. Maybe we could rotate shifts."

Madison was on her way into the room that would decide whether she still had a job, yet she was composed and her mind surprisingly calm. She did her job well and would do whatever it took to get to the bottom of a case—that made her exemplary not worthy of reprimand.

She stopped outside Winston's door, took a deep breath, and knocked.

"Come in."

Opening the door, she faced two scowling superiors.

"Sit." Winston directed her to a chair beside McAlexandar. "Now that we're all here in my cramped office, we need some answers." He consulted a written checklist he had scrawled out on a lined notepad. When he saw she was trying to read it, he moved it out of her view. "Let's start with the search of the boathouse. We'll work chronologically."

I've made so many offenses they need to be discussed chronologically?

"McAlexandar says you were aware the terms of the search were more like a look-see, not a bag and tag."

"The evidence picked up was within plain sight."

"Evidence?" McAlexandar puffed out a loud rush of air. "So, you can tie it to the murder?"

Madison swallowed roughly.

"I take it that's a no." McAlexandar had one leg crossed, his hand resting on his knee. "Besides, that's irrelevant."

Maybe it had been a mistake not calling in her FOP rep, basically a lawyer with the Fraternal Order of Police, a union dedicated to defending law enforcement officers who were members. "Am I on trial here? I'm doing my job." Madison rose to her feet, and the volume of her speech increased. "Is it not my job to find killers? Seriously, if one is going to be reviewed under a microscope—"

"We don't even need one for you," McAlexandar spat.

I could say the same thing about you!

She tried her best to ignore her internal voice, but she couldn't help thinking that Internal Affairs might be interested in knowing her allegations against the chief. "There was a cigar burn on Chris's body. We found a cigar." She calmed down, shrugged her shoulders. "I'm not sure what the big deal is."

"*The big deal* is you were specifically told the property owner authorized a look-over. Nothing more," Winston said.

She felt on the losing end here, and it probably didn't help that the cigar had turned up absolutely nothing useful that she could put in their faces.

"Did your heroics benefit you at all?" McAlexandar crossed his arms, kept his focus on her. It felt like he'd read her mind and just wanted to pour acid on her wound.

"My heroics?"

"Surely that's how you see yourself here. A heroic victim. A hero to the victims, a victim of the justice system."

"That's not—" She snapped her mouth shut. Sometimes it was best to keep quiet.

"Answer the chief's question," Winston told her. "Are you any closer to finding a killer?"

"No."

"No? So, you violated a man's property, his privacy, to no avail." McAlexandar taunted her.

The sergeant clenched his jaw as he fingered his way down the page in his notebook. "Ryan Turner. Why was he here without a lawyer present?"

"He waived his rights in writing."

"But how did you obtain it?" McAlexandar was back to asking the questions—or flinging not-so-veiled accusations. "Is it not true that Ryan Turner was high, that he was drunk, that he was grieved to the point that making any rational decisions for himself was jeopardized? Yet you took advantage of that." He held up a hand to stop her from speaking. "Would Ryan Turner, if he had been in his right mind, have talked to you without his lawyer present?"

"I believe so."

"He tried to speak with you before he snorted a line and drank a bottle of whiskey?" the chief asked.

Madison looked between the two men. It didn't matter what she said.

"Did he?" McAlexandar pressed.

She glanced at the sergeant, who seemed to be nothing more than the master of ceremonies, there to introduce the next segment of the show.

"No," she said.

"Well, then." McAlexandar flailed his arms in the air. "Guess it's settled. You acted against direct orders and put the integrity of this case in jeopardy."

"I did no such thing. You've been hiding behind your claim to find justice for Chris Randall while lobbying with his father to bring the most benefits to your political campaign. It's no secret to anyone your aspiration is to become mayor. You've been greedy for that position for years. Randall has the power to put you in that chair." The words flowed from her mouth like destructive lava she felt powerless to stop.

"Outrageous!" McAlexandar rose from the chair, his finger wagging between her and her superior.

"You're hiding something with Randall. What is it?" She stared at him, provoking the confrontation to a climax. "Did he kill his son?"

"That's enough, Knight!" Winston barked. "I think I've heard enough. You are hereby suspended without pay for one week."

"That's crap."

"That's justice," McAlexandar said.

"Turn in your badge and your gun," Winston demanded.

"Sarge, listen to what you're doing. Can't you see it? The chief is manipulating this case in the direction he wants it to go, the direction Randall wants it go. Why is it always away from that household?" She paused and then continued in a lower voice. "Can you answer that? And why hasn't Chris's file been unlocked yet? Likely because it contains something he doesn't want us to know." She thrust a hand in McAlexandar's direction.

"Knight, we need to know you can follow orders, adhere to management decisions," Winston said calmly. "We can't have you making judgment calls—"

"That's part of the job," she interrupted.

Winston continued. "We can't have you making judgment calls outside of established parameters. We need you to respect authority. That's where the real problem is. One week, get your head screwed on straight, and come back to us."

"That's not fair." With the words out of her mouth, she realized she knew that fact about life already. After all, she'd just been contemplating that very thing not long ago. "What about Terry?"

"You let us worry about him." Winston leaned forward, an opened hand held out to her. "Badge and gun."

"You're making a mistake, Sarge." She found herself wanting to beg for a hearing ear, but the room was full of deaf mutes. Unclipping her badge, she found her hand unsteady. It was only one week, but what would she do? Her job was her life. "What about Ryan Turner?"

"What about him? This meeting's gone on long enough already." McAlexandar eyed her smugly, knowing he'd won this round.

"He knows about the counterfeiting," she said.

"A confession you no doubt received while he was under the influence of drugs and alcohol."

"He's in danger."

McAlexandar wagged his finger. "How the hell would you know?"

Madison ignored McAlexandar and spoke to Winston. "Sergey and Anatolli were watching him." Might have been a stretch, since she never got a clear look at the Navigator's occupants or the plate, but if Dimitre Petrov was going to order men to watch Turner, it would be them.

"The Russians?" Winston said.

"Boss, there's something larger going on here."

McAlexandar laughed. "Now your last-ditch theory is that the Russians killed Chris."

She took his challenge, looking straight at him. "There is no sign of that."

"Your point, then?"

"I won't be here to protect him." She placed her badge and gun on the desk, disregarding the sergeant's hand.

With Madison gone, Winston had this bad feeling that he'd let himself be pressured into the decisions he'd made. Maybe he was too eager to please his superior.

"You made the right decision," McAlexandar assured him as if reading his mind. "It was only a matter of time."

Winston nodded but found it hard to shake the mud Madison had slung on the chief's character. It seemed the closer she got to solving the case or getting more answers, McAlexandar was there to smother the flame of suspicion before it lit into a raging fire. Was there enough kindling to support a fire?

"This Ryan kid," Winston started. "Do we need to—"

"Don't worry about him. It's been taken care of."

. . .

McAlexandar returned to the privacy of his office, but he felt as if he'd never escape the watchful eyes of Detective Knight. She had this determined focus that she would get the truth, even if it meant bringing him down in the process. That would probably bring her extreme pleasure, a bonus that would come with sacrificing her career. But to hell if he'd let her become a martyr. And if only Knight was his sole problem.

He picked up his phone and called Marcus. "It's been dealt with. I have your back."

"You better see to it that you do," Marcus said. His weak bout yesterday had long been buried under confidence and power.

"Has the Secret Service questioned you?" McAlexandar made his point with a rhetorical question.

"Keep it that way, and I promise I'll make good on my end."

CHAPTER FORTY-SEVEN

Madison could go home, brood. She could rouse Internal Affairs, call her FOP rep. But none of those things would get her closer to obtaining answers to all her questions. The primary of which was who had killed Chris Randall. But there were others that were gnawing away at her. How had McAlexandar known about Ryan Turner being downtown in the first place? Was there a snitch inside the department commanded to notify him of everyone Madison brought in, or was it much worse than that? Did the chief himself have connections with the Russian Mafia?

And if they thought they could stop her from finding justice for Chris by taking her badge and gun, they were sorely mistaken. Operating as a civilian, she wouldn't have as many restrictions, but at the same time, if she ever wanted her job back, she'd have to be careful to toe the line. One thing was certain: she couldn't just sit around and do nothing or the emptiness and feeling of uselessness would consume her.

The first thing she did was call the Secret Service agent and place an anonymous tip. They knew about Ryan Turner's partial print on counterfeit cash, but they'd love to hear that Turner could point a finger at Marcus Randall himself. Turner needed protection, and if that took stirring up shit, she was good with it.

Next, armed with a Hershey's bar, she got into her car and headed for Hanigan's Market. It was doubtful she'd catch up with Tony Medcalf, seeing as it was going on ten in the morning, but she might come away with something else that was useful.

She tore a chunk off her chocolate bar and savored the velvety goodness as she meandered through the market.

"Squid, two for one, just for you." A man with a crooked smile held two up for her to see.

She recoiled and swallowed a large mouthful of chocolate. The squid looked like gelatinous goop. *No thanks!* She liked fish but that…that wasn't fish. She waved a dismissive hand at the man and carried on walking.

She finished her Hershey's bar and jammed the wrapper in her pocket. She watched people going by, mostly as a blur of colors. One woman passed her, looking closely at Madison, and it made Madison feel self-conscious, though the stranger wasn't doing anything different than Madison was.

It had to be the suspension making Madison feel insecure and as if as if everyone was watching and judging her.

Her cell vibrated, and she realized Winston hadn't collected her Stiles PD phone. It was a text message from Cynthia.

> *Looked closer at rescue jaw. Has two small insignias. MR. Thought it was a brand name. It's not.*

Madison clipped her phone back on her hip. MR, *as in Marcus Randall?* If so, how did his rescue jaw end up in the Silverman boathouse with Neil Silverman's fingerprints on it? Turner had said that there was usually a rescue jaw in the Randall boathouse, but it wasn't there when she and Terry had looked around.

Adrenaline coursed through her, but she had to simply focus and proceed logically. She didn't have any authority to rush into the Silverman household—assuming Neil was there—and drag him downtown. And even if she did have a badge to back her up, she didn't have enough to go on.

Her phone rang again, and she answered.

"I just heard." It was Terry. "Not from you, of course. You have a problem with communicating. The sarge is always saying it, too."

"Oh, shut up, Terry." She knew he was just trying to lighten things up by mocking the brass, and she would have laughed if she didn't hurt so much inside.

"What happened?" he asked.

"The short version is the chief finally got his way." Her eyes scanned people as they moved past her. It was unbelievable there were so many out and about on a Monday morning. Didn't anyone have jobs anymore?

"Where are you? It's loud there."

A woman with a child in a stroller walked by and kept her eyes on Madison. *What is with people watching me?*

"Sorry, Terry, you're breaking up. Cccch…ssccch…"

"I'm not falling for that crap. Do you know who they stuck me with?"

Her mind went to Detective Benson. He was always complaining of his sore hips and knees. Or it could have been Barkhouse, who had been on the force longer than either of them had been alive and had a catalog of stories to go with the years, which no one could verify. Regardless she wasn't into playing a guessing game. "I don't know."

"No one." He laughed. "And, whoa, the exhilaration of it! The freedom. I might get used to this."

"Well, I wouldn't. I'll be back soon enough."

"They'll just be reviewing my work. Of course, I can always call in backup when and where I need it. The truth is, I miss you a little already."

"I'm sure you do."

"I do. You keep my blood pumping. Never know if I'm going to get yelled at or praised by Winston. Actually, you make me look good."

"Oh, shut up."

"Hey, lady, I'll give you the best deal ever on the squid!"

She was back to that seafood vendor again. She must be going around in circles.

"Oh, you're at Hanigan's Market. You're looking for Medcalf."

She spun and leveled a cold glare at the vendor for disclosing her location to Terry, even if it was inadvertently. At least, by some small miracle, he wasn't holding up squid this time.

Into the phone, she said, "Maybe I'm having a craving for fresh ingredients."

"You don't cook."

"Listen, the sarge knows me well enough to know that a little thing like being suspended isn't going to stop me. I just don't have a leash now." She caught sight of someone who looked like Medcalf. *Could it be?*

She moved toward the man. He wore the same beret as Medcalf had the other day when she and Terry had spotted him outside the market. She was getting closer to him now, and it was definitely Medcalf.

"I really need to go," she said.

"You might like to know something...assuming you don't," Terry said. "But Cynthia's discovered that the rescue jaw we brought in—"

"Has the initials MR on it? Yeah, I got the text, too. You should probably drag Neil Silverman in again, question him about it."

"He's just going to say he has no idea how it got in there," Terry countered. "He told us he never even went into his father's boathouse."

"He's told us a lot of things. It doesn't make them all true."

"Fine, but you might be forgetting that there's nothing on that specific rescue jaw that ties to Chris, either. We need more to justify hauling him again, and you know it."

She could argue with her partner all day, but she didn't have the time. "I've gotta go." She hung up before Terry could get another word out.

Medcalf stopped at a counter and inspected the produce, lifting apples, pears, turning them over, even holding them to his nose. He held four cloth bags in the one hand, and they all looked quite full already.

She moved up to the fruit counter, keeping a distance from Medcalf of about four feet. At the appropriate time, when she sensed he'd noticed her, she turned and smiled as if she were surprised to have run into him.

"Detective?"

Now she had to call on her acting skills, which weren't very good at the best of times. She remembered the man's attraction to her at the estate and would use that to her advantage if it got Medcalf to open up about Randall. "Medcalf?" She put a hand on his shoulder.

"Please. Call me Tony." He put down the imported fruit and closed the gap between them. "What are you doing here?"

"Honestly?" She smiled at him, doing her best to play flirtatious. "I was hoping to run into you." *Sometimes a little honesty went a long way.*

"Into me? Why?" His brown eyes were deep but readable. He was flattered.

She brushed a cheek shyly to a shoulder. "I just thought maybe—" She stopped and laughed. "I can't believe I'm doing this."

"No, it's okay. Continue." He put a hand on her shoulder. She had to fight not to shrug it off, yank his arm behind his back, and flatten him to the floor. She removed her hand from him.

"I really shouldn't." She turned to walk away, but he pulled on her arm to stop her. He had a strong grip, and she faced him. "Well, I'm not supposed to see anyone who is involved in an open case."

His eyes were watching her, studying her.

"But I guess since I have a bit of time off—"

"Time off?"

"They suspended me today." She tried to act devastated, deflated—though those emotions weren't difficult to conjure. She let out a puff of air and pressed her lips downward. "Not fair, really."

"I guess not. You seem like you're excellent at your job."

The best in the entire department. "I'd like to think so."

"As you were saying…" He put a hand on her shoulder again. This man was a touchy one.

"I thought we sort of had a connection."

His lips parted into a large smile. "So did I."

"Pretty pathetic, though, coming to the market to find you." She smiled as if embarrassed.

"No, no, not at all." He paused. "How did you know I'd be here?"

"Well, you mentioned how you go to the market in the morning… Like you said, I'm excellent at my job." She smiled again, her cheeks starting to get sore.

"All right, then. So, you were going to say you can't see me socially, but then said you're on suspension. I guess that leaves your options open now, doesn't it?"

"I guess so."

"Do you have time for a coffee?" He pointed toward where a small food court was located. "Dark Beans serves a great brew and the best croissants."

"What an excellent idea." If she could build up a comradery with Medcalf, maybe she could get him to open up about Marcus Randall.

Terry felt somewhat lost without Madison, but at the same time, he didn't have to follow her lead now. He had more freedom to examine his own gut feelings and intuition. Not that Madison never listened to him, but most times she'd overpower him and exhaust her ideas first.

The one negative to being the one in charge was he'd have to face the superiors on his own. He was used to having Madison as a buffer between him and the brass. Anything went wrong, and she would be blamed for it. He might end up missing that, depending on how things worked out. And he was about to find out, as he was seated across from McAlexandar. He had been called to this meeting after his conversation with Madison had ended.

McAlexandar leaned back in his chair, swiveled slowly, and clasped his hands in his lap. "We need your focus on this case. Can you do that?"

"Of course."

"You know all the facts, the importance of keeping a record of everything, and keeping Sergeant Winston apprised of everything."

He wasn't off to a good start with the test of loyalty already. He'd bet his paycheck that Madison was meeting up with Randall's cook in an attempt to get information from him, but Terry wasn't about to disclose a word of it. "Understood."

"Excellent, then. We'll get along fine." McAlexandar's thin lips turned upward. "If you do well this week, we'll talk about a promotion."

Terry had no aspirations to climb the corporate ladder, but it might be better if he let the chief go on thinking he did.

"See, now, Detective Knight's always had a problem with authority, but you"—he wagged his finger—"I have a good feeling about."

We'll see how long that good feeling lasts.

"I know prior to Madison's suspension, you were going to inquire about getting the camera footage from the boathouse at the Randall estate," Terry said.

"Ah, yes. I've talked with Mr. Randall, and unfortunately, he doesn't want to part with that."

"Is that because there's something on there he doesn't want us to see?"

"Seems like you've learned to be outspoken from your partner."

"I was referring to the drug trafficking. Not implying anything further." Terry wondered how gullible the chief really was.

McAlexandar studied him, trying to read his thoughts. "Mr. Randall feels enough shadow has been cast on his son's memory without adding to it. Then there's always the concern that someone will get their hands on the footage and distribute it." He squinted. "Say on YouTube."

There was too much secrecy surrounding this Randall guy. Madison might have been onto something. If Chris had been his son, Terry would want all the answers—no matter the cost involved. "I can understand his concern," he lied.

"That will be all."

"Actually…would I be able to speak with Mr. Randall?" Terry asked.

McAlexandar eyed him skeptically.

"We believe the rescue jaw we found in the Silvermans' boathouse belonged to him. I'd like to know if he has any ideas as to why it would be over there. I mean, before dragging Neil Silverman in again."

McAlexandar went silent, nodded his head. "I suppose I could arrange a meeting."

With Detective Terry Grant out of his office, McAlexandar leaned forward on his desk. There was no way a meeting between Marcus and the detective would be arranged. There was something about Terry he didn't trust, and it was obvious the guy had picked up bad habits from his partner after all these years.

Detective Knight had won the freakin' lottery to just be suspended. McAlexandar had wanted her badge for good— really stop her from making trouble. Hell, just the thought of Madison made him crave a drink. But it had been six years, one month, and fifteen days. Surely, he could ride this case without one…

Yet he found himself opening the desk drawer. The bottle of double-malt Scotch whiskey sat inside with two crystal glasses.

He looked across the room at the door, reassuring himself that no one would be barging in on him. Any visitors needed to go past Sandy and be approved by him first. But doubts entered in. After all, wasn't every system fallible? Including the justice system. Was he failing Chris Randall?

Just as the thought entered his mind, he felt weakness entwining around him like ivy on the trunk of a tree, a feeling he wasn't accustomed to. Normally, he was the one in control, the one with the power. But he could feel that slipping away. Marcus manipulated him as a marionette on strings. The man flicked his wrist one way, up went a foot, another way, down went an arm, one movement forward, and McAlexandar was on his knees, submitting to his master.

He wiped a hand across his face. He needed to cut the strings. He pulled out a rocks glass, twisted the lid on the bottle. Just the smell of the scotch hit the back of his brain. So potent, so full of body. He remembered the texture on his tongue, the way it made him feel, and how brief a time it would take before he transformed into an animal.

He'd never gotten counseling and had never seen a doctor. He'd just concluded he had an allergy to alcohol and, as such, removed the vice from his life. At least, that's how he chose to recall it. He blocked out his wife's threats to leave him but wondered if they hadn't factored into his decision to adopt sobriety. After all, he couldn't have her following through. It would reflect badly on a man whose life's aspiration was to run for mayor, possibly even a presidential chair. But maybe he was just deceiving himself into thinking those dreams were even possible at this point in his life. He had recently celebrated his fifty-eighth birthday. The sand was running out of the hourglass, but as long as he had breath in him, he'd fight for his dreams, and he knew better than to make an enemy of Marcus Randall.

He shot back a mouthful of the amber liquid. It coated his palate and filled his throat with a soft, woody burn. How he had missed it. He poured himself some more.

CHAPTER FORTY-EIGHT

There were three things Madison wanted to get out of Medcalf. One, confirm that he had served pheasant to Chris on the eve of his murder. Two, find out the brand of cigar Randall smoked. It might not get them closer to the killer, but it could verify Neil's story that Randall had burned his son with a cigar. And three, convince him to give her the camera footage from Randall's boathouse. And if she was going to get any of this, she'd have to finesse it from Medcalf without him suspecting her motives.

She sat across from Medcalf at the wrought iron, bistro-style table. The coffee was no Starbucks, but it was good.

"You really should have tried a croissant. They melt in your mouth here." Medcalf lifted up a piece of the pastry, pinched between his thumb and index finger, and popped it into his mouth. He licked his fingers. "Or are you watching your girlie figure?" He chuckled.

He finds that *funny?*

"Oh, you're not amused," he said backpedaling. "Please forgive me. I say stupid things when I'm nervous."

Stupid was an understatement. If she let this horrific interaction go on much longer, it would be a complete waste of her time and her first day off. She lifted her cup to her lips and blew on the brew, trying to appear seductive while doing so. She kept her eyes on him, took a small draw, and put the cup down. "What's it like working for Marcus Randall?"

He seemed hesitant to speak.

She went on. "I just mean, he's such a powerful man. To be in that presence must be something special."

His face lit up. "Mr. R takes a lot of grief from the media. They don't know him the way I do."

"And how is that?" She asked it in a casual, relaxed manner as if she was just a friend passing the time.

"Let's just say I know the man."

"You are lovers?" she tossed out for a reaction.

Medcalf laughed so hard tears pooled in the corners of his eyes. "Ah, no. I don't swing that way. Neither does Mr. R. I'm into pretty women like you." He reached a hand out to touch her arm, and she allowed it.

"*Women*, as in the plural? So you're not the settling sort?"

He smirked, caught in his philandering ways.

"Don't worry, neither am I." She smiled. "All that commitment crap scares the shit out of me." Blake entered her mind and left it just as quickly. "What do you mean, you know the man?"

"This isn't an interrogation, is it? I thought you were suspended?"

"I'm just curious." She was going to have to back off the intensity just a little. "I'd love it if you cooked for me sometime." *Where the hell did those words come from?*

He smiled, flattered. "I'm sure I could."

Maybe her statement choice hadn't been completely illogical after all. It steered the conversation to food, and she could lead that to pheasant. "What you were going to make the other day was probably divine."

"Fresh is always the key. Don't buy prepackaged or frozen. And the worst offense is to cook with store-bought spices. Chop the actual herbs yourself, and a world of flavors await."

This guy was really into his cooking. "What sort of fancy meals do you make? What about pheasant? I love pheasant." She really had no idea what it tasted like, but acting like she did was a means to an end.

"Yes, pheasant is one of them. Normally, we would have it every Saturday. We don't anymore."

Madison leaned forward. The conversation was becoming more interesting. January tenth—Chris's last night alive—had been a Saturday. "Why not?"

His eyes weren't focusing on her anymore. She was afraid she was losing him.

"Oh," she blurted out. "That was stupid of me."

His eyes snapped to hers. "What was?"

"Just taking a guess here, but was it Chris's favorite meal? Is that why you don't have it anymore?"

"Yeah." He paused, but Madison sensed more forthcoming. "Mr. R disliked it. He prefers venison, but Chris would get whatever he wanted. Mr. R catered to him. He was a spoiled kid and didn't know what he had."

The hairs went up on the back of Madison's neck. "I'm sensing you didn't like him?"

"Oh, no, you're still a cop, lady. Don't make any more of it than is there. I'm entitled to my opinion. That's all this is."

"It must be upsetting to Mr. Randall to have all these things about his son coming to light. The drug dealing, his dalliances with men." She wasn't even going to touch on the counterfeiting allegations, but the two things she did toss out—done in a way to present herself as an ally—should be shocking to Medcalf.

Medcalf gave no visual reaction to what she'd said. He must have known about Chris's affair with Neil Silverman, maybe others.

"The man's very private, but I can tell it does," he said. "You know someone long enough, and they don't have to put their feelings into words. He was disappointed and hurt by Chris's actions. After all that he did for him."

"You said that Marcus spoiled Chis. More than any loving father might spoil his son?"

Medcalf took a deep breath. "Not much to compare him to, so I don't know. I lost my father at ten years old."

"Sorry, I didn't know."

"No, don't worry about it. I don't. I mean, yeah, it would have been nice to know what having a father is like, but my life is full. I'm happy."

Madison nodded. She sensed something different from his vibe when the conversation turned to Chris. It was hard to pinpoint exactly, but it made her uncomfortable.

They sat in silence for seconds, just listening to the buzzing conversations of surrounding patrons.

"All right, I'll tell you this as a new friend," he started. "I didn't care for the kid. I really didn't. But that doesn't mean I killed him."

"Hey, good enough. There are people I don't like." McAlexandar instantly came to mind. "It must have been hard on Mr. Randall to have an unappreciative son. I mean, I'm not a parent, but I can only imagine."

"You can't, actually." He waved a hand. "Not that I'm a parent, either." He smirked. "That I know of."

Does he actually think he's charming?

Medcalf continued. "As far as I'm concerned, that son of his was bad news. He would destroy the company given time. He dragged its name through the mud. All that Mr. R had worked to accomplish became tarnished."

Medcalf seemed enamored with his employer. He saw no flaws.

"Mr. R sets up the flights for him to travel. Chris would complain he was always on the road, didn't have enough time to put down roots. What the hell does a twenty-two-year-old kid need roots for? He should have been thankful for the experiences he was gaining and the women he bedded."

Madison calculated the picture. Randall had placed his son in the position of setting up dummy corporations and depositing counterfeit funds around the world. None of it had been Chris's idea. He could have wanted out, and the father took revenge. "But you don't think he would have hurt his son?"

"No way in hell!" Some people from nearby tables turned to look at him. He lowered his voice and continued. "Mr. R wouldn't hurt anyone."

Such a strong reaction, Madison found herself doubting Medcalf's claim, but it was best she not antagonize him further. "Mr. Randall must be hurt more than people realize, then. As you mentioned, he's a private person."

"Pained beyond belief. He doesn't say much, but I know. I know," he repeated.

"He'd probably really like to know who did it, huh?"

"Definitely. I mean, if I had any idea, I'd tell you what I know, but I don't know anything."

Time to go straight for what she wanted—the cherry on the sundae, the melted butter on the mashed potatoes. "If only there was a camera or something outside of the boathouse." She knew that she'd asked McAlexandar to talk to Randall about the video, but she didn't think he had any of intention of following through. And she wasn't confident Terry could make it happen.

She leaned across the table. "I'll tell you a secret. The evidence points to Chris being drowned within the walls of Mr. Randall's boathouse. Not that Mr. Randall had anything to do with it. But if we just had something to give us eyes on the place…"

Medcalf didn't say anything.

"You know…just to prove that Mr. Randall had nothing to do Chris's murder. You know it, I—"

"Actually…"

"Yes?"

"There is a camera."

She smiled, let the expression fade quickly. "Oh, never mind. There's no way Mr. Randall would want us seeing that."

Medcalf looked around, leaned back in his chair. "Maybe I could arrange something. But on one condition."

"And what's that?"

"You and I go on a real date. Dinner tonight? I can't bring you back to Mr. R's, but I know a terrific restaurant."

CHAPTER FORTY-NINE

"Chief McAlexandar." Sandy's voice thundered through the intercom on his desk, and he jumped.

"What is it?" he barked. He wanted to be left alone to ride out his buzz and salve his regrets for drinking in the first place.

There was a brief silence on the other end. He didn't normally speak to his assistant like he just had.

"Sandy," he prompted.

"Are you okay, sir?"

"What is it?"

"Sergeant Winston is here with two men from the Secret Service, sir."

He tucked the bottle and his empty glass away in the drawer, adjusted his necktie. "Send them in."

"I believe the door's locked, sir."

He must have gotten up at some point and locked the door, not that he remembered doing that. And what the hell time was it? And how long had Sandy been trying to get through to him?

He glanced at the clock. *2:35 PM.*

Last he knew, it was about eleven in the morning. He must have passed out, right in his desk chair.

He got up without another word to Sandy and stumbled his way to the door. His head was spinning. Bracing himself against the wall, he power-talked himself into getting his act together. A moment later, he swung open the door and said, "What can I do for you gentlemen?"

Terry poured himself another cup of coffee, which he had learned to accept as the Stiles PD's mud brew. Yet he kept subjecting himself to it.

Hours had passed since his meeting with McAlexandar, and he was feeling lost without Madison. He tried calling her again, but she wasn't answering, and he didn't like it one bit. He wondered if he should be worried about her but assured himself this was Madison he was talking about.

He'd spent most of his time finalizing some paperwork, interviews, and so on. There seemed to be no end to it, but it could just be the fact it bored him today.

He had tried to reach Neil Silverman, just to ask casually about the rescue jaw, but he didn't get through to him. He could have tried harder, but the location of the rescue jaw didn't get him excited like it did Madison.

He opened a case folder to see if Madison had made any notes from her initial visit to the Randall residence. He was about to quit looking when he found her scribbled text. Who said only doctors had messy handwriting? Madison could certainly rival them. He scanned down the page until he got to the notes about her conversation with Tony Medcalf.

> *He seemed to have pride in Randall's accomplishments, almost like they were his own. Found it kind of strange, considering he is the cook and doorman. Didn't have too much to say about Chris.*

Why would a cook, a hired hand, convey pride in his employer's accomplishments?

> *He talked boastfully about Randall Investments' share in the global market as if it were his own doing.*

Who was this guy? He logged into his computer, typed in *Tony Medcalf*. As the screen filled in with his background, Terry was certain his jaw dropped open. He dialed Madison's cell phone, but only received voice mail again. The time to worry about her safety may have come.

His phone rang, and he answered immediately. "Maddy?"

"Ah, no." It was a woman's voice. "Terry, are you okay?"

"Cynthia, have you heard from Maddy?"

"No. I've tried reaching her. I called you wondering if you know where she is. I heard the news. Wanted to go over tonight, have a girls' night with her. You know, cheer her up."

"Listen, I've gotta go."

"Everything okay? Is Maddy okay?"

"I'm not really sure."

"There has to be some sort of mistake." McAlexandar's head developed a throbbing, reminding him of another reason he'd quit drinking.

"No, the body is definitely that of Ryan Turner." Winston wouldn't look him in the eye, and that was infuriating.

He got the distinct impression the sergeant could no longer be counted on. Knight had ignited his suspicions. "Where was he found? When?"

"The body was found in his house this morning, in the study," Winston answered. "Facedown in vomit."

"An overdose." McAlexandar sloughed it off. In truth, the news knotted in his chest. "It's obvious the kid had a problem. And who found him?"

Winston motioned toward the Secret Service agents. The older agent was pale. The younger agent seemed almost on a high from the discovery. It made McAlexandar question his character.

Agent Weiss said, "We were there following up on an anonymous tip."

Let me guess; it came from Madison Knight.

Weiss continued. "Apparently, Turner had information on the counterfeiting. Our source told us he could have named Marcus Randall as being involved."

McAlexandar would have sworn the Secret Service had been privy to the allegation before, but his mind was jumbled mess.

"Your unnamed source? Do they truly have no name, or are you protecting someone? And you weren't even able to confirm this tip." He rolled his hands, hoping the action would somehow make speaking easier—another horrendous side effect of the booze.

"We spoke with Detective Grant, who confirmed it."

McAlexandar looked at Winston, who was still avoiding eye contact, and his mind cleared—just a bit. If Turner could prove Marcus was guilty of counterfeiting, it was a good thing that kid was dead. Good for Marcus, anyway. And good for McAlexandar.

Weiss added, "The detective confirmed that Ryan Turner had openly discussed the counterfeiting when he was brought in. Did you know about this?"

Who the hell does this punk think he is? "Am I being interrogated here?"

Weiss shrugged.

Winston took a seat in a chair facing the desk. McAlexandar wanted to throw a heavy object at him—hurt him, maim him, something. "Should I be getting a lawyer, gentlemen? Come on...I've done nothing wrong."

Agent Walters cleared his throat and said, "You had information about an open counterfeit invest—"

"Prove it," McAlexandar spat. "Because a detective may have known, it certainly doesn't mean that *I* possessed this knowledge."

"May I remind you that you agreed to keep us fully apprised of any developments?" Weiss asked.

"Maybe if you were out doing your jobs instead of leeching off the backs of the Stiles PD, you'd have your answers by now." Everyone fell silent in the room. Had he taken his aggression too far? "Listen, the kid was high and drunk, not a very credible position. I didn't want to waste your time."

The older Secret Service agent flicked his business card on the desk. "In future, let us be the ones to decide what is a good use of our time. Good luck with your murder investigation, Chief."

The two agents left the room, but Winston remained seated.

"I think we should reinstate Knight," Winston said.

"You've got to be kidding." He put a hand on the drawer that held his liquid comfort. He'd happily gulp it from the bottle. He didn't need the fancy glass.

"Just given the circumstances…" Winston's eyes housed an underlying threat. "We haven't even filed all the paperwork yet."

"What circumstances, exactly? A druggie's overdose? Sad, yet not tragic."

"One we should have kept in our custody—"

"He was convinced to sign over his rights while drunk and high. The case wouldn't even get to court. Any good defense attorney would have it thrown out. If I remember right, his lawyer even showed up!"

"Even if we had only held him until the Secret Service got here and took over, he would have had a chance."

"You're blaming me for his death?"

"No."

"You think the Secret Service would have accepted him in the state he was in? It would have been the same deal."

"I still think we should bring back Knight."

"We'll look like fools."

"Don't we already, sir?"

Was sir *supposed to cover the stench of his remark?*

"I stand by my earlier decision," McAlexandar said gruffly. "Regardless of whether Knight was here or not, whether Mr. Turner was released at that time or not, it doesn't mean he'd still be alive right now."

"Are you certain of that?" Winston moved in closer, his voice lowered even further than with his last words.

"What? Do I have a fucking crystal ball?"

Winston visibly sniffed at the air and moved back.

He knows I've been drinking.

"Do you know anything about Marcus Randall that you're hiding from me?" Winston asked.

"Who are you to—"

"Don't get all defensive like you do with other people. I just want to know before I risk my neck carrying out your orders because of some personal agenda of yours."

He couldn't fight the urge to drink any longer. He opened the drawer with the scotch, poured two glasses, and moved one across the desk toward Winston. The sergeant just stared at it, as if judging his supervisor's choice to drink midafternoon. McAlexandar took a nice draw on his, kept the glass in his hand. "Randall didn't kill his son. This much I know for certain."

"Because he told you that?"

"No, because I know the man, Garry."

"Then you know he worked hard to build his business. But Chris threatened to destroy all of it. He ran around with loose women, apparently dabbled in homosexuality, and to top it off, dealt drugs out of the boathouse."

"I know how it looks." McAlexandar paused to sniff the amber liquid. "But I'm telling you he didn't do it."

"I'm reinstating Knight effective immediately. Due to extenuating circumstances connected to the open case."

"All because some kid is dead?"

"Madison stated her concerns. Do you not remember? You were there. She mentioned the danger he was in."

"He overdosed." McAlexandar's heart palpitated.

"It could have been a murder made to look like a self-inflicted overdose, Patrick."

Very few had the nerve to address him by his first name. He tightened his grip on his rocks glass.

"I don't want us butting heads over this case," Winston stated firmly. "I need you to treat this one like you would any other."

"Hell, I wouldn't even be involved unless it was of special interest."

"I get it. It *is* a special interest case for you, but it's also too close to home." Winston reached for the glass in front of him, downed the entire contents, and set it back heavily on the desk. "I'm sure you want to know who did this to Chris and the truth about what happened to Ryan."

McAlexandar let Winston's words hang out there. With more alcohol fusing through his system, any sobriety he had regained had slipped entirely away. "Of course."

"Then I need you to back off, let us do our jobs."

Who was this man to tell him what to do? The little pissant reported to him, didn't he? Anger surged through him, yet he swallowed it this time. Marcus had the power to ensure he'd reach his full potential. He would never sell him out, but if he could appease law enforcement in this instance by backing off, he'd oblige. He didn't have a choice.

McAlexandar nodded.

CHAPTER FIFTY

The news of Ryan Turner's death hit Terry hard. Madison would take it even harder. They had the kid within their reach. They could have saved him, and Madison had fought for him not to be released. He wouldn't be surprised if she'd told them it would be on their heads if something happened to the guy. Though none of that would bring Turner back from the dead.

He'd tried calling Madison repeatedly but still wasn't able to get through. He'd even stopped by her apartment and got no answer. Unfortunately, there was no way to verify if she was home and simply ignoring him. The parking garage for her building was underground and secured, so he couldn't confirm if her Mazda was there. Driving by Hanigan's Market, he saw there was no blue Mazda parked in the lot there.

Where is she, and why isn't she answering her phone?

His mind went to Medcalf's background. The man had a record, and a volatile past. But maybe Terry was making too much out of it. Madison could take care of herself, couldn't she?

But while he hoped Madison would turn up safe and unharmed, he had to focus on getting some answers. Was the Russian Mafia behind Turner's death, or was it simply an overdose? Was there a partnership or sorts between Randall and the Russians? Did Randall have Ryan Turner killed to protect himself from fraud charges?

Terry left messages for the chief, but after making the last call, his secretary told him he'd left for the day. It must be nice to be corporate with huge pay, big perks, and minimal sacrifice. All the reporting grunts did the work. Anyway, the chief's departure left Terry at a dead end in terms of getting the chance to speak with Randall. He didn't want to contact him directly. No, he would play this as clean as possible, even if that meant sitting on his hands until Madison returned. And she would return. He had to believe that.

If Randall had ordered Turner's death, was he getting desperate, and if so, what was stopping him from taking Madison out?

He had shaken aside the questions as paranoia, chalking it up to Madison rubbing off on him more than he realized. But now he found himself outside the law offices of Golden, Broderick, and Maine. Maybe he could get some answers.

Terry went inside and approached the reception desk. "I'm here to see Blake Golden," Terry said to the secretary.

"Sure, your name?" Her green eyes went from him to her monitor.

It told Terry two things: gone were the days when appointments were kept on paper, and second, Blake was in. "I don't have an appointment."

"Well, I'm sorry. Mr. Golden is booked solid for months, unless it's an emergency."

Terry held up his badge. "I'm sure there's something you can do."

The secretary stared at the badge. "Well …" She moved the mouse wildly, clicking here, clicking there. "He's just in between meet—"

"Detective Grant?"

Terry turned to see Blake Golden standing there in a tailor-made suit. It reminded him of the first time they met. It seemed the suit lent its wearer a certain level of arrogance. He had never made his opinion of the man known to Madison, but he'd never been crazy about him.

"I'm just heading out for a bite to eat, but if you make an appointment with Sarah here, I'm sure she'll be able to squeeze you in between my four and five." He tapped the counter with his palm, and the woman nodded at him and smiled.

Terry read more in her expression, a deeper intimacy perhaps, and he felt a prick of jealousy on Madison's behalf. He really was becoming paranoid. "Listen." He moved in closer to Blake. "Madison is missing."

Blake pulled out on his tie, loosening it a bit. He turned to the secretary. "Hold all my calls."

"Yes, Mr. Golden." She had the voice of a cherub when speaking to her boss.

Blake directed Terry into a boardroom, which was showy and would have cost a mint.

Blake dropped into a chair at the head of the table. "What do you mean she's missing?"

"Just that." Terry took a seat. "I haven't been able to reach her for hours."

"You work side by side."

"She was suspended this morning."

"What? Why?"

"Because of you."

Blake let out a sigh, but his mouth formed a smirk. "Because I was doing my job?"

"Because you took it too far. Ryan Turner called her to talk. Yes, he was somewhat high—"

"There's high and there's not, Detective." Blake cocked his head. He was ready to fight.

"He was alert enough to tell us some things that would put your other client behind bars for life."

"Too bad none of it is admissible, then. I mean, at least for you it's bad."

Madison seems to be missing, and this guy's still about defending himself? Unbelievable.

"Ryan Turner is dead," Terry said coolly.

Blake's eyes enlarged then squeezed tightly shut, creating deep wrinkles in his brow. He opened his eyes, rubbed his forehead. "I didn't… Wow. When?"

"He was found this morning. You didn't know anything about that?" Terry studied Blake's face, and all he saw was surprise.

"Are you investigating his death? Was it an overdose?"

"Kind of funny you went straight there."

"Not really strange." Blake clasped his hands on the table. "He was an addict."

"What is strange," Terry started, "is he had people watching him. Do you know anything about that?"

Blake shook his head.

"You don't know much about anything."

Blake scowled at Terry's jab.

"But you did know we took him down to the police station. How?"

Blake sat back in his chair, not seeming inclined to answer.

Terry balled his hand into a fist and hit the table. "Answer the question!" He got up and walked to Blake at the head of the table. "Does the Russian Mafia work with Marcus Randall? Did they kill Ryan Turner?"

Blake's face twitched like he was fending off laughter.

"I'm glad you think this is all so funny," Terry said, eyes narrowed.

"It's not that. It's just the very idea that—"

"Members of the Mafia were there two nights ago," Terry cut in, "camped outside Ryan's place in their fancy Navigator, watching him. Then you show up at the station demanding he go free. I don't think the timing—or any of that—was a coincidence."

Blake stared through him, smug, arrogant. Terry spun his chair and grabbed him by the scruff of his collar.

Blake swatted at Terry's hands. "Let go of—"

"Madison is missing. God help you should something happen to her."

"Let go…" Blake's face was going red, and he clawed at Terry, trying to weaken his grip.

Eventually, Terry let go, stepped back.

Blake heaved for breath and rubbed his throat.

"Do you care about her at all?" Terry asked, his tone coated in accusation.

"I do, but—"

Terry scoffed. "But? At a time like this you add *but*?"

"It's not meant how you're taking it. We both have our jobs to do."

"You keep overlooking the fact that she's missing. You have a dangerous client."

"So you say. That's speculation on your part."

"Take off your fuckin' lawyer cap for one damn minute!" The swear word was off his tongue before he could reel it in. "She could be in trouble, and to be honest, I'm not sure where else to turn."

"I believe she and I have broken up."

"And what's that to mean? Just like that you don't care about her? It's not your problem to care? Is that the card you're going to play?" He peered into Blake's eyes and attempted to read them. They were devoid of emotion. "Okay, I see how it is."

"You have no fuckin' clue," Blake snarled. "You come in and tell me Madison's missing and in danger. You accuse my client of being in bed with the mob, of killing a kid. And you expect me to sit here and know how to assimilate and respond to all of this intelligently?" He was still rubbing his throat. "I can't."

"You're a lawyer. Shouldn't you thrive under pressure? All I'm asking for is some answers."

"Fine," Blake surrendered.

"How did you find out Ryan Turner was at the station?"

"I received a call."

"Don't play this bullshit game with me. From who?"

Blake's eyes fixed on Terry's. "I'm bound by attorney-client privilege."

Terry nodded. He was cooperating, even if by cryptic means. He might as well have said *Marcus Randall*. "Are you aware of any involvement between Randall and the Russians?"

"No, but I'm not told everything. I'm not his shrink."

Terry wanted to punch the guy in the face, but he took a few deep breaths, cooled down. "What about Ryan Turner? How did you know it was a drug overdose?"

"I didn't."

"You did. I told you he was dead, and your response: 'Was it an overdose?'"

"I was just basing it on his history...addiction."

"Try again."

Blake rolled his eyes, sighed. "Like I said, I'm bound by attorney-client privilege."

Terry had some answers. Randall was behind Turner's death, may even have been in cahoots with the Mafia, but would they ever be able prove it?

Terry had his hand on the doorknob when Blake spoke.

"What about Madison? Is she going to be okay?"

"What do you care?" Terry saw himself out and slammed the door behind him.

The brand was an expensive one, the year exquisite. McAlexandar sat there in his den, in a sofa chair, legs crossed, snifter in hand, watching the fire dance in its marble enclosure. Brandy—almost as good as scotch. It was all he had at the house. He didn't want to detour to the liquor store. Part of him felt ashamed for calling a car service to pick him up, but he knew the right ones, the ones who prided themselves on confidentiality and discretion. At least he hadn't gotten behind the wheel drunk.

He left the office a little past three thirty, just after Winston headed out to take care of business the way he saw fit. When he got home, he remembered his wife was attending a charity event for breast cancer, which took her out of the house that afternoon through the evening. By the time she got back, he'd probably already be in bed. He was already fighting to keep his eyes open and it was only early in the evening.

He took another sip of brandy, contemplating his stupidity, how he'd been transparent enough to draw suspicion. And it's not like he even knew everything. He assumed Marcus hadn't killed his son. But if he had, he didn't want to know.

The house phone rang, and he stood to answer it, hoping the whole while it wasn't his wife checking in. The way his head felt, he wouldn't be able to hide the fact he'd been drinking. How crazy that a small woman put such fear in him. He checked the caller ID and hesitated to answer. Still, he lifted the receiver and gave as robust a greeting as he could muster.

"Patrick?" Randall said. "You don't sound like you normally do."

"No, I'm fine."

"I didn't ask if you were fine. In fact, I don't really give much of a shit how you are."

Did I miss something? What happened after I left the office?

"They came to my work, Patrick. The place where I conduct business."

"Who?"

"Don't play stupid, Patrick. It's not an admirable quality in a man your age."

The Secret Service left his office and went to see Marcus at work?

"On what grounds?"

"It's a free country from what I remember. They can come and go as they wish. What I can't understand is why you don't have this under control. I went to you because I thought you could handle it. I guess you can't." Marcus let his words hang there, letting salt pour into McAlexandar's gushing wound of failure. All he could see was his life going up in flames. "What I need to know is, can you take care of this?"

"They had no grounds—"

"You're boring me, Patrick. Can you take care of this?"

What was he supposed to do about the Secret Service? It's not like they reported to him, and if he interfered too much, he'd draw attention to himself, and they'd start breathing down his neck. And that's the last thing he needed.

"Patrick, are you still there?"

"Yes."

"Yes, you're still there, or yes, you'll take care of this?"

McAlexandar craved his drink and looked at it across the room. "Both."

"Good job, then. Now you can prove it to me." With that, Marcus hung up, leaving him with a droning dial tone.

I'm the one boring him?

How was that even possible when the man uttered repeated threats to find someone else to do his work but never followed through? Apparently, McAlexandar wasn't that disposable after all. He felt a sense of power taking root inside him…or maybe it was just the brandy.

CHAPTER FIFTY-ONE

Terry didn't know his next step. Part of him wanted to storm the Randall estate. The other part of him wanted to head straight to Homeland Logistics, the Russian Mafia's main business front. He sat in the department-issued Crown Vic at a loss as to how to save his partner. He had to trust that she could defend herself if the need arose, but she could be cocky and stubborn. Both could be a bad combination for survival. But then, how could he just sit back and wait for something to happen, or not happen? If he was the one missing, Madison would march right down to Randall Investments and demand to speak with the man himself. She'd get answers. She'd force herself on the estate's grounds. She wouldn't let anyone stand in her way. And he couldn't let her down.

He went to put the car into gear, intent on going to the Randall estate, when his cell rang. "Grant."

"I can't reach Madison." It was Sergeant Winston.

He was one of the last people Terry wanted to speak to. If he hadn't submitted to the chief's strong-arming, Madison would be by his side right now and not in possible danger. "I've been having a hard time myself."

"She's probably enjoying her day off."

Terry clenched his fists. How—in what universe—would Madison go from being suspended to enjoying herself in one day?

"Anyway, you get a hold of her, have her call me," Winston said.

"Can do. Is there a message I can give her?"

"Let me be the one to break the news to her, but you're getting your partner back."

Terry slowly released his fists, but he was still angry. So help the man if something bad happened to Madison.

"Grant, did you hear me? I'm voiding her suspension."

"Yeah, I heard you." Terry hung up, not giving a crap if the sergeant considered the conversation over or not. Before he moved the car, his phone rang again.

Is it too much to ask for some freakin' peace and quiet?

He accepted the call. "Grant."

"Detective Grant, it's Officer Ranson. A package came, marked to Madison's attention." There was a pause. "I heard she was…"

"Well, don't shed too many tears. She's coming back."

"Oh, that's great news. What should I do with the package, then? Just hold it for her?"

"Yeah, though I might be back for it first."

"Okay, will do."

"Thank you. Now, I've gotta go. Later." He ended the call. *Enough conversation*, he thought, and then smiled. Just like Madison at any given moment, he had very little patience right now.

He finally got on the road, but now he wasn't so sure about going to the Randall estate. He would try Madison's apartment one more time. As he drove, he was curious about the package that had come in for Madison. Did it have something to do with the case?

He breezed through an intersection, realizing too late that he had just run a yellow to red. *Good ol' Maddy, rubbing off on him again.*

Madison stood in front of her bedroom mirror, Hershey at her feet. She bent down to pet him. She hated getting dressed up, but felt she needed to play the role perfectly or Medcalf would see through her feigned attraction to him and call her out for using him.

Her hair was cooperating, but it rarely didn't. That's why she went with a short, low-maintenance cut in the first place. The makeup was another story. She'd already poked herself in the eye with the mascara brush—twice—and she wondered if she'd applied the shadow too heavily and looked like she'd been socked in the eye. If Terry was here, he'd be laughing his head off.

Thinking of Terry, she knew he'd tried calling plenty of times, but she didn't need him talking her out of pursuing this angle with Medcalf.

She gave herself one final look in the mirror and found she was missing something. She looked down at her dresser and her eyes fell on her small amount of jewelry. She had so few pieces, she had no need for a jewelry box. All she had was a gold chain, a silver chain, a pair of gold studs, and a pair of diamond earrings. She picked the latter up and thought of Blake. She then put them aside and grabbed the studs. They would do just fine. She matched them with the gold chain. She rubbed her hands down the front of her dress, straightening it out for the fifteenth time. Okay, she was ready to go. She grabbed the purse off her dresser. "Come on, Hershey, in your kennel."

She latched him inside just as there was a knock on her door. She peeked through the peephole and stomped a foot.

Shit! Shit!

"Madison, are you in there? I heard you. I'm not leaving until you open this—"

She swung her door open and pointed a finger at her partner. "Not one word."

Terry took her in from head to toe. "You look good."

"How did you get in? It's a secure building." *Deflect, deflect, deflect!*

"Why are you dressed up?"

"I asked how you got in first."

"I asked why you're dressed up."

His eyes told her he wasn't going to let it go. "I have a date with Medcalf."

Terry winced. "I'm not sure if that's a good idea."

"He's getting us—well, *me*—the footage from the boathouse camera."

"He's a dangerous man."

"What are you talking about?"

"First things first. Why haven't you been answering my calls?"

"I've been busy."

"You've got your job back…Well, I'm just supposed to tell you to call Winston, but that's what he's going to tell you…"

She studied his eyes, afraid to let his words sink in too deep. As it was, they threatened to squeeze the breath from her chest due to relief, but also rage. She shouldn't have been suspended in the damn first place. She plastered on a smile. "You were worried about me, weren't you?"

"I said *you got your job back*."

"You couldn't reach me, and you were worried."

"Damn right I was. Is that what you want me to say? Would it make things better for you, knowing how much control you have over me? Holy shit, Knight, I've been worried about you since I knew you were on Medcalf's trail."

She let the fact he swore, completely out of character, go. "What are you talking about?"

"He has a record. Assault and alleged rape."

"There's a lot of that going around," she said, not dismissing the information lightly, but Terry was making it sound like the guy was one of America's Most Wanted. "Is that all?"

"Nope." Terry shook his head. "Medcalf wanted to be a cop but never measured up."

"So he's bitter against the world?"

"Not sure about the world, but I wouldn't trust the guy."

Madison let Terry's caution sink in, and with it came the memory of how familiar Medcalf had been with Terry and her. He'd known who she was when she first went to Randall's. Maybe the fact Medcalf could never become a cop had made him obsessive—and by extension, dangerous. "Okay, point taken. I'll be careful with the guy."

Terry nodded. "And I have bad news."

"More?"

"I'm not really sure how to say this, so I'm going to get right to the point. Ryan Turner is dead."

She staggered backward and put a hand to her heart. "What?"

"He was found this morning by the Secret Service. They got an anonymous call that he could pin the counterfeiting on Randall. Was that you?"

"Yeah… How did he…?"

"Overdose."

All she could think was they were responsible for it, and not *they* as in a collective party, but primarily one man—McAlexandar. "Please tell me his death is being investigated."

"There's no evidence thus far of it being anything more than what it appears to be."

"That's bullshit." She gripped her stomach; it was knotted so tightly.

"You know it. I know it. I think he was killed—there, I said it."

She needed to sit down and fumbled back into her apartment and dropped onto a barstool at her kitchen counter. "This is my fault. I never should have let him leave."

"You did all you could. His death isn't on your conscience."

If only I could accept that.

All she could do was stare at her partner. The shock of the news was washing over her in waves. "The Russians do this? Randall? Both?"

"They'd both have motive."

"I knew it was too convenient that Blake knew we had Ryan in for questioning. How did he know? The mob tell him?"

"I spoke with Blake."

It was a good thing she was sitting down. "What did he say?" She was grasping, hoping that Blake played no part in Turner's death.

"He said he received a call but wouldn't tell me who it came from. Just that it was bound by attorney-client priv—"

"So, Randall," she concluded.

"I think so."

"Is Randall involved with the Russians?" She let out a puff of air. "I wouldn't be surprised. A man like that has many friends, people who will do him favors. But if Randall was tight with the Russians, the matter of Chris trying to pay them with counterfeit funds would have gone away. There would be no need for them to camp outside Ryan's house."

"Maybe Randall settled the matter with them, paid them up with real cash, put the matter to rest. They got talking, respected each other's work philosophy."

"At what point? And that wouldn't explain why they were outside Turner's house."

"Maybe Randall and the Russians do have a partnership. But it's at least safe to presume that Ryan knew too much about the counterfeiting and was a liability."

Madison realized she'd been pinching her necklace and let it go, dropped her hand. "I don't know. The more I think about it, Turner's death looking like an overdose—and assuming it's murder—speaks more to Randall than it does a Mafia hit. Maybe I can find out from Medcalf if Randall and the mob are in bed."

"You're still going? I don't think the guy's stable."

"And trust me, if you actually met him, you'd know he isn't."

"Don't try to be funny. Why would you go if—"

"The camera footage from the boathouse. He said he'd bring it tonight."

"You believe he will?"

"I'll never know if I don't go."

Terry scanned her eyes. "Fine. But if you're going, I'll be hanging nearby in case you need me."

She rolled her eyes, then hugged him. "I can always count on you."

"Don't get carried away here."

She laughed.

"Oh, by the way, a package came in for you at the station."

"I'm not expecting anything."

"Now I'm more curious."

"You should go and find out what it is."

"No way. I'll be with you, to protect your ass. What time is your date?"

She looked at her watch. *7:50 PM.* "In ten minutes."

CHAPTER FIFTY-TWO

Madison walked into the restaurant where she was to meet Medcalf, turning men's heads as she did so. But she felt ridiculous dressed up in a knee-length black dress and two-inch heels. She preferred jeans and a sweater any day, any time.

"Table for Medcalf," Madison told the hostess, but then she spotted him waving at her from a back table. "Actually, it's okay. I see him."

Medcalf stood as Madison approached, and she actually found herself responding to him; her heart was thumping in her chest. He cleaned up rather well in a collared shirt, sports jacket, and trousers.

Just remember he's not right in the head.

"You made it," he said. "I was starting to wonder if you were going to show."

"Something came up." She was feeling slightly defensive, but she was tired of men pointing out the clock to her. It had only been five minutes after eight when she got here. And apparently, he saw no problem with ordering himself a drink while he waited. A rocks glass with amber liquid sat in front of him.

"Glad to see you were still able to make it." He smiled pleasantly at her, and she clued in that his previous comment hadn't been regarding the time, but rather his fear of being stood up. "I have what you're looking for, but first…"

All Madison heard was his first few words. The rest of what he was saying was of no consequence. Something about purchases he'd made at the market and how impressed Randall would be at the good bargains he found—not that Randall needed to pinch his pennies. Somehow, she would find a way to get herself through this evening, get out with the video and her sanity.

"Madison?" He was looking at her, as if he was anticipating a response.

"Please forgive me. It's been a crazy day, and I missed what you said." She shook her head with a smile on her lips.

"Right, how selfish of me. You were let go this morning, and here I am prattling on."

"Well, I wasn't let go." The words stung, even if all had been righted again.

"Suspended, then. A temporary let-go." He summoned a waiter. "The lady would like a drink." The waiter looked at her, so did Medcalf.

"Go ahead. Tonight's on me. Get what you like," Medcalf prompted. "They have a good house red."

Technically, she was back on the job and probably shouldn't be drinking, but she hadn't been lying when she said it was a crazy day. It had really been *one hell of* a day. "Sure, I'll have a glass."

"There you go." Medcalf sat back, a satisfied smile on his face. He lifted his drink and took a sip.

"You said that you had what I was looking for," she said.

"You're rushing things, Detective. May I still call you that? There's something sexy about a woman with a badge." He reached out to touch her arm, and she smiled innocently and pulled back.

He does have some screws loose…

"A lot of men find it intimidating," she countered.

"I'm not a lot of men." His gaze flicked behind her. "Ah, here's your wine."

The waiter set the glass in front of her, poured a splash, and stood there, grinning. For a few seconds, she had no idea why he hadn't left. Then she remembered. He was expecting her to perform the ritual Blake had taught her. She swirled the wine and watched it coat the sides of the glass, not that she knew what she was looking for. She inhaled, took a small sip, and let it blanket her tongue. It tasted like...wine.

"Does it meet with your liking?" the waiter asked.

Madison nodded.

"Enjoy, madam." The waiter backed away from the table.

Medcalf lifted his glass in a toast gesture. "To new friendships."

She clinked her glass to his, then took a large sip.

He kept his hand wrapped around his glass. "Yes, I find your job very sexy, and I understand how you must be wired."

This clown has no idea.

Medcalf went on. "You are all about the case, even when you've been let go." His eyes suddenly steeled over, and his jaw tightened. He leveled a glare on her. "That's why you were at Hanigan's, wasn't it? You were hoping to run into me. And like an idiot, I fell right into your trap."

"That's not—"

"That's precisely what this is." He pulled the linen napkin from his lap and threw it on the table. "I should have known."

She had to make a play—and quickly. She put her hand on his, took a leisurely draw on her wine. "You're reading this all wrong. I like you."

His hand pulsed under her touch before he pulled it away. "You're using me."

"That's not what was intended."

"You never even had any bags in your hands...at the market. You weren't there to buy anything."

"I picked up some things after seeing you." And that part was the truth. She'd done another loop at the market and found a cigar shop nestled in a corner. She set out on a hunt for any packaging that resembled the cigar box that she'd seen poking out of Medcalf's bag at the house, and believed she'd met with success. Sapphire Label was the brand name. Running with the assumption they were the cigars that Randall smoked, if Cynthia could match its composition to what had burned Chris's hand, they could at least verify Neil Silverman's story about Mr. Randall, giving Neil some credibility. It was a good thing, she'd bought the cigars, because she had a feeling she wouldn't be broaching the subject of Randall's smoking preferences tonight.

Medcalf scanned her face, his expression hardening.

"Okay, fine." She put a hand to her forehead and looked down at the table. "This is embarrassing for me to admit." She dropped her hand. "I don't usually do this type of thing, but I thought I'd have a chance of running into you. I thought maybe we had a connection."

"I guess I can't hold that against you."

For some reason, she had a feeling he wasn't responding from his ego. "Why's that?"

"You weren't looking to hook up with me." It was super hard to read his expression and tone of voice.

"I…wasn't?"

"No. But I get it. You had an important job, and it's hard to let it go. You're wired to find answers."

There is that wired word again.

Medcalf continued. "Your job was one of the things I found attractive about you in the first place. It would be wrong to fault you for doing it…even though you've been let go." He winced, and Madison could have punched him in the face. Instead she pressed her wineglass to her lips.

She swallowed some wine. "I appreciate your understanding."

Nothing more was said about her motives throughout dinner, and it felt like a hammer that could drop at any minute. She ordered another glass of wine, but the alcohol might as well have been a stimulant for the amount of good it was doing to calm her nerves.

While he was scouring the dessert menu, she'd had about enough, and asked casually, "You said you have the footage?"

He reached into his jacket and pulled out a USB stick. "I didn't watch it, but the file's on there. Trust me."

No way in hell!

He extended the drive to her. "This should clear Mr. R."

She bit back her automatic response, which would have been something along the lines of *I thought you just said you didn't watch it, so how would you know who it clears?*

"Thank you." She dropped the USB stick into her purse and pressed a button on her phone to make it ring. She wasn't going to get anything more out of Medcalf and was ready to take off with her spoils.

"Oh," Medcalf said with some surprise. "Is that your phone?"

She winced. "Yeah, I think it is." She pulled it out.

"You could just ignore it."

She looked at the display. "I can't. It's my mother. She hasn't been feeling too good lately."

"Sorry to hear that."

"Knight." She'd need to be more convincing than the last time she'd faked a phone call. "Hey, Mom… Yeah… Oh no… I'm actually on a date, can it wait?" She let seconds pass, trying to allow sufficient time for someone on the other end to speak—if there had been someone. "Yeah, I don't think—"

"That's okay. Go. I understand," Medcalf said, sitting back into his chair.

"I'll be there shortly, Mom. Love you." She closed her cell phone. "Thank you for under—"

"That wasn't your mother."

"Excuse me?"

"You looked at the caller display, said it was your mother, yet you answered with your surname."

It wasn't his deductive abilities that had held him back from being a cop. She had to think quick.

"I always answer that way," she said.

"I'm sure you do." His eyes flashed with a rage that frightened Madison.

"I don't know what to say."

"Start with the truth."

"I've got to go." She polished off the wine in her glass and rose from the table. She felt his eyes on her back. Terry had said he was a dangerous man, and she was starting to believe it.

CHAPTER FIFTY-THREE

Madison slipped into the passenger seat and flashed the USB stick at Terry. "I got what I came for. Let's get out of here."

"You okay?"

"Of course. No need to worry about me." She gave him a toothy grin. "Except I do need a change of clothes."

"You drank on the job. How is that fair?"

"What are you talking about?" Feign innocence.

"There's just enough light coming in from the streetlights. Your teeth are slightly purple."

"Oh, crap." She pulled down the sun visor and looked at herself in the tiny mirror. *Sure enough.* She wiped her teeth with a finger and, after she checked the results, slapped the visor back in place.

"You never let me drink on the job," Terry bellyached. "Remember that time at the pub, when we were working that one case? I wanted a draft beer really bad, and you said I couldn't because we were working."

"You whine a lot when you get fixated."

"Well, same thing, right? Not fair."

"Oh, shut up." She reached over and punched him in the shoulder.

He rubbed at it. "Much better." He was smiling.

"You wanted me to hit you? You really did miss me."

He shrugged.

"And just for the record, I never heard it from the sarge that I'm back yet." She shrugged. "So technically, am I on shift?"

"Well, I think you're going to want to be."

"To watch the video from Randall's boathouse?"

"Something even better. When you were in there romancing it up with Romeo—"

She hit him again and he laughed.

"I'm good and tender now. Thank you."

"You're welcome." She smiled at him.

Terry continued. "I got a call from Cynthia. She made it down to the station already, but you're never going to believe who else is there."

Back at her apartment, Madison changed her clothes as quickly as possible, but she couldn't go to the station until she took Hershey out.

She pushed Terry's number on her phone and wedged it between her ear and shoulder as she struggled to leash up Hershey. When Terry answered, she said, "Listen, I've got to take Hershey out real quick."

"Shit."

"Swearing your new thing now?"

"It's just that I'd like to get there before the entire show is over."

As if I don't!

She hung up on Terry and stuffed the phone back into her pocket. "One minute." She clicked the collar into place. "All right. Let's go."

As she waited on Hershey to take care of business, it felt like the wind had eyes.

Madison tapped on the driver's-side window, and Terry jumped and put the window down. "What?"

"Out. I'm driving." She pulled on the door handle. He'd locked it. "Come on."

"You've been drinking."

"I'm fine, actually. Just being out in the cold breeze while waiting for your Christmas gift to shit helped. Come on." Madison started bouncing up and down. "We don't have all night."

Terry sighed deeply and got out, walked around to the passenger side. "So now you're complaining about Hershey? You've never done that before."

She had to laugh at the density of sarcasm. It reminded her of herself. "You really missed me today, didn't you?"

"We talked about this already."

"I don't think we've explored it enough."

"I think we did just fine."

Her smile faded, and goose bumps spread over her arms. Looking around, she didn't see anyone. "I feel like I'm being watched." She glanced in the rearview mirror. No parked cars in the area. No cloaked figures standing in the shadows.

Terry peered over his shoulders. "I don't see anyone. You think it's Medcalf?"

"I have no idea. But I can tell you one thing—he wasn't too happy about my leaving, and he read through my staged phone call."

"That's because you're not an actress—"

She flashed him a glare.

"What?" he spat. "You're not."

"I just don't like this feeling. It makes my skin crawl."

"There's no one around. Let's just get going."

"Who are you, anyway?"

"What do you mean?"

"Well, I'm away from you for, what…not even a full day." She wasn't about to figure out the number of hours. "And now we're back together, and it's like looking at myself. You're sarcastic, impatient, impulsive."

"I'll take all of the above as a compliment." He smirked at her. "Now get us downtown."

"Okay, okay." With the words out of her mouth, it felt a little twilight zone, everything backward and upside down. Him in a hurry, her more relaxed.

She pulled the department car away from the curb and merged with traffic. It was about ten at night, but there was still a decent volume of traffic on the roads. The sun had long set, and it was drizzling. It left greasy streaks on the windshield that only got worse with each pass of the wiper blades. She pulled back for washer fluid and nothing came out. "You didn't fill up the fluid?"

"It's not my job."

"Terry, if you're going to take responsibility for the ride, then it is." She pulled into the nearest gas station.

"We're never going to get downtown."

"Patience." The word came out, and she was stumped. They had changed roles. "One minute." She flashed a single digit and slammed the car door shut. She could have kept driving with the smudged windshield, but she couldn't shake the feeling eyes were still on her. And that only meant one thing: someone was following them.

A car pulled up beside them and braked quickly, the nose diving down. She jumped, and her heart raced. The driver was a twentysomething male and didn't seem to pay her any attention.

Madison resumed breathing but continued to feel like someone was watching her. Turning around, she saw that a sedan was tucked into the corner of the property. That was their tail. A man, based on the size of the shadow, was behind the wheel.

She could go one of two ways: pretend she never noticed him and go on about her business or walk over and confront him. She'd go with the former for a while, though it wasn't easy. She hated the feeling of her skin prickling on the back of her neck, and for every second it took to fill the washer fluid, she was cringing inside. She snuck in quick glances over a shoulder, trying to make out more about the driver, but it was too dark. She got back into the department car and spoke facing forward. One of Terry's strengths was his ability to recall numbers and sequences even at a quick glance. "Far corner, Buick LeSabre. Run the plates."

He turned and said, "I can't read it."

"Ready?" She pressed the gas harder than she'd intended, and the car lurched backward. The twentysomething at the next pump yelled out, "What the fuck?"

"Smooth," Terry said.

"What is it? What does it say?"

Terry moved his head, trying to read the plate.

"Don't make it so obvious."

"I got it." Terry typed it into the onboard computer. Seconds later, he said, "You're not going to believe—"

"Try me."

"It's Jonathan Wright. Seems to me someone knows you have the video and probably wants it back."

Madison pulled the car out of the lot and watched in the rearview mirror as the car swerved out behind them.

CHAPTER FIFTY-FOUR

The Buick LeSabre followed them until they were a block from the station. Her heart kept an uneven rhythm during the entire drive.

"Does Wright honestly think we didn't make him?" Terry asked.

"I don't think he cares if we did."

"Do you think he wanted us to catch him watching us?"

"He probably feels untouchable, and I wouldn't be too surprised if he's the one who got rid of Turner. He knew about the counterfeiting and probably could have destroyed Randall. He was a liability. Liabilities—in some circles—need to be silenced. And Randall's right-hand man, no doubt also his cleanup man, is Jonathan Wright."

"If that's the case, he probably doesn't want us to see that video Medcalf gave you."

"Makes me want to even more." She pulled to a jerky stop, parking in the station's lot, and practically leaped from the vehicle.

"You dragged my client down here based on the words of a dead man." Blake felt a pulsing in his cheek, and he thrust a pointed finger against the table. Marcus Randall was seated next to him, and the two Secret Service agents across from them. They just kept hurling accusations and hearsay. "We're leaving." Blake motioned for Randall to move.

Weiss said, "I wouldn't be in a hurry to go anywhere. We might be here a while."

"This is ludicrous!" Randall shouted.

Blake put a hand out to silence his client, but the effort was ignored.

"I have more money than you could ever hope to have!" Randall lashed out at the agents. "Why on earth would I make fake bills?"

"Is it true that you would send your son around the world to set up new accounts?" Weiss asked calmly.

Blake advised Randall to keep quiet. "State the relevance," he said to Weiss.

"These accounts were made with dummy corporations, and your client knew this."

"I did not!"

Blake held an arm in front of his client. "I assume you have proof to back up these allegations."

Weiss jutted out his jaw. "We do, and we'll have more when we shut him down for a full investigation."

"Seems to me you had access to my client's financials before and found nothing to substantiate your claims."

"We now have witness testimony to the making of counterfeit funds on Randall's property."

"I have yet to see proof of that."

Weiss thumbed through a file folder and shuffled papers around.

Blake tapped a foot. "You're wasting my client's time and money."

"Everything was right here." The fiery piston looked at his older counterpart. "I know it was…" Papers continued moving.

"Well, since you have nothing to back up your accusations, gentlemen, we'll be leaving."

"We are the Secret Service. We want the answers, and we'll get them."

"Then I suggest you get the grounds before barking allegations."

"The counterfeit money was found on Chris Randall's person at the time of death."

"Proving nothing at all," Blake started. "You can't verify where those funds originated. The money was found on a dead man. There is no connection between the money and my client."

"Chris lived with his father. The deceased's best friend told police Mr. Randall was involved."

"Like you said, *deceased*. Do you have written legal testimony from him prior to death? Also, this is the same friend who died of a drug overdose, is it not? Not a very credible witness."

"Yet a man you had chosen to represent." Weiss let the implication that Blake took on questionable clients saturate before continuing. "It's quite coincidental that someone who can put you in prison for life decides to OD when it's convenient for you, Mr. Randall." Weiss pivoted to face Randall and cocked his head.

"We're leaving." Blake put a hand on Randall's shoulder and guided him out the door.

Madison picked up the package left for her at the front desk and opened it at hers. It was just a white bubble envelope. "Curious."

"Open it today." Terry tapped a foot, and Madison raised her eyebrows.

"I'm nowhere near that impatient."

"Depends on the day." Terry flailed a hand toward the envelope. "You going to open it?"

"Yikes." She pulled out a pair of scissors and slit the top, reached inside. She took out a USB drive. "It's the night for these."

"What's on it?"

Madison smirked at her partner. "We're headed to the lab. Let's just take this with us, shall we?"

They walked into the lab and found Cynthia at her desk surfing the internet. "I was just about to make a big mistake and order five DVDs for thirty dollars." She closed the internet browser. "It's about time you got here."

Madison had called Cynthia on the way to meeting Medcalf and asked her to come back in. She'd been operating under optimism that Medcalf would come through with the video footage. She glanced at the clock on the wall and realized that had been a couple hours ago now.

"You know how I'd love to get into a conversation about time and my poor management of it, but perhaps another time."

"Ha-ha."

Madison pulled out the USB drive containing the video footage from the boathouse and handed it to Cynthia. "And we got this…" She gave Cynthia the drive she just received.

"What's that?"

"To be seen. It came in addressed to me."

"Curious."

"Uh-huh, and I have this." Madison pulled out a freezer bag with—

"A crushed cigar," Cynthia observed. "My, you shouldn't have." Cynthia held a hand to her chest.

Madison looked at the contents and winced. It had started off as a full cigar but must have gotten beaten up in her pocket. "Hey, what does it matter? You're just going to cut it apart anyway."

"And where did you get it?"

"Hanigan's Market. I believe it's the brand that Randall smokes. I'd like to know if it matches the one that burnt Chris."

Cynthia opened the bag, pinched some of the cigar in tweezers, stuck it into a small vial, and put it in a machine. She called it the Dreamweaver. It provided answers for the composition of things on a molecular level. "This won't take long."

"Are you sure we can't just leave this? Come back after we watch the video?"

The machine beeped.

Madison turned to the Dreamweaver. "It's done already?"

"Yep. Not too much longer for popcorn, Maddy. Hold on." Cynthia laughed and took the printout results. "The components look familiar to me. You know, I think this may be…" She left them hanging there as she went to another computer and opened a file. "It's a match. Look." She pointed at the graph on the screen that resembled an element table. "I can tell you with certainty this is the brand of cigar that burned Chris Randall. What brand is it?"

"Sapphire Label." Madison looked at Terry. "It's not solid proof of murder, but it could get us one step closer to being able to believe Neil's account that Randall burned his son's hand."

"The question is, though, did he end up killing him?" Cynthia asked.

"We've decided we were asking for too much from one cigar," Terry said with a little chuckle.

Madison pointed to the TV that was mounted on the wall. "Let's see what we have," she prompted Cynthia. "But you should probably hold off on the butter."

"What's the point, then?" Cynthia laughed. "Boathouse footage first?"

"Sure, why not?"

Cynthia went over to the television and stuck the appropriate USB drive into a side slot, fooled around with the menu, and the footage started to play.

Terry said, "It's outside the boathouse…" Both women looked at him.

"Really? And here I thought it would be college-campus porn." Cynthia started laughing. It was cut short.

"Who's that?" Madison asked. A dark figure served as the footage's main star. "Can you adjust it?"

"I can on my computer, but it will take time."

"The date stamped in the bottom right corner is January eleventh, four in the morning," Madison began. "That would be after Ryan and Chris left the club. Still can't make out who that is, though."

"The figure does look somewhat familiar." The person was headed away from the boathouse. "Wait a minute… Yep, look how he walks. It's Neil Silverman. Maybe after Chris told him to leave…if we were to believe Neil's account."

Another man stepped into the view of the camera. His hands were huddled together in front of his face, and there was a flick of light. His shape was easier to identify.

"It's Marcus Randall," Madison said. "And he just lit a cigar, but it's not adding up. Pause it for a second?" Madison did her best to think clearly, but her mind was all jumbled. "Both men came out of the boathouse within minutes of each other. Silverman first, but I thought…"

"Neil told us that Marcus Randall left first, leaving him with Chris. So he's either a liar or… Why would he lie?"

"To cover his tracks," Madison said.

"But he'd have to know we might see this video," Terry countered.

"He was probably counting on the fact we never would."

"Huh."

"Play more, Cyn."

She hit the button on the remote, and the screen went black.

"What? Where is it?" Madison asked.

"That's it."

"That's all Medcalf gave me," Madison snarled.

"Well, I'd say he just gave you what he wanted to," Terry said. "Who knows if the video was messed with…I'm thinking sections spliced together. That the word?" He looked at Cynthia, who nodded.

"I can take a closer look and see."

"That gets us nowhere, then. If we don't even know the legitimacy of the video, it doesn't mean Neil lied to us. Back to the starting point."

"Let's look at this other USB," Cynthia said with an encouraging tone. "No record of who it came from?" She popped this drive into her computer.

"None," Madison replied.

"Okay, there's two files on here. An audio and a video."

"Let's do the video first," Madison said.

Cynthia took the USB drive out of the computer and swapped it out for the one in the television. All that showed up was the time stamp. *4:55 AM, January 11.*

"Where's the picture?" Madison asked.

"Not sure," Cynthia started. "It was just working."

"Are you determined to destroy everything?" a man's voice said through the speakers.

Madison started toward the door. "I know who that is."

"Hold on. There's more here," Cynthia called out.

Madison stopped moving and listened to the rest of the recording. The audio/video captured a scene that only got more heated, exposing a man who was jealous of everything Chris had and would ever have. A man angry enough to kill for it.

There was yelling and accusations followed by the sounds of shattering ice and splashing water. Screams spoke of the stabbing pains of freezing water, and Chris sealed his fate when he yelled at his attacker, telling him that he was a nobody.

In a voice that smacked of otherworldly, his attacker calmly said, "I would've been thankful!"

More screams came from Chris and splashing water as he would have fought for his life.

"I've heard enough. Let me know what's on the audio file." With that, Madison left the lab, Terry behind her.

CHAPTER FIFTY-FIVE

"Where is he?" Madison asked the officer at the front desk, who must have been new to the rotation because Madison didn't recognize her.

"Who?"

"Marcus Randall. He's here for questioning with the Secret Service."

Madison looked up when a new shadow cast across the floor. It was Blake.

Oh, lucky me.

Terry backed up and then turned, headed in the direction of their desks.

"What are you doing here?" she challenged Blake.

"I think you know why I'm here. Surprised you are."

Terry must have told him about the suspension when he'd paid him a visit. "I've been reinstated," she said.

"Good for you." Blake glanced at the officer sitting at the front desk and back to Madison. "Can we go somewhere private?"

Madison shrugged her shoulders.

"You can use interrogation room one," the officer offered with a smile and a wink. "It's empty now."

If the officer was ever going to advance her rank, she was going to have to work on reading people and situations.

"Fine, let's go," she said coolly. "I trust you know where you're headed by now."

Once they got to the room, Blake shut the door behind them and put a hand on her forearm. "I'm not him you know."

"Really? You're bringing up my past. Toby Sovereign, fear of commitment—none of it—is why we're over."

"You sure it's not a small factor?"

Her earlobes were sizzling with anger. "Everything isn't about that." Besides if Blake really cared for her, he'd fight for her. And he hadn't so much as called in days.

"You need me to come out and say it?" he punched out when she said nothing more.

"Guess I do."

"I want you to let your guard down with me. Despite what you might think, I'm a good guy, Maddy. Not that I should have to say that at this point."

Her head hurt, her heart ached, and she was tired. But she had a killer to apprehend. "I've got to go."

He reached out to stop her, his eyes pleading with her.

"It's just not working for me anymore," she said. "I'm sorry."

"Come on."

She shook her head. "I'm sorry, Blake. And for what it's worth I did really care about you, maybe even loved you."

"Then don't leave me."

She kissed his lips, lingered there before pulling away. Her heart pounded, and she found it hard to breathe. Even if she healed past hurts, she didn't think she could overlook the fact their career paths ran parallel anymore.

"He must have hurt you pretty badly." He paused, trying to read her eyes. "Explain it to Hershey for me?" The corners of his mouth lifted.

"I will." She found herself smiling.

"Stay in touch and take care of yourself."

"It's you who keeps dangerous company," she tossed back.

He was scowling at first, but when she smiled, so did he.

She didn't know when or even if she'd ever speak with him again. No doubt he'd show up in her interrogation room from time to time, but she was okay—*would be* okay—since it was her decision to end it. And really, her heart had been saying goodbye to him for days.

"Okay, let's get this done." Madison jabbed Terry softly in the shoulder before getting into the department car. "You call the chief?"

"Yep."

"He coming in?"

"Nope."

"What do you mean?" Her voice might have hit a higher octave than she liked, but he'd meddled in the entire investigation, and now that it was about to wrap up, he was backing off. *Unbelievable.* "Nope, he's coming." She steered the car in the direction of McAlexandar's house. Once there, she realized *house* didn't do the structure justice. It was a small mansion with columns and a balcony that hung over the front doors.

"Can't believe we're doing this," Terry grumbled.

She pressed the doorbell. It wasn't until the fourth time that the door opened. McAlexandar stared back at them with bloodshot eyes.

"What the fuck are you two doing here?" His speech was slurred, and he could barely hold himself upright. Terry went to support him, but he shrugged out of the way. "I'm not an invalid," he hissed. "Can't a man have a couple drinks?" He held up a glass that was nearly empty. The real question was could a drop of alcohol be found in the place. "Go aw—"

"We need your help," Terry cut in.

"Tomorrow." He lifted his glass, sniffed it, and banged into the doorframe.

"Unbelievable! The guy's wasted out of his mind!" Madison stormed past McAlexandar into his house.

"Hey, where do you think you're going?" McAlexandar pointed a finger toward Terry. "You can come in. She stays outside."

"Too late, Chief." She put her hands on her hips. "Your friend is in deeper than he knows, and we need your help."

"And why the hell would I help you?" He burped, and the stench of bile wafted through the air.

How much booze has he had?

"Terry." She looked at her partner and enlarged her eyes.

"Why don't we get you some coffee?" Terry started out in one direction then backtracked another way. "Where is your kitchen?"

"To the left, you fool." McAlexandar wiped his mouth.

Her stomach soured. "Yes…coffee's always a great idea." She walked ahead of the chief, wanting to put some space between her and his disgusting odor.

CHAPTER FIFTY-SIX

After four cups of coffee, McAlexandar was still about as drunk as an all-star after a championship game.

Madison leaned over to Terry in the passenger seat. "This isn't going to work."

McAlexandar was in the back seat of the department car, and they were headed to the Randall estate.

"You know I can hear you. I'm sitting right here."

She glanced in the rearview at him and shook her head. As if they needed verbal confirmation of his presence. He reeked like a college dorm.

She pulled into the driveway for Randall's estate. Freddy approached the car. "Mr. Randall isn't expecting any visitors."

"Save it," McAlexandar snapped. "We need in."

"Oh, my apologies, sir. I didn't notice"—Freddy bent over, trying to establish a clear line of sight through the driver's window—"you back there. I'll let Mr. Randall know you're coming in."

In the rearview, McAlexandar gave him the one-finger salute.

Madison snickered. The chief was rather likeable and entertaining while drunk.

Medcalf opened the front door, passed a judgmental glance at Madison, and she sensed more than anger in his eyes, but she couldn't put her finger on what.

Randall walked into the room. "Patrick, I must say good timing on you. I was just about to contact you. It seems something has gone missing."

"We need to talk. In private," McAlexandar said.

Randall leaned in and sniffed the air. "We've had a few, have we, Patrick? What a shame to break so many years of sobriety." Randall shrugged, then circled the three of them like a vulture eyeing prey. "It seems some digital footage from my boathouse camera is missing. I thought I'd denied access to it."

"You did." McAlexandar kept his gaze on Randall. "We need to talk in private."

Randall nodded, and he and McAlexandar went off in the direction of the office.

It left Madison with Terry and Medcalf. There was no sign of Jonathan Wright.

"How's your dying mother?" Medcalf asked.

"Oh, my mother. She's—"

"Save it. I'm sure she's just fine. Believe it or not, I've been used before. Just never for video footage."

A door slammed open, and Randall stormed toward them in full-length coat, McAlexandar trailing him.

Medcalf paled. "Sir, are you okay?"

"Put your coat on, Medcalf."

"Sir?"

"You heard me. Put your coat on. We're going down to the boathouse to get this shit over with once and for all. You'll be my material witness."

"Sir?" Medcalf repeated.

"Now. Wright's not here, so you'll have to do."

Madison watched the expression on Medcalf's face morph from one of embarrassment to one of pride.

Randall stood a few feet inside the doorway of the boathouse. "There. This is what you wanted to see, Patrick? A boathouse? How exciting."

Madison glanced at Medcalf but spoke to Randall. "Do you smoke Sapphire Label cigars?" she asked, though she was quite certain he did.

Randall shook his head. "I'm not sure what that has to do with anything."

McAlexandar turned on Randall. "Marcus, just answer the question."

Randall's jaw tightened. "Yes."

"Chris was burnt on the back of his left hand with that brand of cigar," Madison laid out. She knew it didn't mean Randall had killed his son, but it did lend credibility to Neil's account of what transpired in the boathouse between father and son.

Randall's face was getting redder with each passing second. "If you had anything on me, we wouldn't be talking here. We'd be downtown."

"Huh," Madison huffed out. "His lifestyle hurt you badly."

"That's ludicrous! I loved Chris!" Spittle flew from Randall's mouth.

"He used you, and in turn, you killed him," Madison exaggerated and paced, her eyes studying both Randall and Medcalf. The latter stood near the door, his hands clasped in front of him. "Right there!" she shouted, and Medcalf flinched. She pointed to where the ice had been broken and re-formed.

"Tox revealed evidence of boat gasoline in Chris's lungs," Terry interjected. "No doubt a water sample here will help support this as the location where he was drowned."

"You got into an argument with Chris," Madison said. "We have a witness to that effect."

"Who? That faggot? He's a nobody. My boy turned him down."

"That *nobody* can take you down for murder," Madison shot back, pulling from her core to ante up the dramatics.

Randall stiffened. "You can't prove anything."

Madison's phone rang. She put some space between herself and the others and placed her back to them. She was going to play this situation out delicately and tamper with Randall's patience. "Knight." She listened to her caller's message, thanked them, and hung up.

"Who was it?" Randall demanded.

"Are we going to find evidence of your DNA on this?" Madison pulled out another cigar from her pocket, to use as a ploy. This one had remained intact. He didn't even seem to notice it hadn't been smoked.

"What are you talking about? Did you collect something?" Randall turned to McAlexandar. "They were to look around *only*."

"Detective Knight, you're out of line," McAlexandar roared.

Medcalf's lips lifted ever so slightly at the chief's reprimand.

"You've been trying to hide the truth this whole time," she accused Randall. "Well, the truth has a way of coming out. This is the type of cigar that burnt Chris's hand just before he died. We collected a cigar in your boathouse—right here, actually." She tapped a spot on the deck with her foot.

Medcalf put a hand on his employer's shoulder. "Sir?"

"Keep quiet. You shouldn't even be here. Leave." Randall established eye contact with the man.

"I won't let them do this to you, sir. You didn't do it." Everyone's eyes were on Medcalf. He pleaded, "Mr. Randall never would have done this to Chris. Ever."

"Evidence says otherwise," Madison said. She'd wondered how long it would take until Medcalf stepped in.

Terry walked around the boathouse, scanning the walls and studying the deck boards. "No one else fits the evidence and the motives." He stopped moving and faced Medcalf. "It makes sense, unless you know of someone else."

"Why would I know?" Medcalf lifted his shoulders and expelled a large breath of air. When no one spoke, Medcalf shook his head rapidly. "Why? Why ask me?"

Madison stopped inches in front of Medcalf, about to reveal to him this entire thing was a ruse to get him to talk. "Chris had everything you didn't."

Randall's gaze was on Medcalf with homicidal intensity. "You killed my boy!"

"No...no!" Medcalf's chest heaved. "You people don't know what you're talking about. You come in accusing Mr. R of doing something. Something he didn't do."

"Found something." Terry was on his haunches in a far corner of the boathouse.

"What are you doing over there?" Medcalf protested. "What—"

Randall grabbed Medcalf, spun him around, and punched him in the face. There was a loud cracking noise, and Medcalf cried out in pain. He cradled his nose. Blood was dripping through his fingers, and Madison's stomach flip-flopped.

"You killed my son, you fuckin' son of a bitch!" Randall shook his hand that he'd used to hit Medcalf. "You live in my damn house and you killed my only fuckin' son!" Randall's body sagged and tears poured down his cheeks.

Terry hurried over and cuffed Medcalf. McAlexandar stood beside Randall, trying to comfort him.

"This was all a ruse?" Medcalf laughed. "To get me to say something? Well, I've done nothing wrong."

"That's not what the evidence has to say." She paused, and rage flashed in Medcalf's eyes. "We can put you with Chris during his last moments alive. He told you that you were a nobody and you—"

Medcalf's cheeks went a brilliant red, and he turned to Randall. "I didn't kill him. You have to believe me."

Randall spit in his face. "You make me sick." To Terry, he said, "Get him out of my sight."

Medcalf started crying like a man who finally realized he had lost everything. "He didn't appreciate you. You deserved his respect!"

"Don't you dare drag me into this," Randall growled.

"You were like a father to me."

"You were no son of mine."

"He used you and rubbed everything you gave him in your face."

Randall turned his back. "Get him out of here!"

Terry rapped on the door and passed Medcalf over to two cops, who had been stationed outside the boathouse.

"You hit me! I'll sue you!" Medcalf yelled as if one of the officers had attacked him.

McAlexandar addressed both Madison and Terry. "I wouldn't give a shit if one of the officers did hit him. We didn't see anything." He put an arm around his friend's back. "I'm sorry to put you through this, but we figured it might be the easiest way to get Medcalf to confess."

Randall sniffled and held out a hand to Madison. "Thank you."

Madison nodded, feeling like justice was finally going to be served. She turned to Terry, who was hunched down again, this time looking over the ice.

"I might have found the cigar we've been looking for." Terry pointed to one encased in some of the ice that had re-formed.

Madison looked closely where Terry was indicating. It would be easy to mistake it for a twig or piece of brush, but Terry was right. It was a cigar.

In the car, Madison disclosed the details of the phone call she had received to Terry. "Cynthia listened to the audio file and found out that the package came from Ryan Turner."

"Ryan?" Terry gasped.

"Yeah. And the audio file was sort of a verbal tell-all and confessional. He was there the night Chris was murdered. Well, outside the boathouse."

"Why wouldn't he have stepped in to help his friend?"

"He was terrified," Madison started. "And he'd held off from sharing any of this from us because he didn't want to be viewed as a suspect."

"How chivalrous," Terry said sarcastically. "Maybe he was planning to give us the USB when he called us to his house, but chickened out?"

"Could be. Cynthia said that he admitted to struggling with his conscience. He'd wanted to give us the files that night he called us but couldn't bring himself to do so."

"And what about the Mafia? He wanted us to believe they killed Chris."

"Well, apparently he was racked with guilt over keeping his silence and not helping Chris. I think the threat of the mob was real when it came to him, though." Madison went quiet for a few seconds. "Turner also said that if we were listening to his files, he was already dead and got what he deserved."

Silence passed between the two of them.

"Did he say anything more about the counterfeiting?" Terry said.

"Yeah. It was all him and Chris, and he gave the location where they were making the money. He said Marcus Randall had nothing to do with it."

"How convenient."

"Well, you didn't really expect Randall to be serving any time, did you?"

"Did he confirm that Medcalf had killed Chris?"

Madison shook her head. "No. Just said we had to listen to the video file."

"You know it's all good that Ryan had this change of heart, but we can't use any of it."

"We already have. Will what Turner sent us make it to court? Not likely, but we have our focus on the right man now. We just need to round up the necessary forensic evidence and really nail Medcalf to the wall."

"None of this explains why Wright was stalking us," Terry said. "We have nothing that implicates him in the murder of Chris or Ryan."

"I have no doubts that he's behind Ryan's death. We owe it to him to—"

"Oh no, I don't do side missions."

"I just feel like we failed him." She felt herself sinking into regrets.

"Let's go back to Wright. We'd talked about him knowing we had the video footage from the boathouse."

"I think he did. And, really, what was on that video could have been construed as evidence against Marcus Randall."

"Not that Wright would have known either way."

"Well, he wasn't about to take any chances. His job is to look out for Randall," she said. "And Medcalf probably figured that by giving us pieces of the surveillance footage, he'd look cooperative and—"

"Pieces?"

Madison nodded. "Cynthia was able to confirm that the video from the boathouse had been tampered with."

"So, Medcalf gave us what he wanted us to see."

"Yeah." Madison thought about that for a moment. "There were two people who *starred* in the video: Marcus Randall and Neil Silverman. He knew we wanted to see Randall, so he gave him to us."

"Sure, but why Neil?"

"He didn't know we'd get him on the audio/video from Turner."

"Excuse me? Now I'm lost."

She met his gaze, and her chest tightened with an epiphany. "I think that maybe Medcalf didn't work alone." She put the car into gear and hit the gas. "Call Cynthia, make sure she's still at the lab."

"What's going on?"

"I need to listen to the audio/video from Turner again."

"You think we missed something?"

"I do." She took a right-hand turn a little too fast, and the car's chassis rolled like a boat on stormy seas.

CHAPTER FIFTY-SEVEN

Madison and Terry startled Cynthia when they walked into the lab.

She spun in her chair and put a hand to her heart. "It's way too early to be here."

"Catching a killer—or two—doesn't necessarily fall into regular business hours," Madison said as she rushed over to Cynthia. "I need to listen to the audio/video that Turner sent in again."

"Sure," Cynthia said slowly and set off to collect the USB stick.

Madison glanced at Terry. "We never did get a satisfying answer as to why Neil's prints were on the rescue jaw in his father's boathouse. Or how the one that belonged to Marcus Randall had made its way there…"

"And whoever it was would have needed a key to get in," Terry finished.

Madison nodded.

Cynthia popped the drive in and hit Play.

Madison listened closely. "There. Pause it. Rewind." And there is was: unmistakably another voice. She smirked at Terry and Cynthia, and they were smiling at her.

"I'll be damned," Terry said.

Medcalf was in a holding cell, trying to figure out how the hell he was going to get out of here. He'd been so careful. He had been wearing gloves and taken precautions not to leave DNA behind. Who the hell had put him at the scene of

Chris's murder—and how did the detectives know Chris had called him a nobody? Though he had one very good idea. He clenched his hands into fists.

Medcalf should have just walked away. When he'd entered the boathouse that night, he never expected to find Chris in the freezing cold water, yelling for help, trying to grasp the surface of the ice to gain leverage—a man about Chris's age holding him down with the rescue jaw, tears streaking down his face.

But seeing Chris so helpless, floundering about, had felt so empowering. Like righteous payback somehow.

"He doesn't have respect for anyone but himself," the man said with an eerie confidence.

Medcalf remembered studying the man, wondering how Chris had wronged him to such a degree.

"You're not going to stop me?"

Medcalf's eyes were glued to Chris, and he slowly shook his head, then reached for the rescue jaw.

The man handed it over, and Medcalf took his turn pushing Chris under. Adrenaline coursed through him, the power intoxicating.

"Let me again," the man told him.

Medcalf had reluctantly handed the rescue jaw back to him.

When no more bubbles came, the man pulled a wad of hundred-dollar bills an inch thick from his pocket. "Take care of all this."

Medcalf had nodded then, and the man left with the implement of death.

But that was then, and this was now, and Medcalf was far from pleased. He shouldn't be going down for Chris's murder. He technically hadn't killed him, had he? And he'd even provided the detectives a clue with the snippet of video he'd handed over, but they'd failed to see the truth. If he was going down for Chris's murder, he'd be taking the man with him—and he'd better hurry. The first person to speak to the cops received a better deal.

"Hey, officer," he called out to one doing his rounds. "I'd like you to call Detective Knight."

Madison came up on the BMW at the side of the road. The patrol officer had the man cuffed at the side of the vehicle, and he looked away as Madison and Terry walked over.

She studied Neil Silverman. "Did you really think you were going to get off?"

"You need a hobby, lady. You have your arrest."

"And how do you know that?"

"None of your business."

"Your father called you."

Neil shrugged.

"We have your prints," she said, "on Randall's rescue jaw that we found in your father's boathouse."

Neil rolled his eyes. "Here we go again."

"But I don't think it went down exactly the way we—"

Her cell rang as if on cue. She held a finger up to Neil and answered. "You're sure?" She kept her gaze on Neil while on the phone, then hung up, looked at Terry, and shook her head.

"Aw, things are not working out as you had hoped?" Neil whined. "I'll sue the department for harassment. You have nothing on me. Uncuff me!"

"Not on your life."

"You're crazy. It was the cook, not me. I loved Chris."

"When you speak those words, rage fires in your eyes. It was an unrequited love, and people have killed for a lot less."

"I didn't kill him!"

"You even paid someone to help you out," Madison said, pulling from the news she'd received during the phone call.

Neil's eyes narrowed. "And how do you plan on proving that?" he spat.

"You assumed I received bad news," she said, "but we have someone in holding right now who's interested in making a deal."

Neil glanced between the two of them. "No, he wouldn't. You're lying."

"Your prints are on the murder weapon," she said, disregarding his rant. "The rescue jaw came from the Randall boathouse. It was a means of opportunity. It was right there. Then you put it in your father's boathouse, one you told us you've never been. But you do have a key for it, am I right?"

"He pushed him under," Neil said, avoiding her question.

Madison held up a hand. "You took turns," she said sharing another brief tidbit she'd received from her caller.

Neil paled, and Madison motioned for him to be loaded into the squad car and taken to the station.

With them gone, Madison brought up her text messages. She'd seen the icon letting her know she had a new message when she'd answered her phone. She read the message and gave Terry the gist. "Too early for DNA results on the cigar we pulled from the ice, but there's DNA there. Cynthia believes she'll be able to tell who smoked it and confirm that particular cigar was the one to burn Chris." Madison paused to smile at that victory. "And it's the same brand that Neil gave us."

"He's certainly one cocky son of—"

"Terry?"

He smiled and waved a hand. "Nah, I'm just teasing. I'm going back to a clean mouth."

Madison laughed. "We have Neil Silverman, and all the forensic evidence so far nails it."

Silence fell between them briefly.

"But how do we nail Medcalf? It's not like we can use Turner's recording," Terry said.

Sadness knotted her gut. "There's no way I can let Medcalf walk for his role in Chris's death."

Terry stared at her, shook his head, and then smiled. "No need. He was asking for a deal. To me, that's as much a confession to guilt as anything."

She smiled. "I guess it is."

"We also have an ace up our sleeve..." Terry smiled. "Medcalf doesn't know the cigar came back matching to Silverman."

"Oh, I like where you're going with this, partner. We make Medcalf think forensics implicate him, he signs an actual confession, and off to prison he goes. Though we might never know which of them held Chris under until he took his last breath."

"I think I can live with knowing they both had a role."

"Me, too, and don't forget, both will be going to prison for a very long time."

"The deal you mentioned?" Terry prompted. "I didn't think you gave deals."

"Yeah. Medcalf might have been led to believe he was getting one for giving us Neil's name, but like you said, I don't give deals."

Terry smiled.

"There's something we need to take care of," she said.

"Yeah. My twenty." Terry held out his hand. "Come on, pay up. You said Randall was involved in his son's death. I disagreed. Remember? Back at the garage at Randall Investments?"

"Really? I don't remember..." She walked toward the department car. "You should have recorded it."

Madison smiled at Terry, who stood next to her outside Martha Cooper's front door. She'd rang the doorbell once already. "No one ever answers the first time, do—"

The door opened, and Martha stood there.

"Tell me you found my boy's killer," she said.

"We did." The poor woman had been through enough, so Madison got to the point and told her they had her son's killers in custody. It took seconds for Madison's words to set in.

"More than one?"

"Yes, and I'll tell you everything. Can we come inside?"

"But of course, of course." She led them to the living room where they had been before, and everyone sat down. Cooper snagged a tissue from a box and dabbed her nose. She balled it in her hand and looked expectantly at Madison.

Madison proceeded to tell her all about Neil Silverman and Tony Medcalf, while Cooper cried.

"I have something for you." Madison reached into a coat pocket and handed Cooper a small manila envelope.

She opened the top tab and slid out the contents. Fresh tears saturated her cheeks. "You remembered!" She held the necklace with its pendant in the air. "My Chris, my sweet Christopher, may you rest in peace now." She kissed the pendant, and her eyes beaded with tears. "Thank you so very much." She got to her feet, as did Madison. Cooper wrapped her arms around Madison and squeezed. It felt good, and Madison hugged back.

"Will you…" Cooper gave Madison the necklace, turned, and swept up her hair. Madison latched the necklace and tapped a hand on the woman's back when she'd finished.

Cooper laid a hand over the pendant and spun. "The charges have been laid, though? This is final?"

"Charges still have to go before the district attorney, but we have a solid case," Madison said. "They will pay for killing your son." She knew her partner was watching her. He didn't like it when she spoke in absolutes, even with the evidence in their favor. She guessed it was all in perception, because, to her, this was a done deal. Both men would be going away—for a very, very long time if she could help it.

EPILOGUE

Later that week...

"I hate these things," Madison said, standing beside Terry at a news conference. "They're just another way to extend the drama."

Marcus Randall had demanded that all the local paper and television networks assemble at Randall Investments while he discussed the murder of his son, his lifestyle choices, and to announce that the counterfeiting investigation against him had been dropped. But Madison didn't want to think too much about that. She'd turned the audio from Ryan Turner in to the Secret Service, and they had confiscated the printers and plates used in the bills' manufacturing, but nothing was found to implicate Randall. It was like anything that might have existed had vanished into thin air.

Terry leaned in toward her. "Think of it this way, you'll be honored for all your hard work."

This whole affair had nothing to do with them; it was a power move by Randall to protect his interests. Total attendance was an estimated five hundred.

"You know none of that shit means anything to me," she said.

Terry chuckled and rolled his eyes.

Randall took the platform as eager reporters crowded in to get the first word. "As you may have heard, the Stiles PD apprehended my son's killers yesterday. And it is with great gratitude and warmness of heart that I extend this plaque—"

Madison whispered in her partner's ear. "Did he just say *plaque*?"

"—to Major Crimes Detectives Madison Knight and Terry Grant."

She nudged Terry's elbow. "And we have to share?"

People clapped.

Randall extended his arms, raising the plaque for everyone to see. Just another photo op. "Get up here, you two, and accept what you deserve."

"We deserve a cheap-ass plaque for finding his son's killers? Wow, thank you."

Terry laughed.

She hated public speaking—no, detested it. Randall handed the plaque to her, and the audience continued their applause. She smiled and dipped at the hips—a poor attempt at a curtsy, but wasn't that what etiquette called for?

"Speech!" said a man's voice in the crowd.

If Madison could get a fix on who had said it, she'd hunt him down and make their life a living nightmare. Broken taillight? License renewal not current? One mile over the speed limit? There were ways to exact payback.

"Please, I would be honored." Randall moved over, giving her access to the podium.

The room fell silent. Flashing camera lights twinkled.

Maybe the spotlight wasn't that bad. She felt honored, not because of some stupid plaque, but just for getting some recognition.

She looked over a diverse sea of people and felt overwhelmed. "Thank you, Mr. Randall," she started.

"Please, call me Marcus," he said, leaning in to the microphone.

Everyone clapped, and she waited for the applause to die down before speaking. "My partner and I are honored that you chose to acknowledge our efforts in finding your son's killers, Mr. Rand—*Marcus*. But it is what we do every day as Major Crimes detectives. We bring answers to those who don't have them. We dig and uncover truths that most people would rather leave buried under lies and misconceptions." She paused, taking in the moment, everyone's eyes on her. Her hands started to shake, and she glanced at Terry for the strength to continue. He gave her a slight bob of his head, and she went on. "We live to find justice for the murdered and bring some peace back to their families. Again, we are honored. Thank you."

The applause went on for several minutes. As Madison and Terry made their way back to where they were standing before, Randall resumed his place at the podium.

"And I want to call my great friend and chief of police, Patrick McAlexandar, to the podium."

McAlexandar wasted no time joining his friend on stage, and the two men shook hands.

Madison turned to leave. "This is where I'm calling it a day."

A woman's voice called out from the audience, "Chief McAlexandar, is the rumor true? Are you running for mayor in the fall?"

Madison paused in her footsteps, a smile on her lips. All she could think was *That's the way real life works.* So often the unscrupulous went unpunished and even got ahead. And she wasn't just thinking of Marcus Randall; she had no doubt the chief was as dirty as cops came. She'd bet her badge that McAlexandar had made any evidence in the counterfeiting case against Randall disappear.

Good things didn't always happen to good people, and bad things didn't always happen to bad people. It wasn't necessarily fair, but in the end, life had a way of balancing out. And every once in a while, it required a sacrifice.

Catch the next book in the
Detective Madison Knight Series!

Sign up at the weblink listed below
to be notified when new Madison Knight titles are available
for pre-order:

CarolynArnold.net/MKUpdates

By joining this newsletter, you will also receive exclusive
first looks at the following:

Updates pertaining to upcoming releases in the series, such
as cover reveals, book descriptions, and firm release dates

Sneak peeks of teasers and special content

Behind-the-Tape™ insights that give you an inside look at
Carolyn's research and creative process

There is no getting around it: reviews are important and so is word of mouth.

With all the books on the market today, readers need to know what's worth their time and what's not. This is where you come into play.

If you enjoyed *Sacrifice*, please help others find it by posting a brief, honest review on the retailer site where you purchased this book and recommend it to family and friends.

Also, Carolyn loves to hear from her readers, and you can reach her at Carolyn@CarolynArnold.net.

Upon receipt of your e-mail, you will be added to her newsletter mailing unless you express your desire otherwise.

Keep on reading for a sample of *Found Innocent*, book 4 in the Detective Madison Knight series.

CHAPTER ONE

"He didn't do it!"

The hysterical shouting pulled Detective Madison Knight's attention from her monitor to a woman rushing toward her.

What the hell?

Madison rose from her chair and held up her hands to stop the woman. "I'm going to ask that you—"

"Detective Knight." The woman stated this as if they had met before.

"That's me, but—"

Officer Ranson, the female officer who manned the front desk, stepped into view and mouthed, *Sorry*, to Madison.

Another officer brushed past Ranson and slipped his hands under the woman's arms. "Let's go."

He pulled on her, but she stayed still. Her eyes steadied on Madison.

"Please help me." She attempted to shake loose from the officer's grip. Her frown lines were deep burrows, her eyes were sunken, and the flesh around them was puffy. She appeared to be rough-edged, and while there was something desperate about her, Madison wasn't reading anything sinister.

"I've got this," Madison said, though begrudgingly. The only reason she was at the police station today was because it was Sunday, and typically, Sundays were quiet. She had plans to dig into her cold case.

"All right. Your call." The male officer let go of the woman, and he and Ranson left.

"I saw your face in the paper." The woman held up the *Stiles Times* and jabbed a fingertip to a photograph.

Madison passed a glance at the paper. It captured a moment she wished to forget. A day when she had been forced to speak in front of a crowd and take pride in the job she had done. The thing was, though, most good cops couldn't care less about the recognition—and Madison was one of them.

"It's you, isn't it?" Her lashes were caked with mascara, and she blinked so slowly that Madison wondered if the cosmetic had sealed her eyes shut.

"Yeah, that's me."

"Well, he wouldn't have done what they said he did."

Madison summoned patience and took a deep breath. She actually felt like she'd been making headway. A list of local printing companies—which could prove to be a vital link in the chain of evidence against the Russian Mafia—was on her monitor right now, waiting for her review.

She glanced at it and turned back to the woman. "Come with me."

Madison kept the woman to the side of her. Her first impression was the woman didn't pose a threat, but she still wasn't willing to risk her back by leading the way. She took her to a soft interview room with a couch and chairs, and then gestured for the woman to enter first.

The woman dropped her red purse heavily on the coffee table and pulled off her jean jacket, which she folded and put on the cushion beside her as she sat on the couch. She was wearing an oversized pink sweater, but it still managed to display more cleavage than Madison had any hope of ever seeing on herself. The woman rummaged through her large bag and came out with a stick of gum that she popped into her mouth. She chomped on it like a cow on cud.

Madison remained standing and said, "Let's start with your name—"

"Vilma with an 'i.' Thorne is the last name, or it would have been. My God, Kev!" She raised her face upward as if calling out to a greater being, her gum chewing paused momentarily.

"Vilma…" Madison tried to tune out the dramatics. She was getting a headache. "Let's start at the beginning. Why are you here, and who is Kev?"

Vilma stuck her finger through one of the large gold hoops dangling from her ears and leaned in.

Madison inhaled a strong blend of cheap perfume and cigarettes. She risked taking a deeper whiff—maybe it wasn't perfume but whiskey. Though Vilma appeared sober. But maybe it had been an error in judgment to give her an audience… "Okay, Vilma. If you need my help, I need you to talk to me."

"My family is against what he did. But he didn't do it! He wouldn't do it. Not two days before our wedding!" Her voice rose, tears flowed. She stopped chewing and, sniffling, went rooting in her purse for a second time. Madison held her breath—just a little—wondering what was going to come out. This time, the woman held a well-used tissue and dabbed it to her nose. "And tomorrow he's going in the ground and no one will know the truth of what really happened!"

"You keep saying he didn't do it." Madison's patience had hit its limit. "Do *what*?"

A tissue still pinched on the tip of her nose, Vilma said, "Kevin didn't kill himself. Someone killed him."

CHAPTER TWO

The next morning Madison still wondered why she'd ever agreed to look into the death of Kevin Thorne. But Vilma had pleaded and said that he'd only been twenty-seven when he'd died last month, and the ruling that it was suicide had to have been a mistake. She was probably just in denial, which was only made worse because the funeral was today. But suicide doesn't come with the same closure as a natural or accidental death. It leaves behind a myriad of haunting questions. *Did I miss seeing something? Could I have helped? If I had done this or that, would he still be here?*

Madison flicked a pen across her desk and thought about how the interaction had changed the direction of her day. She hadn't accomplished much with her cold case, and it had kept her up most of the night. She knew who was behind the murder, but she had to prove who pulled the trigger.

The victim was a defense attorney who had been gunned down in his driveway after failing to come through for his client, Dimitre Petrov, a Russian Mafia boss. Dimitre was sent away on a life sentence for a single murder, a joke since the man's hands were stained with the blood of many others. With him behind bars, she knew he wasn't physically involved, but she believed he'd ordered the hit. It was a matter of proving her theory and which of his right-hand men were responsible—and all that beyond a doubt to the district attorney and subsequent jury.

The bit of evidence she focused on these days came down to two envelopes, both with an infinity symbol woven into the stationery. A piece of one was found next to the dead lawyer and Dimitre Petrov had sent her a letter in another just like it. She knew her partner would mock her and accuse her of reaching, but she would gather every little thing she could if it would keep the Mafia boss behind bars for the rest of his natural life and get some of his men off the streets.

"So, what did I miss yesterday?" Terry came in holding two Starbucks, and he was grinning.

She closed the internet browser with the list of printing companies. That was as far as she'd gotten again today, and the way things were going around there, she might have to work on this at home. "You heard," she said. His grin had given him away. She took a cup he extended to her.

"Oh yeah." He started laughing. "I'd say eccentric, but everyone said she didn't appear to have any money." He spun his index finger around his right ear. "Cuckoo for Cocoa Puffs."

Madison laughed. "You have such a way with words."

"You're jealous of me." He sipped his coffee and then put it on his desk. "Seriously though. Coming at you, all upset, and screaming, 'He didn't do it!'" He steepled his hands. "What didn't he do? Spill it."

"Kill himself."

Terry sobered. "Oh. That's disappointing."

"Disappointing? A man's dead."

"Well, I thought maybe she was going to say the butler didn't do it. I don't know. I just expected something better."

"She says her fiancé never would have killed himself." As Madison verbalized the situation out loud, she found more empathy for Vilma.

"If I had a penny every time I've heard that—"

"You've heard that before?"

"Nope, not really, just thought I'd bug you with a cliché. Too bad it didn't work." He pouted.

"Terry, I'm going to kill you." She rose and lunged toward him.

He took off in a slow jog with his Starbucks. "First you'll have to catch me."

She hated running more than she hated beer—and that was saying a lot—but she would catch him, and then he'd stop laughing. At least that was her goal until her sergeant, Garry Winston, rounded the corner.

He was scowling, with his hands on his hips, his round belly becoming more pronounced with the stance. "Don't you two have work to do?"

She and Terry stopped moving.

"We're a little slow this morning." She felt her cheeks heat.

"As I can see. Well, now you're not. A body was been found at nine twenty-three Weber Street."

"That's a residential area." Terry drank some coffee like they hadn't just been busted fooling around.

"You're a genius, Einstein," the sarge stated sardonically and added, "The remains were found in the backyard. Of a house." He seemed to add the latter part for the purpose of mocking Terry. "Some poor sap thought it would be a good time to turn the dirt in his garden and came up with a finger on the point of his shovel."

It seemed a little early to start on a garden, given it was only March. They often had warmer springs in Stiles than in more northern states, but she would have guessed the ground would still be hard. Cold soil could have preserved the remains though. First to verify what they were looking at… "Originally you said 'body,' then 'remains.' I'm to assume there's flesh?" Madison asked.

"There's flesh."

"Do we know if the remains are male or female?"

"It's looking like a female based on the finger they unearthed." He paused there and let his gaze drift over them. "Don't tell me you're both still standing here. You were moving quicker a moment ago."

"Leaving now." Madison hurried to her desk for her coat.

"Damn right, you better be."

"I call the driver's seat," Terry said, coming up behind her.

"You can call whatever you want," she said. "It still doesn't mean it's happening."

CHAPTER THREE

Weber Street put them right in the middle of the shady east end, which was a popular spot for druggies, prostitutes, and gangbangers. Narcotic detectives had recently shut down a meth lab in the area, resulting in charges against three people. It was certainly the type of neighborhood where people could slip away without being missed.

But as Madison drove, she appreciated that it was also a neighborhood of contrast, with some well-maintained houses showcasing a modicum of pride, while most properties were dilapidated and hosted mini junkyards. The section they were passing now fell more into the latter category. Paint was worn off the siding, and front windows were broken and covered with plywood.

"I wouldn't want my kid growing up here," Terry said.

She looked over at him, and he was facing out the window. His wife Annabelle was five months pregnant.

"Speaking of it—"

"*It?*" Terry turned to her from the passenger seat. "Nice."

"Well…" She didn't have a mothering bone in her, but that was beside the fact. "How else do you refer to a baby when you have no idea which sex it is?"

"As *him*. It's a *he*. I can feel it."

She wasn't looking at him, but she heard the smile in his voice. "You sound pretty positive."

"A father knows these things."

"Yeah, what does Annabelle say?"

"Want to stay on the topic of the baby's gender? If not, I need to vent. Most of the time, it's 'pick up a burger' or 'get me black-cherry ice cream.' The woman's got the strangest cravings. You'll never believe what she had for dinner last night."

Madison smiled. "Amuse me."

"Canned salmon with a little dab of mayo and pickles. That's it. No bread, crackers, nothing else."

"Sounds healthy."

"Sounds like a boy." Terry flashed a goofy grin.

Madison parked in front of 923 Weber Street behind the Stiles medical examiner's van and the one belonging to the Crime Scene Investigation Unit. Her conversation with Terry faded under the scrutiny of onlookers. People stood on the sidewalks, arms crossed, heads tilted, seeming none too pleased cops were in their neighborhood, but too nosey to resist gawking.

The house offered no driveway, and its two stories of wood siding were pitted with dirt and the passage of time. The front yard was small and outlined by a four-foot-high chain-link fence, but a look down the side of the house revealed a long backyard with a garden along the property line.

"There's room for more than one body," she said.

"You've always been a positive thinker."

"Well, it wouldn't be the first time. Right area for it."

Officer Higgins came over to them.

"Hey, Chief." She addressed him by her nickname for him. Reggie Higgins had been her training officer when she came to the Stiles Police Department and, as far as she was concerned, could have been police chief if he'd so desired. Truth was, he wasn't corrupt enough to be promoted to office.

"Not too nice around here." Higgins lassoed his hand around his head, indicating the neighborhood, and the movement drew her attention to a pair of sneakers hanging by its laces over a power line.

Higgins continued. "I've been called out for domestic complaints here so many times, the car knows the route. I should have known it would be for the girl's death one day."

"We know for sure it's a woman?" Madison asked.

He nodded.

"Do we have an identity yet?"

Higgins slowly shook his head.

"Oh, I figured when you said you've been here…"

"Well, you know how it goes. Once we get here, the girl doesn't want to press charges, claims everything was her fault."

A ribbon of anger coursed through her. She had zero tolerance for men who used women as punching bags.

"Sadly, there's no ID on the body," Higgins said, "but I remember her face."

"Has she been fully exhumed at this point?" Terry asked.

Higgins glanced at him. "Yeah. It still makes me sick. I know he beat her, but there was nothing I could do. The only time I had the pleasure of hauling his white ass downtown was when he answered the door with a handgun. Turned out it wasn't registered. Thought I really had him. Threatening an officer with an unregistered firearm. But nope, he wasn't behind bars long and was back out to beat on her. That must have been over a couple of months ago now. That was the last time I was called out here."

"What's this asshole's name?" Madison wasn't sugarcoating the loser for what he was.

"Don't even need to consult the records for that one. Ralph Hennessey. Unfortunate for us we can't find him right now."

"He's probably in the wind," Terry said, and when she and Higgins looked at him, he shrugged.

"I'd have to say I agree." Madison gestured for Terry to start making notes, but he didn't make any move to do so.

Instead he said, "Did the girl live here?"

"Not sure. I had always assumed so, but maybe she had and moved out. The only sign she had been around inside was a package of prescribed allergy medication that Crime Scene found under the couch."

"We have a name for her, then," Madison assumed.

Higgins shook his head. "Unfortunately, the label was torn, so we only have her first name. Lacy, no E. I know you have a niece named Lacey, with an E."

"That's right." Now this case felt a little personal.

Higgins went on. "There isn't a script number either, but we have a partial logo and the pharmacy phone number. It might help."

"Guess it's better than nothing," she mumbled.

"Well, hopefully something comes together. We officers will be out canvassing soon. If anything comes of it, I'll let you know."

"Thanks," Madison said.

"Of course." He moved like he was going to leave when Terry spoke.

"If Hennessey did kill her, he'd want to get rid of all the signs she was in the apartment. The pills could have just been overlooked," he said.

"Suppose that's true," Madison agreed and turned to Higgins. "How many apartments are in the house?"

"Two. Hennessey lives on the main level, and a guy by the name of Elroy Bates rents the upstairs. He's got a record too. Breaking and entering. Got out a year ago after serving three years. We've gone to pick him up. He works at a gas station down on Bakker Street."

Madison rattled off another question. "Anyone contact the property owner?"

"No need. He's the one who called us."

"He's the green thumb who wanted to start the garden?" Terry surmised.

"Yep. Donald Giles. He got a ride downtown. You can talk to him there."

Madison glanced at Terry, who tapped the names into his phone. She rolled her eyes. He had discovered technology recently, and it often replaced his traditional notepad. Madison didn't put much faith in his new system. For one, scribbling something down was much faster than pecking away. And two, what if the phone crashed?

"Terry," she prompted.

"What?" He kept his focus on the screen.

Higgins smiled at Madison, knowing that she wasn't the biggest fan of electronic gadgets to start with. As far as she was concerned, some things were better old-school.

She snapped her fingers inches from Terry. "By the time you're finished there, I'll have caught the killer."

"And the problem with that?" He smiled at her, and she narrowed her eyes.

She should never put getting out of work past her partner. He was always ready to call it day.

"Fine." He stuck his phone back in its holder and pulled out a notepad. He held it tight to his chest, close to his face, a black pen poised over the lined sheet. "Yes, boss. What can I do for you?"

She imagined him with small, round reading glasses perched on the end of his nose. "Don't be a smart-ass." She smiled. "The names are Ralph Hennessey and Elroy Bates."

Terry wrote down the names and looked up at Higgins. "Does Richards know the cause of death?"

"It's looking like she might have done herself in with a gunshot to the head. Such a damn shame." Higgins toed the ground with his shoe. "Even looks like a .22 caliber. Hennessey's confiscated handgun held .22s. Maybe he got himself another one."

Madison patted Higgins's arm on the way to the backyard. She didn't say the words *It's not your fault* but hoped her touch communicated that.

"Keep safe out there, Maddy."

"You too, Chief."

Terry leaned into Madison, "What about me? He didn't tell me to be safe. Are you two involved and I don't know about it?"

"Seriously? The guy is the same age as my father. Now, if he were at least twenty years younger…maybe." Her partner really needed to stop prying into her love life.

The property was teeming with life as Crime Scene crawled through every blade of grass. A barn-shaped shed was in a far corner, and Mark Andrews, an investigator, shadowed the doorway for a minute before returning inside.

The back door of the house opened, and Cynthia Baxter came out. She headed up the forensics lab, was Mark's boss, and Madison's best friend. Cynthia stood there as if she were lost in thought. She pulled her sunglasses down from her nest of brown hair where they had been resting. Her regular studious eyeglasses were nowhere in sight, so she must have been wearing contacts today.

Madison waved at her, but Cynthia walked back inside.

"Huh, she must not have seen me," she said.

Madison shook it off and headed toward Cole Richards, the medical examiner. He was braced beside the victim's head—*Lacy's* head. Madison never cared for labels. The body was on a black tarp near the side of a shallow grave.

She stopped next to Richards and took a long look at the girl. Probably in her early twenties—if twenty. Very thin. Blond hair. Pretty face despite the dried blood and dirt caked around a mouth that was agape, exposing chipped front teeth, and circled by a muzzle burn. The front of her shirt was bloodstained and dusted with dirt, as were her jeans and shoes and any exposed flesh.

"Higgins said it looked like COD was a self-inflicted gunshot," Madison said.

Richards looked up, his expression clearly saying he was disgusted that an officer made that judgment. "I haven't officially concluded yet."

Richards's personality usually accommodated for some small talk and lightheartedness. Obviously not the case today, but maybe it had been her approach. In a way, she had managed to insult his profession by relegating what should have been his determinations to a uniformed officer.

"Just a misunderstanding," she said, backpedaling. "How long do you think she's been in there?"

Richards rose to his feet and squinted from the sunlight. "I'd say probably not much longer than one month, but it's hard to pinpoint exactly."

She'd been hoping for a narrower window than that. "A month? Wouldn't the ground have been too hard to dig?"

Richards gestured toward the body and the mounds of dirt. "Apparently not, but whoever buried her didn't make a deep grave either."

"It was probably just a holding spot until they could put her somewhere else," Madison speculated. "They hadn't accounted for someone wanting to get an early start on a garden."

"We'll need to find people who last saw her alive to get a better idea on timeline," Terry said.

Madison looked down at the woman again, her heart aching for her. "First we need to figure out who she was."

Richards bent back down and opened Lacy's jaw with gloved hands. "I'd say the damage could have been caused by a .22."

"If that's the case, we might not have a bullet to trace," Madison said. "It would have fragmented in her brain, especially at such a close range. Is that right?" It was the muzzle burn around her mouth that told her the gun had been against her skin.

"Possibly," Richards replied.

His succinct responses and cool demeanor were message enough that their relationship was still fragile. There wasn't a day she didn't regret prying into his personal history and exposing a wound that still cut him deep.

"Well, if we can find the casing, we could tie it to a gun." Terry looked around the yard.

"For that we'll need the scene of the crime." Madison's gaze drifted again to the young woman. She wasn't just thin; she was anorexic. Her hipbones protruded as knobs under her jeans. "Is there any indication she was a drug addict?" The categorization would fit with the demographics of the area.

"I didn't see any visible signs at first—"

"At first?"

"Uh-huh." Richards moved down the body and separated two of her toes. Between them was a definite pinprick. "I'd say she shot up here. I'll be requesting a tox panel to determine what she was into and if that at all factored into her death."

Madison's gaze drifted to her ankle and the rose tattoo there.

Richards went back up the body and pointed to abrasions on the knuckles. Madison now noted the girl's slender fingers and that some of her painted nails were broken. He said, "It looks like she may have been in a bit of a struggle."

"I know you haven't officially concluded anything," she started, "but even if she did shoot herself, there's no way she could have buried herself. So either someone wanted to make it look like she shot herself and screwed up by burying the body or…whoever buried her had found her dead, panicked, and then buried her." Madison paused, then added, "Regardless, someone has something to hide."

Also available from
International Bestselling Author
Carolyn Arnold

Found Innocent

Book 4 in the Detective Madison Knight series

She put a hand over her stomach. She had wanted to start over and make a new life for herself and her baby. But once the trigger is pulled, all of that will come to an abrupt end...

Called to a residential property after **the discovery of a pregnant young woman in a shallow grave, Detective Madison Knight arrives to find a perplexing crime scene**. It looks like suicide, but the dead don't bury themselves.

The victim is soon identified as **Lacy Rose**, and it appears she was working to turn her life around, but **Madison thinks clues to her death may lie in the shadows of her dark past**. The investigation reveals a dangerous ex-lover and an estranged father, both of whom had motive to kill her. But evidence also surfaces that connects Lacy to a dead man found in a motel room a few days prior. His death was ruled suicide, but Madison's convinced it was murder too. To find out the truth of what happened to both victims, she'll be staking her reputation and risking her career. **And while Madison has never let anything stand in the way of finding justice before, the shocking outcome of this case shakes her core.**

Available from popular book retailers or
at CarolynArnold.net

CAROLYN ARNOLD is an international bestselling and award-winning author, as well as a speaker, teacher, and inspirational mentor. She has several continuing fiction series and has many published books. Her genre diversity offers her readers everything from police procedurals, hard-boiled mysteries, and thrillers to action adventures. Her crime fiction series have been praised by those in law enforcement as being accurate and entertaining. This led to her adopting the trademark: POLICE PROCEDURALS RESPECTED BY LAW ENFORCEMENT™.

Carolyn was born in a small town and enjoys spending time outdoors, but she also loves the lights of a big city. Grounded by her roots and lifted by her dreams, her overactive imagination insists that she tell her stories. Her intention is to touch the hearts of millions with her books, to entertain, inspire, and empower.

She currently lives near London, Ontario, Canada with her husband and two beagles.

CONNECT ONLINE
CarolynArnold.net
Facebook.com/AuthorCarolynArnold
Twitter.com/Carolyn_Arnold

And don't forget to sign up for her newsletter for up-to-date information on release and special offers at CarolynArnold.net/Newsletters.